The Loneliest Magician

The Dragon Nimbus #3

Irene Radford

BOOK VIEW CAFE

OTHER BVC TITLES BY IRENE RADFORD

Merlin's Descendants Series

Exciting periods of history, insert a descendant of the Merlin who has to nudge events to match what we remember.

Guardian of the Balance

Guardian of the Trust

Guardian of the Vision

Guardian of the Promise

Guardian of the Freedom

Trance Dancer

After the apocalypse, a young woman can only dance until she collapses to bring vision of how her community can find a path through a strange wilderness filled with predatory humans and wildlife.

Trickster's Dance

Artistic Demons

Music may soothe the savage breast, but sometimes it incites demons to murder.

Confessions of a Ballroom Diva

Confessions of a Piano Demon

Confessions of a Siren Singer

Confessions of a Changeling Dancer

Pixie Chronicles

The greatest calling for a Pixie is to be a friend, even if that means playing tricks on people so they don't take themselves so serious and can look beyond their problems to find a true path to their destiny.

Thistle Down

Chicory Up

Dandelion Twist

Whistling River Lodge Mysteries

Cozy mysteries set in an historic lodge that may be haunted. Or maybe it's just the hotel mascots creating mischief.

Whistling Down the Wind

Whistle While You Plow

Whistling Bagpipes

Ghostly Whistles

THE DRAGON NIMBUS SERIES

"Go see an invisible dragon," the senior magician said. What he didn't say was save the world while you are at it.

The Glass Dragon

The Perfect Princess

The Loneliest Magician (coming 2023)

SHORT STORY COLLECTIONS

Fantastical Ramblings

Speculative Journeys

Steampunk Voyages

Magical Meanderings

NON-FICTION

Magna Bloody Carta

Committing Novel

Irene Radford writing as C.F. Bentley

Confederated Star System

A spiritual journey with a literary twist, set in a space opera landscape.

Harmony

Enigma

Mourner

Copyrights & Credits

The Loneliest Magician
Dragon Nimbus #3
Irene Radford

Copyright © 1994 Phyllis Irene Radford Karr
Book View Café Edition August 29, 2023
ISBN: 978-1-63632-162-2
Originally published by DAW BOOKS, INC. 1994
Original ISBN: 088-6-777-097

Production team:
Proofreader: Brenda W. Clough
Cover artist & designer: Maya Kaathryn Bohnhoff
Ebook formatting: Jennifer Stevenson
Print book formatting: Diana Pharaoh Francis

Book View Café
304 S. Jones Blvd. Suite 2906
Las Vegas NV 89107
www.bookviewcafe.com

BOOK VIEW CAFE

Praise for Irene Radford's Dragon novels:

"Ms Radford's considerable gifts as a mesmerizing story-teller shine with undeniable luster." —*Romantic Times*

"A rousing adventure of magic and treachery." —*Library Journal*

"Plenty of popular elements: an intelligent cat, an enchanted wolf, a redheaded witch, a missing prince, the apprentice mage with misunderstood powers, and, of course, dragons." —*Locus*

"A big, adventurous, satisfying climax to the trilogy by one of the more interesting new voices working with the traditional quest story." —*Science Fiction Chronicle*

"This action-packed plot makes for engaged and thoughtful reading. The author manages to keep the story clear, and the characters interesting to follow. Several themes interplay successfully, with the reader caring what happens. Not surprisingly, the volume resolves one conflict, but keeps the door open for continuing obstacles. This reader, for one, is eager." —*KLIATT*

*This book is dedicated to the members
of the Portland Lace Society,
active and retired.*

Prologue

Lord Krej and his sister Janataea are lost to the coven. Zolltarn, king of the Rovers, betrayed them both and deserted our ranks. No other has enough power to become the focus of our magic rituals. Our numbers are depleted; a miserable six when we need nine, and I am but half-trained. The Council of Provinces and their puppet king have triumphed.

But only for the moment. I am making plans for when we are a full nine once more. Then the Twelve will die for what they have done to us.

I have not the power or knowledge to break the reflected magic that transformed Krej into a tin weasel with flaking gilt paint. No honor for him, tricked by Darville and caught in the spell's backlash. If only our Lady Janessa could be revived. She would know how to release her son. But she died and was honored by being transformed into an idol at the moment of death. I sense that Lord Krej still lives within his statue prison. His life-spirit fades little by little.

I will have revenge. Before Darville is crowned, when all eyes are on the gaudy display of the coronation festival, my agents will kill the self-righteous king and his trollop of a queen.

The great winged god Simurgh will demand blood for the power needed to carry through with the plan. A mere slave will do for the initial spells. When all is done, I will need a triple sacrifice for the return of Krej. Yes! I sense the balances moving into place as I plan.

Jaylor is boon companion to Darville. His wife, Brevelan, is bastard daughter of Krej. And their babe is an innocent. They should die together.

Chapter One

Apprentice Magician Yaakke downed the last of his ale, purchased with illusory coins. Sullenly, he elbowed his way out of the makeshift tavern and into the rowdy coronation crowd. He'd lingered too long.

Time never flowed at the speed he wanted it to, and now he was late. One more infraction of the rules to prevent his promotion to journeyman.

A crow scolded him with raucous cries from atop his perch on the tavern tent's ridgepole. Guilt and shame burned Yaakke's ears at the reminder of his tardiness.

He'd idled the hours with forbidden eavesdropping on the thoughts of drunken revelers. He liked to imagine these simple folk were his family, since he had none. Every farmer or merchant could be his father come to visit him during the week-long coronation festival. . . .

Now he was late.

"Disgusting filth!" A lean man of middle height spat a bite of meat roll into the gutter. His bright scarlet tunic with gold braid proclaimed him a senior member of the Guild of Bay Pilots. The wily boatmen were an integral part of Coronnan's defense. No one else could guide shipping through the constantly changing channels in the mudflats of the Great Bay. Invading navies had ceased trying to negotiate the mudflats centuries ago.

"That's good meat and pasty. How dare you insult my wares!" A young woman with blond curls escaping her kerchief glared at her customer. She planted work-worn hands on narrow hips, presenting a picture of outraged determination. "You took a bite, now pay up."

The noisy black crow swooped down from the ridgepole of the tavern pavilion and devoured the discarded food in one gulp. Not a crow, a jackdaw. As it lifted its head and croaked in triumph, Yaakke noted the white tufts of feathers above the bird's eyes, much like the bushy eyebrows of an old man. The bird rolled its eyes before launching itself back to its high perch. The movement caused the white tufts to waggle, just the way Old Baamin's eyebrows had whenever he admonished his apprentice.

Grief threatened to choke Yaakke. The irritable old man would never again correct him for an error in magic or in manners.

The argument between the girl and the Bay Pilot drew Yaakke's attention back to the present. His telepathic senses amplified the anger, distrust, and fear that surrounded this typical market argument. He considered turning his back and slipping into the throng of revelers, unseen, unknown.

"Uncooked pig offal. I'll not pay to be poisoned." The pilot's hand reached for the long boat hook that dangled from his belt.

Violence spilled from the man's aura, infecting other members of the crowd. Warning prickled the length of Yaakke's spine. He searched the crowd for help, anyone with a hint of authority to intervene. A ring of avid observers formed around the arguing couple.

"Give the arrogant bastard what for, Margit!" one of the watchers yelled.

"Don't let the chit cheat you, Guildsman!" another voice answered from the other side of the crow. Violence simmered around them, inviting their participation with more than words.

The pilot looked over his shoulder at the crowd. Uncertainty flickered in his eyes and in his aura. Then the mask of arrogance, so typical of his kind, dropped back into place. He waved the boat hook in front of Margit. The girl didn't retreat.

Yaakke silently applauded Margit's courage. He'd had his meals stolen from him by bullies often enough to understand the girl's need to stop this one thief before another took advantage of her weakness.

"You'll pay or I'll have the guard on you!" Margit's eyes grew large at the sight of the Guildsman's sharp boat hook. Her aura pulsed red. Anger or fear?

Power?

No. Her eyes were too clear and innocent for her to possess the sudden surge of magic Yaakke sensed in the air.

"What guard?" the boatman snorted. "Only my Guild keeps Coronnan safe!"

More jeers from the crowd, for and against the Guildsman. Yaakke decided he'd better step in before a riot started. If he prevented a dangerous disturbance at the king's long awaited coronation, maybe the Commune would consider him reliable again. He also needed to track down that sudden surge of magic he'd felt. Maybe Jaylor would give him his journeyman's quest after all.

Yaakke sought the pilot's name within his mind. The information hid from a light probe. Yaakke concentrated harder. *Paetor.* Unusual. The syllables grated on his tongue like a foreign language. The Guild tended to be separate from the rest of Coronnan, inbred to the point of alienness. But the name was strange even for the Guild. Curiosity and admiration of Margit's courage propelled Yaakke forward.

He threw an illegal spell, a small delusion. The surge of magic didn't return to combat him. Reflection from the Guildsman's eyes showed the short apprentice as an army officer twice the man's height and double his breadth of shoulder.

"You'll pay for the pasty, or I'll lay you out as fish food," Yaakke hissed at Paetor, grabbing the haft of the boat hook with one hand.

His little boot knife suddenly appeared in his other hand looking very much like a foot-long dagger tickling the pilot's throat.

Paetor's jaw opened, then shut.

The crowd edged backward, suddenly silent.

"She gave me refuse from the gutter to eat!" Paetor fingered his purse but didn't open it. Some of the arrogance slid out of his posture. His eyes darted to the thinning crowd.

"That's good sausage!" Margit protested. "If you don't like it, fine. But you ate it, now pay for it."

An angry tirade from Paetor's mind filtered through to Yaakke's mental ears, in a very foreign language. This was no Bay Pilot with a few strange ways, but a foreign smuggler up to no good. The strange source of magic must come from him.

Jaylor! Yaakke sent a telepathic plea to his new master, the Senior Magician. *We've got trouble.*

No answer. Jaylor's thoughts were normally easy to find and separate from a crowd. Something must be terribly wrong in the Grand Court, where the coronation was about to take place, if Jaylor didn't answer a message of trouble.

The smuggler wrenched himself free. He took off at a run over the bridge to the next city island. Yaakke followed him. He discarded his spell of delusion and became, once more, the undersized, name-less drudge from the University kitchens he had been until last spring. No one took much note of his running pursuit of the smuggler except to protest his jabbing elbows as he cleared a passage.

He lost sight of the smuggler in the crowds of dancing and singing citizens who thronged along the processional route. More tavern pavilions sprang up along the way, offering a dozen places for the man to hide.

Think! Yaakke admonished himself. *Think like a smuggler.* The docks were too obvious. Where else would a fleeing foreigner head?

Yaakke calmed his panic-driven heart rate and focused his psychic powers on one specific accent. The physical and telepathic din from the crowds dropped to a murmur. Two men thought with that peculiar clicking rhythm to their mental voices. Yaakke tuned in to them. One was at a distance, probably the other side of the capital. One was just ahead.

Yaakke fine-tuned his listening and heard surface thoughts in a foreign language. He probed deeper, seeking meaning in images rather than words. He encountered a little resistance, then the man's thoughts became clear.

I've got to get to the boat and close the cargo hatches, the accented mental voice hummed anxiously. *Can't let the guard find those s'murghing Tambootie seedlings before the assassination.*

What? Yaakke sought the source of that desperate thought. The smuggler had to be stopped. He had to discover who was going to be killed and when.

But the significance of the Tambootie bothered him more. If Coronnite Tambooties grew anywhere else, the dragons would seek it, and they'd never be enticed back to their homeland. Magic and magicians would be illegal in Coronnan forever without the dragons. The border to keep out King Simeon's invading armies would remain collapsed without dragons and dragon magic. Yaakke listened for the elusive mental voice again.

Nothing. Almost as if the smuggler and his thoughts had been swallowed whole by the void. Further probes from Yaakke's mind met a wall of resistance. Some kind of internal armor.

He sniffed the magic that surrounded the foreigner's mind as he edged his physical body closer. The magic didn't come from within the smuggler. Only a powerful and well-trained magician could impose that kind of subtle protection on another man. And this magic didn't smell like anyone in the Commune.

Carefully, Yaakke probed the "nothing" with a finely honed magic dart. In his mind's eye he saw the witch bolt of questing magic pierce the armor. The invisible arrow came up against an undulating wall of power and slid around it. Glaring white light filled the dart with explosive menace as it rounded the curve of armor and headed straight back toward its sender at double speed and intensity.

Yaakke recoiled in horror. If the probe pierced his mind, then the hidden magician who had placed the layers of armor on Paetor would know everything about Yaakke, about the Commune's secrets and the disguises used by the Master Magicians today.

Yaakke needed his staff to counteract the probe. If he opened his magic senses to keep track of the questing spell, his own power would attract it like a magnet. The staff was inert, unless charged by Yaakke, and could absorb the magic safely. But the staff was hidden, along with his pack, back at the inn. If he'd carried it today, he would have been marked as a magician and hustled off to gaol hours ago.

On the edge of panic, he ducked the speeding probe and ran, scattering diverting delusions in this wake. The dart of magic swung around to Yaakke's new direction, seeking the mind that had launched it.

Rejiia de Draconis peered at the coronation spectacle in the Grand Courtyard from behind a magical mask. Resentment of her cousin, the new king, colored her perceptions with black auras. Counting slowly, she controlled her breathing. "I have to see things clearly if I am to succeed," she whispered to herself.

Calm spread through her body. Knotted muscles in her back and shoulders relaxed a little.

The royal steward flung open the massive doors of the King's Gate, signaling the beginning of the coronation ceremony and a major interruption of Rejiia's plans to become queen.

A hush fell over the crowd. Gold- and green-clad musicians sounded the fanfare. Rejiia winced at the harsh sound.

"Do you think the king will actually show his face?" she whispered into the silence that followed the trumpet blast.

"Sshh," a woman held one finger to her pursed lips, signaling silence to her husband.

Rejiia smiled. The thrown-voice spell worked! "I heard Darville's face was horribly disfigured in his battle with the magicians," she commented louder, meaning for all to hear. King Darville's face hadn't been touched in the fateful battle with her father and aunt, but his sword arm was badly burned.

With mischievous glee she fed the mundane superstition against the outlawed magicians of the Commune. Her purposes were served well if the crowd believed all evil sprang from the Commune—especially the coming assassination.

Acolytes in white, swinging censers of burning incense, began the procession from the palace around the dais in the center of the courtyard. A choir of green-robed sisters of the stars followed next, bearing lighted candles. Their songs invoked blessings from the Stargods in six-part harmony.

Behind the women marched a bevy of red-robed priests, silently carrying the books of wisdom left by the Stargods. All three groups circled the cloth-of-gold-draped dais.

The crowd followed the clerics with their eyes. Rejiia was totally forgotten and ignored. Good. She could continue her assignment undisturbed. She faded backward, toward the protection of a guardroom.

The priests took up positions around the dais. The sisters and the acolytes joined them, alternating silence, song, and incense.

A ritual the Stargods stole from Simurgh. Rejiia felt the blood drain from her face as she realized the significance of the processional. Nine priests, nine sisters, and nine acolytes marched sun-wise around a place of reverence. *Widdershins, you fools!* she screamed within her mind *'Tis a ritual designed to raise power and inspire awe. Who knows what demons you will spawn by performing the ritual incorrectly?*

The incense thickened into a purple haze. Too sweet and cloying. Witchbane. Rejiia retreated farther from the dais. She had too much to do today to fall victim to her own plot. If any magicians hid behind delusions in the courtyard, the witchbane would cause their minds to wander aimlessly while their vision bounced and circled. If they tried to use magic to bring their senses back to order and restore their disguises, they would discover all power had deserted them, including their disguises. The mundanes wouldn't know anything was amiss.

Lord Andrall, most loyal to the crown of all the Twelve Lords of the Council of Provinces and a royal relative by marriage, emerged from the palace. He carried the Coraurlia, the splendid glass crown shaped into the head of a dragon. The crown that should have come to Rejiia. Costly rubies, emeralds, and star sapphires adorned the crown in gaudy splendor, none more precious than the rare glass of the crown itself.

Lord Krej almost had the Coraurlia while he was regent. But Jaylor and the Commune had interfered. She wanted the crown, the title, and royal authority so much her teeth ached. She unclenched her jaw and concentrated on her tasks.

"Aaah!" the assembly gasped. Many of them had never seen the dragon crown before.

But I have seen the crown before. I know firsthand the magic power embedded into the glass. The Coraurlia protected King Darville in his battle against my father. By rights it should be mine. 'Twill look hideous against Darville's golden hair and eyes. My raven hair and bay-blue eyes will enhance the glory of the Coraurlia when it is finally mine.

I will be avenged for Janataea's death and Krej's humiliating imprisonment. Darville has to have the crown on his head to invoke the protection. He won't live that long.

Chapter Two

Yaakke gasped for breath, pressing his back against the outside walls of the Grand Court. He had nowhere else to run. His lungs ached with each breath. Darkness pressed at the sides of his vision. How could he hope to escape his own probe turned malevolent?

He blanked his mind, as if preparing himself for a trance. The all-but-invisible magic dart paused, seeking. It avoided the mundane minds of the dancers as they leaped and spun with wild abandon. Musicians increased the tempo of flute and drum. The probe sped forward as if enticed by the whirling music.

Yaakke dove into yet another party of celebrants, letting their overt thoughts and conversations mask his mind.

"Can you imagine the audacity of the healer?" a fat ore broker protested to his clinging companion. "He refused to use magic to banish the pox. Insisted that only herbs were legal now!"

The companion-for-hire nodded and made sympathetic noises. She arched her back, displaying more of her bosom.

The ore merchant wandered off with his companion, leaving Yaakke alone in the crowd. The magic probe slid around and through the musicians straight for Yaakke's eyes. Nothing stood between the apprentice and the witch bolt.

A dark shadow flitted across Yaakke's vision. For a moment he thought the probe had found him. Then, miraculously, a large black bird dove between him and the glittering dart of magic.

The probe couldn't divert its path around the bird and plowed directly into the shining black breast feathers.

"Braaawk!" the bird screamed. A cloud of tiny feathers burst from his breast. His flight faltered and the bird dropped heavily and clumsily to the ground at Yaakke's feet. The splash of white head feathers over its eyes rose and fell several times. Angrily the jackdaw stabbed at the wound with its beak.

"Yuaaawk!" The bird spat more feathers from its clacking bill in disgust as it danced in a circle. The bird's body jerked forward with each step in a rhythm peculiar to his kind.

Yaakke breathed a sigh of relief. The probe had found a victim. Wouldn't the armored magician be surprised when the only information revealed was a litany of abuse from a bird! A raw wound in the jackdaw's breast marred the smooth velvet of his coloring and reminded Yaakke of the sacrifice the bird made for him. What would happen to it now? Did a jackdaw have enough of a mind to be stripped by the probe?

"Thanks, bird." Yaakke saluted the cranky creature still preening and pulling damaged feathers from its breast.

"Corby, Corby, Corby." The bird cocked its head and repeated the sounds as if speaking directly to Yaakke. Its beady black eye probed him almost as deeply as the witch bolt would have.

"All right. Corby you are. I owe you one, Corby." Yaakke turned to push his way through the crowd toward the Grand Court entrance —where he should have met Jaylor over an hour ago.

"Owe me one. Owe me one. Owe me one," Corby repeated.

Yaakke paused a moment at the shift of the pronoun. The bird was just mimicking sounds. Wasn't it? Whoever heard of a jackdaw smart enough to speak? Unless the probe had given the bird the intelligence it would have stripped from Yaakke. He twisted his neck to look at Corby one more time. The white tufts above his eyes waggled again. The resemblance to Lord Baamin was so strong in that instant, he almost saw his dead master peering out of the black, beady bird eyes.

"No. You aren't Old Baamin. You're just a bird."

"Corby. Corby. Corby," the bird repeated as it flapped its wide wings and launched itself into the sky.

Yaakke dismissed the bird with a shake of his head.

Jaylor needed to know about the smuggler and the foreign magician running free in the capital, not about weird birds. Right away. Yaakke sent another message to Jaylor. Still no answer.

At the entrance to the Grand Court, Yaakke dropped to his hands and knees in the middle of the crush of people. He found paths between legs. He avoided trouncing feet with the skills he'd learned as a child while avoiding bullies and thieves. He dared not throw a spell of invisibility to let him pass through the tight crowd. One jostling elbow would rip right through the spell and get him into more trouble.

Already today he'd passed magic coins at the tavern, revealed his magic to an alien magician, and lost all trace of the smuggler. He really needed to avoid any other problems.

No one noticed his natural thin and ragged urchin body as he crawled between the legs of a cloth merchant and under the crossed pikes of the guards. All attention seemed directed toward the center of the courtyard where King Darville and Queen Rossemikka moved in stately procession toward the dais.

"But I provided the queen's gown. I have a right to view the coronation," the cloth merchant above Yaakke argued with the guard.

"You'll have to wait for the procession across the city bridges, sir," the guard repeated the same phrase he'd probably been saying all morning. "One more person in there and the whole court will sink back into the river."

Breathless and sweating, despite the autumn nip in the air,

Yaakke crawled through the crowd to the wall of the court where it hung out over the River Coronnan. He tried to stand up, but couldn't force himself through the mass of legs and brocade robes, velvet slippers and leather boots.

"May you all wallow in dragon dung," he grunted as he pushed his back against the wall and inched upward. Stone and mortar scraped his skin through his simple homespun shirt. He ignored the burning scratches until he was fully upright, staring straight into the bay-blue eyes of a tall, black-haired girl with beautifully clear, pale skin. His heart almost stopped beating as he gasped at her beauty. Long black lashes framed her big eyes. She lifted a hand to sweep a stray lock of hair back behind her ear. Graceful. Elegant. She was taller than he by half a head or more and seemed to be about his own age. But those eyes spoke of knowledge and pain, and were old beyond her years.

Something about the set of her jaw and the penetrating look she gave him was familiar. Brevelan's eyes. Another of Lord Krej's get. The deposed regent had scattered his seed as indiscriminately as his magic. Which of his many daughters was she? Before he could remember, she turned and dissolved into the crowd. None of her thoughts were open to his telepathy. She didn't seem to be armored, just elusive. He watched the spot where she had disappeared into the crowd, hoping to catch another glimpse of her.

"I don't have time for this," he muttered.

Yaakke searched the crowd for Jaylor and Brevelan. All he saw was satin and brocade and jewels, fortunes in jewels. Wealth and prestige were the only things that counted in the Grand Court today. His everyday country trews and tunic, as well as his youthful face and small stature would mark him as an outsider and unworthy to attend the coronation. He draped a little delusion about himself, making sure that each citizen saw his tunic and trews as equal in cost and grandeur to their own.

And he'd better avoid the numerous guards scattered throughout the crowd. Palace guards were notoriously strong witch-sniffers. One whiff of his magic and he'd end up in the same dungeon cell as the hideous statue that Krej had become with a heavy dose of witchbane to keep him there.

"I don't mind King Darville wanting more money for the army," a lavishly garbed town dweller complained. "We've got to protect our borders since the magicians deserted us and took their protective barriers with them. But Darville thinks we should feed the poor, too. I say let the wretches find honest work or join the army. I have trouble enough keeping the wife in SeLenese lace." He and his equally elegant companion strained anxiously to see the king he discredited.

SeLenese lace? All imports and exports from SeLenicca were banned. Could that be where the smuggler aimed to take the Tambootie seedlings? Yaakke strained to follow the speaker with his eyes, but lost him among the throng of taller observers.

The mood of the crowd seemed to echo the speaker—half wildly enthusiastic for the king and half faddishly bored, unable to approve of anything.

With the slightly crossed eyes required for TrueSight, Yaakke scanned the courtyard for any hint of Jaylor. All he could sense was a tiny tune of peace and love just ahead of him. That had to be Brevelan, Jaylor's wife. An island of calm radiated outward from her delicate frame. Her witch-red hair and magic were disguised. No one who didn't know her would suspect that the quiet tune she *Sang* to her new baby was really a spell to keep the overwhelming emotions of the crowd away from her empathic sensitivities.

Disguised or not, Jaylor wasn't beside her.

Yaakke climbed to the top level of seats erected around the central dais, almost to the top of the wall. He ignored Corby perched atop the wall ten arm-lengths away as he preened scorched breast feathers. Tendrils of black floated on the wind, like ash, with each stab of his sharp beak.

Scanning the crowd for anyone wearing a magic disguise or delusion—friend and enemy alike—Yaakke avoided jostling elbows that threatened to push him over the outside wall into the churning river that encircled Palace Isle. The jackdaw cackled laughter at his concern.

"Rotten weather for a celebration." A sergeant in the green-and-gold uniform of Darville's personal guard remarked beside Yaakke.

"Yeah, could rain any minute." Yaakke looked at the sky where the jackdaw now flew, rather than at his unwanted companion. He swallowed heavily and tried to ease away from the young sergeant.

"Do I know you?" the Palace guard asked, peering closely at the black-and-silver tunic Yaakke had chosen for his magic disguise. He thought it went well with his dark hair and eyes. Then he remembered the girl with raven hair and bay-blue eyes. She had been wearing black and silver too.

"I don't think we've met." Yaakke looked around nervously. He wished he could dissolve into the crowd like the girl had, without using any magic. This curious sergeant looked as if he might be trying to "smell" the presence of magic.

A bizarre purple haze clung to the area around the dais. Yaakke wrinkled his nose against the odor of the incense. Cautiously he eased a light shell of magic armor around him. The overly sweet smell subsided.

The sergeant opened his eyes wide and shoved his way down the tier of seats, like a boat forging upriver against a strong current, pushing noble and wealthy citizens aside without regard. Apparently, he didn't like the smell either.

Yaakke watched, wondering at the sergeant's haste and determination. Then he saw what had disturbed the sergeant. One of the acolytes wasn't a young boy. Beneath a dissolving spell of delusion, he was a short, middle-aged man with a square-cut beard. No respectable citizen of Coronnan would wear a beard trimmed in the style affected by King Simeon of SeLenicca, the sorcerer-king who waged war against Coronnan.

A sorcerer-king who ruled a land notorious for the absence of magic, A dragon could provide Simeon with enough magic to work his spells. He'd need Tambootie trees to feed the dragons who had deserted Coronnan last spring.

Was the smuggler headed for SeLenicca and King Simeon?

Assassin! The outside thought came into Yaakke's head unbidden.

He sent an invisible probe into the false acolyte's head. *Poison.* The man was going to shoot poison into King Darville. Yaakke had to stop him.

But how? He was too far away to get to the dais before the assassin acted.

If he threw any magic at all—at this distance he'd have to summon power and focus the spell with gestures and a trance—the guard standing one tier away would arrest him for using outlawed powers. The guard might even think he, Yaakke, was the assassin.

Rejiia eased out of the guardroom toward the King's Gate. The magician boy had seen her. That meddlesome apprentice of Jaylor's, who seemed to melt into walls and fade into obscurity while listening to the most private of conversations, was skulking around the corona-tion. She had no doubt he could penetrate her delusions. Perhaps he could eavesdrop on her private thoughts and telepathic conversations as well.

If he overheard, the coven's plans were in danger. The safety of many depended upon her role in today's actions. She darted into her new hiding place, just inside the corridor to the throne room. She peered around the edge of the door to watch the coronation.

King Darville and his foreign queen approached the dais with slow, measured steps. The gold of the king's tunic seemed a perfect match to his barely restrained mane and yellow-brown eyes. He knew how to manipulate the crowd's loyalty by projecting an image of beauty and power. Rejiia aimed for the same aura of authority with her black and silver gowns and sapphire jewelry—though her husband disapproved of her dramatic clothing. When she was queen, he'd not be around to scowl and whine at her.

The crowd's attention strayed from the majesty of the new king to the audacious display of bosom by his queen, Rossemikka. Her golden gown didn't dip nearly as deep as her wedding gown had, but still, she challenged the modesty of all the other women present. Rejiia wished she dared expose so much of her own breasts. Her meek little husband and his father, Lord Marnak the Elder, had beaten and bruised her the one time she'd tried. They'd pay for that. Soon. When Darville was dead and she was queen.

If all eyes were on the queen, then no one would see the magically armored assassin make his move.

One of the acolytes ceased swinging his censer. Rejiia held her breath in anticipation as he lifted a small cylinder from the center of his incense holder. The assassin's SeLenese beard poked through his disguise, making him look much older. *Demon spawn!* The armor did not work in the presence of the witchbane.

No outcry rose against the hired killer. Perhaps no one noticed him amid the dazzle of the Coraurlia and the queen's white breasts.

A tiny dart head protruded from the bottom of the tube in the censer lid. The assassin held the tube up to his lips. He took a deep breath to blow. Rejiia filled her lungs as well, willing the poison dart to find its target.

Almost done. A few more seconds and she would be queen.

Hands reached out from beneath the dais and encircled the ankles of the assassin. One mighty yank from those hands and the hireling fell forward. *Thunk!* His face slapped the pavement with a hideous sound. He opened his mouth in a soundless protest and he inhaled the dart. The assassin's eyes rolled up and his mouth foamed as the poison penetrated the delicate membranes of his mouth and throat.

Another yank on the assassin's ankles by the person hidden

beneath the dais and the body disappeared from view. No one in the crowd seemed to notice the slight disruption in the ceremonies.

Stunned by the failure of her plans. Rejiia stared at the place where her agent had disappeared beneath the dais. Jaylor, the youngest Senior Magician in history and King Darville's childhood friend, peeked out from beneath the platform. His eyes searched the courtyard and rested on the King's Gate where Rejiia stood.

"Dragon dung!" Rejiia gasped. "I've got to get out of here."

She turned and ran down the corridor toward the throne room.

Failed! We have failed to execute Darville. What kind of demon is he to pervert fate and remain alive?

Calm. I must force myself to accept the failure and find another plan. Sooner or later the king's luck will run out. The magicians protect him, even though I arranged for them to be outlawed. I must separate Darville from the Commune. Will they still protect him if he and Jaylor are no longer friends?

Today I must settle for rescuing Lord Krej from the dungeons. That should cause Darville some trouble. For only a magician can break the spells surrounding the cell, and the only magicians he knows belong to Jaylor and the Commune.

Yaakke slipped behind a broad-shouldered petit-noble. He watched warily as Jaylor peeked out from beneath the dais searching for someone in the crowd. If Jaylor couldn't find his apprentice, then he couldn't punish Yaakke for succumbing to cowardice and failing to intervene against the assassin. To protect the Commune, Coronnan, and the king was the most sacred oath of magicians.

Yaakke suspected his journeyman's quest would be delayed once more because of his failure. A new commotion stopped him.

"Look, up there. A dragon!" A sharp-eyed priest shouted and pointed. All eyes lifted to the heavens.

Yaakke fought the compulsion to look upward as well. A vision of the court wallowing in dragon dung brought a smile to his face. He'd have to take more care how he cursed. Best he slip into the city and get as far away from his master as possible for the rest of the day. Jaylor had peered right at Yaakke and known he hadn't done a bloody thing to save the king. Maybe by nightfall he'd forget Yaakke's short-comings.

He'd have to send a brief telepathic message about the smuggler when he was a safe distance from Palace Isle.

"It's a blue-tipped male dragon," King Darville added to the crowd's murmurs.

This time Yaakke couldn't resist looking up, as he eased closer to the guardroom exit. The outline of the winged creature hovered and shimmered in a shaft of sunlight over the courtyard, almost visible against the dark gray sky. The beast's crystal-like fur directed light and sight around him, challenging the coronation crowd to look everywhere but directly at him. Yet their eyes needed to linger and seek a glimpse of the dragon.

"Grrower!" The gray overcast dissipated in the blink of an eye, as if commanded by the dragon's trumpeting call.

Sunlight danced across translucent wings and arced downward. Rainbows sparked the Coraurlia with life and color. A giant aura spread around the glass dragon crown for all to see.

This was the Coraurlia of legend; forged by dragon fire to protect the rightful king and no other.

Lord Andrall lifted the crown high and turned within the circle of prismatic light to face King Darville. His face glowed with the same wonder Yaakke saw reflected in every face in the court. Warmth and joy tingled from Yaakke's toes to his ears.

The dragon shifted. The rainbow followed his wing movement

and bathed King Darville and Queen Rossemikka in the light of magnificent blessing.

The young king and his consort mounted the six steps of the dais amidst applause and cheers. The dancing rainbows seemed to follow them, bursting into bright auras for all to see, magic and mundane alike.

Yaakke smiled and lingered outside the guardroom. Darville deserved to be king. The few times Yaakke had encountered him, the young ruler had been kind, almost friendly. Rossemikka had to be the most beautiful woman in the kingdom, maybe in the three kingdoms.

An image of black lashes surrounding huge blue eyes flitted across his memory. Well, maybe there was one girl, almost-woman, more beautiful than Queen Rossemikka.

The procession followed Darville and Rossemikka, ready for the ancient ritual to consecrate them monarch and consort of Coronnan. An overwhelming sense of pride and joy lingered in the court. In a tradition not seen in living memory, the dragons had validated Darville's claim to the throne.

Come to me. The dragon voice came into Yaakke's head.

"What?" Yaakke whispered. Only royals were supposed to hear dragons. He looked up again, searching the clear sky for a glimpse of wing or tail.

You are needed.

"Did a dragon speak to me?" Maybe the dragon spoke to someone else and Yaakke merely overheard. He eavesdropped on people's thoughts easily, why not a dragon's?

Meet me in Shayla's old dragon lair. Above Brevelan's clearing, two weeks hence. The dragon disappeared above the remaining fluffy white clouds.

"What would a dragon need me for?" He craned his neck in search of one last glimpse of blue-tipped crystal.

I know of your parents, Boy. Come to me and we will discuss those who left you with no name and no heritage. Tell no one of our tryst. You must not be followed.

"Two weeks? I only need that much time if I bother taking a travel steed. I have the transport spell. I can be there tomorrow." His parents? Maybe he had a real name after all and needn't borrow one from history.

No. You use the transport spell too often. Danger follows it. Steal a steed if you must, but come in two weeks.

"Steal? What if I get caught?" A thrill of danger almost replaced the awe of speaking to a dragon. A real live dragon who spoke to him and wanted to meet with him in secret.

You will not be caught. I will tell you of your heritage two weeks hence. No sooner.

"If I sneak out through the dungeon tunnels, I can be out of the city before sunset." Who would miss him? Yaakke lifted the latch on the guardroom door.

Don't be late. The chuckle in the dragon's voice reminded Yaakke of Old Master Baamin. Grief touched his eyes with moisture for just a moment.

Then he straightened his shoulders with pride. "I'll follow the dragon for your sake, sir," he whispered to the memory of an old man who had cared for him when he was nothing.

Do it for your own sake, or you won't find the lair.

Chapter Three

Katrina Kaantille halted her quest for a cup of milk or a cracker to stop her stomach growling. The door to the family kitchen was firmly closed. Raised voices beyond the door made her uncertain she wanted to overhear yet another fight between her parents.

Cold seeped from the floorboards into her feet. Winter had come early to Queen's City—to all of SeLenicca according to market gossip. Just a moon past the equinox and frost made the front steps slippery every morning. She should have stopped to slip clogs over her velvet house slippers. But she'd put down her study of geometric grids for only a moment. A sudden growth spurt had made her stomach clamor for food all the time lately. Often she couldn't concentrate for the discomfort.

"What do you mean there isn't enough money to buy Katrina's apprenticeship!" Katrina's mother, Tattia, hissed.

Katrina pressed her ear against the kitchen door to listen more closely. Her entire body shivered with apprehension.

Money was hard to come by all over SeLenicca these days. Yesterday the price of milk was twice what it had been last week.

P'pa had dismissed the scullery maid, valet, and governess last week because he couldn't pay them. Cook would go next week.

But Katrina's father, Fraanken Kaantille, was a wealthy merchant. M'ma worked as the queen's Lace Mistress. Exporters and lace factory owners valued M'ma's new designs. Surely her father could find enough money for her apprenticeship somewhere.

Katrina loved the fine thread work that had become SeLenicca's primary export. She'd reached her thirteenth birthday last moon, the age of apprenticeship. Only a few weeks' more work and she would complete the entry requirements. That future now seemed in jeopardy.

"There will be enough money. Just not right now. Upon King Simeon's request, I've invested all our money in a ship," P'pa explained.

Katrina could almost see her father place a soothing hand on M'ma's shoulder before her volatile temper exploded.

"And just what cargo do you expect to put in the hold of that ship? The mines are played out and the timberlands are nearly barren. Lace is the only thing left to export and the queen controls every shipment," M'ma argued. Her voice was growing louder rather than softer.

Katrina nearly winced at the acid in her mother's tone. Talented and highly respected artist that she was, Tattia Kaantille had never learned moderation in her emotional reactions. Lesser beings were expected to jump to her commands and bow to her superior knowledge.

"But what do you make your lace with, my dear?" P'pa's wide and generous smile shone through his voice. That endearing grin usually soothed M'ma.

"Inferior cotton and short-spun linen. Since the war with Coronnan, we can't get any decent Tambrin. Our own Tambootie trees are too small, too tough and irregular in their fibers. And there's barely enough of them in a few isolated spots to bother seeking."

Katrina breathed a little easier. M'ma's angry tones continued, but now her temper was directed toward the enemy of SeLenicca and not her husband of fourteen years.

"How much would one ship filled with Tambootie seedlings from Coronnan be worth, *cherbein* Tattia?" P'pa used an intimate endearment meant to soothe and flatter. His voice lifted with pride and greed. "Seedlings that will grow into thread-producing trees in a few years."

Katrina gasped. The long, silky fibers of six-year-old Tambootie trees made the best lace in the world. One tree supplied enough Tambrin to make a hundred arm-lengths of finger lace, symmetrical insertions as wide as the queen's ring finger was long. Of course, some of the trees would have to be saved to produce seeds for the next crop. Even so, a shipload of seedlings, once grown to proper size, but before they were mature enough to sprout flowers and seeds, could save SeLenicca and make Katrina's family as wealthy as the queen.

But trade with Coronnan was forbidden. Military ships inspected every cargo. What if P'pa's ship was stopped? The entire family would be in deep trouble. He'd invested all of his money in that ship. All of it?

Too excited and frightened to be hungry anymore, Katrina returned to the workroom on the third floor of the tall, narrow townhouse. Vents from the kitchen fires kept this room warm enough for the entire family to pursue their daily occupations.

Dolls and miniature clothing lay scattered around the workroom floor. Katrina's two younger sisters had obviously used her brief absence as an excuse to abandon their lessons in keeping household accounts for playtime. The limited pictorial language of household ledgers might be all they ever learned to read, but women in the Kaantille family could add and subtract better than any merchant who might try to cheat them.

"Katey, Maaben says my dolly isn't as pretty as hers. Tell her it isn't so," six-year-old Hilza wailed and tugged at Katrina's long woolen skirt.

"Your doll is ugly and broken," nine-year-old Maaben rejoined.

"Tell the truth, Katey. Tell her how ugly her doll is. Its hair is dirty and doesn't look blond anymore, and the eyes are dull, not blue like a real lady's. Only peasants and outlanders have dark hair and eyes. It's ugly," Maaben quoted the often-heard prejudice. "And peasants can't wear lace. Give my doll that shawl and cap!"

"Maaben, Hilza, stop it! Now get back to your lessons. I can't waste time on such stupid squabbles. I . . . I have to work at my lace for a while," Katrina brushed aside the grasping hands of her sisters. She needed the soothing thread work to banish the frightening argument she had overheard in the kitchen. What if P'pa lost *all* of his money?

She walked past the long study table to the cupboards beneath the single glass window—the greatest luxury in the house. Her agile fingers pressed the lock buttons in the proper sequence and the doors sprang open to reveal her finest treasure.

She caressed the tubular pillow stuffed with unspun wool, from sheep bred half a world away. Her hand traced the dimensions of the pillow—as long as her forearm and as thick as her fingers stretched wide. Tucked inside the center of the tube was a compartment designed to hold the strips of stiff leather that were a lacemaker's patterns. Pinholes in a geometric grid covered the patterns, guides for the weaving of the lace. Katrina had inherited nearly one hundred patterns from her father's mother, irreplaceable patterns that had never been duplicated and that she alone could legally work.

The velvet-covered pillow rested in a wooden frame that kept it from rolling. Gently, Katrina carried the precious pillow and frame to the study table. She placed it in the one spot the autumn sun brightened the most. Only when the pillow rested securely in place did she remove the loose cloth draped over the top to reveal an arm-length of a simple piece of lace. Two dozen spindles of carved bone wound with thread dangled from the unfinished end of the lace.

This lacemaker's pillow and the patterns were Katrina's thirteenth birthday present as well as her heritage and her dowry. Gentlewomen of SeLenicca had always made lace to adorn their wardrobes. In the last three generations, lace had been elevated to a national treasure. Only the export of lace could replace the money lost from the failing mines and empty timberlands. Only lace could buy food and wine and woven cloth from abroad, for the land of SeLenicca had never been farmed.

"Can we watch?" Maaben crossed the room on reverent tiptoe. Her blue eyes widened with wonder.

Hilza crept behind her sister, moon-blond curls glistening in the weak sunshine. The dolls lay abandoned in a heap.

"If you are quiet, you may watch. I can't think if you ask questions or argue." Katrina caressed the first two pairs of bobbins, thrilling at the texture and wonderful lace they would produce. Engravings etched some of the thin bone spindles. She examined tiny pictures of mythical animals, or the names and birthdays of the relatives indentured to the royal family SeLenicca as lacemakers, including herself. At the bottom of each bobbin was a circle of precious beads, some wood, others metal. The bangles added weight to the slender bobbins and kept them from rolling and over-twisting the thread. Only the bobbins commemorating a Lace Mistress, like Tattia and Granm'ma, contained a single, priceless, glass bead within the circle.

Peasant women who worked in the export factories couldn't afford slender, beaded bobbins, light and smooth enough to work Tambrin and the finest long cotton and linen threads. The factory owners supplied their workers with heavy, barely sanded, wooden bobbins with fat bulbs on the ends, as well as pillows covered in rough homespun and stuffed with straw. The factory tools, including the pins, were so clumsy that only thread heavy enough so it wouldn't suffer damage from rolling bobbins and overtwisting could be used on them. The light in the factories was poor, restricting patterns to large, open, and symmetrical designs. Katrina pitied those women for a moment. Her family was wealthy. She would learn the art of lace and design at the palace, as well as how to finish the lace onto garments. She owned her own equipment and could work at home if she chose, once she'd finished her journeywoman's work. She also had a treasure trove of exclusive patterns to keep her work unique. These wonderful tools would grant her special privileges at court, and if she managed to design a truly glorious pattern, she could be named a national treasure.

M'ma was still working for that status. Granm'ma had achieved the prestigious title days before her death last winter.

Deftly, Katrina worked a stitch, double twist right over left in both pairs, single cross, left over right between the pairs, and push a very slender pin into the proper hole in the pattern that encircled the bolster. Then, another double twist of right over left and a cross of left over right to enclose the pin in thread. Set aside one pair of bobbins, pick up the next in line.

The ancient rhythm of the bobbin weaving settled into her hands as a work tune brushed her mind. She hummed the soft clicking rhythm of the song—the first lullaby she'd ever heard—in time with the movements of her hands. Double twist, cross, and pin.

This third of the beginning patterns already seemed too simple and she longed for a more complex one. The first few finger-lengths of this lace, where she'd made two mistakes, had become the disputed doll's shawl and cap. Katrina had started and restarted the pattern several times until the work was perfect. Two arm-lengths of lace from each of three patterns were the entry examination for apprenticeship. A few more days of concentrated work would finish the requirement.

She had more than a few days to finish. She had until P'pa's ship returned with its precious cargo.

Double twist, cross.

"When will you get to use Tambrin thread?" Hilza barely breathed her question.

"Not for years yet. I've got too much to learn before I can use anything but short-spun cotton and thick linen," Katrina replied. Double twist, cross, and pin. "Only lacemakers as smart as M'ma can use Tambrin. It's too expensive to waste on beginners."

Double twist, cross.

"Maybe by the time Queen Miranda's baby is of an age to marry, I'll be skilled enough to make the wedding veil out of Tambrin." Provided P'pa found the money for her apprenticeship.

Maaben and Hilza continued to watch, mouths slightly open, breathing shallow, and eyes fixed on the lace.

Double twist, cross. Double twist, cross, and pin.

Yaakke crept up the back stairs of the Bay Hag Inn to retrieve his staff and pack. Twilight had fallen early, along with a new onslaught of rain. He hadn't been able to communicate with Jaylor by telepathy all day. News of the smuggler would have to wait a little while. He had to get out of town tonight if he wanted to meet the dragon's deadline.

He munched absently on a thin slice of purloined meat stuck between two slabs of coarse bread. Not nearly as tasty as the sausage rolls Margit had offered him when he'd questioned her about the smuggler masquerading as a Guild Pilot. She'd thanked him prettily for intervening on her behalf. Her clear blue-gray eyes had offered him more than a pasty. He didn't have time or inclination to linger.

His eyes and mind focused on the essence of each piece of wood in the steps, picking out stress points that would groan and betray his presence to anyone in adjacent rooms. Finding the creaks on the stairs with his magic was better than thinking about the half-cooked fat and gristle.

But what else should he expect from the Bay Hag? Isolated on the mainland from the river delta islands that made up Coronnan City, this was the kind of place where a man could rent bed space well away from prying eyes and ears, without questions.

The Bay Hag Inn seethed with life tonight. Mostly lowlifes who couldn't afford shelter from the rain in the city proper. Patches of fresh thatch dotted the moldering roof. Damp salt air from the Great

Bay was hard on thatch. This nearly forgotten hostel beside the river didn't look prosperous enough to reroof with slate, or even wood.

Brevelan and Yaakke had both turned up their noses when Jaylor chose to lodge his family here. The Senior Magician had insisted it would be easy to guard Brevelan and baby Glendon against theft and physical attack at the Bay Hag. Protecting them from suspicious neighbors who might report the presence of magicians to the Council might prove impossible.

Yaakke extended his senses into the wooden planks and beyond. The loft where he'd hidden his staff and pack was empty of people. Maybe he should just transport them to his hand. He could grab them and leave right now. No, Jaylor and Brevelan were constantly reminding him that magic was for need, not convenience, and he'd wasted too many spells on inconsequential things today. Witch-sniffers might be on his tail already.

"If he needs healing, I must go to him. I can't return to the clearing yet." Brevelan's urgent whispers to her husband penetrated Yaakke's thoughts through the closed door at the top of the landing.

Why hadn't they answered his telepathic call?

"We don't dare stay in the capital any longer," Jaylor returned. "The witchbane is still in me. I can't whisk us out of here at the first sign of trouble. We have to leave on foot with the rest of the crowds before someone recognizes us."

Witchbane? That explained Jaylor's silence. Yaakke sent a tendril of self-healing through his body, searching for something wrong. Nothing. Wherever Jaylor had encountered the dreaded drug, Yaakke had escaped an accidental dosage that would temporarily rob him of his magic. He shuddered. Without magic he was just another nameless kitchen drudge.

"I'm not leaving until I see Darville and I know that he is well," Brevelan announced.

Yaakke knew from experience that Jaylor might as well give up his arguments when Brevelan used that tone of voice.

"NO!" Jaylor's denial echoed across the landing.

Baby Glendon set up a howl of protest at the angry words circling around the room.

The king must be very ill indeed if he needed Brevelan's special brand of empathic healing. He'd looked a little pale at the coronation, wincing when he jarred his injured arm. Not many people in the Grand Court looked beyond the joy of the coronation to see the deep creases in the king's forehead that suggested the pain was never very far away—a legacy of his last battle with the witch Janataea.

Yaakke was glad he wasn't an empath like Brevelan. The churning discomfort he felt in his gut from just listening to this fight was bad enough. To actually experience other people's anger and grief, their pain and illness, as Brevelan did, was more than his body and mind could handle.

Did he dare linger long enough to deliver his message about the smuggler, or should he wait until he was out of town and Jaylor free of the witchbane?

Yaakke stretched his ears a little closer to the closed door.

"Conventional healers can't help Darville. He needs me!" Brevelan said.

Yaakke bit his lip. He had never before heard these two fight. He knew nothing of how a marriage worked, even less of women and their moods. Could a loving bond recover from angry words? *Stargods*, he needed to be away from this argument.

"And just how do you intend to get close enough to the king to heal him? When do you propose to do this—before or after the witchbane wears off? You got a pretty good dose of that purple smoke, too. Don't deny it." Jaylor's voice started to rise. Then he dropped it to a hissing whisper.

Yaakke's toes began to tingle with the urge to depart. He didn't want to stay here at the inn and listen to his only two friends argue and hurt each other. He didn't want to watch their bruised feelings dissolve their love.

He turned to make his way back down to the kitchen level. He'd have to risk retrieving his few possessions later by magical transport.

Jaylor threw open the door of his private chamber and grabbed his apprentice's collar. "Not so fast, Yaakke. Where have you been? You should have been back hours ago."

"How'd you know it was me?" Yaakke squeaked. He cleared his throat, almost glad rather than embarrassed by his lack of control over his voice. Maybe, just maybe, he was finally growing into manhood. Fifteen was kind of late for the change.

By tradition he couldn't face the rite of passage with the Tambootie smoke until his body entered puberty. He needed that trial to achieve journeyman status. Technically he couldn't leave his master or be inducted into the Commune of Magicians without the trial. He needed to set out tonight if he was going to reach Brevelan's clearing and the dragon in two weeks.

"I have eyes and ears beyond my magic." Jaylor closed the door to the bedroom, separating them from Brevelan and the now quiet baby. "You were supposed to report to me before the coronation began. Where have you been, Yaakke?"

"I—ah—I overheard—ah—" How did he explain how he heard the smuggler when he wasn't supposed to use any magic at all?

"Just this once, I wish you would answer a direct question. I'm not going to steal your dinner or beat you for impertinence."

Yaakke fought for the right words. His long habit of keeping his mouth shut and his mind sharp to avoid bullies and punishment stalled the words in his throat.

"*Stargods*, I'm not an empath like Brevelan. I can't read you," Jaylor ground the words through his teeth.

Yaakke hung his head. Fear of punishment clawed at his throat, killing the words. He had to try. He had to make Jaylor see how valuable he could be to the Commune.

"I overheard a smuggler. . . ."

"Criminals aren't my problem. I need your help now. Did the witchbane in the Grand Court affect you?"

"Witchbane?" Yaakke shuddered again at the thought of losing his magic and therefore his right to call himself anything but "Boy."

"The purple smoke one of the acolytes was dispensing instead of incense."

"I didn't like the smell, so I armored against it right off." Yaakke looked at the food still clutched in his fist. "The smuggler might be important to the king. He's taking . . ."

"That isn't important now. The king's health is. Is your magic intact?" Jaylor pressed for an answer.

"I guess so." He'd tell about the smuggler and SeLenicca and the dragons later, when Jaylor was ready to listen.

"Show me your magic."

Yaakke shrugged and brought a globe of witchlight to his outstretched palm. Shadows dissolved in the direction-less glow. He extinguished it with the pass of a hand before anyone from the kitchens below them could investigate.

"Good. You can eat on the way to the palace." Jaylor latched onto Yaakke's arm and pulled him toward his room.

Yaakke crammed the last of the bread and meat into his mouth. He didn't wait to swallow before he mumbled: "But, Jaylor, I've got to go . . . to tell you . . ."

"You need to follow my orders." Jaylor dragged him into the private room, still holding his collar. "We're ready, Brevelan." He grabbed his staff and headed back down the stairs. Brevelan slung a shawl around herself and Glendon, hurrying in her husband's wake. She didn't even notice the smell of the meat Yaakke had eaten. Usually the smell of an animal's death pained her.

"Where are we going?" Yaakke asked, swallowing the last bite of his hasty meal. He figured he'd need all of his strength for whatever Jaylor planned.

"The king is ill," Jaylor announced grimly, checking the back stairs for privacy.

"Did the assassin get him after all?"

"So you know about that."

"I'm sorry I didn't help, Jaylor. But I was too far away and there was a guard standing very close to me. I couldn't throw any magic without . . .”

“Never mind apologizing. Fred and I handled it. Now get a move on. We're needed at the palace.”

“Fred?”

“Darville's personal bodyguard. The sergeant.”

“Oh, him.” Yaakke relaxed as if a weight lifted from his shoulders. “Is it okay if he sorta recognized me?”

“He's loyal to Darville first and the Council second. He won't betray us.” They hurried into the muddy yard at the back of the inn. The hoarse caw of a crow or jackdaw greeted them, then faded with the last of the daylight.

Yaakke looked toward the roof of the ramshackle stable for signs of Corby, the jackdaw who seemed to have followed him all day. The lumpy thatch betrayed no unusual outline.

“Is the king's sword arm acting up again?” he asked to cover his search for Corby. If that was all that was wrong with the king, maybe he could get Darville to listen to his news about the smuggler.

“I'm afraid so. The wound, where the rotten magic in Janataea's witch blood burned him, is getting worse. If we can't reverse the damage tonight, I'm afraid he might die.” Jaylor choked on the words.

“I need my staff.” Yaakke “listened” to the loft. No one remained up there, awake or asleep. Another croak from Corby seemed to confirm the absence of patrons above the private rooms. Yaakke wondered briefly where the bird was, and if it truly was speaking to him.

The long walking stick appeared in his hand. Transporting things through the void from one place to another was easy—transporting people was hard. The distinctive grain of the oak staff from the Sacred Grove was already beginning to twist from the magic he had forced through it. “And our errand with the king is so urgent, I'll transport us.” Yaakke halted in his tracks. He closed his eyes a moment and sent his pack to a concealed corner of the stable. He could retrieve it from there later without arousing suspicion. While he was at it, he might as well get an apple from the barrel in the cellar.

"No transports." Jaylor shook Yaakke's shoulder to keep him from sliding into a deeper trance. "The spell is too dangerous. The last time I used it, I nearly got lost in the void."

Chapter Four

Yaakke peered over Brevelan's shoulder as she stirred herbs into a steaming pot stolen from the palace kitchens. Brevelan and Queen Rossemikka knelt on the floor before the hearth in the royal bedroom. Whenever instructed, Yaakke repeated the words of a spell Brevelan gave him, infusing power into the words and thence into the healing mixture. The conversation between Jaylor and King Darville intruded into his concentration for making the hot poultice. He forced his mind back onto the symbolic power behind the words while still half-listening.

"You shouldn't have risked coming here tonight." King Darville sounded weary and excited at the same time. His coronation day had been a long series of exhausting formal rituals culminating with the dragon's blessing. By ancient tradition, he now ruled by Dragon-right. No one could contest his possession of the crown.

Yaakke desperately needed to start his journey to meet that same dragon. He also needed to impart the information about the smuggler —if anyone would listen. Flusterhen feathers quivered in his belly.

"Have you ever tried arguing with Brevelan?" Jaylor answered his king and friend with a chuckle.

"Not since Krej enchanted me into the body of a golden wolf and I tried to bring my freshly killed supper into her hut," Darville replied. Laughter tinged his voice, too.

"Then you know I had no choice but to sneak her in here by way of the tunnels." Jaylor's restless eyes surveyed the room.

Yaakke had already searched the room for signs of eavesdroppers. There weren't many hiding places left in the apartments since the new queen had cleared away the clutter of generations.

"Take off your tunic, Darville." Brevelan stood in front of him, a steaming bowl in her hands. Noxious fumes rose from the contents. Yaakke and Queen Mikka stood right behind her.

"Help him, Jaylor, please." Mikka lifted her slanted eyes to plead with the Senior Magician. Her pupils were round now. Yaakke had seen them slit vertically when her cat persona dominated her body. "My stubborn husband won't admit how much the burns still hurt him, or how difficult those fitted tunics are to get out of. Now if court fashion allowed him to wear a decent robe. . . ."

"The court is already outraged at your foreign costumes, my dear." Darville struggled upright, but his smiling eyes never left the expanse of bosom showing above her gown. A place Yaakke hadn't dared allow his own gaze to linger.

"And I have difficulty coping with the immodesty of unveiled hair and skirts that reveal the ankles! A woman's breasts are a source of pride. And when I have proved my ability to bear and nurse a child, I intend to decently and proudly display my breasts." Mikka stared her husband down, amusement tickling the corners of her mouth. Her fingers flexed and curved like cat's paws. Her very long fingernails scratched at the velvet nap of her skirt.

Mikka had participated in a binding spell to heal Jaylor's warped magic. By accident she had joined with her pet cat. Her dual personality was the Commune's most closely guarded secret—except for the transport spell.

Yaakke yanked his eyes away from Mikka's catlike caress of her gown to Darville. He noted how the king kept his injured left arm close to his body and used his right arm to brace himself against the chair arm. Darville paused before standing, as if gathering strength against the pain he knew would come. Jaylor hurried to assist him. Yaakke stood on the opposite side with a polite hand beneath Darville's elbow.

The king shook off any help from Yaakke while he leaned heavily on his best friend. Yaakke remembered the tales of mischief that still followed these two around the city from when they were adolescents. Ten years of close friendship was a long time.

Once he'd read a person's thoughts, Yaakke knew their selfish motives. He couldn't think of anyone he'd liked and trusted for more than a few moments. Well, maybe Old Baamin.

Tonight he made a serious effort not to read the thoughts of these two couples. He didn't need to know what it was like to be half-cat, or a new mother. He didn't want to develop jealousy of the love they all shared.

Darville winced as Jaylor lifted the stiff tunic over the injured arm.

"Now roll up your shirtsleeve. This poultice may sting for a while, but it should draw more of the poison out and allow your body to heal itself." Brevelan set the bowl on the side table and began soaking bandages in the odoriferous liquid. "I've shown Mikka how to brew the solution. Between us, we'll have you well in no time."

"I certainly hope so. It's getting harder and harder just to sign my name to the infinite number of documents the Council comes up with. Then there's the problem of eating like a civilized man." Darville shook his head. "Life was easier when I was just your 'Puppy,' Brevelan."

"But not nearly so interesting." Mikka smiled and bent to kiss him.

While Darville was distracted by his bride, Brevelan placed the first of the steaming cloths on the exposed black burns that snaked up Darville's arm.

"Yaiyeee! What is in that demon brew!" Darville gritted his teeth. The cords of his neck went rigid.

"You don't want to know." Brevelan's expression didn't change until she turned to look at Jaylor.

Worry furrowed her brow and whitened her naturally pale skin. The spray of freckles across her nose appeared darker in contrast. Jaylor placed a supporting hand on his wife's narrow shoulder. Fear crossed Jaylor's face.

Yaakke couldn't penetrate the wall of Jaylor's thoughts. The apprentice touched the bandages as if to check them. A raw tingle traveled from the wound up through his arms. The weird sensation turned to a burn and then a pulsing jolt that tried to push his hand away or invade his entire body. He wasn't sure which. He didn't like the magic scent that suddenly tainted the room.

"Do what you have to, love," Jaylor whispered to Brevelan.

"What does that mean?" Darville clung to Mikka while he fought the pain.

"There is magic in that wound, Darville. Dark and dangerous magic." Jaylor refused to look at his friend.

Yaakke suddenly found the pattern in the rug fascinating. He'd felt death in that wound.

"We know that. Janataea's blood was rotten with Tambootie and evil magic. Everywhere it touched me, it burned through clothes and flesh almost to the bone." Sweat dotted Darville's brow and his breathing became shallow.

"This is something more, my dearest friend. I'm going to have to *Sing* the magic out." Brevelan clutched her hands in her lap.

Her healing talent required her to take the alien magic into her own body as well as Darville's pain. Her healthy body would gradually absorb, then dissipate, whatever was eating away at Darville. Someday, her ability to heal just might kill her.

"I'll lend you strength." Jaylor sat on the floor beside Brevelan, where she knelt at Darville's feet.

"As will I." Mikka plopped down on Brevelan's other side.

Yaakke dropped to his knees behind Brevelan, hands on her shoulders. The witchbane was still in her. He'd have to fuel the magic for her *Song*.

"No, Mikka." Jaylor put up a hand to keep the queen beside Darville. "The Council would burn you and depose Darville if they ever found out you participated in magic."

"I'm not the one throwing magic tonight." Mikka planted her clenched fists on her hips and glared at Jaylor. Stubborn determination creased her brow and set her lips into a straight line. "Is lending physical strength magic?"

Jaylor didn't answer. Queen Rossemikka had a reputation for single-minded determination. Several headstrong servants reported she had the patience to outstare and out-wait a stone statue.

"Well, is it?"

"Not by our definition. But it might be by the Council's," Jaylor hedged.

"He's my husband. I will help him however I can." Mikka plunked herself down beside Brevelan.

Yaakke placed his hands on Brevelan's shoulders. They took a deep breath in unison. The beginning of Yaakke's magic trance extended through his hands to include her. Jaylor and Mikka mimicked the calming exercise. Breathe in three counts, hold, breathe out. Again. A third time. The rhythm drew them all halfway to the void. Reality shifted in layers of past and present.

As usual, the ritual sent Yaakke's mind above his body. From there he could reach below the mask of the witchbane in Brevelan's body and tap her empathic healing ability. Her tune started low and melancholy.

Unusual. Brevelan's healing tunes tended to be light and cheerful, replacing pain and illness with joy and life.

Except that one time last spring when Jaylor had poured his life into the spell that released Shayla, the last female dragon, from Lord Krej's glass prison. Brevelan had called Jaylor back to life with a tune as soft and poignant as this.

Yaakke forced calm upon his mind. Panic and worry would end the spell. If Darville's injury was as bad as the tune indicated, then Brevelan needed every fragment of help he could give.

The tune grew in volume. The melody took on a richer more complex tone. Dimly Yaakke heard Jaylor's deep baritone seeking the harmony of the *Song*. The apprentice needed to add his own wavering voice in harmony an octave above Jaylor. The *Song* circled and wove and blended around the three voices. Mikka's untrained alto voice joined the spell, complementing Brevelan's piercingly sweet soprano.

Colored mists danced around the room in rhythm with the *Song*. The music lifted higher, enticing the poison out of Darville's body, urging the blackness to dissipate into the colored fog.

Darville dropped his head against the back of the chair. Gradually the lines of pain etched around his eyes and down his cheeks eased and flowed away.

Brevelan brought the *Song* to a glorious high note and lingered there. Jaylor took his harmony to a complementary fifth an octave below her. Mikka found the third.

Communal magic, fueled by dragons, must feel like this. Unity, companionship, binding them all together.

Yaakke opened his mouth to silence. The large room in a stone palace faded and shimmered. Different walls, older, unhewn bones of the Kardia curved around a cave. Cold dampness. Loneliness and pain.

He fought the vision and shook it from his mind. Reality was here in Coronnan City. He needed his concentration and strength *here* to heal the king.

Darville opened his eyes in wonder, then screwed up his face in agony. His scream caught Brevelan's shriek as they all collapsed in utter failure.

"Shayla!" Darville and Brevelan breathed together.

Yaakke forced himself to rouse from the exhaustion of strong magic. Shayla was lonely and hurt in her self-imposed exile from Coronnan. Had his vision shown him where the dragon hid?

"Did you see the dragon in your vision?" Jaylor asked wearily.

"She's hurt, trapped by an injured wing, and she can't fly," Darville panted. The pain seemed to return with double intensity.

"We've stabilized your wound with this spell. But I can't heal you, Darville, or Shayla. This wound is more than Janataea's poisoned blood. Your body is tied to the health of the dragons. The Coraurlia and the dragon blessing compound the link of your royal blood to the dragon nimbus. As long as Shayla ails, you will, too." Tears flowed down Brevelan's face. "I should have tried this yesterday, when I was in full control of my talent, before the dragons sealed your ties to them."

"Then why aren't you hurt, too, Brevelan? Your blood is almost as royal as mine. Shayla is linked to you."

"My link with Shayla was severed, Darville." Brevelan hung her head in regret.

"If Shayla is hurt that badly, then I'd best go find her." Jaylor stood, his hand already reaching for his staff.

"No!" Brevelan and Darville commanded in unison.

"I'm Senior Magician. 'Tis my duty to go," Jaylor protested.

"And you are the only one who can hold the remnants of the Commune together. You have to stay in Coronnan, Jaylor." Darville leaned back in the chair, cradling his injured arm against his body.

"A Commune that is now outlawed by your Council."

"All the more reason for you to stay. You have the strength of will and body to fight the Council. Our government is an intricate balance among twelve lords and the monarch, with the magicians as neutral advisers. That balance has been destroyed. Dragon magic allows magicians to join and amplify their powers by orders of magnitude to overcome any solitary rogue magician who won't obey the ethics of the Commune or laws of the land. Those restrictions have been shattered by the absence of dragons. Only you can hold the Commmune together and advise me until the balance is restored.

Send someone else. I need you here, Jaylor, even if your counsel is given in secret."

"Who else could I send? My class of journeymen never returned from their quests. The Master Magicians agreed to my elevation to Senior because they are all too old or unfamiliar with solitary magic to guide the Commune. There is no one else. I have to go." Jaylor tapped his staff against the floor with each word for emphasis.

"Excuse my presumption, sir," Yaakke interrupted. He forced politeness into his words to mask his excitement. "You have an apprentice, sir. You could give me this quest, now, like you said a few weeks ago. 'Tis my quest when I'm ready . . . when I've proved I'm reliable."

"Reliable and trained," Jaylor countered. "And of an age to undergo the trial by Tambootie smoke."

Yaakke refused to be disappointed. Somehow he had to make Jaylor see that he was *meant* to take this quest. Tonight. Before he left for his appointment with a dragon. Maybe if he told them about the smuggler now . . .

"Excuse me, Your Grace." Fred slipped into the room unannounced through a mere crack in the doorway.

Darville sat up straight and alert. "Yes?" Only a dire emergency would bring the king's bodyguard into his private quarters unsummoned.

"There's a ruckus in the dungeons, sir. Someone has stolen Lord Krej."

Chapter Five

*C*hild's play. The telltales Jaylor left around Krej's dungeon cell evaporated too easily. I wasted precious minutes looking for additional traps that weren't there. I watched him set the spells and knew some of their secrets. When I ran out of time, I took a chance and levitated the statue that is now Krej through my escape route.

Would that the spell enchanting Krej dissolved as readily. At least a member of the coven now has possession of his entrapped spirit. He will be kept safe by the one person who can guard him best while we research the nature of the spell.

"Every one of Jaylor's spells has been released." Yaakke announced as he examined the outside of Krej's now empty dungeon cell. "Whoever sprang the magic traps either did it before the coronation or while the witchbane was spreading around the Grand Court," he continued as he sniffed with his magic senses.

"Shayla is hurt so that I won't heal, there's been an assassination attempt, and now someone has liberated my enemy!" Darville paced the dungeon corridor, anger simmering just below the surface of his kingly posture. "This coronation day is not turning out particularly joyous."

Yaakke looked around for anything Jaylor's sharp eyes might have missed. He'd placed several balls of the shadowless witchlight in and around the cell to make sure no clue remained hidden. Krej's cell was empty; there was no straw on the stone floor, no bedding on the cot. Not even a chamber pot or bucket in the corner. Ensorcelled into a tin statue, Krej wouldn't have needed any of those bleak comforts.

Krej had been alive when his own spell to capture Darville into a sculpture had been backlashed by the Coraurlia, trapping the rogue magician in his own evil.

Had the magic reached Darville as intended, the king would have assumed the figure of a golden wolf—the image dictated by his aura. The tin weasel reflected Krej's personality.

"Who did this, Yaakke?" Jaylor asked. He searched for minute traces of evidence with his master's glass, a rare piece of magnifying glass, as large as a man's hand, framed in gold. Jaylor could use the precious instrument to direct spells, as well as enlarge cramped print and seek clues.

"Don't know." Yaakke breathed deeply and allowed his eyes to cross in the first stage of a trance. "Something's wrong. The little bits of magic left over are really weird, but I can't say why." The cell next to this one smelled equally strange, too, as if the thief had lingered there but hadn't thrown any spells within the room. The grisly statue of Krej's mother, Lady Janessa, was still there. She'd been dead when Krej and his sister Janataea had ensorcelled her into an onyx statue of a harpy. She couldn't be revived and was useless to the coven. Krej still lived within his tin prison. He might revive if they could figure a way to break his own backlashed spell.

"Well, if we can't tell who and how let's look at where," Darville ceased his restless pacing a moment. "Where could the thief expect to take Lord Krej when he's been transformed into a statue of a weasel?"

"Somewhere close," Jaylor pronounced. "The statue might be the size of a real weasel, but it contains Krej's full weight and mass. That much dead weight concentrated in a small form would challenge a very strong man."

"A strong magician could transport him," Yaakke interjected. That's what he would do.

"If the magician who sprang the traps doesn't have the secret of transporting a living being unharmed, I don't think he'd risk damaging Krej." Jaylor finger-combed his beard; a familiar gesture when he was deep in thought. "But he might try levitation. That's how Krej got Shayla back to his castle last spring after he'd turned her into glass."

Yaakke thought back to the magic probe he had dodged this morning. He hadn't revealed the secret of the transport spell to the smuggler from SeLenicca. Nor the queen's dual personality. He was sure of it. But maybe . . .

A blush crept up from his toes to his hairline. In all the rush and excitement he'd forgotten to relate important information. A smuggler. A ship to SeLenicca. Were all the mishaps connected?

"Does this corridor lead to the tunnels and maybe access to the river or another part of the city?"

"It does," Darville said. Traces of suspicion crossed his eyes. "But only if you know the tunnels exist, how to get out, and which walls hide doors."

Jaylor and Darville looked at each other for a long moment. If Jaylor's magic weren't dormant, Yaakke would swear they were talking mind-to-mind.

Yaakke looked down the dark length of the nearly empty prison carved out of bedrock. He squinted his eyes for traces of magic. Patches of red-and-black mist glowed in the shape of footprints.

"Who's red and black?" Yaakke asked Jaylor while following the faint traces of a magician's path. Magic tended to take on the color of the magician's personality. No two alike, though shades of a color might be similar.

"Red and black?" Jaylor looked surprised.

"Maybe not black. Something very dark. And the red is bright, like blood." The footprints were small, the stride short. Traces of delusion faded in and out, altering the shape and length of the tell-tales. Who was this magician?

"The assassin in the Grand Court was short!" Yaakke exclaimed. "And his beard was cut square, like he was from SeLenicca. There's a smuggler's ship going to SeLenicca tonight!"

"What? Tell me everything you know, Yaakke," Jaylor ordered. "Why didn't you tell me earlier?"

"You wouldn't listen and then we got caught up with the healing and I forgot." Yaakke's mind and mouth closed with a firm snap. Survival depended upon keen observation and keeping his secrets. He hadn't really forgotten to relate this information. Long habits of silence had pushed the incidents to the back of his mind. Ten years as the smallest and weakest kitchen drudge had taught him that.

"This is too important for you to hide behind big innocent eyes and silence." Jaylor grasped Yaakke's chin and forced him to look directly at him.

Yaakke saw anxiety and authority in Jaylor's gaze. He also saw a potential for violence within this big man. But none of his anger and aggression was directed toward Yaakke.

"Tell me what you know, Yaakke," Jaylor pleaded.

Yaakke filled his lungs and forced himself to trust his master. Never, in the months they'd been together, had Jaylor raised a hand to him. Not once had he given Yaakke reason to doubt his intentions.

"Yes, sir." Carefully, Yaakke related his morning's adventure, including his first suspicion that Margit the pasty seller had thrown a defensive spell at the beginning of the argument, finishing with an assurance that he hadn't leaked the transport spell to a foreigner nor revealed the queen's potential for magic.

What if he had revealed that information without knowing it?

"Where is that damned crow now?" Jaylor asked.

Yaakke fell silent once more. One of the shadows in Janessa's cell looked suspiciously like a bird sleeping with its head under one wing. If Corby followed him, everything the jackdaw did was special. For years, all he'd owned were his secrets. He had to keep Corby to himself a while longer.

"More important, how were the smugglers planning to get through the mudflats to the Bay proper?" King Darville resumed pacing the dank corridor, more restless than Yaakke had ever seen him. He nodded to the hovering Fred to send troops to investigate any ship leaving the Great Bay tonight.

"Only Bay Pilots know the ever-changing channels, and they are the most arrogantly close-mouthed demon spawn I've ever encountered!" The king yanked the golden queue restraint from his hair and shook the mane free. Once more he appeared the barely tamed wolf. The theft of Krej had challenged Darville's kingship and done more to invigorate him than all of Brevelan's healing spells.

"Can we assume that the theft of Lord Krej is related to the abortive assassination attempt?" Darville pressed.

Sounds of merriment from the banqueting hall drifted down into the higher levels of the dungeon as Fred opened the door a crack and slipped back to watch over Darville. He nodded that his errand was complete.

"I can't afford to absent myself from the festivities much longer, Jaylor. Can you find other clues, anything?"

"Sir," Yaakke interrupted. "Whoever stole Krej was strong enough to throw a delusion over the assassin and armor another man who was headed for the smuggler's ship. That's a lot of magic to throw and clear the cell, too."

Soberly silent, the three of them turned their attention back to the slim pieces of evidence. Jaylor placed a few threads of black cloth on a pewter tray alongside some flakes of gilt. "When was Krej last checked?"

"There is supposed to be a regular check of every cell by the guards at least once an hour. Every cell, not just these two." Darville extended his pacing to bypass half a dozen unoccupied cells. A coronation pardon had emptied most of them. Only two foreign spies and a few of Krej's steadfast followers remained.

"Could the backlashed spell have worn off?" Fred asked from the shadows.

Yaakke added more witchlight to the corridor to eliminate concealing darkness.

"I doubt it. Krej's original spell was meant to be permanent," Jaylor replied. "Krej himself would have to remove the spell, and he can't do it until he's animate again." He shifted his weight as if shrugging away an uneasy memory.

Yaakke looked at his master and knew he relived the scene in Krej's great hall last spring when Jaylor had freed Shayla from her glass prison. That spell was supposed to be unbreakable, too. The great effort of throwing the mighty magic had nearly killed Jaylor. Only Brevelan's love and healing *Songs* had brought him back from the void between the planes of existence.

Darville stopped square in front of his oldest friend. "Our thief must also know the tunnels. There are no maps of these passages. Few know they exist, fewer still know where they lead."

"I don't know who it is," Jaylor replied. "The magic signature doesn't belong to any of my Commune. *We* don't want Krej free to cause more trouble." He looked directly at his apprentice for confirmation.

Yaakke nodded, free of guilt. He'd thought about freeing Krej just to see if he could do it. For once he hadn't followed through. All of Coronnan, including Yaakke, was better off with Krej frozen into his tin weasel statue.

"I've got to get back to the banquet before people start asking questions." Darville ran a hand through his hair.

His right hand, Yaakke noted, not his normally dominant, but now damaged, left.

Jaylor reached his left arm out to clasp Darville's in friendship before they separated. Darville responded in kind. The lightest of squeezes on his forearm caused his brows to furrow and his shoulders to tense.

"We've got to do something about that arm," Jaylor whispered. Yaakke heard, but he doubted Fred did. "Maybe another session with Brevelan?"

"No." Darville stood firm. "I miss you both, terribly, but you have to leave the city before the Council guesses that you've been here."

"The Council of Provinces couldn't keep me away. I've awaited this day since I was twelve and you were fourteen." Jaylor's smile lit his eyes with merriment.

"The day I ran away from home to join your band of renegade boys. The best day of my life, even if it lasted only a few hours." Darville returned the grin. Much of the pain drained from his face with the memory.

Yaakke burned with jealousy. He'd never had a friend. Never had a family to run away from.

"I've got to go." Darville broke the hand clasp and took a decisive step toward his personal guard. "Jaylor." He stopped his progress. "I miss your counsel. I'm working hard to rescind the banishment of magicians."

"I know, old friend. I'm working hard at it, too."

"How? You're supposed to be in exile."

"Sometimes it takes an exile to find an exile."

"Shayla! You've got to find her." The king winced as his left arm brushed against Fred.

"I guess I have to send Yaakke on that mission."

"Everything will be fine, Your Grace, once I return with the dragons," Yaakke burst forth. He had his quest. Jaylor had forgiven his earlier shortcomings and given him his quest!

Dragons take them all! Almost we reached open water. Almost, we sailed free of Coronnan. Darville's men followed in a fast galley. They overtook us and shot burning arrows into the sails. Then they boarded my ship with unsheathed weapons. My captain and his crew fought valiantly for our freedom. When all was lost, I planted the idea of suicide into their feeble minds. Better they all die than betray my spell of invisibility. Darville must never know 'twas I who stole Lord Krej.

I can no longer flee to SeLenicca with my treasure. Where can I hide? Right under their noses, where they are least likely to look.

Black mists chilled Yaakke to the bone. Utter blackness that had never known light. All of his senses stopped. He'd shiver with fright if he had a body to respond to his mind.

All of his previous trips through the void had been brief—darting in and out in the middle of the transport spell. Familiarity didn't make a transport spell any easier or less frightening. If he slipped in his concentration for even as long as a blink of the eye (presuming he still had eyes), he could end up permanently lost in this black nothingness.

Yaakke fixed an image of Brevelan's clearing in his mind. He saw the one-room thatched hut in the center, with a new lean-to affixed to the back: The coop where the flusterhens laid their eggs and the goat munched on her hay. A new weed in the kitchen garden and the layers of mulch Jaylor had laid on the big field to protect the last of the yampion roots. The closest thing to home Yaakke knew.

Brevelan wasn't there to open and close the barrier around the clearing. He'd have to shape-change into a wild animal to slip through. Remembering to change back into his human form afterward was the hard part of that little trick. He hoped Brevelan never learned he'd found a way in and out of her protected home.

The blackness faded just a little. He pulled the image of the clearing into sharper focus and aimed his spell for the open space before the hut.

Pulsing colored lines crisscrossed the lightest patch of nothingness. Could that be a door out of the void and back to reality? He reinforced the image of the clearing. The web of lines brightened. A sensation of speed propelled him toward the colors, and he braced himself for contact with solid ground.

He bounced against something soft. At least he thought that was the sensation. The only softness in the clearing might be the upper branches of a tree, or the thatched roof. But he hadn't visualized either as his landing place.

Carefully he scanned his surroundings with every sense available to him. Wild tangles of throbbing umbilicals, in every hue imaginable, wrapped around and around him like the tentacles of a giant sea monster. Between and behind the colored symbols of life forces the void continued, on and on. Nothing between here and eternity.

He pushed a few cords away from what should be his face. Memory struck him. The time he'd entered the void with Jaylor to search for Queen Rossemikka's life force when Krej had kidnapped her, these threads of life had encircled them both. During that spell, the sight of a magician's blue umbilical fading to nothing had told Yaakke the moment Baamin died.

The shock of the old man's death had dropped him out of the void and the spell, leaving Jaylor alone, without an anchor to his corporeal body.

Yaakke was stranded in the void now, body and all. He needed to find a familiar life and follow it out. He didn't care where he landed as long as it was out of this sensation-robbing blackness.

Dozens of life forces coiled around his body and tightened. Suffocation squeezed his mind to blankness. Desperately he clawed at the life lines, seeking an exit. One shimmering white thread clung persistently. He grasped it to pluck it away from his heart. New images filled his head.

A girl with moon-bright hair braided in a foreign style fell to her knees crying. She clutched a tubular pillow to her skinny chest. Wooden spindles dangled from the pillow by slender threads. An older man with similar features and hair ripped the clumsy bundle from her arms. Her father? One of the wooden spindles broke free of the pillow and fell back into the girl's lap. She covered it with a fold of her dark skirt to hide it from the man. The well-dressed father then thrust the bundle into the greedy grasp of a tall, dark-eyed merchant. Money changed hands and the father grabbed the girl by the arm and dragged her away. She continued to clutch the hidden spindle.

Yaakke dropped that life-thread as if it were hot, sensing danger to himself in the vision. Shame heated his mind as if he were responsible for the girl's distress. Who was she? He was sure he'd never met her, never seen a woman with two four-strand brands that joined into one halfway down her back. Why was her life wrapped around his as if they were soul mates?

He resisted the pull to view more of the girl's life. One more vision of her might answer his questions and quiet the longing that surrounded his heart. No time. He had to get out of the void.

Somewhere there was an exit. But where? Blackness and the coils of lives stretched on toward infinity.

Chapter Six

"Where can the boy be?" Jaylor paced the flat roof atop the central keep of the last monastery dedicated to the priests of the Stargods. Its remote solitude had, so far, left it untouched by the purges of all enclaves of magicians. He feared their safety was only temporary. When the extremists ran out of targets for their venom, they would remember that a man must first be a magician before he became a priest. Temples and monasteries might lose their sacred protection.

Jaylor glared at a long telescope mounted atop the crenellated wall as if the arcane instrument could provide answers. His concern for his missing apprentice demanded more immediate answers than his worry over political purges and the omens his study of the heavens offered.

Master Fraandalor, known as Slippy within the intimate enclave of the Commune of Magicians, shrugged his shoulders in reply and positioned his eye to look through his own priceless equipment. "A quest is by necessity a solitary endeavor," he said, still squinting through the lens toward the northeastern sky.

"But he left the capital alone, before Brevelan and I did. He didn't collect any drageen to buy supplies or wait for special instructions. I haven't been able to find him in the glass for weeks and I'm worried about him." Jaylor ran his left hand through his unrestrained hair, then finger-combed his beard. "He didn't have the benefit of the trial by Tambootie smoke."

"We couldn't put him through that, Jaylor." Slippy made a notation on a piece of parchment without lifting his eyes from the telescope. "He hasn't reached puberty yet. He wouldn't have survived the ordeal."

"What happens when his body does make the change and his magic runs as wild as his emotions?" Jaylor resisted the urge to slam his fist into the long black tube that had been bequeathed to the first magicians of Coronnan by the Stargods.

"I don't know what will happen to Yaakke, Jaylor. The ritual of the Tambootie smoke is older than communal magic. If there were any records of what happens when a magic talent runs wild at puberty—especially a talent as strong as Yaakke's—those records were destroyed. We lost so much knowledge by suppressing solitary magic." Slippy shook his head in regret and returned to stargazing, the time-honored duty of all men of talent: magicians, healers, and priests of the Stargods.

The knowledge gained by observation of the sun and moon and stars would become as scarce as true glass if the fanatics rallying around the Council of Provinces destroyed the Commune. The precious instruments could not be replaced. New ones made by the Sisters of the Stars never quite measured up to the originals. Only dragon fire was hot enough to burn the Kardia's impurities out of sand to make glass clear enough for lenses. Normal furnaces left the glass too muddy and brittle for much of any use. Dragons hadn't been cooperative or predictable for several generations. There were many reasons Yaakke had been sent to seek them.

"I stalled Yaakke's quest as long as I could, hoping he'd exhibit some signs of maturation while he learned something of responsibility."

"You did the best you could. He's a headstrong boy with a mind of his own. Almost as determined and imaginative as you were at that age." Slipppy chuckled without looking away from his telescope.

"He's at least thirteen, maybe as old as fifteen, and shows no sign of puberty. Do you suppose there's something wrong, that he'll never mature?" Jaylor asked the older magician.

"Sometimes that happens. Usually when the boy has been the victim of privation and cruelty as an infant. Or if his mother was the victim of those conditions during pregnancy. Sometimes it just happens."

"We'll never know if that's the case with Yaakke. He was dropped off at the poor house when quite young. We have no idea how old he was. One year old, based on his size? Or closer to three, based upon his manual dexterity? By the time he was indentured to the University no one thought to test him for intelligence because his language skills were retarded." More likely, he'd learned to keep his mouth shut in self-defense.

"I have heard of some distant races where maturity comes late—people who tend to live to very advanced ages," Slippy mused. "Could the boy hail from across the seas?"

Jaylor shrugged. Yaakke's thick dark hair, big lustrous eyes, and olive skin weren't common features in Coronnan, but they were not unknown.

"He'll turn up eventually, Jaylor. Now get back to work. This unexpected meteor shower won't last much longer. We need to record the data for interpretation later. Perhaps the unusual pattern is an omen of the dragons returning."

"Or a sign of disasters yet to come," Jaylor grumbled as he bent to look through his instrument. "I wonder if I could sniff for his magic in the void?"

"Don't even think about it!" Slippy looked up aghast.

"The last time you ventured into the void the dragons almost kept you."

"Yaakke never feared that damned transport spell. Sometimes I wish my apprentice had never discovered it."

"Next time you wish that, remember how important the spell is in keeping the Commune and our scientific equipment safe from that new cult, the Gnostic Utilitarians. Whoever heard of preferring to earn something by hard work, study, and sweat rather than requesting it by magic?"

"Our enemies don't want knowledge and hard work, they just resent the fact that magicians have secrets and power beyond mundane control. I just hope our spy in the capital manages to stay out of their way."

Yaakke thrust the shimmering white umbilical away from his heart. As fascinating as the girl seemed to be, he had to find a familiar thread and follow it out of the void—no matter where it led.

He plucked the nearest coil of colored life away from his face. Cool and gold except for a black spot that looked as if disease burned into the shiny metal. This should be King Darville. A bright iridescent thread entwined with the gold one had to be Rossemikka.

Slowly Yaakke sorted the cords by the colors of the people who had come close to him. Copper for Brevelan, rusty soil tinged with magician blue must be Jaylor. He deserved the blue now that he was Senior. A silver line dangled from where Yaakke's belly button should be. An early lesson in magic theory tickled his mind. No one ever saw the true colors of his own aura until tested and found worthy by the dragons.

Could he follow his own life back out of the void? That might lead him right back where he started—into the suspicion-riddled capi-

tal. An abrupt materialization would earn him witchbane and imprisonment at the hands of the Council.

Then a grayish-green cord wrapped around his waist and
squeezed until a sensation akin to belly cramp demanded his attention. More cautiously than before, Yaakke plucked at it. The keeper
of the Bay Hag Inn appeared before him, thrashing around his filthy
kitchen and pantry. He screamed and searched the cupboards.
Though Yaakke couldn't hear his words, he knew the man needed
bread and cheese and dried meat to supply the last group of travelers.
Every cabinet, basket, and shelf was as empty as his cash box. Illusory
coins passed and exchanged by Yaakke during the coronation festival
had vanished. Behind the innkeeper stood a tax collector. Without
the journey rations to sell to the travelers, the innkeeper didn't have
enough cash left to pay his due. Yaakke had stolen a large portion of
those rations for his fast trip away from the capital.

An unpleasant taste penetrated Yaakke's overloaded senses. He
couldn't remember why he'd had to steal or where he was going. He
thrust aside the innkeeper. The man was a cheat and overcharged for
everything from his rooms to a single mug of ale. He deserved a hefty
fine for overdue taxes.

Maybe Yaakke should search out the single crystal umbilical that
was Shayla. Certainly the dragon would be willing to help him.

Help him do what?

He thrust his shadowy hand past another bluish cord. A vision of
Nimbulan, the greatest magician in Coronnan's history, shimmered
before him. The exhausted founder of the Commune said a sad
farewell to his beloved wife as she left Coronnan for a lonely exile.
All magicians who couldn't gather dragon magic were banished from
Coronnan at the end of the great War of Disruption. All women of
magic, led by Nimbulan's wife, Myrilandel, were included in
that ban.

Yaakke knew what it was like to be alone.

Other scenes from Coronnan's past fled by him. He watched,
fascinated, as lives wove themselves into the web that trapped

Yaakke. Curiosity propelled him forward and back through time. He caressed the umbilicals, searching for . . . searching for . . .

He couldn't remember. Somewhere in the compelling interplay of life, he lost track of himself. Yet something told him he couldn't waste any more time here. He had to go. But where? What was time?

The copper umbilical glided beside him. Copper. That was important. Copper, a planetary element, anchored to the core of Kardia Hodos. Copper for Brevelan and her unique nurturing magic.

Partial memory lightened fading corners of his mind. Brevelan, the first woman to care enough about him to teach him manners and give him hugs without attempting to pick his pockets. He had to find her clearing deep in the southern mountains. From there he needed to make his way to Shayla's old lair higher yet in those mountains.

He picked up the copper cord, seeking an image to guide him back out of the void.

Instead of the clearing, he saw a cave. Jaylor and Brevelan. The two were frozen in time, reaching out in protest, Reaching out to Shayla. Yaakke watched, horrified, as a dancing Krej used his magic to transform Shayla into a glass sculpture. Every transparent hair that cloaked the dragon's gravid body changed into a real crystal. The elegant all color/no color wing veins and spines dulled from natural iridescence to clear glass. The life within her and the lives of the twelve babies she carried stilled, stumbled, glimmered, just barely aware. Yaakke nearly dropped the copper thread of life in despair.

The images faded and something alive and wonderful died within Yaakke. One of Shayla's babies hadn't survived that spell. When freed of the magic prison, the dragon's anger over Krej's betrayal of the pact between Coronnan and the dragon nimbus caused her to fly away, leaving magic chaos in her wake.

Now it was up to Yaakke to find her again and restore the controls that existed only in dragon magic. Those controls would also end his own magic career. Because he couldn't gather dragon magic, the Commune would exile him or dose him with witchbane.

The blue-tipped male dragon had asked for a meeting in the very cave where Krej had worked his evil. Could he provide clues to Shay-la's location?

Solid ground rocked Yaakke's body and jarred his teeth. Slowly he opened one eye. Did he have an eye to open, or was that an illusion of the void?

Morning light, slanting through the thick forest pierced his vision. By contrast to the emptiness of the void, the watery sun trying to break through the clouds and fog seemed blindingly bright. Cautiously, he checked around him.

The clearing! Familiar, homey, isolated. He gulped the fresh mountain air filled with the clean and natural scents of trees and ferns, of animals and life. Real scents and sounds, not the dulled echoes of memories tangled together in the void.

"Late. Ye'r late," a jackdaw's mocking greeted him from the bird's perch atop the hut's roof. White tufts of feathers above his eyes waggled in stern disapproval.

"Shut up, you stupid bird. How'd you get here so fast?" He'd given up questioning why Corby was so intent upon following him.

Yaakke's stomach growled. The tiny discomfort was a wonderful reminder that he lived. He reached for the journey rations in his pack. Gone. His pack hadn't survived the transport. Memory of the innkeeper's frantic search for something to sell so he could pay his taxes flashed before Yaakke's mind. The sour taste returned to his mouth. Had he been responsible?

Food first. Think later.

Before leaving for the coronation, Brevelan had stashed a sack of oats by the hearth. The flusterhens would probably have laid some eggs in the coop. The goat would need milking. Enough to fill him up once he started a cooking fire.

His stomach growled and roiled at the same time. He was so hungry he almost fainted; so hungry the thought of food sickened him.

How long had he been in the void anyway? A day, a week, a year?

"*Stargods*, I hope the dragon waits for me. I can't afford to lose any more time." He thought about transporting up to the lair. Brevelan's copper life force had left an indelible memory of the cave in his mind to direct the spell.

Coils of colored lives, and one shimmering white one, enticed him back into the void, invited him to linger and learn.

"Ye'r late! Late, late, late," Corby reminded him again.

"I'll be later yet if I don't get something to eat," Yaakke protested. The blue-tipped dragon was right. Yaakke had used the transport spell once too often. Next time he might not have the will to leave the void.

"I'm still hungry!" Hilza whined, her voice little more than a whisper.

"We're all hungry," Katrina tried to soothe her sister. Was there any way to ease the pangs that gnawed at her belly? Two weeks of anxious waiting for the ship while bankers hounded P'pa for repayment of their investment; then two more weeks of small, meatless meals as P'pa scrambled for every coin he could gather to repay the bankers lest they send him to prison.

"Just try to think of something else, baby." P'pa looked at his plate as if by a miracle he'd left a tidbit to give Hilza. Flesh had fallen from his face since the day his ship hadn't sailed into port on time.

"Don't coddle the child," M'ma pouted. "She's old enough to learn that we are all paying for your mistake, Fraanken." M'ma's face was still full and bright. Only P'pa made the effort to give some of his share to his children.

"There is still time, Tattia. The ship may have been delayed by storms," P'pa protested.

"Tell that to the bankers and King Simeon!" M'ma screamed.

Hilza wailed in fright. Katrina choked back her own fear. Fear that tomorrow there would be no food on the table. Cold and upset, she reached over and pulled her youngest sister into her lap. Every meal lately ended with someone in tears. At least Maaben had the sense to spend her afternoons with Tante Syllia and Oncle Yon so she would be invited to stay for dinner. P'pa's brother and sister-in-law were childless and doted on Maaben, but had no time for studious Katrina or timid little Hilza.

"I've tried and tried for an audience with His Majesty," P'pa explained. "He won't see me. He won't admit that he ordered me to invest in that ship or that he has already borrowed and spent his share of the profits. Profits that will never be. He won't accept any part of the blame." P'pa seemed to shrink within his altered robes.

Yesterday, Katrina had cut all the costly embroidery from her father's clothing and reshaped the fabric for him. The ornaments had been sold to buy tonight's meager supper of rice and stale bread. The price of the food equaled what a full banquet would have cost six moons ago.

"If the ship doesn't come tomorrow, the day after at the latest, we'll have to sell Katrina's patterns," M'ma pronounced. "Without the patterns to work, we might as well sell the pillow and bobbins, too. She'll never be accepted into the palace school without her own patterns. Do you want to be responsible for ruining your daughter's future?"

"Perhaps if you spoke to the queen?" P'pa looked hopefully to his wife.

"The queen dismissed me today and impounded my pillow and patterns." M'ma dropped her eyes and her voice. "Please, Fraanken, you have to do something before we starve."

Katrina had never seen her mother so reduced, so helpless. Always, Tattia Kaantille's talent and experience with lace had placed her above ordinary people, granted her privileges and secured her place in society. Now she was lost. Katrina feared they were all lost as well as hungry.

"What will it take to make the king forgive you, P'pa?" Katrina whispered around the lump in her throat.

"Too much."

"What, Fraanken?" M'ma raised her head, hope bright in her eyes.

P'pa stood so fast he knocked over his chair. "I will sell myself to the slave ships before I sacrifice any of my daughters to The Simeon's bloodthirsty god, Simurgh!"

Hilza wailed again in fright and hunger.

Katrina lost all heat from her already shivering body.

Chapter Seven

"This doesn't seem right, M'ma." Katrina shuffled her feet on the wooden sidewalk of Royal Avenue. This major thoroughfare ran straight through Queen's City on a true east-west axis. To the north lay the tall, elegant houses of the merchants. Beyond them on the hillside were the palaces of the nobles. To the south lay the commercial district and warehouses that fronted on the SeLenicca River. M'ma walked toward those warehouses.

"Right doesn't put food on the table, Katey. With King Simeon's threat hanging over our heads, we dare not add any more debt, lest he take you and your sisters as sacrifices. Last week he announced that he needs the deaths of all the queen's prisoners to fuel his next battle spell and win through the pass into Coronnan." Tattia Kaantille charged ahead on the crowded street. "If I don't sell this pattern today, we'll have to sell your patterns and pillow, then next week the house will go. Though the Stargods only know if anyone in SeLenicca has the money to buy it."

"Sell the house?" That would mean moving outside Queen's

City. The homeless and dispossessed must leave this side of the river after sunset each day.

In recent months Katrina had watched the south bank of the River Lenicc become a veritable city of tents and hovels in its own right. Large numbers of desperate and destitute people fled there daily from all over SeLenicca as mines and timberlands closed.

Signs of a collapsing economy and the trade embargo with Coronnan affected Katrina's family faster than most residents of their neighborhood. No servant walked ahead of Tattia as a symbol of her wealth and favor with the queen. Katrina supposed the cook, the governess, the butler, and scullery maids were now part of the crowds who pressed against her, hands out begging, or attempting to creep into her pockets. There was nothing in her pockets to steal. Indeed the only signs that she and her mother had ever been privileged were the still sturdy black cloth of their skirts and cloaks and the two braids that started at their temples and joined into a single plait at their shoulder blades. Peasant women wore a single braid. Noble women wore three. Only the queen wore four plaits.

"But why must we tell the factory owner I designed the pattern?" Katrina hurried her steps a little so she wouldn't be separated from her mother by the press of people. They stepped off the sidewalk into a muddy alley.

"Because the queen has forbidden my designs. That's one of the prices we have to pay for your father's foolish investment." Tattia set her lips in a grim line. She scanned the narrow alley for unfriendly elements hiding in the shadows before proceeding farther.

"Do you think the factory owner will buy the pattern? He'll never believe that I drew it. I'm not even an apprentice—officially," she hastily added. M'ma had been teaching her at home, pushing her through the apprentice patterns and into journeywoman work faster than the palace normally allowed.

"No, but you are my daughter. We must make these men believe that you have inherited my talents."

"I'm not sure I can . . . I don't know enough about lace." Katrina bit her lip in uncertainty.

"Nonsense, Katrina. This is a simple T'chon pattern that uses twenty pairs of bobbins. I designed it for apprentices. It's so easy, the factory girls ought to be able to produce leagues of it for export. Just mention symmetry and geometric grids. They'll believe you. These are businessmen, not lacemakers!"

The alley suddenly narrowed and veered off to the right. Refuse grew thick in the gutter, as if it were some exotic plant with a life of its own. Shops with houses above gave way to warehouses—windowless, bleak, and huge. Empty. The air smelled of fish and garbage. They emerged onto a planked walkway beside the docks.

Katrina stared at the pier where P'pa's ship was supposed to rest at anchor, hoping for a miracle. If only the black-hulled vessel with red Kaantille sails bumped gently against the dock, all their troubles would be over.

"I don't like this district, M'ma." Katrina slipped her hand into her mother's.

"Who does? But thread has to be kept moist or it becomes brittle and breaks. The best place for a lace factory is near the river. These old warehouses are rotten with damp."

"I bet the lacemakers are, too."

"Yes, well, I suppose many of the women suffer from the cold and the damp. It's necessary. There wouldn't be any money in SeLenicca at all if we didn't have lace to export. Stargods only know if there will ever be any timber or enough ore to supply overseas markets again," Tattia whispered.

"Perhaps if we went to the temple first and prayed, M'ma. Not many people do that now. Maybe the Stargods have time to listen to our prayers."

"Don't even think that, child!" M'ma looked around hastily for signs of eavesdroppers. "We're in enough trouble with King Simeon. We daren't ask for more by being seen at the temple."

"But going to temple isn't forbidden," Katrina protested.

Suddenly she felt an overwhelming need to kneel before an altar and release all of her family's problems to the Stargods.

"No, prayer in the temple has not been forbidden by the king—yet. But such action earns his extreme displeasure."

For centuries the people had believed a never-ending supply of resources to exploit was their gift from the Stargods. To nurture and replant the land was blasphemy—denial of SeLenese status as the Chosen.

Now the resources were gone and no one knew how to replace them.

King Simeon preached a new philosophy. The people of SeLenicca were the Chosen of Simurgh, not the Stargods. The ancient bloodthirsty god required feeding for SeLenicca to regain its dominance in world trade and politics. King Simeon said he would get SeLenicca new resources through conquest, not farming or praying. Those who agreed with the king's religion—at least in public—found favor at court and in the marketplace.

A dark-green wooden door suddenly appeared in the otherwise blank brick wall of a factory. Freshly painted, with shiny brass hardware, the doorway invited business people within. Tattia paused long enough to take a deep breath before turning the doorknob.

Katrina followed her into the murky depths of the entry with heavy feet and a lump in her throat.

"This is necessary," she muttered to herself. "We have to get enough money to buy food and firewood."

A tiny bell jingled above them as the door swung shut of its own accord. A man approached them from the open office to their left. Tall and thin, he moved with an odd grace.

Katrina thought anyone that tall and long-limbed should jerk and wobble his way toward them. Dark eyes burned from his gaunt face beneath a fringe of sandy-blond hair. He wore a square beard.

"Outland half-breed!" M'ma hissed through her teeth.

Katrina hoped the man hadn't heard the insult. Success today depended upon his goodwill.

"We are not hiring today." The man looked down his nose at them. A long way down.

"I do not seek employment." M'ma stood tall and straight. Every bit of her artistic superiority added majesty to her posture and high-lighted the man's inferior breeding.

"Then why do you disturb my busy schedule?" The man didn't back down before M'ma's glare.

"I wish to discuss a matter of business with the owner." M'ma sniffed as if the hallway smelled as badly as the gutters outside.

"You do not have an appointment." The man withdrew two steps. He reached to close the office door with long, slender fingers. Katrina thought his hands ideal for making lace.

"Tell your superior that Tattia Kaantille wishes to speak with him."

The man's eyes widened a little at the name then closed to mere slits. "No man, or woman, is my superior, madam. And I am the owner of this establishment. You do not have an appointment."

The door slammed in their faces.

"Hmf!" M'ma sniffed her disgust. "I'll have your father track down the true owner of this factory. That ungrateful peasant will be fired for his insolence to us. Everyone knows you can't trust dark-eyes. They are born stupid and dishonest."

"You shouldn't have insulted him, M'ma," Katrina whispered.

"I don't want to do business with anyone who hires outland half-breeds." M'ma marched back up the alley. "No wonder the country is falling to pieces. First the queen marries a foreigner, and now infe-riors are allowed positions of authority."

A few more twists and turns in the back streets brought them to another grim factory. This time the green door wasn't newly painted and the brass fittings needed a good polish.

The man inside the office was small, wiry, and as filthy as M'ma thought the outlander had been. He bought the design, but only after M'ma had sworn that no one else in the city had it.

"We will try the next two factories. That should give us enough money to last the month." M'ma smiled brightly as she secreted the coins inside her embroidered vest. "But, M'ma, you just swore that no one else in the city had the design!" Katrina protested almost as loudly as her empty stomach.

"And no one else does. Yet," M'ma replied.

"Isn't that illegal?"

"This is a matter of survival, Katey."

"Oh, M'ma, this seems so wrong so . . . so dirty. Please, don't make me come back here."

"Lord Jonnias?" Rejiia whispered into her father's glass. "You could depose Darville and rule all of Coronnan if you destroyed the Commune. You know where the Commune hides." That piece of information had come to her with the cost of many spells and the lives of several informers—none of them Jaylor's spy here in the capital. Now she revealed the secret to Jonnias.

The image of the sleeping lord squirmed within the candle flame behind Rejiia's glass. The basic summons spell worked better than a compulsion with mundanes, if she spoke to them in their dreams. When they awoke, her words seemed her victim's own ideas and they didn't build up resistance to the spell as Rossemikka had to Janataca.

"Take a witch-sniffer, Jonnias. Take him to the ancient monastery in the foothills of the southern mountains." She waited a moment for that idea to settle in the lord's mind. "You will need the troops of Marnak the Elder and the Younger plus your own. The wife of the Younger will provide you with a copy of the king's personal banner to grant you authority. She will demand to go with you. Accede to her wishes."

The image of Jonnias smiled in his sleep. Pompous and arrogant he might be. But he wasn't stupid. He knew that Darville and Jaylor had been friends most of their lives.

"Jaylor will blame Darville for the attack when he sees the banner. If he survives the attack, their friendship will be broken. Then they will both be vulnerable.

"You have followers within the new cult. They will make you king if you destroy the Commune."

"Yes," Jonnias whispered in his sleep. "Yes."

Rejiia extinguished the flame, breaking her contact with the odious lord. She allowed herself a moment's rest before she repeated the summons to Lord Marnak the Elder. The two were easy to manipulate. Their inflated sense of self-importance made them vulnerable to her plans. When their conspiracy failed because they overstepped their abilities to lead, she would abandon them. Until then, they served a purpose.

A chuckle tickled the back of her throat. She wondered which one of them would be first to order a new crown made. The Coraurlia contained the taint of magic. They wouldn't be able to justify using it if they used the Gnuls to achieve their goals.

But the Coraurlia was the crown Rejiia sought. Its magical protection *Sang* to her in her dreams.

She caressed the tin statue that sat beside her chair. "Soon, Pappi. Soon I will be queen. Then I will be able to set you free. By then I will have learned more magic and you must recognize me as your equal. I will not submit to you demeaning me in public again. Until then, I must send you by fishing boat and other secret ways to a place of safety."

You are late. A deep voice bellowed the words from the depths of the cave through Yaakke's physical and mental ears. He stopped short before passing through the black entrance into the heart of the mountain.

"Ye'r late, late, late." Above him, the attendant jackdaw circled and echoed the dragon's proclamation.

Late? Yaakke knew he'd lost time in the void. How much time? Certainly not two weeks. Autumn weather hadn't deepened by more than a day or two at most. The sun had warmed his back quite nicely on his long walk from the clearing. When he'd discovered the barriers around the clearing were down, probably because Brevelan wasn't there, he'd started the trek uphill rather than wait to recover his strength for a shape-change. The single night he'd spent sleeping rough had been cold, but not intolerable as long as his campfire glowed within a bubble of armor.

"I . . . got lost in the void," Yaakke stammered his explanation.

I told you not to use that spell. Light shifted and distorted within the cave entrance. Star bursts of light exploded before Yaakke's eyes.

He blinked and refocused and blinked again. The brightness settled into sunbeams refracted off the faceted points of a huge oval jewel. He forgot the journey dust that clogged his throat.

Tremors traveled beneath the ground, telling of something heavy moving across the stony plateau in front of the cave. The jewel took on a more definite shape. A fold of a nearly transparent membrane closed over an all color/ no color kaleidoscope.

A dragon's eye! Yaakke sighed in relief. The blue-tipped dragon had waited. But how long? Now for the first time, Yaakke wished he'd learned to center his magic so that it tracked time accurately.

Gradually the rest of the dragon emerged from the depths of the lair. Hazy, autumnal sunshine slanted off his crystalline fur, pulling Yaakke's sight around the dragon rather than directly toward him. He blinked and forced his mind to concentrate on the outline of the huge creature before his eyes tricked his mind into believing the dragon invisible.

Larger than Shayla, the dragon rested back on his haunches. Blue veins outlined the shape of wings folded against his back. More blue marched across his head and down his back in a showy display of horns. On his shortened forelegs, blue claws flexed, much like human fingers.

Yaakke waited, expecting the dragon to offer his name according to dragon protocol.

The dragon remained silent while surveying Yaakke with those penetrating eyes.

Yaakke squirmed in guilty self-consciousness. "I'm sorry." Finally he offered the apology he knew he owed the dragon.

You have become arrogant with your power. The dragon words came into Yaakke's head unbidden.

"I'm sorry," Yaakke's murmured again. "I should have guessed you have more knowledge of the void than I." He hung his head a little, peeping up at the dragon through lowered lashes.

I hope your trip through the realm of the dragons taught you something useful.

"I don't know . . . um . . . sir. What do I call you anyway?"

Sir will do.

"Anyway, *sir,* the images came so fast I didn't recognize half of what I saw." A memory of moon-bright hair and tears on a girl's pale face flashed through his mind. "Who is she?"

You will learn that when your time reference catches up with what you observed. Time has no meaning in the void. Past, present, and future are all the same. Dragons observe it all and learn.

"Why did you call me here?"

Shayla needs assistance from the magicians.

"Shayla!" Yaakke breathed through his teeth. His quest was almost over. He'd be the youngest Master Magician ever. Without ever having been a journeyman!

Your journey is long, apprentice. Long in distance and long in maturity. The dragon speared Yaakke with a compelling gaze. *There are things you must know before you face the dangers ahead of you.*

The ominous tone of the words in the back of Yaakke's mind was so like Old Baamin, the boy automatically keyed all of his attention to the huge beast.

Drink, Boy. Then we will discuss your future and perhaps your past. The dragon gestured with his muzzle toward a crystal cold stream trickling down the mountain face beside the cave entrance.

"You promised to tell me about my parents, sir," Yaakke reminded the dragon.

I know of your sire and your dam. The knowledge will be given to you at the appropriate time.

"When will that be?"

At the appropriate time. Drink and refresh yourself. You have much to learn in order to find Shayla.

Curiosity flared. Yaakke was always eager to know more about magic. He'd taught himself to read so that he could steal books from the University library before he knew for sure he had any magic.

Yaakke knelt beside the little pool that formed in a hollow made by the falling stream. He cupped his hands in the water. Colors and images swirled before his vision, then faded to reflections of sunlight on water. He drank deeply, twice, then splashed his face and hair reasonably clean.

One more drink. He'd never known plain water to taste so sweet before. Head bent over the pool, he was about to dip his hands once again, when the dragon's reflection shimmered in the water.

The beast loomed behind him, magnificent head higher than two sledge steeds. Sunlight sparkled. Water reflected. Crystal fur shimmered and those huge, faceted eyes showed access to the void and all of those tempting umbilicals.

Chapter Eight

Pinpoints of light speared Yaakke's eyes, then burst into a myriad of stars. Suddenly the dark cave entrance and the crystal spring disappeared.

A thundering cascade of water filled his ears. His gut reverberated in response to the deep *boom* of a river tumbling hundreds of feet into a deep pool. He shivered as cold spray dampened his clothes and drizzled down his face. A wall of algae-slick granite, older and paler than the jagged basalt near the lair, pressed into his face, but he didn't dare jerk away from the slime until he found secure footing. He glanced at his feet without moving his head. A narrow shelf of rock jutted out from a cliff side, barely wide enough to contain both of his feet.

Finger-length by finger-length, he eased his body around to face the roaring waterfall. Tiny droplets tumbled, joined, separated, fell hundreds of feet below him into a wide pool. Turbulence from the waterfall thrust small waves across a deep pool to a long rolling meadow. Steep walls on three sides defined a wide vale that narrowed at the far end into a canyon leading to the outside world. His only exit from this unknown mountain hideaway?

A wide undercut yawned deep into the base of the cliff behind the waterfall. He knew instinctively that a series of caves wandered back into the bowels of the mountain from that barely glimpsed opening. Shadow within shadow moved behind the lacy curtain of water. Was that the outline of a dragon head, its glittering eyes the same color as the water drops?

He'd found Shayla! But where?

Then Yaakke scanned the setting for clues. He looked up. A black bird with funny white tufts on its head soared up the cliff a hundred feet above him. Scrubby everblues seemed to hang out over the edge. The water poured over the lip around and through them. Ferns, lichens, and wildflowers clung to the rocky face, adding spring vibrancy to the scene.

The waving grass in the open field appeared lush with moisture and new growth. Clumps of tall shrubs offered shade and shelter on this bright afternoon. More than just shrubs, stunted Tambootie trees. Dragon salad.

Above the hidden vale, sharp mountain peaks, still covered in snow, rose in undulating tiers into the distant, hazy horizon. Jutting out from closer crags and pinnacles, wind-sculpted lumps of stone pointed toward the cloudless sky. Dragons standing guard?

Yaakke sniffed the air and wrinkled his nose. "Woodsmoke." Alarm sent his heart racing. Corby cawed loudly in distress, then disappeared. Soon, the mindless destruction of fire unleashed would envelop this lovely glade. Tambootie smoke would poison all living creatures within two leagues or more.

He sought the magic power that should be entwined with the rock and soil of the cliff. No energy tingled through his body. "Rain. *Stargods*, I need rain to stop this!" Concentrating the failing reserves of his own body, he reached up into the sky for every drop of moisture available.

A small cloud formed. Then another. Tiny, fluffy white clouds. Not big enough or heavy enough to release a single drop of rain.

Cease!

Dragon thoughts sent him tumbling down, down toward the pool. Cold water numbed his mind and body. Pain lanced through his temple.

You may not change a dragon-dream.

Yaakke sat up from the plateau outside Shayla's old lair. "Dream? It all seemed so real." Delicately he probed his temple with shaking fingers. Aches spread outward into his jaw and ear. No sticky blood. Just a bruise from collapsing onto the ground.

Reality changes from eyeblink to eyeblink. What you see is real until you disprove it with new perceptions.

"Where is this place you showed me? Not in Coronnan. The mountain shapes were wrong. Too jagged and bare of trees." Yaakke inspected the rest of his body for damage, glad that he hadn't ceased breathing because he thought he fell into a pool and drowned.

Your quest ends in a place that appeared to you in the dragon-dream. The jackdaw will guide you.

"Do I still have a quest? I left Jaylor without an explanation. I disobeyed you. Will anyone trust me after that?"

Seek Shayla with your heart as well as your mind. She will trust your heart.

"What is that supposed to mean?"

Shayla's life depends upon you. Without Shayla the Nimbus of Dragons will die.

"I need to talk to Jaylor first. He'll help me understand . . ." His voice trailed off. Yaakke wasn't certain what he needed to understand. His bizarre trip through the void followed by a dragon-dream seemed to have scrambled his insides as well as his thoughts.

You may discuss this with me. The dragon sounded sad or upset that Yaakke sought advice from another.

"You're just a dragon. You wouldn't understand."

Uncomfortable silence stretched between them.

If only I could tell you.

Was that a dragon thought? Yaakke wondered if he truly caught a glimmer of hurt and resignation in the droop of the dragon's muzzle and half-closed eyes. He shook his head, trying to clear it of confusion so he could be sure.

More silence.

Jaylor's hiding place is on your way.

"On my way where? Is Shayla hurt like King Darville? Can she fly?"

Yaakke twisted his neck to peer at the dragon. Gone! The dragon was gone, disappeared.

"I know you are nearly invisible, but this is too much." Silence except for the distant call of a jackdaw. Yaakke staggered to his feet and blundered toward the cave entrance that had shadowed the dragon. With outstretched hands he examined the lair entrance. Nothing.

"Is this whole thing a dragon-dream?" No one answered but Corby. "*S'murgh it*, I could still be in the capital for all I know."

Jaylor squinted through his telescope one last time. The other Master Magicians had deserted him for the warmth of their beds hours ago. There wasn't anything particularly interesting in the sky tonight. But Jaylor needed the practice. And he needed some time alone.

A year ago, when he'd begun his journeyman's quest, all he'd wanted was to "Go see an invisible dragon" and earn the right to be a Master Magician. He had no idea, then, precisely what master status entailed. Now he knew.

Master Magicians charted the stars, tabulated the paths of celestial bodies, and searched for anomalies and omens. Closer to the mundane population, magicians used their powers to minister to the sick, communicate with distant outposts, test the soil, and advise the people about proper nutrients and crop rotation and efficient breeding of stock. The secret knowledge entrusted to them by the Stargods provided them with guides. They experimented with tools and inventions, striving for improvements in production. They kept records and wrote chronicles. In better times, magicians advised the rich and powerful about diplomacy, economics, and alliances.

Those responsibilities were child's play compared to Jaylor's duties as Senior Magician. Endless lists of supplies, maintenance and observation schedules, keeping track of every member of the diminished Commune, and placing the magicians where their talents could be maximized and their limitations augmented by others. And a constant monitoring of the defensive war being waged at the pass near Sambol. How many magicians dared he post there without raising superstitious fear among the troops, generals, and Council? The number had to be enough to counteract King Simeon's indiscriminate use of battle magic. Where did they get the power to wage war? Everyone knew there were no ley lines in SeLenicca to fuel magic.

These late hours on the roof seemed to be the only time Jaylor had alone, to think, to plan, to worry. He couldn't remember the last time he'd gone to bed at the same time as Brevelan.

His wife and son were always sound asleep when he crawled beneath the covers and still asleep when he rose before dawn to his morning duties.

He checked the position of the wanderer he had been monitoring for twenty-one nights. Then he measured its position between two fixed stars. His eyes blurred and he placed the point of light on the wrong chart, in the wrong position.

His geometric calculations on the chart tangled.

One more time. A deep breath for calm. A second deep breath for clear vision. His third deep breath sent him into a light trance. With the aid of his magic, he looked, measured, and calculated once more. The numbers fell into place. The wanderer had definitely shifted its position relative to his location. Precisely what it was supposed to do at this time of year.

The calculations on the chart, combined with the recent meteor shower, predicted chaos. The same conclusion the other masters had drawn a week ago.

At last he'd done something correctly. He bent to touch his toes, stretching his back in relief. As he stood again, his shoulder bumped the telescope.

"Dragon dung. Now it's out of alignment." He looked into the lens, still maintaining his extended senses, to see how far off he'd knocked the sights.

Shimmering pinpoints of light responded to his magic senses. Not starlight. Too green, wrong shapes. He extended his TrueSight and hearing through the telescope into the distance beyond.

At the extreme limits of his magic, woodsmoke caressed his nose. The sounds of drowsy steeds cropping grass within their picket line tickled his ears. Jaylor drew upon FarSight and the scene jumped as close as the exterior grounds of the monastery. Seventy-five, no, one hundred campfires. One thousand men. Herds of war steeds. He spotted a sentry patrolling a perimeter.

An army camped out there, half a day's hard march away.

Whose army? His spy in the palace had said nothing to him about an army on the move.

He wished for Yaakke's listening talent, or for the boy himself. No word from him for nearly two moons now. Curse the boy for his secretive ways and stubborn disregard for others.

Jaylor sought and found a silvery-blue ley line filled with magic power, running through the foundations of the monastery. Slowly, he urged the magic energy to rise through the walls. The stones caught the power, resonating with their internal music. The magic picked up the natural harmonics and amplified them within the ageless bones of the land. Jaylor listened to the singing of the power. His body vibrated in harmony with it. Only then did he draw upon the power, forcing it upward when it wanted to dart out into the world through his fingers. Up and up into his neck and his mind. The *Song* of the Kardia grew. He *Sang* the magic into his eyes and his ears.

Only then did he look through the telescope again. Bright

banners atop gaudy war pavilions came into focus. He identified the flags of Marnak the Elder from Hanic in the southwest and Jonnias from Sauria in the northwest. Neither lord was particularly fond of Jaylor or his magicians, but they had sworn loyalty to Darville.

A third banner caught Taylor's attention. Marnak the Younger of Faciar. Through his wife, Rejiia, that sniveling little upstart had claimed Krej's old province. He, too, had sworn loyalty to Darville, but only after Jaylor had purged the young man of all traces of Krej's magic manipulation. If Marnak and Rejiia hadn't been so young and naive about Krej's corruption, the Council of Provinces would have forced them into exile with Krej's wife and six younger legitimate daughters. No one bothered counting his bastards.

Rumor in the capital claimed the tall, determined, and still very young heiress to the province intimidated her shorter husband, and that the marriage had never been consummated.

Rejiia had tried to renounce her marriage along with her father when the extent of Krej's evil became obvious. But the Council of Provinces had held the adolescent marriage to be legal and Rejiia's husband governor of her province.

The three lords encamped beyond the next line of hills were an odd confederation to lead an army. None of them had ever shown interest in the arts of war before.

Jaylor puzzled over the implications, listening to the small sounds of nightlife in a military camp. He swung his vision around the perimeter of pickets and steed lines, tents, and provision sledges. One more large pavilion stood off to the side, but still within the perimeter of the camp, as if seeking privacy and protection at the same time. The royal banner of a dragon outlined in gold against a midnight blue field surrounded by silver stars flew from the ridgepole. A golden wolf stood in the corner of the flag.

Darville's personal emblem. The presence of the king explained the other three banners. None of those lords would be willing to remain idle in the palace when there was a chance to kiss royal ass in the field.

The tent flap opened and a shadowy figure slipped out into the fresh night air. A tall man, broad of shoulder, slim of hip, stretched and yawned. King Darville. Jaylor's best friend.

As Jaylor watched, the king walked to the perimeter, speaking with each of the guards. Darville's personal contact with his soldiers had won their loyalty and made him a better general.

Why would Darville bring his army within two days' ride of where Jaylor and the Commune hid from the Council of Provinces?

Jaylor yawned and stretched. He couldn't think straight until he'd indulged in some much needed sleep. Darville would never deliberately harm him. Time enough to puzzle this out in the morning.

He thought of Brevelan's warm body and inviting arms. Already he ached to hold her tight against his chest and sleep with her sweet scent filling him with her serenity and calm.

Hilza coughed and coughed again. Katrina looked up from her newest lace pattern to check her sister. Hilza's thin body collapsed jerkily with each new spasm. Dots of sweat popped out on the little girl's brow though the workroom was icy. The kitchen fires that heated the whole house had been extinguished right after a meager breakfast of thin porridge, in order to conserve firewood.

Hilza coughed again, nearly choking from lack of breath. Maaben dropped her tablet of figures and dashed out of the room, slamming the door behind her. Distantly, Katrina heard the front door bang shut. She knew that Maaben would seek refuge from the stress of little food and less heat, of sickness and short tempers, with Tante Syllia and Oncle Yon. Their relatives welcomed Maaben, fed and cosseted her, where they rebuffed the rest of the family. King Simeon's displeasure with P'pa had extended to anyone seen assisting the Kaantille family.

Tears streamed down Hilza's face. "I can't help it, Katey. I can't stop coughing. Why does Maaben blame me?" She choked out the words around a raspy throat.

"I don't know, Hilza." Katrina cradled her youngest sister against her chest, rocking her gently, humming an old lullaby to soothe her.

> *All is quiet, all is still,*
> *Sleep, my child, fear not ill,*
> *Wintry winds blow chill and drear,*
> *Lullaby, my baby dear,*
> *Wintry winds blow chill and drear,*
> *Lullaby, my baby dear.*

"Maybe Maaben is afraid," Katrina cooed to her now quiet sister. "She hates me," Hilza whispered around a sniffle. "Hush, little one. Hush."

> *Let thy little eyelids close,*
> *Like the petals of the rose;*
> *When the morning sun shall glow,*
> *They shall into blossom blow,*
> *They shall into blossom blow,*
> *When the morning sun shall glow.*

"P'pa is trying to raise more money. He'll come home tonight with bundles of firewood and a fat chicken for our dinner." Katrina's mouth watered at the thought of meat, so long absent from their table.

"And M'ma?" Hilza murmured drowsily.

"M'ma has made a wonderful lace shawl for the queen. If Queen Miranda accepts the gift, then M'ma can go back to work at the palace." M'ma had worked the shawl with weaving silk, a thread much heavier than most lacework. Yet the fibers worked up to appear filmy and frothy. If M'ma started a new fashion trend, then she would be in demand to design more shawls and maybe veils. The Kaantille family would be rich again.

"But the queen may not like the gift," Hilza protested. She partially roused from her sleepiness but didn't raise her head. The cords of her neck stood out rigid and hard under Katrina's caressing fingers.

"She must accept it, little one. No one makes lace like M'ma does. The shipments of lace overseas are fetching less and less money since M'ma left the palace. Queen Miranda has to take M'ma back." She hoped.

The lace factories had stopped buying M'ma's designs. She'd falsely promised exclusive rights to the patterns once too often.

The front door slammed again. A heavy reluctant tread on the steep stairs. That would be P'pa. If his steps dragged, then his mission had failed. There would be no chicken for dinner.

Another step behind P'pa. This one springier and lighter. A stranger. The door to the workroom opened slowly. P'pa stood there, a deep scowl on his face. Defeat seemed to drag his shoulders down, shortening, reducing him to a haggard old man.

"What is it, P'pa?" Katrina looked up at her parent, frightened and insecure. She kept Hilza's weary body cradled within her arms, face buried in her lap.

"Is your mother home?" P'pa looked around the room, peering into shadows He seemed to fear what he might find.

"No" Katrina answered.

"Good." Was that relief in his tone and the raising of his shoulders?

A tall, hooded stranger appeared behind P'pa, pushing to gain access to the room. "Almost as cold in here as it is outside, Merchant Kaantille." The thin man rubbed his long-fingered hands together, not with cold, but with some kind of eagerness.

Katrina had seen those hands before. "Take the blasted patterns and be gone!" P'pa bellowed impatiently.

"Patterns? P'pa, you didn't!" Katrina darted across the room to her lace pillow, heedless of Hilza. She clutched the velvet bolster with its cache of patterns to her chest, letting the bobbins tangle. Pins that held her latest lace into the pattern pressed through her clothes, pricking her skin.

"I'm sorry, Katey. I had no choice." P'pa looked at the floor.

"Give me the pillow with the patterns, girl." The thin man stepped closer, hands reaching for her treasure. His hood fell back revealing the dark-eyed owner of the first lace factory she and M'ma had approached. The man M'ma had insulted.

"No. I don't care how much money you paid him. The pillow and patterns are mine. My dowry. He can't sell it." She swung around so her back was to the stranger. She hated the gleeful revenge that burned in his brown eyes.

"Give him the pillow, Katrina. Give it up or watch your sister die of the lung rot and the rest of us starve or freeze to death," P'pa ordered. His voice was as weak and reluctant as his steps.

He was right. The patterns contained within the pillow with its engraved bone bobbins were the most precious things left in the house. Even the glass window in the workroom had been sold, the opening covered with scrap wood. M'ma's pillow and patterns had remained at the palace when she was dismissed and could not be retrieved.

"I can't, P'pa. If I give this up, I have no future." Katrina dropped to her knees, her legs suddenly too weak to hold her upright.

"If you don't, we'll all starve, Katey." P'pa pried her fingers up and yanked the bolster out of her arms. He thrust it at the eager stranger.

A single bobbin broke loose from the tangle of fine cotton threads. Katrina caught it within the folds of her skirt. The men wouldn't notice one bobbin missing. Not one lonely little bone bobbin out of forty pairs.

"Take it and be gone. I don't want to ever see your face gain." P'pa ushered the stranger toward the door.

The man shoved a fat purse into P'pa's still outstretched hand. It slipped through his fingers and dropped to the floor with a clank that echoed around the silent room.

Katrina glanced at the bobbin still clutched in her skirt. "Tattia Kaantille" the engraved letters spelled in a spiral around the slender piece of bone. She traced the letters from bottom to top. Something sharp caught on the threads of her skirt. The glass bead on the bangle had shattered in the fall.

Chapter Nine

Rejiia listened through the night for magic on the wind. Not long after midnight, she sensed a spell of braided magic winding its way through the encampment like a ghost of stray mist, questing but not disturbing.

Red and blue. The Senior Magician was scouting the army with that spell. She had watched Jaylor work magic in the capital often enough to know his signature colors.

Silently she crept from her bed behind a heavy screen in the largest pavilion. Marnak the Younger, her husband, snored on a cot on the other side of the screen. A year of marriage and he still hadn't found the courage to join her in bed. A shiver of loathing coursed through her as her nightrail brushed against his cot.

She thought she might have more respect for him if he'd raped her on their wedding night, as her father had advised. But now? The weak little lordling was still dependent upon and submissive to his father. Rejiia would rather sleep with the sergeant who patrolled the nobles' section of the encampment than with her lawful husband.

Outside the tent, she sniffed for the magic again, clearer and sharper in the fresh air. Half invisible, she followed the drifting red-

and-blue braid to the edge of camp. Earlier, she had ordered a single tent set up here. A delusion slipped from her fingertips. She smiled in delight as she transformed the miserable private's shelter into a huge royal pavilion with Darville's personal banner flying above.

The magic circled the delusion briefly then hesitated at the opening, scanning Rejiia's form. She gave the questing magic an image of Darville tall, blond, dynamic in his masculinity. The red-and-blue braid persisted, wanting reassurance.

Reluctantly, Rejiia ambled around the edge of the camp, cloaked in the image of her royal cousin. She paused and spoke to several of the sleepy soldiers, as the king would do.

Darville had stolen the crown that should have been hers. She hated him and resented his presence even in this imaginary form.

At last Jaylor's magic was satisfied and retreated to the monastery. It smelled of curiosity partially satisfied.

Rejiia hummed a joyful tune she'd heard the troops singing as they marched from the capital. More than slightly bawdy and confident, the song collapsed the delusions. Her body tingled with power. Maybe she should seduce the sergeant, right under Marnak's nose.

No. Not tonight. She should save her maidenhead until she needed its destruction to fuel a spell of real importance. Her bed and a well-deserved sleep enticed her back to the camp. "Perhaps I'll dream of looting and rape and fire. Tomorrow the Commune dies along with my bastard sister and her brat. Brevelan stole my father's love from me. Now she will pay."

Yaakke forced himself to walk west, away from familiar jagged peaks toward the more rounded mountains of SeLenicca. Shayla's hiding place was in a valley near rounded mountains, stripped of timber. The only mountains like those were west of Coronnan. He counted four more steps and then four more.

"Shay-la needs me. Shay-la needs me," he recited in rhythm with his steps.

The more space he put between himself and the dragon lair, the less worn and confused he felt. Every time he looked at his body, he was afraid he'd start to fade into transparency—like the dragons.

Hunger gnawed at him constantly. He'd devoured all of the food he'd been able to scavenge in Brevelan's clearing—including one of her precious flusterhens. Villagers were shy and suspicious of strangers in this part of Coronnan, so he'd had to steal a few provisions here and there, including a pack and cooking utensils. Still he ached with fatigue and emptiness.

How long had he been in the void?

He looked at the sky for some indication he'd chosen the right direction. A deep overcast didn't betray the position of the sun.

Corby the jackdaw cawed enthusiastically above him, dropping a smelly blob on the trail behind Yaakke. He looked from the bird to his deposit, then along the trail. Sure enough, Corby had spotted a crested perdix lurking in the scrubby grasses. The characteristic head bobbing and twisted topknot were not fully developed in the bird. Probably a youngster without the sense to migrate.

Yaakke stood hunter-still. His mouth watered at the thought of a true meal cooked over a campfire. A palm-sized rock appeared in his fist. Desperation enhanced his reflexes and trued his aim. He flung the stone directly onto the perdix's bobbing head.

"Thanks, Corby. I'll save you some!" Yaakke plunged toward his prey.

"Owe me one, owe me one," the jackdaw cawed.

Almost, Yaakke considered eating the meat raw, feathers and all. Then something deep inside him sickened at the thought. Methodically he sought a campsite.

One good thing about being a magician: he could start a fire even when the wood was wet. He settled his pack beneath an overhang where the soil was reasonably dry. His tin pot came readily to hand. It always did, no matter where he'd stuffed it.

He'd seen a Rover trick once that might help him find Shayla or Jaylor—or someone who might help him. He needed food and rest first. When he had some grains and the gutted perdix simmering nicely, he granted himself the luxury of a quick wash and a fresh shirt. As he ran his fingers over his jaw and neck, the texture of his skin seemed changed, coarser, rougher. Using a calm pool at the edge of the creek as a mirror he checked for cuts or rash or just leftover mud.

Nothing quite so usual greeted his reflection. Dark shadows creased his jaw and upper lip. The beginning of a beard! A rather complete and dark beard at that. Well, several days' worth anyway. The facial hair seemed soft and fine now. Soon enough it would grow thicker and heavier.

At last!

About time.

"La, la, la, la," he sang, testing the quality of his voice. To his own ear the notes sounded his same childish soprano.

"Loo, loo, loo, loo," he sang again, on a lower tone. Much lower than he used to sing.

"La, la, laeeeeek," he tried the high notes and lost all control.

Good. By the time he found Jaylor, maybe he'd be through the worst of the change and be able to speak like a man. Jaylor could authorize his trial by Tambootie smoke and promote him to journeyman. Once promoted, he could claim a larger piece of glass for focusing his spells. The trial might also grant him a vision to guide him to Shayla.

"Shayla needs me."

Yaakke tried the notes again and didn't croak until almost two tones lower than last time.

Corby jeered from his perch atop the boulder at Yaakke's miserable attempt to sing.

"Your voice doesn't sound much smoother, bird!" Yaakke returned to his campfire, anxious to try the Rover trick.

Just before leaving Shayla's lair, he had seen something very frightening reflected in water. More than reflections. A vision, or another dragon-dream. Jaylor and Brevelan and the baby had stood in the middle of a raging inferno, desperately seeking escape.

The vision had ended before Yaakke had seen an accurate picture of *where* Jaylor and Brevelan were. He needed to know where, or what direction in order to direct a standard summons spell.

Yaakke knew deep inside himself that Jaylor and his family needed help.

He'd been granted the vision for a reason. He had to find Jaylor and warn him of the fire. Or help him escape.

If the trick worked.

The trap is set. By an hour after sunrise, the Commune will cease to exist. An hour later my agent will inform King Darville how it happened and who was responsible. Jonnias and the Marnaks will never be trusted in Council again. When they realize the depth of the rift between themselves and their king, the three sniveling lords will revolt. The rest of the Council will blame Darville for the newest civil war. He won't be allowed to survive as king of a country tearing itself apart and he without an heir and with a witch for a wife.

Within a few moons Coronnan will be in such chaos, the coven will be able to step in and enforce law and order on their own terms. Soon, so very soon.

Four horsemen backed by a thousand soldiers rode up to the gates of the monastery. Jaylor watched the three noble banners fluttering above the lieutenants who each represented a lord: Jonnias, Marnak the Elder, and Marnak the Younger. Higher than the three fluttered a fourth banner. The man carrying the symbol of a crystal dragon and a golden wolf didn't wear a uniform of the royal household or army.

An aura of hate shimmered over the entire army.

"I don't like the smell of this," Jaylor growled to Brevelan who stood by his side at the window of their tower room.

"I sense a great deal of anger out there." Brevelan edged behind Jaylor, putting a physical barrier between herself and the roiling emotions of a thousand armed men. "Anger and fear. They do not come in peace."

"Can you isolate Darville in the throng? I want to talk to him privately before I face those emissaries at the gate." Jaylor leaned against the windowsill, trying desperately to find one familiar blond head among the battle-hardened men.

Brevelan's eyes closed in concentration. Her pale skin turned whiter; but shadows hollowed her cheeks and furrowed in her brow. Jaylor resisted the urge to reach out and offer her strength and comfort. If he touched her right now, her contact with the army below would shrivel.

"No. There are too many people out there to find one soul." She shook her head. Huge blue eyes, clouded with bewilderment and pain, looked up to his. "Our king is the one person I should be able to isolate at any distance. He hides himself from me."

A momentary pang of jealousy brought a red mist to Jaylor's eyes and judgment. Brevelan might be his, Jaylor's, wife now. Darville might be very much in love with his own bride, Rossemikka, *now*. But he could never forget that a little less than a year ago, Brevelan had made a very hard choice between the two men.

The possibility that the king's seed had fathered Glendon remained.

"You know it is you I love, Jaylor," Brevelan reached across the barrier of his emotions.

A hard spot in his heart dissolved. Her small hand sought his. With those few words the jealousy died and love reblossomed in his chest. He clung to her hand, the simple gesture binding them together.

"What do we do about them?" She gestured to the horsemen who were pounding on the gates for entrance.

"I know Darville's banner gives this army authority. But I cannot find any reason our friend would betray our location to those three lords. He might tell Lord Andrall—his loyalty has never been questioned. But those three?" He shrugged in disbelief.

"Could it have been a trick to disarm your suspicions. You would open the gate willingly for your king."

"Aye. But not to Jonnias and the two Marnaks."

The wind shifted slightly, carrying the babble of voices from the army. The aura of hatred intensified.

"I believe we have been betrayed, Brevelan." By whom? An agent of the fanatical Gnostic Utilitarian cult which decreed that all knowledge must come by hard work and experience, not magic? His best friend? Jaylor faced that painful possibility reluctantly. His spy should have told him about this army before it left the capital. Perhaps the Council had decided to secretly remove Glendon, the king's bastard son, from Jaylor's and Brevelan's custody.

Never! Jaylor resolved. "Show Master Fraandalor an image of Shayla's old lair and have him begin transporting the library and the telescopes there. The time has come to find a new sanctuary for the Commune." Regret hung heavily on his shoulders.

The sanctity of this remote retreat for aging magicians, priests, and healers should not be violated by an army bent on destruction. Darville should not have succumbed to any of the forces that wanted an end to all magic in Coronnan.

"Will we be able to protect everyone there?" Brevelan looked out over the undulating sea of soldiers that spread across the hills. The noise of their coming increased.

"If Krej couldn't find the path up the mountain without help, then this mundane army won't be able to either. There is shelter, water, and privacy." He snatched a quick kiss from her. "Go quickly.

I'll stall the lieutenants at the gates." The ancient wooden barriers were beginning to buckle from the pounding of sword hilts on the planks.

Brevelan's departure emptied the stark room of warmth and sunshine. Jaylor emptied his mind and body of emotion, allowing keen thoughts to focus without distraction. Only by eliminating his beloved from his consciousness could he generate the spells necessary to save her. To save the Commune.

"Why, Darville? Why are you with these men?" he asked the wind.

Below him, in the courtyard, the gatekeepers peered out the viewing hole of the right-hand gate. Anxiety written in their posture and the wringing of their hands, they looked up to the tower window for guidance.

Jaylor uncoiled a thread of magic, linking him to the gatekeepers. He fed them instructions to keep the gates barred, but not to retreat yet.

The banner-toting envoys drew back a pace. "Yield this sacred stronghold of the Stargods to Darville III, by the grace of the dragons, King of Coronnan!" bellowed the man carrying the banner of Jonnias of Sauria.

"This enclave belongs to the Stargods, not to any mundane king," one of the two gatekeepers squeaked a reply. His frail old voice barely carried through the massive wooden barrier.

The lieutenants growled and consulted among themselves for a stronger command.

Jaylor directed the gatekeepers to withdraw to the safety of the library.

"Yield or be taken by force!" the lieutenant of Jonnias cried once more.

No one was left at the gate to reply.

The lieutenants hoisted their banners high, Darville's symbol highest of all, and returned to their comrades.

The ranks of soldiers lunged forward, anxious to begin. A strange chant issued from a thousand throats. Waves of violent sound chilled Jaylor's mind. "Kill magic. Kill all magicians." The chant grew in volume and aggression, fed by a whiff of magic from some unknown source. Battle frenzy swelled, binding the men together for the coming fray.

"Kill magic. Kill all magicians."

Weapons drumming on shields took on the rhythm of a thousand hearts beating in unison; a thousand minds with one goal. Battle. Blood. Heat. Lust.

"Kill magic. Kill all magicians."

Determination rose and rose again as the chant became a shout and then a roar.

Horror ran before the swelling noise, growing like a living thing. Fear filled the tower chamber and laid a heavy pall of doom on the once-quiet monastery.

No spell could combat the power of unity and relentless drive generated by the chant. Anyone caught between the men and their objective would be torn limb from limb.

Small points of deadly fire bloomed on the tips of arrows. Bright blossoms of green flame became a hailstorm of destruction.

Chapter Ten

Yaakke sat beside the creekbed, replete and rested for the first time since he'd left Coronnan City. He folded his legs under him, palms resting on his knees, open and receptive. He stilled the twitching muscles of his back and thighs. His mind opened reluctantly.

Three times he had dropped pebbles into the quiet pool at the edge of the creek. As the dropping rock created ripples in the surface of the water, raindrops had interfered with the pattern of ripples. He'd caught glimpses of scenes from his past. Yaakke and Baamin clearing debris from the cache of forbidden books in the tunnels. Yaakke in Brevelan's clearing with Jaylor, teaching him the secret of transporting live humans without danger . . .

But no glimpses of the future. The old Rover woman had sworn to Yaakke that the pebble always told what was to come within the next few hours.

Maybe if Yaakke could properly center his magic, he'd work the Rover spell correctly.

Fire. Smoke. His vision back at the dragon lair had been so real . .

.

Corby perched on a rock in front of him, head cocked curiously at his strange inactivity. Yaakke resisted the urge to shoo him away. He didn't need an audience, but he had to remain still or lose his concentration.

Stargods! He hated meditation. He couldn't think of any other way to align himself to the Kardia. Knowledge of where he was and what direction he was headed in would follow. He hadn't seen the sun rise or set beyond the ominous cloud cover for days. His youthful confidence melted with each new onslaught of rain, until he was totally lost and disoriented.

Once he managed to center his magic, maybe he could sense Shayla's power. *Shayla needs me*, he reminded himself.

The urge to let his muscles move plagued his attempts at stillness. He resisted, forcing his mind to accept the wind and rain as an extension of himself. He heard only the creek rushing over stones. Then his heartbeat filled his ears just as loudly. He breathed deeply, listening.

Slowly his pulse and the rhythm of his breathing tuned to the rhythm of the land around him. He heard birds on their perches fluffing their feathers against the cold. He felt the sap drift sluggishly within the tree that sheltered him. When his body cried out for him to move, he concentrated on the worms opening new paths through the soil, seeking tiny rootlets.

Gradually a pull of energy tugged at his back. With eyes closed and a minimal shift of position, he turned to face the tug. This must be south, the nearest planetary pole. The world adjusted its orbit to include him. He merged with the four elements and the cardinal directions, one more piece of the whole.

Behind his eyelids, his vision centered. Mountains to the south and west. Rolling plains to the north. The Great Bay to the east. The creek flowed north and east. Therefore he must be in the foothills of the south.

A year ago, Jaylor had taken refuge in a monastery in this general vicinity, one day's hard walk from Castle Krej. Yaakke had helped Jaylor hide there while they protected an injured Brevelan and Darville, who pranced at his heels, ensorcelled into the body of a golden wolf.

This morning Yaakke had passed a boulder with a tall everblue growing out of a crack that nearly split the rock in two. He'd marked it, deep inside his memory, as a pointer during that adventure last spring. Now, as his consciousness floated free of his body, he remembered the landmark. How far away was the monastery? The last time Yaakke had come this way, he'd been on steedback, compelling the animal to move faster than normal. Distances were badly distorted in his memory.

Yaakke took a deep breath and roused himself from the silence. The rain had ceased and Corby was gone. His campfire smoldered within a ring of rocks three paces away. He fed it a few dry sticks. Flame glowed on the ends, then licked upward to consume the wood.

He set his pan of water before the fire, allowing it to settle. Green-and-yellow flames reflected in the water. Their gentle movement enticed Yaakke to look deeper into them. He dropped a smooth white pebble into the water.

Pictures appeared in the watery surface, more flames, bigger, hotter—destructive rather than friendly. Jaylor and Brevelan trapped by falling beams. Yaakke blinked and cleared his eyes of smoke.

Anxiously Yaakke fixed an image of Jaylor in his mind and sent it through the water to the monastery. He had no shard of glass to direct a summons properly since he'd lost his pack in the void. The reflective surface of the water would have to do. The vision of flames grew higher, fiercer. The Senior Magician appeared in their midst. Frantically Jaylor lifted a fallen beam from a crumpled form. Flames licked at his hands. He ignored them. The muscles of his broad back and shoulders strained, and he grunted as he moved the beam aside with brute force. Why didn't he use his magic?

Yaakke watched in horror as his master gathered the unconscious form of Brevelan to his breast, and then they both disappeared as another flaming beam crashed down on top of them.

Yaakke breathed deeply, sending his mind toward the void in preparation for transport.

"Naw!" Corby warned him from the top of a tree. Yaakke couldn't rescue Jaylor and Brevelan if he got lost in the void again. He cast around him for another solution. Smoke drifted on the wind from the west. He tried fixing his magic on Jaylor and Brevelan. He'd never transported two people at the same time before.

His magic darted around and around the images in the flames. There was no one to latch onto and transport to safety.

Yaakke took off at a run, over hummocks, around boulders and through a number of icy streams, taking the straightest route toward the smoke. Uphill he ran. Above him and to the left the land rose in a series of grassy plateaus. He crested the first ridge and pressed onward.

Familiarity tugged at his memory as landmarks flashed past. On and on he ran, until his lungs burned and his legs begged for collapse. Still he ran, stumbling, panting, crying.

Time and distance ceased to have meaning as he pressed his body to cover more and more ground. The only reality lay in the column of smoke that appeared beyond the next hilltop. He crested the steep rise. Terraced hills came into view half a league ahead.

The refuge of the Commune should be on the third level, set back from the ridge about two hundred arm-lengths. The smoke thickened in that direction.

If only he hadn't taken so much time to center his magic—if only he hadn't gotten lost in the void—

The smell of smoke was stronger here, sour and vile. Halfway to the third ridge, Yaakke slowed his pelting progress. He couldn't breathe. His legs and arms felt like jelled meat broth. His newly awakened contact with the wheel of sun, moon, and stars hummed a warning.

A pile of boulders, a hundred arm-lengths beyond, offered

shadows and a view of the next ridge. He stretched and pulled himself up the rocks, seeking hand- and footholds by instinct. He barked his knuckles and scraped his shins in his haste. At last he crawled on top of the tumbled boulders. Lying flat, barely breathing, he scanned the horizon.

Ahead, above, and below him stretched an army of jubilant soldiers. Cadres of men capered and jeered as they tossed plunder back and forth in a vicious game of keep away with slighter, less aggressive men. Lean, battle-hardened men in well-used armor. Their evil grins gaped like bottomless pits in their smoke-blackened faces. One scarred sergeant made obscene gestures with a gnarled and twisted staff—the kind of tool favored by magicians.

The plaited grain in the wood looked suspiciously like Jaylor's staff—broken and mended by magic at three points. Yaakke sent out another mental probe addressed to his master. His questions dissipated and died. No mind received or responded.

On the next ridge, smoke rose in a dense black column. The monastery was gutted, the roof collapsed, and the walls breached in a dozen places.

Incompetent fools! Couldn't those bumbling generals tell that Jaylor had whisked his Commune to safety before they entered the buildings? Not a shred of paper left in their library. None of their fabled viewing equipment shattered from the heat of the flames. NOTHING!

They used the transport spell. I will have that secret. As long as the Commune can jump from place to place without pursuit, none of the coven will be safe. We have to master that spell for our own escapes and secret raids.

Jaylor's escape is merely a setback, not a destruction of my goals. His suspicion of Darville's involvement must remain. I have broken their friendship. I have had a minor success.

I will not resort to the Tambootie to soothe my irritated nerves. That was the biggest mistake made by both Krej and his sister Janataea. Let us hope The Simeon doesn't stoop to the drug as well. I need him in the coven and I need his base of temporal power as a sanctuary for Lord Krej.

"Don't give up, Hilza!" Katrina sat beside the little box bed in the kitchen holding her sister's limp hand. Fever had dried the shrunken palm to parchment.

At least the kitchen was warm now. Last moon, P'pa had overcome M'ma's prideful objections and rented the upper levels of the narrow townhouse to street merchants, students, and artists. The money they paid Fraanken Kaantille bought firewood to heat the entire house and enough plain food to keep the family alive. But no amount of money could buy medicine to combat the lung rot that gripped half of Queen's City.

The rasping wheeze of Hilza's lungs was the only reply to Katrina's plea. Apprehension clawed at Katrina's heart. Her little sister had slipped into unconsciousness last evening as her fever soared.

Now, in the darkest hours before midwinter dawn, Hilza opened her eyes. Katrina bit her lip as she saw the hazy film covering her sister's vision. Hilza's breath grew shallower, more labored.

Katrina rolled a blanket and stuffed it behind Hilza's head, propping her as upright as possible. Her sister's head lolled loosely on her weakened neck. Spasms racked her frail body as her lungs tried one more time to clear themselves of the accumulated fluid. Violent tremors passed through her limbs and bloody spittle trickled from her parched mouth.

"P'pa, wake up. I need your help!" Katrina called.

"I'm awake," Fraanken answered as he rose stiffly from the straight-backed chair where he had dozed fitfully most of the night.

Sadly he lifted his youngest daughter, supporting her head on his shoulder.

Always, since the lung rot had grabbed hold of Hilza last autumn, P'pa's cradling comfort had been able to overcome the worst of the cough. Not tonight. Hilza continued to choke and bleed with the disease that killed its victims, young and old, hale and weak.

"Awaken your mother, Katey." P'pa stroked Hilza's back, trying desperately to soothe her.

Katrina ran up the stairs to the guest parlor on the ground floor that was now her parents' bedroom.

A lamp on the dresser cast a dim glow on the room. Frightened at this sign of negligence and waste on the part of her mother, Katrina hastened to extinguish the tiny flame. Her eyes strayed to the wide bed where her mother should be asleep. The down quilts—remnants of better times—lay flat and empty, undisturbed by any sleeper.

"M'ma?" Katrina searched the dim corners for some sign of her mother's presence. No flicker of movement or shadow out of place. "M'ma!" she called louder.

A cold draft made the lamp flame flicker. Katrina raced to the entry seeking the source of the frigid air. The inner door stood wide open. Beyond it, the outer door was closed but not latched.

"M'ma!" Katrina screamed in fear. She tugged on the outer door. Three filaments of white silk hung tangled in the lock. The finest yarn available that Tattia had woven into a lace shawl for Queen Miranda last autumn. A present the queen's husband had rejected as unworthy of his wife because it had been made by a disgraced Kaantille. Queen Miranda hadn't been allowed to view the gift and decide for herself to accept or reject it. Just yesterday, M'ma had tried again to see the queen and present her gift. She'd been evicted from the palace at the kitchen gate, before she reached Miranda.

Katrina stared at the threads. Her chin quivered in uncertainty. She returned to the bedroom, seeking some sign of her mother. Tattia's last woolen gown lay draped over the clothespress. Her cloak and shoes were in place. Nothing seemed missing except Tattia and the infamous lace shawl.

Tattia had worn the shawl as a badge of honor ever since the rejection by King Simeon. A merchant, unknown to Katrina or her father, had offered to buy the shawl several times. Proud Tattia had refused to let it go. Now she had gone out in the predawn freeze wearing nothing but her nightrail and the silken lace.

Katrina ran back to the kitchen. Her father gently laid Hilza's slack body on the straw mattress. Tears streamed down his careworn cheeks.

"P'pa?" Katrina choked on the fears that swamped her.

"There is nothing more we can do, Katey. Our baby is gone. We must be grateful that she is no longer in pain, no longer struggling for every breath." He stood over the body of his youngest daughter, shoulders slumped.

"P'pa, I'm frightened. I think M'ma ran away. She didn't wear her cloak or her shoes."

Fraanken looked up from his contemplation of death. His chin trembled with the effort to control himself. "Stay with your sister. One of us must watch over her until her spirit is prepared for passing." There was no one else. He didn't need to remind Katrina that Maaben no longer considered herself part of the family. "I will search for your mother. Perhaps she finally agreed to sell the shawl. She would have to go in secret because of King Simeon's ban on her work."

"M'ma would not have left the house at midnight without her gown, or shoes, or cloak if she merely wanted to sell the shawl."

A fierce pounding on the kitchen door roused them both. Katrina's eyes widened in greater turmoil. *Stargods!* What other disaster could plague them? For only the direst emergency would bring unannounced visitors to the basement door in the dead of night.

Fraanken yanked open the inner door and unlatched the outer with fumbling haste. A dour-faced man in the black uniform of the city guard glared at them. "Do you recognize this?" He held up a sodden and filthy length of lacy silk.

"M'ma!" Katrina gasped.

P'pa held the shawl as if it were a great treasure. He suddenly appeared old, shrunken, feeble.

"We found that floating in the river right after a passing member of the palace guard reported seeing a woman jump from the bridge."

Chapter Eleven

Yaakke concentrated on the clouds. He forced a clump of moisture to gather above the ruined monastery.

"You can't save them." A feminine voice interrupted his spell.

He whirled on top of his rock, almost losing his balance. A black-haired young woman, with incredibly beautiful white skin, stood at the base of the boulders, hands on hips, huge blue eyes angry and accusing. The skirts of her black traveling gown and the length of her unbound hair billowed out behind her in the rising wind.

Vaguely he realized his manipulations of the clouds and temperature had created the wind.

"I've got to try!" Yaakke returned to his task. The clouds above the ruins sagged, heavy with water. A little shift of the temperature beneath them and they dumped their load of thunder and lightning, but no rain.

Yaakke tried again, lowering the clouds into the ruins of the monastery. Still no rain, only a dense oily fog rolling through the crumbling masonry.

None of the soldiers noticed the strange weather. They were too busy mauling tapestries depicting the descent of the Stargods. Crude ale splashed from golden winecups. But no one burned a book or smashed delicate glass and brass instruments.

"Trying to smother the enemy with a mist?" The girl laughed, rich tones sliding up her white throat. "Like as not you'd have more success putting out the fire if you spat on it."

Yaakke blushed from his ears to his toes. "You destroyed my concentration." His voice cracked into an embarrassing squeak.

"You still can't save them. You're too late," she stated. "But you can exact vengeance from the lords who sent the army to destroy your precious Commune."

The clouds above the monastery thinned and drifted back to a more natural pattern. The wind faded with them. Once more Yaakke sought Jaylor's spirit within the ruins.

Nothing.

With mounting anxiety he probed for any member of the Commune: prickly old Lyman, wily Fraandalor, gentle Brevelan, or even her baby, Glendon.

No response.

"I told you, you're too late. But I will reward you mightily if you blast Lord Jonnias and the Marnaks—Elder and Younger—to hell and back again." Her eyes smoldered with fanatical hate.

"Who are you?" Yaakke twisted into a sitting position on top of the boulder. He rested his head in his hands, massaging his temples. Where were Jaylor and the others? They couldn't all have died. He'd have felt their passing, he was sure of it.

The barriers surrounding Brevelan's clearing had been down. Surely not because she had died! That was weeks ago.

How had the spell gone so wrong? He'd been careful to visualize rain, torrents of rain to douse the fire.

"Don't you recognize me?" The girl hiked her skirts and began climbing up to Yaakke's perch. She revealed an indelicate amount of ankle and calf beneath the black cloth.

"Danger! Danger, danger," Corby croaked, circling above.

"I saw you at the coronation," he muttered.

"I'm Rejiia." She sat beside him, mimicking his cross-legged pose.

"Krej's daughter?" He barely acknowledged her presence. Why hadn't he centered his magic and found Jaylor by summons as soon as he'd departed from the dragon? He could have reported everything and maybe received some more clues on where to look for Shayla. Jaylor would then have known where Yaakke was, so he could have sent a summons for help in time.

The barriers around the clearing were already down. How long had he been in the void? Long enough for all his friends to die?

"Aren't you going to ask why I want you to kill my husband, Marnak the Younger, his father, and their best friend, Lord Jonnias?" She sounded aggrieved that his attention had wandered away from her beauty. What good would he do helping Shayla if there were no more Commune to gather the dragon's magic?

Rejiia's pout dragged his attention back to her question.

"You must have your reasons for wanting those men dead. They don't concern me. I've got to save the Commune." Yaakke dismissed her. Why hadn't the king stopped his lords from waging war on the magicians?

"King Darville doesn't know this was their mission," Rejiia answered his unspoken question.

"You read my thoughts. Do you have magic?" Yaakke hastily erected some armor around his thoughts lest she read his lonely pain and find him vulnerable.

Yaakke started scrambling down from the rock. He had to see for himself that the monastery was destroyed and that all of his friends were dead.

"I have some magic," Rejiia said interrupting his descent. "Not enough to do more than a few parlor tricks. My father never saw fit to test or train me. He had no use for his daughters, except to marry us off for power and wealth."

"And now you want freedom from your chosen husband." Yaakke let his eyes wander away from her toward the mass of soldiers behind them, seeking a sign of Marnak the Younger, or evidence of Jaylor's demise.

"You won't find Marnak in the field. He directs things from the safety of his tent," she spat the words with disgust. "And yes, I want my freedom. Faciar is *my* province—from the capital to the southern mountains, from the Great Bay inland five leagues. All of it is *mine*. I won't let my husband destroy it with his greed."

"Why not destroy him yourself?" Yaakke completed his slide to the ground, prepared to fight his way up to the smoking ruins if anyone stopped him.

"I told you, I don't have enough magic to kill him with suitable subtlety and get away with it." She frowned petulantly. "What good is killing him if I am caught and burned at the stake?"

Yaakke dismissed her petty anger. She might have reason to dislike and distrust her husband, Marnak the Younger. Yaakke had the more immediate grudge. The greed of both Marnaks—Elder and Younger—as well as Jonnias' superstition, had destroyed the Commune. Yaakke's Commune. His friends and family.

A great ball of magic built within him on the heels of the grief turned to anger. Not enough. He found more magic beneath his feet. He pulled energy from a storm building to the east. His newly awakened alignment with the magnetic pole centered the magic. All he had to do was shape it into a weapon, address it, and send it forth.

"That's right, use your magic. Wreak havoc through this army of destruction," Rejiia coached in excited whispers. "Revenge is sweet." She licked her lips in almost sexual satisfaction at the power he gathered.

Yaakke didn't know why he hesitated. An image of a young woman with moon-bright hair and pale blue eyes reddened with sadness came between himself and Rejiia's excited face. Then a memory of the blue-tipped dragon superimposed upon his preparation to hurl the magic.

"There is never a right time or place to throw magic for harm." The dragon spoke with Old Master Baamin's voice, reciting the first rule of Communal ethics. "Magic is for health, for growth, for the benefit of Coronnan and all who live within our boundaries. Magic can never be used to destroy lest we destroy ourselves in the process."

"What does right have to do with this? They killed my friends!" Yaakke screamed into the wind. The magic fireball burned for release within his gut.

"Do it, boy. Do it and I'll take you to my bed. A bed where I never allowed Marnak to exercise his privileges." Rejiia's aura pulsed with sexual vibrancy.

He needed no reward, only vengeance. The magic came into his hand. He shaped it with anger and addressed it to the image of skinny, sniveling Marnak the Younger, Krej's puppet, whose loyalty landed wherever was most convenient to Marnak.

With a mighty thrust of his shoulders, back, and arm he lobbed the magical firebomb into the air in the direction of the field tents behind the massed soldiers.

The magic sought the symbols on a standard raised above one particular tent. Through the air it flew, heedless of wind or missiles thrown to divert it, with Yaakke's mind close on its heels. Faster and faster the bomb flew. Yaakke became the magic fire as it fed on his mind. They gathered speed and intensity from the cries of fear and horror growing within the army; horror that invaded Yaakke. He tried to jerk his mind away from the bomb but found himself trapped within it.

The bomb slammed into the standard with crackling intensity. Magical blue light glowed from the flagpole and raced down, down into the tent. It consumed wood and fabric as it sped toward its target, greedy for more interesting fuel. Marnak, wearing light field armor, lounged against the tent pole. He rejoiced with his coconspirators, a cup of pilfered wine in one hand, precious altar linens edged in SeLenese lace in the other.

His smile turned to shock and then to agony as the firebomb leaped from tent pole to head, to hand, and body. Flames burst upward, followed by screams.

Indiscriminate screams gathered harshly on Yaakke's conscience and slammed him back into his body, but he still sensed all that happened within range of the bomb he had exploded in Marnak's face. The smell of burning flesh and cloth, of hot metal and pain beyond imagining, violated his senses. Rampant emotions from a thousand sources filled his mind, contorting his perceptions. He became the instrument of destruction and, in turn, was its victim.

Hate. Fear. Greed. Desperate prayers. Revenge. Mindless flight.

Every soldier, officer, and lord broadcast his feelings directly into Yaakke's being. No magical armor could block the intimate sharing.

The onslaught of foreign emotions tore at Yaakke's sanity. Who was *he*? Which thoughts were his own? Whose body did his mind inhabit? What did *he* feel? Painful wounds stabbed and burned into his heart.

Suddenly the riotous noise of a thousand men swelled within Yaakke's ears. The wind increased to a howl and seemed to stab his skin with the force of arrows. His blood pounded and roared within his body.

He had to get away. Away from the noise. Away from Rejiia. Away from himself.

Jaylor coughed the smoke from his lungs. Desperately, he heaved the fallen beam away from Brevelan where she had fallen when the roof collapsed. With blackened hands, he clutched his wife tightly against his chest and transported them out of the inferno that had been the monastery library.

The shocking cold of the void roused them both from the stupor induced by roiling smoke and blistering heat. Reality slowly formed around them. Still kneeling in the position he'd been in when he transported out, Jaylor coughed again and blinked his gritty eyes. He clung to the sensation of holding his beloved in his arms while he concentrated on maintaining his balance.

"Where's the baby?" Brevelan whispered, then coughed.

Other coughs and grumbles penetrated Jaylor's awareness. He counted bodies, eyes still too blurred to distinguish faces.

Forty-three. "Where's the baby?" he asked louder.

"Glendon?" Brevelan asked again.

"Right here." Elder Librarian Lyman stepped forward with a grimy bundle cradled in his arms. "Took to the void like he was born there. Little tyke never uttered a squeak." He clucked and shifted the baby against his shoulder, rubbing his back and cooing nonsense as if he'd always cared for infants instead of living the lonely, celibate life of most magicians.

Brevelan reached for Glendon before Jaylor could settle her onto the rough cave floor. Anxiously she removed the smoky blanket and checked her baby for any signs of distress. Little Glendon looked up at his mother, eyes focusing in his narrow field of vision. A slurpy gurgle followed by a toothless smile brought a sigh of relief from the entire gathering.

"My son wasn't born in the void, but he was conceived there," Jaylor murmured to himself. Stiffly he stood and faced the ragtail gathering. "We're all safe. Did the equipment make it through?"

"All except one shelf of books—duplicates most of them." Slippy surveyed the array of books and observation equipment littering the floor of the cave that had once been a dragon lair.

"It's damp here, Jaylor. Not good for my books," Lyman reminded him. "Not good for my old bones either. At least we're safe from those heathen lords and their troops. For now."

"There's a broad valley between here and Brevelan's clearing," Jaylor told them. In his mind he saw a meadow at the base of a cliff. A small waterfall tumbled down the cliff into a scattering of boulders. That same cliff Prince Darville had fallen over when Krej ensorcelled him into a wolf and left him for dead. Neither of them had known at the time that Shayla, the resident dragon, was so tied to the royal family by honor, blood, and magic that she would compel Brevelan to rescue the injured wolf from the snowdrifts. Jaylor could think of no better place to rebuild the University: to honor a now dead friendship.

"We'll begin building as soon as we have recovered from our journey and the weather warms enough to fell timber. By summer we'll have a refuge for all those who flee the persecution of magic. This attack against us smells like the work of that new cult, the Gnostic Utilitarians."

"The Gnuls have less of a sense of morality when it comes to magicians than the coven does," Lyman grumbled.

"I fear the attack on our monastery was just the beginning of some very hard times to come for our people," Jaylor said sadly. He had to contact his spy among Queen Rossemikka's maids. Surely the girl had eavesdropped on enough conversations to know what Darville meant by sending the army to the monastery. If Darville had authorized it at all.

Rejiia latched onto the boy's magic, sucking and feeding upon it as a leech draws blood from its victims. She had watched her father do this. A little giggle escaped her. She ignored the hysterical quality of the mirth. If the mighty and arrogant Lord Krej could see her now, he wouldn't dismiss her as worthless.

She had every intention of murdering the loathsome boy as soon as she'd drained him of his magic and his secrets. He wasn't hard to follow. The flaws in his magic screamed at her through the tentacle she'd attached to him. His power rose to amazing strength and then fell abruptly to nothing in unpredictable waves. He committed the ultimate folly by allowing his emotions to affect his magic.

She took a deep breath in preparation. At the next hint of a waver in his talent, she'd drop a compulsion on him.

He ran furiously. Legs pumping. Arms straining.

In her mind, Rejiia followed, feeling what he felt, seeing what he saw. She couldn't read his thoughts and his secrets yet. The power was still rising in him.

"Give me the transport spell!" she whispered through her tentacle of magic. "The coven will reward me well. They'll have to give me full membership if I discover the secret. I'll surpass my dear father in power and prestige. Then when I revive him, he will have to look up to me!"

"Spirits of the dead, spring forth in freedom from fleshly concerns," the magistrate implored as he released a sack of ashes into the River Lenicc. "As these last remnants of your corporeal bodies dissolve, so shall your attachments to this life. Your possessions are dispersed. Your families are reconciled to your passing. Your next existence beckons. Release your hold on this one!"

Dry-eyed and numb, Katrina watched as Hilza's ashes spread across the icy water like a gray blanket. The sluggish current caught the smothering cover of ashes, swirled them into an ugly soup, and dragged them down. All that remained of sweet little Hilza sank into watery oblivion.

A commoner's funeral. No expensive priests, no professional mourners. Not even a proper grave. Merely ashes of the dead cast into the almost-frozen river by one of King Simeon's officials. A duty the man had performed too often these last moons.

The ground was frozen deep. No one could dig graves this winter. There was barely enough wood for a single funeral pyre. So, the numerous dead—from hunger and disease—were heaped together in a common bonfire, their remains mingled, and their funerals held at the same time. There was no way to separate the ashes for the grieving families. The poor and the homeless gathered around the pyres in a morbid search for warmth, cheering as each new body added fuel to the noisome black smoke.

Katrina wouldn't have an urn to set beside the hearth to cherish, for either Hilza or Tattia. Tattia's body had not been found. All that remained of her was the lace scarf. P'pa had wanted to burn it along with Hilza's body. Katrina had cleaned the precious reminder of her mother and hidden it where her father and the persistent merchant would never find it. Why was the stranger so eager to purchase the piece, tainted as it was by Tattia's suicide?

Ten other families joined Katrina in mourning the loss of a loved one on this cloudy day. Families huddled together for warmth, comfort, and shared memories. No one stood beside Katrina.

Oncle Yon and Tante Syllia refused to be seen near the family of a suicide. Tattia's ghost would haunt her kin for five generations.

Lawsuits had been filed with Queen's Court and Temple to sever all bonds of blood and law between Fraanken Kaantille and his brother Yon. Maaben's name was included in the suits. Maaben would be kept safe and secure from this latest, and worst, scandal in the Kaantille family.

The river marched toward the sea. A few traces of gray ash clung to the bobbing ice floes. Gradually they passed out of sight, under the bridges, on and on toward open water. Nothing remained of the dead but the grief within a few hearts.

"Be warm, Hilza," Katrina murmured. She could think of no other wish for her little sister. It was the same wish most citizens of Queen's City prayed for.

The stranger who was eager to buy Tattia's shawl separated himself from the crowd of mourners. Katrina turned her steps away from him and the scene of the funeral. She ducked into a narrow alley wishing for the release of tears. Her eyes continued dry. Her grief built within her until she thought the pain would choke the breath from her.

Aimlessly she wandered until the tears flowed freely, releasing the paralyzing grief in her throat. Only then did she seek her own kitchen door.

"P'pa!" she called as the inner door banged behind her. "P'pa, I'm home." Silence rang through the cold and empty kitchen.

"Curse you, P'pa. The tenants will complain and refuse to pay their rent if you let the fire go out." She gathered fresh kindling and a fire rock as she rushed to the stove that filled one whole corner of the room.

Since Hilza's death and M'ma's suicide, P'pa rarely moved from his chair by the stove, where he sat in morose silence. The loss of his wife and child preyed more heavily on his mind and spirit than all of his financial woes combined. He started in fear at every moving shadow and sharp sound. He was the first person Tattia would haunt and plague until he, too, joined her in self-inflicted death.

Only his fear for Katrina had prevented him from committing the ultimate sin.

He was not in the kitchen today and had not attended Hilza's funeral.

The bell on the front stoop rang, loud and imperious.

"P'pa!" she called again, as she fumbled with the kindling. The fire was more important than a visitor. Who would visit the disgraced Kaantilles?

The bell rang again, impatient as a sick old granm'ma.

Still no sounds from above or the front room. Where had P'pa gone? Katrina struck a spark and fed it enough fuel to keep it lit until she answered the bell.

She flung open the inner door. Harsh pounding rattled the outer door. Her heart leaped into her throat.

With shaking hands and trembling heart she opened the outer door. Three men-at-arms, in the gray uniform of the palace, stood on the front step. All the same height, all the same coloring and uniform. All with identical grim expressions.

The center man stepped forward. Two bands of silver on each cuff marked his rank as above the other two. "Katrina Marie, daughter of Fraanken and Tattia Kaantille, you are summoned to the presence of His Majesty, King Simeon the First, Lord of SeLenicca, Emperor of Hanassa, and rightful Heir of Rossemeyer."

Katrina swallowed the lump in her throat. It wouldn't go down. She swallowed again and almost choked on her fear.

"I . . . I must tell my P'pa, and I must damp the fire." Wildly she looked around. A million questions pounded at her. She couldn't make sense of any of this.

"Your hearth is cold, the tenants dismissed, and your father is already in custody," the ranking soldier informed her. No flicker of emotion crossed his face, and his eyes stared straight ahead, above Katrina.

She backed to the inner door. *Flee,* her feet urged. *Hide,* her mind overruled. *Faint,* her heart joined the clamor of emotions.

A harsh hand gripped her arm. Pain shot up to her shoulder.

"You will come now," the soldier said.

She hung back. His fingers dug deeper into the muscles of her upper arm. Numbness spread down to her fingers and up into her brain.

"You will come, or you will die here and now." Knives appeared in the right hand of each of the three soldiers. Their blank faces awoke with ugly grins.

Chapter Twelve

"**Y**ou must flee now, boy. Escape before the troops turn on you. Teach me the transport spell, so I can flee with you," Rejiia whispered to Yaakke from behind.

Yaakke halted his flight from the scene of destruction and turned to ask her what she knew about the spell, the Commune's most closely guarded secret. Only a grimy soldier, gaping at the flames in the center of the camp stood there. A flash of black skirts, or maybe black feathers, flitted through the trees above him.

"Teach me the spell; I will take you with me!" Jaylor's voice demanded from the mouth of the grimy soldier.

"No," Yaakke formed the word without sound. The glare of the sun through the pall of clouds and smoke intensified. Pain lanced from his eyes to his mind.

"The transport spell. Give me the spell." This time Rejiia's haunting voice came from the jackdaw perched in the tree above him.

"Quickly, boy! Give me the spell." The whispers bombarded him from all directions. Rejiia, Jaylor, Baamin, and Corby. A compulsion grew within him, insisting he whisper the secret.

Frantically Yaakke opened every listening channel in his mind to find the source of the demanding voice. Was it Rejiia who haunted him, or a true magician using Yaakke's suppressed attraction for the Lady of Faciar to trap him?

Every mind in the army was firmly closed to him. Only the demanding whispers leaked through to his telepathy. They grew louder.

Sun and the fire he had unleashed blazed before his eyes. He closed them. Still the blinding light penetrated.

Then, suddenly, the wall between the thousand troops and his mind broke apart. A myriad of mental voices made a jumble of his thoughts and weakened his knees. His senses stretched beyond normal limits to include field mice, cats, and panicky steeds. Images of his firebomb exploding within a tent and burning all it touched with lethal intensity, including himself, replayed in his memory again and again. Mental and physical screams racked his aching body.

Pain, blinding light, noise, demands. Always the demand. *Give me the transport spell!*

Yaakke resumed his run uphill until his lungs burned. Away from the voice; he had to get away from the voice. The smoke from the monastery ruins thickened. Heat, trapped within the building stones, seared his hands when he touched them. He pressed his palms harder against a half-standing wall, ignoring the pain, seeking the lives that once dwelt within.

More pain, more screams: his own and others. Escape. He had to escape.

There was nothing left of his own thoughts or identity. Confusion. Noise. Pain. Bewilderment. Screams.

"I've got to get out of here!" Yaakke searched blindly for an avenue of retreat from the noise, from the light, from his own guilt. Quickly, he built a picture of cool, quiet, darkness around his stretched and oversensitive nerves. Three deep breaths into a trance. Another lungful of air whisked him across the void and plunged him down, down, down, into the bowels of Kardia Hodos, the living planet.

A guard on each side of Katrina held her arms tight and high, barely allowing her feet to touch the ground on the long walk up the hill toward the palace. Her knees were so weak with dread she doubted they'd hold her up.

Along the wooden sidewalk the men marched her, following in the rapid wake of their two-stripe leader. Merchants, shoppers, and homeless wanderers stepped out of their path, gaping at her.

"Where are they taking her?" a frightened housewife whispered.

"Hush. She's a Kaantille, getting what they all deserve. No doubt this is the last we'll see of that clan." Disgust colored a man's voice. "If King Simeon executes them all, then the ghost will be banished."

Katrina felt the blood drain from her head. *If King Simeon executes them all . . .* Images of dark, dank prison cells, torture, and death built tremendous pressure in her chest and sent her heart pounding. She lashed out with both feet in a desperate attempt to escape.

The relentless guards kept their grip on her arms, marching faster as they approached the villas of the nobility. At the end of the long Royal Avenue stood the palace and her doom.

Darkness encroached on her vision from the sides. Cold sweat broke out on her face and back. The burning grip of hard male hands on her arms deepened and spread. At the last moment of consciousness the uniformed men turned left away from the palace. Her mind revived slightly as questions rose within her.

Huge marble mansions lined the hill becoming more and more opulent farther away from the river. Evidence of the luxury afforded the nobility in the crowded Queen's City was revealed in the wider spaces of open land that lay between each of the homes, cropped grass and sculptured shrubs, and large gardens.

They passed between two of the sprawling mansions and proceeded to the back entrance of nearly the last villa before the end of the road and the beginning of the rolling hills. The two-stripe leader entered without knocking. Obviously, they were expected.

Katrina looked at her grim escorts, hoping they would allow her the dignity of walking on her own. Neither man varied his grip, his expression, or his rapid pace.

At a double door on the left of the long corridor, the leader paused and knocked lightly. A grunt from within responded. The door slid open without a touch from the guard and Katrina found herself carried into the presence of King Simeon where she was abruptly dropped.

Her knees buckled, and she scrambled, ungracefully, to an upright position. Through a swimming haze she focused on the carpet rather than the man who held her fate in his unpredictable and often tyrannical hands.

Her royal judge sat behind a large desk. Witchballs of shadowless light sat atop silver stands. The room was nearly as bright as daylight. King Simeon need not squint and hunch over the parchment he wrote upon. He needed no inkwell, for his quill pen flowed with dark liquid at the precise level required. At his left elbow, in a place of honor, sat a life-sized tin statue of a weasel. Gilt paint flaked from its molded fur. Mouth agape in a vicious snarl, the weasel's teeth seemed to drip venom.

Katrina shuddered in repulsion at the sight of the ugly statue and the loving caress King Simeon gave it as he raised his deep blue eyes from his work. His gaze seemed to bore right through her, delving into her innermost secrets. An aura of power shimmered around him and extended to the hideous statue. The rest of the room seemed dim and unimportant compared to the broad-shouldered man with bright, outland red hair.

"So this is the last of the traitorous Kaantilles?" King Simeon leaned back in his thronelike chair. Hooded eyes continued to probe and appraise her body. "Remove her cloak," he ordered.

The guards whisked off the heavy oiled wool and stepped back. A chill rippled through Katrina as the king's penetrating eyes lingered on the budding curves of her body. A spark of interest flashed within the deep blue orbs and a mocking half smile touched the comer of his mouth.

Katrina crossed her arms in front of her, trying to hide from his gaze a body she was not yet familiar or comfortable with.

"Where . . . where is my P'pa?" Katrina whispered.

"Never speak until you are spoken to! I am your king. You must show respect." Anger propelled Simeon up into a half-stand behind his desk. He leaned forward, hands pressed against the massive wooden top until his wrists and knuckles grew white. A shudder coursed down his body from neck to arms. Then he seemed to relax.

The king sat again and dusted invisible specks from his fire green tunic. "Now, my dear, I have some news for you, some good and some bad."

She bit back her alarm and her questions.

"Very good, Katrina. You're learning respect. As a reward, I'll tell you about your P'pa. Your brave and smart P'pa who ruined me and himself with his investments." The king rose and sauntered around to the front of his desk. There he perched on the edge of the furniture, his thick and powerful legs thrust out in front of him, arms crossed on his chest in mocking imitation of her own stance.

Shoulders hunched, back curved, Katrina tried to huddle deeper into her arms. The solid presence of the guards prevented her from backing up to put more distance between herself and the king's penetrating gaze. She wondered if this acknowledged sorcerer saw through her vest and skirt, through her shift to her naked body. Lumbird bumps rose on her arms and chest. Beneath a loose breast band, her nipples tightened into yet more bumps. A ripple of fear and disgust added to her discomfort.

"The bad news first. Your esteemed P'pa has sold himself to the slave ships." Mocking amusement touched King Simeon's lips but didn't light his eyes. "In return for his five years of servitude, Fraanken Kaantille demanded I forgive his debts and allow you to inherit the house. He claimed you could earn enough to maintain yourself and the house by renting out the upper rooms. Of course he forgot that under the ancient laws of SeLenicca, the daughter of a slave—freeborn or not—has no rights and can possess nothing, least of all a valuable house in the middle of a respectable neighborhood."

"You can't turn me out!" she protested.

Cold. So very cold. The room, her body, the king's smile. Everything was so cold.

"Quiet, or I'll increase his indenture to seven years in the mines. Your P'pa might survive five years in my galleys. But no one survives the mines. No one! Do you hear?" the king shouted.

Katrina nodded, too frightened to do more. The tin weasel seemed to raise a lip to bare more teeth. She stared at it in shock rather than look at her king.

"Now then, the good news." King Simeon smiled in abrupt and capricious change of mood. He thrust himself upright from his perch on the desk and took two steps closer.

She didn't like his tone. Didn't trust his volatile temper. She feared the way he looked at her.

"Leave us." He nodded to the guards.

Behind her, Katrina heard the door slide open, footsteps retreated, and the door whispered shut again. She was alone with the most feared man in the Three Kingdoms.

"My dear, I have a proposition for you." King Simeon walked around her, his eyes appraised her front and back, from her two plaits of blond hair to the hem of her skirt. "Only you can save your father. Indeed, I'm willing to forgive his debts and return him to a place of honor in the mercantile community. In return, all I ask is a favor from you."

She didn't dare ask the nature of that favor. Rumors followed this man. Rumors of black sorcery and sacrifices to a foreign and bloodthirsty god. No one dared repeat those rumors to Queen Miranda. According to Tattia, the hereditary ruler of SeLenicca was so besotted with her outland husband she wouldn't have listened to

them anyway. She hadn't listened to her advisers when she granted
Simeon all the rank and authority of a king.

Could Simeon have thrown a magic spell on his wife to force her
to give him all her rights and power?

"Only you can grant me this favor, Katrina. Think of it, your
beloved P'pa restored to his home and his fortune, your sister Maaben
returned to the loving arms of her family. You can achieve this for
them." He toyed with the lacing on her shift, tugging playfully until
the neckline started to gape open; then he released the tie to finger
the buttons on her vest.

"H . . . how?"

"My coven has need of a willing virgin." He uncrossed her
protective arms with gentle hands and opened her vest with a swift
movement she barely saw. "I presume you are still a virgin?" One
mocking eyebrow reached nearly to his full head of red hair.

Her jaw dropped, aghast at the immodesty of his question and his
actions.

"I see by your reaction that you are untouched, by your P'pa or
any other man. Good. Good." His finger traced the line of her shift,
opening it until her undergarment was revealed. His finger stopped
on the tip of her breast.

How could he imply such a horrible thing? P'pa was good and
kind and honorable. He would never do . . . do *that* to her. But the
king could. The sensuous caress of that single finger rasped against
her taut nerves. Hot shame vied with a need for him to continue his
teasing of her nipple. Shame won.

"Did you know, my dear, that the next Vernal Equinox occurs on
the night of the dark of the moon? 'Twill be a night of powerful
magic. I will be able to build spells of such magnitude, all other magicians will be forced to bow to my will. But I need a virgin." His gaze
captured her eyes and bound them together with alien power. His
thumbs traced erotic circles on her breasts.

"A willing virgin."

"Wh . . . what will become of me?" She couldn't look away

though she tried and tried. Lightning seemed to flash across her vision, then leap from his hooded eyes into hers. Of its own will, her body arched toward him.

Disgusted with herself, she fought the heated longing he built within her.

"There is power buried deep within you. With proper training between now and the Equinox, you have a good chance of surviving the ritual. At the end of it, you would no longer be a virgin, but your power would be released. Only I have a matching power that will bring yours to maturation, ready to be tapped. I might even allow you to bear me a son. A child raised to rule the coven as Miranda's son will rule SeLenicca." Finally he blinked and released her. The spell that bound them together slid away, and he retreated to the edge of his desk once more.

"And if I don't agree to this?"

"Then I will take you for my own pleasure—and yours, my dear—and your father will rot in the mines!" Anger exploded from him like a living being. Katrina recoiled from him.

All traces of longing for his renewed touch vanished, replaced with cold hate. "Then I have no guarantees that you will honor the bargain even if I give myself willingly to your vile purposes."

"You can trust me. I am your king, after all."

" 'Twas not P'pa's fault the ship was lost at sea. Why are you blaming him?" She blinked back tears of bewilderment.

"Fraanken Kaantille organized the plan and supervised the investment syndicate. If the ship had won through, he would have been a hero. But the ship was betrayed by a dark-eyed magician boy. My agent barely escaped alive." He petted the thin weasel once more, almost cooing to it. "The plan failed. For all I know, Fraanken Kaantille may have sold out to the agents of King Darville's Commune of Magicians. So, 'tis only right your father be considered a traitor for that failure," he stated evenly.

"P'pa would never sell out to an outlander. He loves our land and our queen."

"Answer me now. Do you give yourself freely to my coven for the Equinox ritual?" A sneer marred his handsome face. No spell bound them together this time. She was free to make a rational decision.

"Never."

"Perhaps a few moons of humiliation and unrelenting toil in a factory will change your mind. Did you know a factory owner has offered to buy you from me? You, with your moon-blond hair, fair skin, and blue eyes of a true-blooded woman will be the slave of an outland half-breed. He hates all true-bloods and will make certain you suffer. And you condemn your father to death in the mines."

"No, I don't. You do."

"Remember my offer when hunger, cold, aching back, dimming vision, and humiliation drive you away from the factory. I'll wait for you, Katrina Kaantille. You will come back to me."

"Simurgh save me!" Rejiia gasped. "Come back here, Yaakke. I'm not finished with you. You can't do that. I won't let you!" She stamped her foot in rage.

Gone. Without a trace. She flung a web of magic outward to snare any life within her range. One very cranky crow screamed at her as he beat his wings against her entrapment. Nothing else. The soldiers were too far away, all rushing to douse the fire in Marnak's camp.

"Where are you, boy?" she screamed as she released the crow with the funny white feathers on its head. She cast the net again, more carefully and in a wider pattern. Still nothing.

"What did I do wrong?" All her dreams of power faded. Having probed his magic, she should be able to find him anywhere on Kardia Hodos. Still he eluded her.

That kind of power was unheard of, outside of legend. Only one of the Stargods could disappear so completely. "I'll get you yet,

Yaakke. Then I will take you to the coven for judgment. And I shall preside as your judge and executioner."

Quiet. Blessed quiet surrounded Yaakke. Darkness soothed his eyes. He'd transported himself to some unknown sanctuary. Yet still he heard the echoes of thoughts and saw flashes of light.

The sound of dripping water penetrated his exhausted mind and body. His hands hurt, burned by the fire-blasted stones of the monastery. He opened his eyes to seek the source of water to soothe the burns. The light flashes continued to blind him.

Footsteps upon stone. Flickering light from lanterns. The harsh smell of lamp oil and stale air.

More voices. Real this time.

"Gimme the whip! Here's another one broken his chain.

See how his hand is burned from the barracks fire? Have to make an example of malcontent slaves." A harsh voice spoke, made deeper by malice. "We'll have this mine up and running again in no time once we punish the leaders of this little rebellion."

"There are no slaves in Coronnan!" Yaakke croaked.

"Yeah, so you said 'afore you killed three guards. Tell that t' the army what sends us prisoners and t' judges what sends us criminals." The man laughed.

Yaakke looked up, a long way up into a craggy face and ugly harelip. An evil, malicious grin added another broken seam to the filthy face. This man enjoyed inflicting pain.

Frantically, Yaakke sought a spell, any spell to protect himself. Armor. Transport. Another firebomb. He had to be free to help Shayla!

His mind went blank and his magic died with the first bite of the whip across his chest, followed by a blow to his temple from the pommel of a sword.

Chapter Thirteen

Time dragged forward. The man called Muaynwor—the dark mute—marked the passage of days in the number of breaths he could take during the one-hour sun break each noon. He measured days in strokes of the sledgehammer. He counted the stars as he marched with his fellow slaves in iron chains from mine adit to barracks.

Each day and each night he counted and wondered why. He'd stopped wondering who he was or how he had come to be a slave in the mines when slavery had been outlawed a millennium ago. Counting seemed safer than speaking or remembering. Remembering brought the lash across his back. A word to his chain partner for the day earned them both the sweat box.

Heft the hammer, breathe. Slam the hammer down, breathe. He found solace in the rhythm. Heft, breathe. Slam, breathe. One stroke, two and three, shift the spike. One, two, three. Four, five, six.

The familiarity of the count brought a tingle of awareness to his mind. Breathe in one, two, three, as he raised the hammer. Hold one, two, three, as he gathered his strength. Breathe out one, two, three, as he lowered the hammer. Hold one, two, three. Raise the hammer one, two, three . . .

He swung downward with the hammer. The force of his blow sent shock waves from the hammer head up the shaft and into his hands. His arms ached and his head threatened to split open with the backlash of pain.

Numbly he lifted the hammer again. One, two, three. Breathe one, two, three. Something wasn't quite right. The hammer was too light. He stopped his movement, midstroke, unsure how to proceed.

A guard patrolled the length of the cleared shaft to enforce the no talking rule. Muaynwor continued to stare straight ahead. What was wrong?

"Stupid slave," the guard grunted. "Broke your hammer and don't even know it." The guard bent and retrieved a different tool from the pile. He thrust a shovel into Muaynwor's hands.

The dark mute continued to stare. The new tool wasn't right either.

"You'll probably break that one as well. Get yerself a new handle. That one's too worn. You know how to do it." The guard pushed Muaynwor toward a pile of wood in various shapes and sizes.

Muaynwor hobbled the last few steps, anxious to avoid the guard's touch. The manacle on his right ankle dragged his chain partner with him. The partner seemed familiar, safe, unlike the guard whose touch sometimes brought pain.

He reached for a new handle. The first piece of wood was too thick and short, meant for a sledgehammer. The second piece was wrong, too. He discarded them both and reached deeper.

His hand curled around something smooth and even grained. A long straight piece of wood. Power pulsed up his arms. He looked at the handle more closely.

A tree branch cut to the length of a walking stick, smoothed and polished. Good, solid oak. The grain was obscured by a thick layer of dirt. Warmth caressed his tired hand. The wood seemed to glow and pulsate with unnatural blue sparks.

Light. A glowing warmth just out of reach beckoned. Something huge and shinning and winged at the core.

"Ja . . . Jack . . ." he croaked at the urging of the shimmering presence in his mind.

"Hold your tongue, slave!" The guard flicked his wrist. The lash bit deep into Muaynwor's cheek. "Ain't spoke in nigh on three year. Don't need to start now."

Three years? Three years of counting hammer strokes and breaths. The oak staff shot a flame of awareness to his mind.

Jack, he thought. *My name is* . . . Not Jack, almost . . .

Jack closed his eyes and shook his head. When he opened them again, the glow in the staff intensified. The tingling warmth spread up his hand to his arm and tight shoulder muscles. The peculiar warmth invaded his toes and soothed his aching arches caused by the ill-fitting boots.

"Git back to work, y' worthless slaves. Fix the shovel, and start clearin' the debris around that *s'murghing* boulder."

The guard shoved Jack and his chain partner toward the rubble.

When the guard moved on around a bend in the passage, Jack examined the staff. Knowledge and memory jolted through his mind.

He'd taken innocent lives. He hadn't even stopped to offer healing magic to the victims. Shame and disgust for some unknown action washed over him.

"What do you remember?" his partner whispered, barely audible.

"Too much and not enough," Jack replied, still staring at the staff. A magician's staff. *His* tool and focus for spells. He didn't know if he had any magic left within him.

He and the staff had been separated for three years. His magic had been dead an equal amount of time. "Is it too late to find the power again?" he asked the staff.

Katrina sat before the rough factory pillow, an alien in the only world she knew. Her neat single plait gathered from the crown of her head to the nape of her neck, her plain dark skirt, and her meticulously clean hands and nails, showed how different she was from every other lacemaker in the cold and dark factory.

She was a slave and could never leave the building without permission. She had to wear the clothes provided for her by her owner and had no salary to spend on the cheap, gaudy jewelry the other lacemakers delighted in. The only similarity was her single plait. Unlike the other women, Katrina kept hers neat, tight, and clean. Most of the others merely clubbed their dirty hair together at the nape of their necks and braided it loosely.

Her owner, Neeles Brunix never ceased to remind her that her slavery was his revenge for the way Tattia Kaantille had insulted him that day three years ago when he refused to buy her patterns.

Katrina shifted in her straight chair, willing her bladder to hold out a little longer. Another hour to the noon sun break. Three years she had been a slave in the factory, and she still hadn't learned to adjust her body to the daily routine. Another wiggle eased her back, a little.

She tried to dismiss the whispers and covert glances from the other lacemakers. Constant, disquieting murmurs filled the workroom on the third floor of the largest factory in Queen's City. Each exchange between two lacemakers was followed by a pointed look over a shoulder or across the room toward the coveted window position occupied by Katrina. She fought the urge to shift her back and ease the pressure on her bladder.

No work song lightened the long and tedious day. Katrina's soul cried out for music.

Alone in the world and in the factory, Katrina bent her head to her work. The heavy bobbins didn't fly through the pattern as her lighter, more slender bobbins had. Rhythm was difficult to maintain without music.

In defiance of factory rules, Katrina hummed an ancient work tune to aid her as she worked her pattern.

Meet together, crossing paths.
Work together, twisting threads.
Sing a little, friends are fast.

The snickering whispers and slightly turned shoulders told her more than words how unwelcome any contribution from her would be. They would never be her friends.

Katrina flipped her right-hand pair of bobbins in a triple twist. The outside thread caught on the imperfections in the pillow cover, throwing her timing and tension off. The pin-hole in the pattern was out of alignment as well. The song died in her heart as the flow of work was interrupted.

"Ooooh! Not again," Maari, the newest lacemaker in the darkest corner of the Brunix factory, whined.

Katrina put down her bobbins with a sigh and crossed the large workroom to the new girl's pillow. Owner Brunix had given Katrina extra food and new blankets for her bed in return for helping the beginners keep their work straight and error free. After three years she had proved her skills above and beyond any of the free workers.

Somehow, someday she'd find a way out of this miserable factory and back to her rightful place in society where she could wear two plaits again. Becoming the best lacemaker ever was the key to her survival and eventual freedom.

Brunix had offered many times to change her slave status to employee if she willingly shared his bed. That course was no more than another form of slavery.

"This pattern is too hard," Maari protested.

She sounded so much like Hilza before her last illness, Katrina had to restrain the urge to hug the girl to her breast. She hadn't allowed that wound to heal. The reminder of the deprivations inflicted upon her family by King Simeon kept her angry. Made her strong enough to survive and to resist Owner Brunix's sexual offers.

Allowing any man to take liberties with her body was too close to King Simeon's ugly demands for Katrina to agree to her owner's lewd suggestions. Why didn't he just rape her? He had the right. He owned her body.

She'd never give up her soul.

"There is nothing new in this pattern, Maari," Katrina explained brusquely. "I've added two extra pairs of bobbins to the fan and reversed the rose ground with the half-stitch diamond."

"But it *looks* different. And the half stitch is always tangled." Maari's lower lip stuck out. Hilza had pouted the same way. In a moment the girl would cry. Big fat tears that garnered sympathy but did nothing to mar her clear skin and sweet blue eyes.

Katrina hardened her heart lest she shatter three years of reserve and give in to Maari's sulks. Fixing the problem for her wouldn't help the girl overcome her lack of proper training. Nor would it give her the skills to survive in the fierce competition of factory life.

"Half stitch always looks tangled until you get four or five rows into it. Look." Katrina extracted a long pin with a costly amber bead on the head from the thickest part of her single plait. She was supposed to use this expensive gift from Owner Brunix to separate her growing clumps of bobbins into sections. It was more useful as a pointer. The tiny insect trapped in the amber was a constant reminder of the prison she had made for herself in accepting slavery in the factory over King Simeon's coven.

She laid the length of the pin along one thread running through the questioned part of the pattern. The mistake jumped into view.

Maari nodded, eyes wandering around her pillow.

"Watch the threads, not the bobbins."

Maari's eyes jerkily followed the path of the pin along the threads.

"Oh!" Maari breathed. "I twisted twice instead of once." Hastily she reached for her bobbins to unweave the lopsided diamond.

Katrina halted Maari's hasty movements with a touch of the pin. "And never throw the bobbins! Lay them down neatly, in order. That is your true problem, Maari. You do not respect your bobbins or your work. You led a pampered life, and your teachers always rescued you. Now you have to take care of yourself and fix your own mistakes."

Maari had come from a wealthy mercantile family brought to ruin by the war and changing times, just as Katrina had. No one had helped Katrina during those early days in the factory as she struggled to keep up with more experienced lacemakers. No one had protected her from their cruel insults and sneaky tricks. Jealous rivals within the factory sometimes stole a bobbin from a pillow—usually from a place that required extensive reworking to add a replacement thread.

She jerked her head around to view her own pillow to make sure no one did that now. Taalia, one of the senior employees, stood halfway between her own work stand and Katrina's. She scuttled back to her chair at Katrina's fierce glare.

Katrina returned her attention to her pupil. "Tomorrow, I expect to see every half-stitch diamond worked correctly. I also expect to see your hands scrubbed and your fingernails *clean*." She retreated toward her own work.

"Did you give Owner Brunix the new design?" Taalia asked as Katrina passed by. Her tone was as breezy as ever, not acknowledging her previous attempt at trickery.

"Not yet."

"Afraid he'll notice there's more to you than lacemaker's hands and sharp eyes? I'll take him the pattern and claim it as my own. Maybe he'll offer me the same bonus he wants to give you." Taalia shifted in her chair, thrusting her bosom forward and wiggling her hips provocatively.

"I'll deliver the pattern when it is ready." Katrina bit her lip. Neeles Brunix's sexual innuendoes were getting harder to turn aside or ignore.

She wondered yet again why the owner hadn't forced her into his bed. He seemed to prefer his women willing—just like Simeon, who needed a willing virgin.

The most recent increase in privileges could be a bribe, or perhaps merely a reminder that Neeles Brunix controlled every aspect of her life. Why shouldn't she take a step toward earning her freedom by granting the owner a few favors?

Because the touch of his hand on hers reminded her over and over of the filthy suggestions made by King Simeon. She'd never give herself to any man without marriage, without respect. She didn't dare hope to find love.

"I'll give him the pattern during the sun break. He won't make lewd suggestions with all of the others around," Katrina said to herself.

"Don't underestimate him, Katey." Iza came up behind her. Iza no longer made lace. She was nearly blind and hunchbacked from a lifetime of working her pillow in dim light. She wound bobbins or straightened pins and did other useful, time-consuming chores. Working in the factory had deprived her of a life and family of her own. She was now too old and her skin too yellow, from the enforced restrictions on trips to the necessary during work hours, to catch Brunix's lustful eye. Iza had no other place to go.

"Brunix wants you, not just for your body. He wants to use your talents to gain the respect of the other owners. If he can flaunt a fair-haired woman with palace training as his mistress, then he believes the other owners will accept his dark eyes and dusky skin. Hold out for marriage." Iza urged Katrina back to her work.

"I don't want to marry Owner Brunix. Marriage to an outlander won't earn me two plaits. I've been betrayed by dark-eyed men before. I'll never let it happen again." A magician boy with dark eyes had betrayed her father's ship and ruined her entire family.

Katrina had never met the apprentice responsible for stopping her father's ship full of Tambootie seedlings, yet her hatred and mistrust of him grew with each year of separation from her old, comfortable, and stable way of life with a family she loved.

"Design is your entrance to the palace and out of this rat's maze," Iza reminded her. "Show him the design today at the sun break. I'll stand behind you."

"At the sun break," Katrina affirmed with trembling hands and quaking heart.

"Are you sure the queen is pregnant? So soon after her last miscarriage?" Jaylor asked the flickering image in the glass.

A slight tickle in his mind told him that Brevelan listened to his conversation with the Commune's informer.

Three years ago, on the night of Darville's coronation, he and Brevelan had been anxious to leave the capital before the Council discovered them. But he'd taken the time to recruit the spy. He needed information to keep his Commune safe. He couldn't risk talking directly to Darville or Mikka.

Though Margit had confirmed that Darville had not been with the army that attacked the monastery three years ago, Jaylor and his best friend had agreed to end all association and communication until prejudice against magic subsided throughout Coronnan. That couldn't happen until the dragons returned. Bringing control back to the magicians.

"I overheard her tell the king. She isn't well, Master Jaylor. She's as likely to lose this baby as all the others," the spy said. Her voice was clearer than her face.

Was it her lack of control of this spell or something else that interfered with the summons? Jaylor had only had time to teach her the basics of a summons and extending her listening senses when he recruited her.

Yaakke had noticed her carefully hidden talent without recognizing her as the source. After three years, her powers hadn't increased. She'd never qualify as an apprentice. She made a very good spy, however, despite her chafing at the confines of her work as a maid in Rossemikka's household. Her need to be away from people and buildings had prompted her to dress as a boy and follow the king on a wild tusker hunt the day he appeared to be outside the old monastery. Her unauthorized actions had given Darville a welcome alibi.

"Do the king and queen plan to announce this pregnancy?" Jaylor pushed a little of his own magic into the spell, though the girl had initiated it. Her image remained dim and flickered in and out of focus.

"Not for a while. She's miscarried so often, they're afraid of offering false hope of an heir." The girl paused. Swirls of gray and blue clouded Jaylor's glass. "I've got to go. The queen is calling for me. I wish you would allow me to find other employment in the palace. I hate being indoors all the time as much as I hate cats."

"I need you where you are, Margit. Take care of the queen. Try to make her stay in bed as much as possible. Brevelan says . . ." His glass cleared. All he could see through it was the candle flame, greatly magnified.

"I have to go to Mikka," Brevelan said from behind him. She grabbed several handfuls of herbs drying in the rafters of their home and stuffed them into her small satchel.

"You can't go. It's not safe, for you or for our baby," he replied. Gently he touched her slightly swollen belly where she carried their third child. "Our children need you here. You can't take Glendon with you. One look at him and everyone would know who his father is."

"I can help Mikka. I can prevent a miscarriage. I should have gone a long time ago." Grief and guilt crossed her face.

"What if you had gone and helped her through a full pregnancy? If anyone suspected her new midwife had any magic, the child would be removed from the succession. They'd suspect the child as a potential witch or, worse, a changeling. Mikka might be put aside, too. No. The fear of magic is too strong in the capital. I won't risk you.

Darville won't risk the Council sending Mikka back to her brother. That might start a new war with Rossemeyer. We have to find another way to help our friends get an heir."

"Mikka loves Darville too much to allow her brother to start a war. She's close to Rossemanuel. He'll listen to her." Brevelan continued packing medicines.

"Rossemanuel may be king, but he's still very young. Their uncle's party rules Rossemeyer. They still control hordes of mercenaries anxious to fight. Coronnan is as good a target as anyplace."

"If they are so anxious to fight, why haven't they joined our war against SeLenicca? Maybe with their active support we could end this stalemate." Brevelan set her carry pack on the table, next to Jaylor's glass and candle. "I'll take the boys over to the apprentice dormitory. Your students need practice in controlling our two hooligans." A small grin touched the corners of her mouth. Three-year-old Glendon and his two-year-old brother, Lukan, managed to find more mischief than any ten normal boys combined.

"You must stay here, Brevelan. The journey to the capital is too long. I won't risk you and the baby." Jaylor picked up the satchel and began replacing the small crocks and vials of medicine on their shelves.

"Then send me by the transport spell." Brevelan returned her potions to the satchel as fast as he removed them.

"No! I have forbidden the use of that spell except for the most dire emergencies. We haven't any dragons to guide us through the void. I can't allow you to go." Panic sent his heart racing. The thought of losing Brevelan to magic or to those who feared her magic made his world bleak and empty. "Think, Brevelan. Think of the consequences."

"Then you will have to find us some dragons. Quickly. Mikka needs me!"

"I have no one to send in search of Shayla yet. The only alternative is to let me go, as I should have gone three years ago." Yaakke's death still weighed heavily on his conscience. When would he have the courage to send another journeyman in search of the dragons?

"I can't let you go, Jaylor." Brevelan clung to him, crying silently.

Queen Rossemikka seems to be barren. The Council looks elsewhere, outside of Coronnan to distant relatives of Darville, for an heir. Rejiia's son died at birth. Now she has deserted her husband and disappeared from Coronnan. Lord Andrall's son is mentally defective and hasn't been considered a possible heir to the Coraurlia for more than twenty years. The Council and the increasingly powerful Gnuls will not countenance an illegitimate birth. If they did, they would have to look at witchwoman Brevelan as next heir. If they could find her. Krej acknowledged her as his eldest. If the Council insists on a male, they would look to Brevelan's oldest son, Glendon—likely a magician born and bred. She never claimed Darville to be the father. We all know he is. Descended from two royal lines, her son has the strongest blood claim to the throne—if the people of Coronnan could put aside their prejudice against magic.

The coven is so close, and yet so far, from achieving domination of the Three Kingdoms. I have waited years for events to move themselves. My patience is at an end. I must stir some mischief to move events forward.

Chapter Fourteen

Mid-afternoon brought a thinning of spring clouds. All of the lacemakers gratefully grabbed their cloaks and trooped onto the narrow walkway that separated the factory from the river. Katrina wasn't sure where or when the custom of a sun break had begun, but it was now a time-honored tradition. Fines for denying workers their right to an hour of sunlight in the middle of the day—even when it was storming—could financially ruin an employer. Too bad she spent most of the time waiting in line to use the necessary.

The men who worked in the factory warehouse would have their sun break after the women returned to the workroom.

Katrina looked askance at the welcome sun. Neeles Brunix did not always join his lacemakers on the walkway. A break in the clouds almost guaranteed his presence. He was here today, ahead of the women. His long body leaning against the sand-brick wall of the factory, almost the same color as his hair, he stared at the rushing river. No flicker of his dark, hooded eyes acknowledged the presence of his employees until Katrina appeared at the end of the line. As soon as she threw back her hood and raised her face to the sun,

Neeles Brunix stood straight and his eyes sparked with unconcealed desire.

The younger lacemakers scurried out of his way, not willing to have tht intense gaze rest on their bodies.

"I hear you treated the new girl very harshly this morning." Brunix appeared at Katrina's side before she had a chance to gather her courage and take a deep breath.

"You make me responsible for her training. Therefore, I am also responsible for her mistakes and dirty lace." She looked at the river rushing past the levee. It smelled clean today, refreshed by snow melting in the hills. An unwelcome urge to follow her mother in the water's endless journey to the sea gripped her. To end the struggle. To know peace.

She didn't want peace. She wanted to avenge the wrongs done to her and her family by King Simeon and a dark-eyed magician boy. In her mind the magician looked very much like a younger Neeles Brunix.

"I would free you from slavery if you would add certain other responsibilities to your . . . work." His eyes opened as they skimmed her cloaked body.

Did he know she made certain her clothing was too large for her and that she bound her full bosom extra tight to disguise her figure from his gaze?

Just then, Taalia sauntered by, her wrap drooping on her shoulder to reveal the deep neckline of her bodice. Her heavy breasts swelled above the white cloth. A dusky shadow peeked out from the skimpy confines of her clothing in blatant invitation to Brunix. She rotated her hips as she walked, making little thrusting movements with her pelvis.

Katrina turned away, embarrassed.

Brunix never took his eyes off Katrina.

"This is the only additional responsibility I ask." Katrina thrust the new pattern under his nose so he couldn't ignore it. "I want to draw new patterns."

"I have no need for new designs. I have all of the patterns you inherited and I bought. I do need you to warm my bed," he stated as he took the pattern from her and examined the flowing lines of the floral motif.

"No." Katrina stood her ground, wishing she could turn him into a living torch like the witches of legend.

"I own you, Katrina Kaantille, just as I own your inheritance. I could order you to submit."

"But you prefer your women willing, just like King Simeon."

Brunix blanched at her comparison.

"I am not willing."

"Compromise!" Iza hissed as she pushed her frail body between them. "The pattern is good and it is unique. You will make money from it, Brunix."

"It is also complex. Only the most skilled lacemaker could work it. I'm not certain Tattia Kaantille could work the design, let alone her half-trained daughter."

Katrina gasped at his audacity. By invoking her mother's name, he reminded them all of the taint of suicide that clung to Katrina. Tattia's ghost was said to haunt the workroom at night. Superstition claimed that Katrina, too, would become a ghost upon her death because of her mother's sin.

"We seem to be at an impasse," Brunix sneered at Katrina. "I will examine the design. If it is worthy, I will consider adding it to my stock."

"No." Katrina grabbed the pattern from him and walked over to the edge of the walkway. There she held the strip of leather over the rushing river. "I have many more ideas for new patterns—exporters always need new designs. All of my ideas are exclusively yours in exchange for my freedom. End my slavery, or I destroy it."

"That pattern is mine! And so are you." Brunix lunged to grab it away from Katrina. As his hands curled around her arm, she opened her fingers. A puff of wind caught the contested prize, swirled it, and then dropped it at Brunix's feet. He retrieved the strip of stained leather before the next breeze drowned it in the river.

"Stupid bitch. You'll pay for your insolence!" Brunix screamed. "I'll make a fortune from this design and the others. You owe me your life and I intend to keep you my slave for a very, very long time."

"I hope the cost of a license for Tambrin to work the design properly will beggar you." Katrina stalked back to the workroom alone.

Jaylor raised his head and listened to the clearing. "Someone comes," he announced to Brevelan across the open space where she hung the laundry.

"Another victim?" She cocked her head as if listening. "Build up the fire and start some water boiling. Fetch some bandages, too. I sense pain. Serious pain." She hurried toward the west path.

Glendon ran ahead of his father into the hut. Two-year-old Lukan planted a reluctant lop-eared rabbit onto his hip and toddled in her wake.

Light shimmered in a sense-lurching flash of colored arcs as the forest shifted and the entrance to this hidden clearing opened.

A nondescript young man dressed in common trews and home-spun shirt used his sturdy staff for balance as he dragged a smaller body up the hill.

"Another victim," Jaylor acknowledged, knowing his wife had been correct in her assessment of the newcomers. He hastened to set a cauldron of water to boil for whatever healing herbs and poultices she might need. Bandages. The stock was low. This was the third refugee in the past moon. He sent Glendon to tear strips from the store of linen in the loft.

The young man he recognized as Journeyman Marcus. One of the few boys of talent who had remained with the Commune since Baamin's death and the disbanding of the University. Journeyman quests now revolved around rescuing the victims of the Gnostic Utilitarians. In the last year the cult's hatred had gained momentum. Why?

Whether the child with Marcus had true magical abilities or was hounded away from his home because of unfounded accusations of witchcraft remained to be seen.

More than two dozen refugees had found shelter in the southern mountains with the remnants of the Commune. Most of them had some talent; one or two had the potential to become true magicians and join the continual fight for the survival of the Commune.

Unfortunately, most of the girls who found their way to the clearing were so traumatized by the rape gangs that wandered villages in search of "potential" witches, they'd never be brave enough to try magic. The mistaken belief that only virgins could throw magic was just an excuse for bullies to run wilder than magicians were reputed to.

"Good thing we started a new cabin to house apprentices," Jaylor remarked to the greenbird perched above the doorway of his own newly expanded home. The cluster of wooden buildings at the base of a cliff an hour's walk from the clearing had grown from a single library to include Masters' quarters and now apprentice dormitories. The two journeymen, Marcus and Robb, parked their weary bodies where they could when they were about. Mostly they wandered Coronnan, supplying Jaylor with information and new apprentices.

Jaylor's biggest worry lately was to find ways to feed them all without arousing the suspicion of the countryside.

"News from the capital, Master." Marcus eased his companion onto a cot before the hearth at Brevelan's direction.

While his wife tended the pale and frightened boy, Jaylor ushered his two sons and the journeyman ahead of him, out of the cottage. "How badly is he hurt?" He handed Marcus the length of linen and gestured for him to start ripping it into bandages.

"A broken arm, I think. Straightened and splinted it as best I could, but I'm no healer. Lee's da threw stones at him when he stopped plowing and ran to help a steed in distress foaling twins." Marcus shook his head in dismay. "The boy was only trying to help the mare and save the foals."

"I know, Marcus. I know. 'Tis the same story we've heard over and over. The Gnostic Utilitarians have spread dire tales of the evils of magic. They encourage lawless vengeance against innocents. I wonder that King Darville allows it."

"I don't think he sanctions the Gnuls, sir. King Darville is a good king and Coronnan has prospered these last three years, despite the war. I think the Gnuls have invented evidence of evil magic to regain the followers who aren't afraid of magic now that life is getting comfortable again."

"Does this boy have true talent?" Jaylor changed the subject rather than dispute the issue with Marcus. The Gnuls claimed Darville had led the attack on the monastery three years ago. Revealing the truth—that Margit had followed him on a wild tusker hunt in the opposite direction—might jeopardize the girl's position.

"Can't tell what's talent and what's sensitive hearing. Lee feels guilty for having any magic. He's bottled it all up so tight I couldn't find it with my probes. But I think he must. The mare went into labor weeks early. She was pastured well away from where the boy was tilling. Yet he knew. Just reared up his head, nostrils flaring and eyes wide, like he felt the pain himself. Or heard her distress well beyond the reach of normal senses."

"Another empath? Brevelan does that."

"Good thing I was in the area. I 'heard' the boy cry out when the first stone knocked the wind out of him. If I hadn't thrown a delusion of Lee running away and diverted the attack, he'd be dead now. Good thing he's a boy."

A fearful father might have raped his own daughter to kill her magic. Boys were just murdered.

"Someone is compounding the ugliness. I've heard reports of animals being stolen from secure pens and being found slaughtered—

throats slit, blood drained in a ritual manner—miles away." Marcus swallowed heavily as if keeping down bile.

"I've heard those rumors, too. No evidence, though. It's always in the next village."

"Now it's in the capital. I talked to a woman whose cat was stolen from her arms, on her doorstep, by a gang of older boys. She found the cat on her doorstep the next morning. She claims she saw a cloaked man in the shadow of the next house directing the gang. Later the boys involved each had a gold piece they had no explanation for earning. Some of her neighbors are calling her a witch now. Just 'cause she's old and alone."

"Hearsay again."

"I've alerted Margit. She's looking for hard evidence. I've tried to teach her new spells, but she can't seem to learn anything beyond a basic summons. She'll have to rely on her knowledge of Coronnan City."

Regretful silence followed while Jaylor tried to calm his fury at events in the capital. He hugged both his sons tighter, savoring their innocence. Glendon responded by wrapping one arm around Jaylor's knees. Lukan plopped his thumb into his empty mouth and snuggled into his father's lap.

"Any other news from the capital?" Jaylor diverted his thoughts and his anger away from the persecution of magic. How could he stop the torture and murder of innocents? The rumors of sacrificed animals had to stop before they amplified into tales of stolen children.

The time for the Commune to intervene and show that magic was not something to fear was fast approaching, with or without dragons. But their numbers were so few!

With luck and a lot more training, Marcus and Robb would be ready to go on a real quest in search of Shayla within a year or two. Too late. Something needed to be done now. Before the Gnuls discovered the University in exile and murdered them all.

"The king still wears a sling on his left arm. But he attends banquets now and eats with his right hand. Until recently he hasn't been seen to eat in public since the battle with Janataea and Krej."

Jaylor knew that. Margit had reported the Council's complaints that the queen's miscarriages and subsequent illness shouldn't keep Darville from attending banquets and other festivities.

"There's something else you should know, sir." Marcus looked about the clearing as if seeking information.

"Did you find a trace of Yaakke?" He asked the same question every time either Marcus or Robb returned with reports.

"Not him. But sort of like him. Robb and I have noticed some of the outlying villages disappear."

"What?" Jaylor roared. His sons slipped behind him to avoid his wrath. He reached out and hugged them both, drawing calm from their innocence.

"Sometimes when we pass by at a distance we see houses and people, fields and flocks. And then as soon as someone spots us, we can't see them anymore. If we weren't stretching our senses looking for magic, I doubt we'd see these places at all. It's like this clearing. If Brevelan doesn't want the path open, ain't no way in Simurgh's hell anyone, magician or mundane, is going to find our refuge."

Darville walked the streets of Sambol on the old border between Coronnan and SeLenicca. The stillness in the air that foretold dawn enhanced the scents of spice and cut lumber, of salted fish and too many people crowded within the walls of the merchant city. All was silent, as if Kardia Hodos held its breath in anticipation of the new day, the Vernal Equinox.

False dawn glimmered on the eastern horizon. The near-constant wind funneling down the mountain pass to the west returned.

The troubled king turned his back on the wind and the last bite of winter in the mountains. At the far end of the pass, his army would be preparing for the first battle of the season. A first battle that would carry the war out of the pass and into SeLenicca, hopefully crushing the next invasion before it began. He'd kept King Simeon's army out of Coronnan for three long years. Now, at last, he was in a position to end the conflict.

He didn't think he'd have been allowed to achieve that advantage if Lord Jonnias and Lord Marnak still sat on the Council of Provinces. Heavy fines for their attack on the monastery and banishment from the Council until those fines were paid had ended their dissension. For the first time in too many years the Council worked with their king as a team and the war progressed, however slightly. A defensive war only. Until now.

Both Coronnan and SeLenicca were exhausted and running low on resources.

Dark shadows still lay between the steep walls of the pass. Night would linger longer there, hiding ambushes and stalling messages. 'Twas one message in particular that had brought King Darville to the city on the edge of the battlefront. His spies in the enemy army had sent a coded letter by a long and circuitous route. The generals of King Simeon of SeLenicca were willing to discuss an armed truce, with or without Simeon's approval.

Frost clung to the trees and paths this cloudy equinox morning. But yesterday had been balmy. Any disarmament had to take place soon, so that soldiers could go home in time for spring planting.

Darville heaved a lonely sigh as he continued his ritual walk. Fred, his trusty bodyguard and confidant, now that Jaylor remained in hiding, was somewhere behind him, hovering protectively. Dawn was almost here and Darville had yet to make the decision that drove him to walk the streets at dawn.

"Jaylor knew before I did that I think better on my feet," he mused. Then he looked up to the sky and addressed the wind as if it were Jaylor. "I miss you, old friend."

He lengthened his stride, almost hoping to lose Fred and his loneliness in the tangle of alleys and warehouses. No questions arose in his mind about the tentative offer of peace. That he would grab.

But what would he do about the Council's request that he put aside his beloved wife in favor of a woman who could bear him a son and heir?

More than three years had passed since his coronation, and Mikka had miscarried seven times. He feared her current pregnancy would also end in disaster. For her own health, she shouldn't have conceived again so soon. She had enough magic talent in her to prevent it.

But Mikka was a princess born and bred. She *knew* how much Coronnan needed an heir to provide a clear line of succession. The country wouldn't survive a dynastic war compounded by the exhausted reserves from the current war with SeLenicca.

He walked on. The tangle of alleys opened to a market square. In the center stood a proud Equinox Pylon decorated with the first greens and flowers of the season. As soon as the sun topped the horizon, citizens would be dancing and singing a welcome to spring. The celebration and fertility rituals would go on all day and well into the night. He should be with Mikka.

The wind shifted once again, and new odors assaulted the king. Death.

Recent death. And not a clean one. The hair on the back of his neck rose in preternatural fear. He cast about him for the source of danger, left hand reaching automatically to the short sword on his hip.

"*S'murgh it!*" he cursed as an aching burn snaked up his arm and his hand grasped nothing. "I'll never learn to fight right-handed." With a conscious thought he grasped his weapon with his undamaged hand.

"What is it, Your Grace?" Fred appeared at his left elbow, ready to guard his vulnerable side. Then he wrinkled his nose.

A flicker of movement by the Pylon drew their attention. No one stood near the focus of celebration, but an ugly brown nest of twigs at the base crackled with new fire. Atop the fuel lay the gutted body of a cat, intestines and blood feeding the growing flames.

Fred dashed forward to stamp out the fire before it spread to the Pylon and spring decorations.

"Who would sacrifice a cat?" Darville asked the air. Painful memories of Krej and his coven sacrificing the body of one particular cat came to mind. Thanks to their efforts, there was no feline body to receive the alien spirit sharing Mikka's human form.

He'd heard about ritual slaughter of livestock around the country. This was the first report of the carcass being found at a Pylon. The action brought back childhood horror stories of the days before the Stargods when Simurgh, the winged god of death, had reigned throughout Kardia Hodos.

Krej's old coven had worked to restore that bloodthirsty religion. They'd had three years to restore their numbers after the death of Janessa, Krej's mother, and Janataea, his sister. Krej himself had been locked into the tin statue of a weasel. And Zolltarn had deserted their ranks for the Commune. Had Krej broken free and restored the coven?

Had a cat been sacrificed this time because they were the symbol of a witch's familiar and fearful citizens targeted the poor animals? Maybe a malcontent chose a beloved pet to stir up fear of witches.

Or had the coven sent a warning that they knew Mikka harbored the spirit of a cat in her human body? If that knowledge leaked to anyone, Mikka would be named witch and exiled or executed. He didn't know if he had enough authority to save her.

"Looks like the work of the coven. I heard there was a village up north that found a sacrificed child by their Pylon at the last Solstice."

"Unconfirmed rumors," Darville said sharply, breathing through his mouth to reduce the stench. "I have to have hard evidence to confirm or refute these stories of human sacrifice. Remind me when we get back to the city. I'll have to send out a trusted agent."

"We'd best hide this before anyone else sees it and panics," Fred suggested. "The coven would love to involve you in suspicion of witchcraft, so's the Gnuls would depose you or start a new civil war."

"I wouldn't put it past the Gnostic Utilitarians to plant this fake sacrifice so I would lead a witch-hunt. When we get back to the capital, I'll find a spy to infiltrate that group, too." Darville found a sturdy branch among those gathered for the bonfire that would be lit at midnight.

Together the two men scooped up as much of the grisly evidence as they could. "Throw it into the river, Fred. And not a word of this to anyone."

"Evil rumors have a way of starting without evidence."

"Rumors that must be squashed before they become fact. I'll not fall victim to the plots of either the coven or the Gnuls. I have had enough of my citizens becoming vicious, prying spies. Those lavish rewards granted to informers by the Gnuls must stop. People invent evidence of magic against their neighbors, family, and business rivals for money." And courtiers followed Queen Rossemikka, hoping she'd betray her rumored magic talent. Was that why the Council pushed him daily to put aside his queen?

Darville set his jaw in determination. No one would make him set aside his wife. Not even Mikka herself.

Chapter Fifteen

"Good thing the old commandant wandered off and drowned himself in a creek two inches deep," Jack's chain partner whispered out of the side of his mouth. "Died with a smile on his face, I hear."

Dragon-dream! He'd heard of that happening before. Where? When?

Jack didn't reply until the black-uniformed guard making his rounds passed beyond them. Speaking was forbidden in the yard during sun breaks as well as in the mines.

"Why is it good?" He kept his faced turned toward the sun, absorbing as much warmth and light as possible. His body turned toward a natural tug, and he knew that direction was south. Without knowing why, he checked the position of the sun against the length of the shadows. The sun had just passed the Vernal Equinox.

"The old commandant would have ordered you whipped for disrupting the routine when you broke that hammer." The partner also continued to bask in the sunlight.

"Not my fault the equipment is shoddy and worn out," Jack protested, still in whispers.

"That was the old commandant. The new one knows that slaves are in short supply. Most criminals are sent to reinforce the army at the front rather than here. Now that Coronnan is setting up an invasion, Simeon doesn't have enough troops." News of the last battle had come with a private message to the commandant a few days ago. Two dozen of the youngest and healthiest miners were due to be shipped out when the pass cleared. Jack and his partner weren't among them, though both could bear the hardships of army life.

Something was wrong with Simeon sending slaves from this mine to battle Coronnan. Jack didn't know what.

"We live longer and work harder when the commandant feeds us and goes lighter on the lash," the partner finished.

"How long has the new commandant been here?"

"Two years. Maybe more. Hard to keep track of time in a place like this."

"Why can't we speak?" Jack muttered into his beard and turned his back on his companion as another guard strolled around them. He'd counted four uniformed men in the yard, armed with clubs and whips. Nearly one hundred prisoners—he refused to think of himself as a slave. The weapons were not formidable. Surely one hundred prisoners could overpower four guards and escape.

"Same reason chain partners are changed every few days. They don't want to give us the opportunity to plan an escape or learn to trust each other." The partner stretched his arms over his head as if offering prayers to the sun.

"Who needs plans? We're strong from hard work. Why can't we bash a few heads and break out?"

"Where would we go?"

That stunned Jack. He hadn't thought further than escape.

"CRAWK, Crawk, crawk, crawk . . ." A jackdaw, perched atop the commandant's quarters, mocked Jack's shortsightedness with a raucous cackle. He watched the bird preen himself, absorbing the familiar movements in a memory that seemed to have been washed as clean as a cooking pot.

His hand hovered over an imaginary kettle as if wielding a dishrag. He'd washed pots before. But where or when?

"CROOAWK, Crooawk, crooawk . . ." the jackdaw cawed again, this time as if encouraging him to drag more memories out of his tired brain.

"So far, the guards have allowed me to stay as your partner for three weeks," his partner said, breaking into Jack's thoughts.

"Because I've been walking in my sleep for three years?"

"Probably. You haven't spoken or even acknowledged anyone with a flicker of an eye or a nod of the head. They don't consider you a threat."

"Hmf." Jack looked away again.

A slight, stoop-shouldered, man with a thin, patchy beard edged closer, as if listening. Jack turned his back on the man. The listener was new to the mine, new since . . . yesterday!

Jack smiled inwardly at this minor triumph of memory. Then he frowned. A newcomer eavesdropping bothered him.

He allowed his eyes to focus on the jackdaw with the white spots above its eyes—almost like bushy white eyebrows. Why did that thought resound through his body as if it were important?

"CRAWK, Crawk, crawk," the bird encouraged him again.

Jack suddenly knew he'd awakened to the same raucous call every morning since arriving in the mine. The bird was tied to him in some way. He longed to go back into the mine and hold his staff again. His tool of magic had to be the key to his memory. It was still lashed to a shovel inside the mine.

"Don't blame you for existing in a fog like that. We were all sent here to die. Not thinking, not remembering the pain we've caused others makes it all easier to bear," the partner said.

"I don't think I was sent here for that purpose," Jack said, more to the jackdaw then to his partner. "If only I could remember!"

"Don't force it. Memories are like quicksilver. They look solid until you try to grasp them, then they slip away just out of reach, still looking solid but more than ready to escape again. What are some of the things you do remember? Do you have a name?"

"Jack." That didn't sound exactly right, but it was close enough.

"I'm Fraank."

The jackdaw glided to a fence post on the south side of the yard. It cocked its head and looked at the pair as if listening to their muted conversation. Perhaps the bird had been a familiar. He knew he was a magician, so why not?

"Corby, Corby, Corby," the jackdaw called.

Jack had heard the bird speak in just that way once before. "Corby." He formed the word soundlessly. "Your name is Corby." He smiled at the memory of Corby scolding him, listening to him, spotting game for him.

"What else do you remember?" his partner prodded him.

"I remember things. I can't remember me. Look at me, I'm half a head taller than I think I should be, I'm strong instead of skinny, and this beard is full when I've never had a beard before."

"What things do you remember?"

"Things, like this is Coronnan and the Stargods outlawed slaves here a thousand years ago. So how can King Simeon of *SeLenicca* draw slaves from here to fight in his army?"

"This isn't Coronnan. We're in SeLenicca and King Simeon owns this mine."

"No." Jack shook his head. He knew that information was wrong. "None of the guards, nor the commandant, cuts his beard square. The guards speak both languages. Some of the prisoners might be SeLenese, but we aren't in SeLenicca."

"But I was sent here by King Simeon in punishment for my . . . for crimes against him!" Fraank protested.

"I know that when I fled to this place, it was within the boundaries of Coronnan. I know that in my bones. We are within the borders of the land once reserved for the dragons."

"Fled here? You came here by choice?" Fraank's voice squeaked in apprehension. "Jack, no one comes to this death camp by choice.

Not unless you wanted to die or you were running away from something too hideous to remember."

Like me.

A death camp. No one left here alive.

What had he fled that a hard death in the mines was preferable to?

"Margit, would you summon my cousin the ambassador?" Queen Rossemikka looked up from sealing a long letter. "I wish to place this letter to my brother in the diplomatic pouch."

"Yes, Your Grace." Margit dipped a polite curtsy and fled the queen's study eagerly. Her lungs grew heavy and clogged every time she was alone with Rossemikka. If she didn't know better, she'd swear a dozen cats filled the room.

Margit hated cats. She hated them even when they provided a necessary check to rats and mice in barns. But at least she could breathe in a barn, cats or no cats. Maintaining her pose as a devoted servant to the queen was getting harder all the time.

Kevin-Rosse, the ambassador from Rossemeyer and Rossemikka's cousin, lived in a different part of the city from Palace Reveta Tristile. Margit breathed easier knowing she had a legitimate excuse to leave the crowded confines and stale air of the palace.

If only she were a real apprentice magician. Then she could live in the mountains with Jaylor and Brevelan and the other magicians. She could breathe clean air and sleep out-of-doors if she chose. Eventually she'd be given a quest and allowed to roam Coronnan freely like Marcus and Robb.

She hurried past the market square between Palace Isle and University Island. Three years ago, she'd sold sausage rolls and other savory pasties here, enjoying the opportunity to escape her mother's hot and stuffy shop every day. Then Yaakke, the strange magician boy, had sent Jaylor into her life. He'd tapped the power in her brain that she'd kept carefully hidden from the Gnuls and her mother. No one in her family had ever been tainted by magic. At least no one Margit knew about.

Jaylor had freed her from her mother's shop and opened many possibilities for the future. A position in the queen's household had seemed like a small temporary step upward. Temporary had dragged into a third year and approached a fourth.

She skimmed over three more bridges on her way to the ambassador's residence. The rushing waters between each of the city islands cleansed her of the weight of living in the palace. At the end of the next bridge, a line of heavily laden sledges blocked her way. She wove her way among them, speaking softly to the huge steeds harnessed in front of them. The placid steeds nuzzled her pockets for treats she didn't have.

"You'll have to settle for a scratch," she whispered to an animal in the middle of the caravan as she ran her blunted fingernails up and down the center of its head.

The steed snorted and stamped with pleasure. The sounds muffled the approach of a merchant and the steed's wrangler. Their whispered words stopped her in her tracks.

"Do you have the poison?" the Rover-dark merchant asked the blond wrangler.

"I have it hidden." The wrangler touched the scrip at his waist, right next to his long dagger.

"As soon as the ambassador gives me the diplomatic pouch, I'll pass it to you. You'll only have a few moments while I distract him. Then we'll have to strap the pouch onto the courier's chest where it will stay for the duration of the journey. The queen's letter to her brother will be on top. The last item added. Will you be able to do it?"

"Three drops on the queen's seal will kill King Rossemanuel within an instant of opening the letter. He always caresses the seal as if touching his beloved sister. The poison will be traced to Rossemikka. She will be executed for murder."

Margit suppressed a gasp. She couldn't let them discover her now. She had to find out who wanted to murder the queen's brother and depose Rossemikka before she bore an heir to Darville. The delicate political balance among the Three Kingdoms would be terribly upset. Who would inherit the thrones of Coronnan and Rossemeyer?

"Ordinary poisons might not be enough. If the boy has inherited any magic talent from his mother's family, he could detect and neutralize it," the merchant protested.

"The ingredients were prepared by King Simeon's mistress. Who knows what magic she added to the formula." The wrangler shrugged, unconcerned. "She distilled it right after the Solstice when the coven's rituals created some very powerful magic for her to tap."

"Good. Once the little king is out of the way, his younger brother will pose no problem. His health was compromised years ago by Janataea when she was governess to all three Rossemeyer brats. The coven has agents in place to name Simeon the rightful king of Rossemeyer. We'll have control of all three kingdoms before the year is out."

Margit slid behind the huge sledge steed. Who did she tell first? How could she keep the queen's letter out of the diplomatic pouch? Her first thoughts flew to Marcus, the journeyman magician who took her reports whenever he wandered into town.

No time for that. She had to summon Jaylor with a candle and a glass. No time. Ambassador Kevin-Rosse expected her. He could arrest these assassins. Unless he was part of the plot. He and Queen Rossemikka rarely agreed on anything, especially Rossemeyer's limited involvement in the war against SeLenicca.

Who could she trust?

Only herself.

A smile crept across her face. "I've never practiced the invisibility delusion on anyone but Mama. Maybe it's time to see how well it works on strangers," she said to the steed. The animal nodded its massive head as if in agreement. Probably only a beg for more scratches. Margit complied as she thought out her plan.

Three minutes later she replaced the tiny vial in the wrangler's scrip. He didn't react to her presence at all. Now the vial contained only plain river water.

She had leisure now to reveal the plot to Jaylor, and only Jaylor, on the next full moon when she summoned him.

"Look, there's the queen!" Iza tugged on Katrina's sleeve to watch the processional. The lacemakers and other factory workers had been given a day away from their work to celebrate the third birthday of Princess Jaranda.

"Queen Miranda does not look well," Katrina observed. Tight lines of fatigue and worry creased the hereditary monarch's eyes. Though barely two years senior to Katrina, the queen looked much older. Her body was too thin; her four plaits pulled so tight against her scalp her facial bones seemed devoid of flesh. The platinum crown set with priceless jewels was so heavy that Miranda's thin neck strained to support her head. Her white and silver ceremonial gown did nothing to enhance her complexion.

"She looks unhappy," Katrina murmured. The gradual hush that fell over the crowd echoed her sentiment. "So unhappy with her husband she's withdrawing the Edict of Joint Monarchy. Rumor claims she'll sue for peace with Coronnan when she deposes The Simeon."

Peace was an idea that met with mixed popularity. The unemployed and homeless, who flocked to the army, loved the war effort. Merchants, who imported arms and supplies, profited. The widows, orphans, and other victims of the war hated it. Katrina couldn't forget the war had caused the trade embargo with Coronnan that led to P'pa's bankruptcy.

She fingered the lace shawl she'd retrieved from her father's house during her first year of slavery. The gleaming white fibers added a festive touch to her plain skirt and vest on this day of celebration. It should have adorned the queen.

"Oh, the little princess, all dressed in purple and silver!" Iza continued her litany of praise. "Isn't she pretty, Katrina? I think she's the prettiest little girl in the whole world."

A purple canopy carried by four half-naked slaves rose above the princess' open litter. She was too young for even the most placid ponies. The little girl smiled and waved shyly at the crowds of people gathered along the wide Royal Avenue.

A sickly child, Katrina thought. Waxy skin, too pale to be fashionable, and too small for three years old. Her hair shone in the sunshine, red highlights obvious in her four thin plaits, too short to join into a single braid below her neck. Queen's City hadn't seen much of the princess. The queen, too, had remained mostly in seclusion these last three years. King Simeon was the only member of the once-beloved royal family much in evidence. And he wasn't loved by many. Certainly not by the families of his Solstice victims or those who had lost men in the endless war against Coronnan.

Three once-proud men, former military heroes who had secretly sought peace with Coronnan, followed a troop of elite military guards in the parade. Raw wounds marred their naked backs. One man's face had been beaten until his left eye was permanently closed. He dragged his left leg painfully. Soon they would join the criminals sacrificed to Simeon's god at the next solstice. Unless Queen Miranda removed her husband from power before then.

Why had the queen tolerated his cruel religion all these years? Or was she so isolated in the palace she didn't know? More likely, Simeon had bewitched her so she couldn't intervene and outlaw his sacrifices.

Rumors from the palace suggested the bewitchment was waning, though.

Katrina had trouble maintaining interest in the parade of dancing steeds with ribbons plaited in their manes and haughty noblewomen flaunting three plaits and fortunes' worth of Tambrin lace on their gowns.

Katrina searched the faces of the slaves for Fraanken Kaantille. P'pa wasn't carrying the canopy. The little flame of hope died within her heart. Royal servants were born into slavery and knew their lot in life. They were treated well and trusted. Criminals, prisoners of war, and traitors, like her father, were sent to die in the king's galley ships or in the mines.

"I could buy your freedom from Neeles Brunix if you gave me that shawl," a man said quietly into Katrina's ear.

She looked around startled by his unsuspected presence. The man wore a hooded cloak that shadowed his face. The voice was familiar. Where had she heard him speak before?

"What?" Hope kindled a tiny light in her mind. *Freedom!* "Why?" She damped any possibility he could truly offer her freedom.

"That shawl is valuable. More valuable than your slave price." His voice barely reached her ears.

"Does this offer include employment once I am free of Brunix?" Once he released her, the factory owner wouldn't allow her to continue working for him. Not unless she shared his bed. What use freedom at the cost of the shawl, the only tangible link to her mother she still had?

"I have not the resources to help you beyond the purchase of your slave papers." The man bowed his head, increasing the shadows around him.

"I have no use for freedom without a promise of employment." Katrina dismissed the offer reluctantly.

"I may not be able to meet the price again. Think long and hard. I will try to speak to you again. Later." The man faded into the crowd, as if he'd never been there at all.

Iza continued to prattle, unaware of the exchange. "Look. Look, there behind the Lord Chancellor rides the king. So far back from the queen and princess. Do you suppose the rumors are true, that Miranda will divorce him and outlaw his hideous religion?"

Katrina returned her attention to the parade, deliberately pushing aside all thoughts of the strange encounter with the cloaked man. She sought the figure of the outland king who had bewitched young Miranda and mercilessly ruled SeLenicca ever since. What had happened to weaken the adoration that used to shine from the queen's eyes? Katrina didn't care as long as the man she hated was brought low and stripped of power.

"The outland woman riding beside Simeon, who is she?" Katrina asked. The tall beauty with black hair and blue eyes rode a sleek black steed draped in silver-and-black ribbons. Her black gown trimmed in silver lace dipped immodestly low into her bosom. Undoubtedly, steed and gown had been chosen to set her apart from the sea of blond citizens riding equally light-colored steeds.

"Her?" Iza spat. "His latest mistress. He calls her 'niece.' But everyone knows he has no siblings. Gossip in the city says he flaunted her at the palace once too often. Miranda threw him out. That's why she's going to rescind the Edict of Joint Monarchy."

"Simeon's niece looks pregnant." Katrina scanned the elegant curves of the tall woman. A noticeable bulge filled her black gown.

"She does, doesn't she? And Miranda isn't. The nobles call us workers immoral. They should look to themselves before they condemn us," Iza sniffed.

"Simeon can't be trusted. Someone should warn Miranda." Katrina eyed the man she hated. "He'll kill her before he relinquishes power."

"Don't be silly. Guards and councillors and lacemakers surround the queen day and night."

"Guards won't stop a sorcerer."

As if he heard her sneer, Simeon turned his burning gaze directly to Katrina. His eyes widened as he stared at her. Then his lips curled up in a mocking, self-satisfied grin. Insolently he blew her a kiss.

Katrina stepped back, shocked and revolted. Her hand reached to her throat in surprise. She gathered the lace shawl protectively around her. The king's gaze followed her hands. His eyes narrowed and seethed with emotion.

Why do you wait so long to come to me and meet your destiny, Katrina Kaantille?

The words echoed around her head. She hadn't really heard them. Her imagination had interpreted the flirtatious gesture and fed upon her fears.

"He saluted you!" Iza gasped. "You didn't tell me you knew the king."

"I don't." Katrina turned her face toward the head of the procession so she wouldn't have to look at King Simeon. "He's a notorious flirt."

Queen Miranda twisted her body to speak to the princess. Her steed chose that moment to shy away from the noisy crowd. A flash of blue light stabbed the skittish animal's hindquarters. The frightened mare reared high, screaming in pain. Miranda fought for control of the reins.

Another flash of blue light pierced the frightened steed in the chest. The animal reared again and circled, trying to bolt away from the magical dart. Miranda lost the reins and control of the headstrong beast. She bounced out of her saddle. She lay unmoving on the cobblestones, blood staining her four white-gold plaits.

Chapter Sixteen

P eople screamed. Steeds reared and circled in confused panic. Princess Jaranda cried out. Noble ladies swooned. Guards rushed forward to form a protective ring around the queen. King Simeon pushed the converging crowd aside.

Hastily he knelt and cradled his wife in his arms, the picture of a devoted husband. Katrina watched him closely, not trusting the concern written on his face. He tested Miranda's pulse, then lifted his head, eyes searching the crowd. Briefly he exchanged a look with the black-gowned woman. She nodded slightly, knowingly.

Then Simeon looked up, directly at Katrina, as if he always knew where to find her in the crowd. His gaze locked with hers. A malicious smile played across his face.

Unbidden, his thoughts invaded her mind. *You won't get away from me this time, little lacemaker.*

Katrina shook her head and pulled the hood of her open cloak over her face to break mental contact with the sorcerer-king. Her mother's lace shawl seemed to squeeze the breath out of her as she hid from his gaze.

Queen Miranda moaned and stirred. Tension returned to her

muscles. Her mouth opened on a silent scream. A look of panic crossed Simeon's face. He pressed his fingers to her neck once more as if testing her pulse. The queen slumped back into unconsciousness at his touch.

"Seize that woman! The one with the lace shawl," Simeon cried, pointing at Katrina. He held Miranda's face close against his chest, smothering any sound she might make. "She shot an arrow into the queen's steed. Seize the one in the black cloak and lace shawl!"

All eyes turned in the direction he indicated—to stare directly at Katrina. She shrank back behind Iza.

"I didn't," she whispered anxiously.

"Quick, leave your cloak. Take mine. Blend in with the crowd. Don't run," Iza directed as she slipped her ordinary brown cloak over Katrina's shoulders, obscuring the distinctive lace.

"I didn't do it," Katrina protested, too stunned to follow her friend's advice.

"I know that. Only a magician could throw an arrow made of blue light. Now drift away. Don't call attention to yourself." Iza shoved Katrina back into the depths of the crowd, then turned to face the grim guards converging on her. Katrina's thick, black cloak of oiled wool now draped Iza's shoulders, standing out from the cheap and ordinary coverings protecting working-class citizens. The same cloak Katrina had brought with her from her father's house three years before.

More aggressive onlookers elbowed Katrina aside. Shame and guilt warred with her need to put a safe distance between herself and the palace guards. What would they do to Iza, her only friend? She couldn't watch.

She had to watch. With renewed determination, Katrina pushed her way back toward Iza. The crowd resisted her efforts.

"Lose yourself quickly," an unknown woman whispered as she stepped in front of Katrina. "We can't hide you much longer."

"But Iza . . ." Katrina protested.

"Save yourself." The man who had spoken to her earlier picked her up by the waist and set her back down, facing in the other direction. He shoved her hard. "Lose yourself in the alleys; don't go directly back to the factory. I've searched for you and that shawl for a long time. I'll meet you by the side door of the temple," he hissed.

Katrina stumbled. Hands helped her up and eased her away from the center of the action.

The guards carried Iza away amidst bitter protests from the bystanders. Mud and rocks pelted the guards. More gray-uniformed men entered the fray, clearing a path for their prisoner.

Katrina was pushed farther and farther away from the core of the riot. Tears streaming down her face, she allowed her anxious feet to speed her toward safety.

She ran and ran until her sides ached and her lungs threatened to burst. The temple loomed in front of her. The man with the shadowed face offered her safety, freedom. Where had she met him before?

I've searched for you and that shawl for a long time. His words burned into her memory.

Who was he? A friend of her father's perhaps. More likely an agent of King Simeon, sent to trick her.

The familiarity of Brunix and his factory beckoned her. Her life there was hard. But it was safe. She turned and ran again.

At last the familiar blocky outline of the Brunix factory loomed ahead of her. Grateful for the sanctuary offered by its dark corridors and damp rooms, she pelted headlong for the green-painted doorway.

Abruptly her flight stopped as she ran into the tall, lean body of Owner Neeles Brunix. He grabbed her shoulders and forced her to look up at him. Up and up she looked to his hollow cheeks and sallow skin. His dark, outland eyes captured hers in an angry gaze.

"The king's men will be here soon to search for you," he announced matter-of-factly as he escorted her inside to his ground floor office.

"I did nothing but watch!" she sobbed, trying to catch her breath.

"I'm innocent." She leaned over the back of a single straight-backed chair to ease her heaving lungs.

"No matter. Simeon has decided to have you back. This time you will choose to participate in his ritual rather than suffer death by torture. He has violated his pact with me."

Katrina took a long series of deep breaths fighting the panic Brunix's words evoked. Finally her vision cleared and her pulse ceased pounding behind her eyes.

Then she saw an expensive, velvet lace pillow resting on a stand beside her chair. Dangling from one of her grandmother's patterns were a hundred or more slender, bone bobbins with bright bangles on the ends.

She peered closer, still bent over the chair. Her eyes focused on the bobbins while she gathered her thoughts and courage. She picked out a bobbin with a spiraled inscription and a familiar blue bead at the center of the bangle. "K-A- . . ." the next letters wound away from her. ". . . I-N . . ." And above those letters "A-A . . ." was visible. She didn't need to twist the slender spindle to know that this bobbin along with the pattern was part of her dowry, sold to buy food and medicine for Hilza.

Food and medicine purchased too late to save her little sister.

Anger at King Simeon, who had brought her family low and still pursued her, replaced her fear. Hot hatred filled her veins and eased the pain in her lungs.

"Why does the sorcerer-king persecute you, Katrina Kaantille? I know he wants your body as much as I do, but there must be more. He has access to many women. What makes you so special?" Brunix took the cloak from her shoulders and hung it on a tall rack alongside his own.

"I don't know. He picked me out of the crowd as if he were looking for me." She closed her eyes against the sight of her own bobbins gracing this man's pillow.

"Perhaps he is anxious to retrieve something he considers his own. What passed between you the night you chose slavery to me, an outland half-breed, rather than joining his ritual?" His voice sounded devoid of emotion, as if he calculated possibilities and advantages with the same scrutiny he weighed imported goods taken in trade for exported lace.

Katrina kept her eyes closed to help control the painful memory of that night still brought her. "I have done him no hurt, yet he pursues me and threatens me for a crime I have not committed. He shot the bolt of blue light into the queen's steed, not I. How could I? He's the only magician in SeLenicca!"

"Perhaps he hunts you because you did refuse him. How many women in SeLenicca would sacrifice much to become the king's mistress?"

"Or be sacrificed to him?" she added.

Criminals and outlanders were routinely burned at the stake as part of the king's rituals. So far he had not publicly sacrificed one of the queen's citizens.

"I heard he likes his toys young and virginal, dismissed as soon as they become boring." Brunix paced a circle around her and the lace pillow. "Marriages are discreetly arranged for the girls he ravishes. Those girls he rapes without guilt. But you . . . you he demands must come willingly to him. My contract with him forbids me to force you. As if he didn't know that rape is a most heinous crime among my mother's people. But I am supposed to . . . never mind. He has broken that contract." He fingered the lace still draped around her shoulders. Gently he removed it and hung it beneath the cloaks.

"He told me that if I survived his Equinox ritual, my power would be released and I would be worthy to bear him a son. But I must come to his altar willingly. He hoped the humiliation of being *your* slave would drive me back to him. Willingly."

"The black-gowned goddess!" he hissed. "She carries a child, conceived near the Autumnal Equinox. And she wears the aura of one with much power. Was she willing? Eager perhaps?"

Crashing footsteps on the wooden walkway, loud shouts, and

angry questions brought Katrina upright. Her balance shifted to her toes, as she made ready to flee again.

"I can save you," Brunix stood between her and the door, the only exit from the room. Another man had offered her the same thing. He'd asked for her mother's shawl in repayment.

"What will it cost me?" She sought frantically for a window, another door, a place to hide.

"You know my price. Come to my bed *of your own free will.*"

The door buckled on its hinges from the fierce pounding on the painted planks.

Katrina bit her lip. There was no way out.

She nodded, too frightened to speak.

Brunix reached behind him to unlatch the door. Six broad-shouldered men wearing the gray uniforms of the palace guard filled the narrow hallway.

"In the name of His Majesty, King Simeon the First, I place you, Katrina Kaantille, under arrest," the leader, wearing three silver stripes on his cuff, informed them. He stepped into the office so his companions could flank him.

"What crime has my wife committed?" Brunix remained firmly in place between Katrina and the uniformed men.

"Wife?" Three-stripe raised an eyebrow in surprise. "I was told the girl is a maiden."

"My *wife* has been with me all morning, developing a new pattern." Brunix waved a hand at the bolster pillow. "What makes you think she is the person you seek?"

"The queen was struck down during the birthday parade. His Majesty picked that woman out of the crowd as the perpetrator. She was wearing a black cloak and a wide lace shawl about her neck and shoulders. We arrested another woman wearing her cloak, but not the lace shawl. She is being detained until we find the true culprit and the lace." The officer's eyes strayed to the hook where the cloaks hung. Brunix's outdoor garment was dark green. Katrina had been wearing Iza's brown. The shawl was draped beneath them both, not visible to the guard.

"How can my wife be guilty? She has been here with me all morning. And though we make lace to sell, who but the nobility can afford to wear it?"

"Your lies won't protect her, outland half-breed," Three-stripe sneered. He raised his arm as if to backhand Brunix across the mouth.

Brunix caught the man's wrist well away from his face. He squeezed and twisted the guard's arm backward. "My father was a true-blooded citizen, my mother half," he ground out. Brunix's eyes grew darker with cold anger. "How much true blood runs in Simeon's veins? He is the outlander, and a sorcerer. Yet you trust him over me, a lawful citizen of the *queen*. How did he single out the name and address of one woman in the crowd, who was not there, as the assailant? Look to him for answers before you arrest and accuse innocent citizens."

He wrenched his hands away from contact with the guard as if the man were dirty. The guard hopped back a step, shaking his arm and wrist.

Three-stripe's mouth opened and closed without a sound. Indecision marred his posture. He suddenly seemed shorter and less imposing. The two men flanking him edged backward, toward the hall.

"We will be back." Three-stripe turned on his heel and retreated with less noise than he had come.

"And now, my dear, the time has come to pay what you owe me." Brunix gathered the cloaks and the lace shawl from the rack as he gestured toward the staircase. Up the long series of steps to his apartment on the top floor.

"Hmm, distinctive design." He studied the shawl as if unconcerned with her obedience to his wishes. "Unusual concept. We will discuss payment for this design after I teach you the delights of sharing my bed."

"You are certain you can do it?" Jaylor asked Marcus for the fifth time. "Sensing a concentration of dragon magic is crucial in this quest."

"I'm certain, sir," Marcus replied tiredly. "I was gathering dragon magic before Old Baamin died."

Jaylor turned to his other journeyman. "What about you, Robb?"

"Master Jaylor, I was levitating winecups long before any of my class." The young man looked indignant at the question. "Successfully."

"Then I charge you both with the quest to go see an invisible dragon," Jaylor said quietly. Unconsciously he'd used the same phrase Master Baamin had spoken when giving Jaylor his journeyman's quest four years ago.

But Jaylor was Senior Magician now. So much had changed in the intervening years. Coronnan needed journeymen magicians to seek Shayla and bring the dragon nimbus up to full strength more than ever. Without dragons, Communal magicians could not combine and augment their magic by orders of magnitude to overcome the solitary rogues. Only with the enhanced power of several magicians joined together could the Commune hope to impose and enforce honor, ethics, and justice into all uses of magic.

Until then, judges, lords, and mundane citizens looked to the Gnostic Utilitarians to protect them from all magic, good and bad. Good thing the Gnuls and the coven hadn't worked together on their separate plots to depose Darville and his queen.

"I hope you are more successful in restoring the dragon nimbus to Coronnan than I was." Jaylor draped his arms about the shoulders of his journeymen.

"You freed Shayla from Krej's glass sculpture. That was a start," Marcus reminded him.

Jaylor paused a moment, remembering his lengthy recovery from that spell.

"You had better return as full masters of your powers, or I'll come find you to make you regret it," he added sternly, shaking them with affection.

"As if Brevelan would let you chase after us without her," Marcus mumbled.

"We know who really runs the Commune." Robb grinned at his partner.

"What did you say?" Jaylor glared at the young men.

"Nothing, sir. We'll come back. With the dragon." Marcus winked at Robb.

"Or if she can't fly, we'll summon Brevelan."

"Good. Now remember your instructions. Stay in touch. I want a summons every night at sunset." He'd said this all before, but it deserved repeating. "Keep together and blend in with the locals any way you can. You'll have to be doubly careful avoiding detection at the battlefront. SeLenicca is gearing up for a major push to drive our army back toward the pass. There is no magic in SeLenicca to augment your own reserves, so you'll have to keep your delusions to a minimum. And whatever you do, don't rouse King Simeon's suspicion. The battle mages report small concentrations of dragon magic across the border, but not enough for all to gather and combine. That convinces me that Simeon is holding Shayla hostage. He won't want to give her up. You will be executed as spies at the first suggestion that you come from Coronnan."

"We know, Jaylor." Robb patted the Senior Magician's shoulder reassuringly. "We've been over this a dozen times."

"Keep going over it. I can't afford to lose any more journeyman. Keep a look out for Lady Rejiia, too. She's been missing since her child died."

"But Queen Rossemikka is pregnant again. We don't need Rejiia as heir to the crown," Robb grumbled.

Jaylor bit back the bitterness of that news. Margit reported that

Mikka ailed with this pregnancy. A few whispers had begun that the queen's inability to carry a child to term was clear evidence of witchcraft.

Between the whispers and the difficult pregnancy, Jaylor had decided to keep word of the plot against the queen's brother to himself. Mikka and Darville didn't need the extra worry. The plot had been temporarily foiled. King Simeon's mistress, whoever she was, would need time to replace the poison.

"Better off without Krej's daughter. I never trusted her," Marcus added.

"More reason to bring the dragons back, to protect the queen's baby—the long-awaited heir. Take care of yourselves." Jaylor saluted them with a fist clenched over his heart, then offered his left hand, little finger, and ring finger curled under. A mild shock of power that only another magician could feel went into the handshake—the new recognition signal of the Commune.

He watched the young men gather their packs and march toward the edge of the clearing.

"Will you keep an eye on Margit, sir? She's feeling kind of abandoned with both of us going off on quest." Marcus paused at the edge of the clearing barrier. "Maybe you can teach her to tolerate cats better. I really like cats."

"I'll make contact with her every week instead of every moon," Jaylor promised.

Marcus nodded and smiled his thanks as the edges of the clearing blurred and the journeymen passed through to the path.

Jaylor raised his hand, as if to delay their departure once more. Surely they'd forgotten something. He should call them back, delay their leave-taking a little longer.

"They are older than you were when you were given the same quest. And better equipped." Brevelan placed a gentle hand on his shoulder. "Those boys have scoured Coronnan for apprentices these last three years. They know how to live rough and fend for themselves," she reminded him.

"I guess I can spare the boys for a while. They must succeed where I failed. Coronnan depends upon them."

"Thanks to those 'boys,' you have ten new journeymen to take their place and fifteen apprentices eager to join them." Brevelan urged him away from the sight of the path closing behind the retreating steps of Robb and Marcus.

"We still don't have enough magicians to resume our traditional roles in society, if and when we are ever legal again. I wonder if I should leave the University in Slippy's care while I go with the boys?"

"Don't you dare!" Brevelan's hands fluttered trying to reach for him and curve protectively around her swelling belly at the same time. If the mundanes could see Brevelan and her children, they'd never again believe that witches couldn't bear children. That was an action he dared not allow.

Jaylor smiled anyway. Brevelan's dragon-dream was coming true. Shayla had promised her a clearing full of healthy children. In the vision, the oldest boy was as blond as King Darville, all the rest as red-haired as their mother.

Jaylor's eyes automatically searched the clearing for blond Glendon, now three, and his redheaded brother, Lukan. The boys were rolling around the freshly tilled kitchen garden, wrestling with a wolf pup. As usual they were filthy, healthy, and laughing.

"We have been blessed, Brevelan." He patted the evidence of their new child. A tingle of awareness shot up his arm. The child was already asserting its personality.

"Twins this time." Brevelan sighed happily. "Girls."

"What! I thought this was to be another boy. Next time is supposed to be twins. Dragon-dreams don't lie."

"We make our own future, dear heart. This time we made twins," she laughed at him and with him. "Gossip from the capital says that Darville is much better since he learned to sign his name and wield cutlery with his right hand. He's learning to live with the pain. His wound isn't worse," she continued happily.

"If the boys don't find Shayla and heal her, then Darville will always have a useless left arm," Jaylor reminded her. Memory of Darville's situation sobered the bubbling joy of impending fatherhood.

He and Darville had wrestled in the mud as boys, much like Glendon and Lukan. They'd been happy and healthy then, blond- and auburn-haired, just like Glendon and Lukan.

Yaakke had spent his childhood as a kitchen drudge, without much happiness, love, or companionship. Jaylor wasn't sure why his thoughts turned to his lost apprentice. Sending two journeymen off on the same quest as Yaakke must have reminded him of the boy's failure.

Had the wild fluxes of a maturing body caught up with his unbounded magical talent? If so, perhaps he was better off dead. The massive, uncontrolled powers unleashed in such circumstances must have been lethal to Yaakke's spirit as well as his body.

"I am reluctant to authorize a full-scale invasion of SeLenicca, Andrall," Darville informed his most trusted Council member. He paced the small retiring room behind the Council Chamber.

" 'Tis sound military strategy, Your Grace," Andrall reminded him. "We control both ends of the pass through the mountains. Our position will be reinforced if we hold more territory on their side of the border."

"The battle mages we employ at the front fear there is not enough magic in SeLenicca for them to protect our troops from Simeon's mages. I would give a fortune to know where they get their power! Besides, invasion will put us on the offensive. If we keep to defensive resistance, we have leverage in convincing other countries to honor the trade embargo against SeLenicca."

"The Council of Provinces intends to push for an invasion, and override your veto if necessary, Your Grace," Andrall whispered, though no one had access to this room except through the empty Council Chamber.

"I need something to bargain with. Something that will . . ." Darville stopped in mid-sentence. A shift in the tapestry that separated them from the main room alerted him to the presence of an eavesdropper. Both men stood absolutely still, hands holding ceremonial short swords at the ready.

"Ahem, Your Grace?" Fred called from the main room.

Darville relaxed and thrust aside the wall hanging. "Yes, Sergeant?"

"I have someone important for you to interview, sir." Fred clamped his mouth shut and stared pointedly at Lord Andrall.

"You can trust His Lordship, Fred. Who claims my attention now?"

"The spy, sir."

"Which spy?" There were so many, in SeLenicca, in Rossemeyer, in the households of his lords, at the front . . . He dared not trust anyone these days. Not with the Gnuls gaining influence with the Council and the Council paying people to spy on himself and Mikka.

"The one we sent from Sambol last year, sir. The one who knows about cats . . . dead cats."

A frisson of alarm ran from Darville's spine to his hands, making him itch to wield his sword. If ever he needed Jaylor's counsel, it was now. How did he deal with people who left gutted cats in places where he was likely to find them? The one he and Fred had found at the Equinox Pylon in Sambol was the first of many.

Every time he rode through the country, they found another. The placement of the corpses was no coincidence.

"Bring the man to my office. I'll fetch the queen. If I can pry her away from that nosy maid, Margit." Mikka was his best adviser since Jaylor had deserted him. Raised to be a queen, Mikka knew how to listen and observe. From a quiet place in the corner she often saw things that Darville missed, like gestures and postures suggesting lies and deceit. "We will discuss the military situation later, just before the lords regather, Andrall," he said as he dismissed the lord.

"They will be here momentarily, Your Grace," Andrall reminded him. They'd met here, behind the Council Chamber for that reason.

"Then tell them I am detained. I need an hour."

"Yes, Your Grace." Andrall bowed his head in grudging acquiescence.

Three years ago the Council might have taken advantage of Darville's absence to vote for invasion. Now, however, he knew they'd wait for their king.

Minutes later, Fred hustled a slim young man wearing the white robes adopted by the Gnostic Utilitarian cult into the king's office. Cut in the same manner as the red-robed priests of the Stargods, the white was symbolic of their purity from the taint of magic.

Mikka's eyes narrowed at first sight of the man. Her nose twitched with suspicion and she withdrew deeper into her window seat. If anyone had reason to fear this cult, 'twas the queen. Magic was still illegal in Coronnan and she possessed a great deal of magical talent. The cult had been known to denounce those who claimed to be the victims of magic as well the perpetrators. Knowledge of the cat persona trapped within Mikka's body would draw their outrage and fuel the pleas for Darville to put her aside as his queen.

So far he'd been able to avoid confronting the issue of her inability to bear him an heir. How much longer before he was forced by lords and populace alike to bring in a distant and foreign relative or divorce Mikka?

"Your Grace," the spy bowed deeply, but his eyes darted furtively into every corner as he moved. "I have not much time. I must either return to my dwelling before I am discovered missing or leave the country within the hour." He continued to search the shadows for any sign of listeners. His eyes lingered on the queen in the window seat, then darted back to Fred for reassurance.

"I will protect you . . . uh, your name was not given to me. Please sit down." Darville leaned back in his demi-throne, adopting a position of ease. He hoped the spy would become comfortable enough to speak freely.

"My name is best kept secret from all but the Stargods. No one is safe from the Gnuls, sir. No one. They'll torture and kill me without hesitation if they suspect where my allegiance lies." His pale skin lost more color as he shivered inside his robe. He remained standing, poised to dart out of the room at the first sign of trouble.

"Then tell us quickly. What have you learned?" Darville sat forward, frowning. None of his appointed magistrates had the authority to overlook such outrages.

"Life has been quiet and prosperous for nearly three full years. People don't really fear magic when life is good, and the Gnuls have lost a lot of followers. The sacrifices at the Equinox Pylons have been engineered by the Gnuls to frighten the people. Cats and dogs at first. Pigs and goats will come later if they have to. They discuss bringing suspected witches and magicians to justice at the next holiday." He stared at the queen a silent moment. "But I've never found evidence of an innocent or a child becoming a victim. The evidence of human sacrifice always comes from someone in the next village who heard it from a cousin's sister-in-law, or some such." The last words faded away and he refused to look up from the floor.

"There is more," Mikka whispered. They all heard her quiet words. "What do you fear telling us, Spy?" Her hands trembled as they stroked the nap of her gown.

The spy looked to the door again as if he needed to escape immediately.

"Tell me, Spy," Darville demanded. "What else have you learned?"

"Rumors only."

"Rumors! I hate rumors. Tell me so that I may squash them before they are lifted into the wind and become the truth for all who hear them."

"The queen, sir," he said so quietly Darville had to strain to hear him.

"What about my wife?"

"I have met with the leaders of one cell of Gnuls. They have orders to prove that she is a witch of the first order. Everyone knows that witches can't bear children." He swallowed deeply. "And . . . and they say she has bewitched you so you won't put her aside, just as King Simeon has bewitched the Queen of SeLenicca. Some say that Her Grace is in league with Simeon and that is why you won't invade SeLenicca and end the war. The leaders plan to drug the queen so that she will miscarry. Then they will present the deformed fetus as 'evidence' to the Council of Provinces in time for her to be exiled or burned at the next solstice."

Chapter Seventeen

Fear for Mikka drained the blood from Darville's head and limbs. Shakily, he dismissed the spy with a handful of gold to buy passage out of Coronnan that very day.

"I must return to my brother's court," Mikka whispered. "For your sake, I must go." She rose gracefully from her window seat and the bright sunshine she loved. "If you wait to divorce me until I get there, I can persuade Manuel the fault is mine and he needn't invade Coronnan to avenge my honor."

"No." Feeling and heat began to return to Darville's body. "If you scuttle away now, like some beetle frightened of the light, then you have given the Gnuls control over our lives, over all of Coronnan. I cannot allow that to happen. I will not let them take you from me." He knelt in front of her window seat, clutching her hand between both of his.

"What else can we do?" She pulled free of his touch and buried her face in her hands.

Darville gathered her into his arms, holding her close against his heart, where she belonged.

"First, I will order your maids to taste all of your food before you do. Everything, even a cup of water. Then, I will set forces in motion to hunt down members of the cult who commit outrages against my citizens. No more will I bury myself so deeply in military tactics and trade agreements that I lose sight of what is happening in my own country. The Gnuls will be brought to justice."

"But their followers are many. They will not tolerate a banning of the cult. Executing the leaders will make them martyrs." Mikka raised her head, once more a dignified queen advising her husband.

"They will be brought to justice, not banned or outlawed. If they commit the crimes of kidnap, torture, and murder, then they will pay for their crimes, like any other citizen."

"That will not stop the rumors. I am still suspected of witchcraft."

"We will do what we must to put the rumors aside. Though I know in my head and my gut that the action is a tactical error, I will authorize an invasion of SeLenicca."

Military men must wear blinders. They can see forward only in a straight line. Darville has foolishly invaded SeLenicca. At first his troops penetrated deep into the interior along the trader's road.

But that movement outraged all of Simeon's citizens, even the ones who hate and fear him. They rally to defend their land. War fever grips them. The homeless and unemployed flock to join the army. Merchants double the price of lace overseas to buy more weapons and supplies. Outlanders react to the inflated value of lace by ordering even more and demanding greater variety.

Now Darville is in danger of losing control of the pass between the two countries. His Council will not tolerate defeat. They bring Jonnias and the Marnaks back into their ranks in defiance of Darville, though the rebel lords have not paid their fines or made public apology for burning the monastery all those years ago. The younger Marnak wears a ring with a black diamond. His wedding ring, presented by Lord Krej himself. Marnak does not know that the diamond is really precious glass. With a candle and my own glass, I can see and hear through the ring all of the Council's private discussions. I should have forced him to pay the fines earlier so I could spy on the Council.

Soon young Rossemanuel of Rossemeyer will receive the poisonous letter from his sister. His death, traced back to Rossemikka, will start a new war against Darville and Coronnan.

Jack awakened gradually from his dream of a woman with pale blond hair, like moonlight on water. He'd dreamed of her often in the last three years, wondering who she was and why she haunted him.

He'd been reaching out to pull her away from something dangerous. But he couldn't quite touch her.

The sounds of men grunting and scratching, shifting in their hammocks and whispering quietly banished the last images of his vision. Several men coughed, long spasms that threatened to turn their lungs inside out. They were dying and they knew it.

They were all dying unless they escaped. The sense of having left something undone nagged at Jack and urged him to push forward his plans to escape—even before he had regained full memory and before the mountain passes cleared of snow.

He wondered if the tiny spell he had tried last night had succeeded and what good it would do if it had.

The gray light of false dawn seeped beneath the closed plank door. Knotted muscles in his shoulders protested every movement he made. Not that he could move very far or very fast with his right ankle chained to the post.

"Uhrrgh!" he moaned and rolled over. Another day of opening a new mine shaft. In a few minutes the guard with a harelip would slam the door open and glare at the thirty men. His small, deep-set eyes, would seek out the last one to remain in his hammock. That laggard would likely feel the tip of the lash all day long for the tiniest infraction of the rules. Harelip enjoyed seeing other men in pain.

Jack fingered the scars beneath his ragged shirt. All of them had been inflicted by Harelip. They didn't hurt anymore. The new one forming on his cheek still stung. Memory of the pain kept him wary and obedient.

"You awake, Jack?" Fraank whispered from the hammock above him.

"No," he replied.

"The birds aren't up yet. You have a few minutes to rest. Though I've never known you to be a slug-a-bed before."

"I've not been able to think about options before—or the lack of them."

"One way or another, we all chose to come here," Fraank replied.

"You're an educated man, surely you didn't choose this hell hole."

"I came here to die a slow death. My punishment won't bring back my wife and child, nor will it restore my family to wealth and honor. But perhaps Tattia's ghost will rest easier knowing I suffer for my sins."

"What sins?"

"A foolish investment. Greed and ambition above my station in life."

"All men make mistakes. Surely an unwise investment isn't a sin."

"King Simeon asked me to form an investment syndicate. He had plans to smuggle a shipload of Tambootie seedlings out of Coronnan. The fibers of immature trees can be spun into the most wonderful thread for lace. My wife was a lacemaker. The best in the kingdom. I wanted to please her with an unlimited supply of Tambrin."

"So?" Jack shivered. An almost memory tasted bad in his mouth. He knew something about this shipload of Tambootie. What?

"I borrowed heavily, sold almost everything I owned so I could finance the venture myself. I wanted to reap all of the profits. King Simeon would have taken half of the money as his portion for arranging the shipment. I didn't want to share the rest. I wanted to buy prestige for my wife. She deserved to be named a National Treasure."

"The ship didn't make it through the blockade," Jack stated. He could have guessed the fate of the ill-advised venture. But he knew. Knew in his gut that he had something to do with Fraank's fall from grace.

Fate or the dragons had brought him face-to-face with the consequences of his actions.

"And I lost everything. My brother disowned me and stole one of my daughters. Another daughter died of the lung rot. She died in my arms, too weak to cough, too worn out to breathe. I couldn't afford to keep the house warm enough to protect her. None of us had enough to eat to stay healthy. I couldn't . . ." he choked on his litany of grief.

Jack gave him a moment of silence to recover, sensing the man's need to tell someone of his internal pain.

"Tattia was dismissed from the palace. She was lost. If she couldn't make lace, she had no place in life, no identity, no reason for living. Because of my failure, she threw herself into the river. And now her ghost will haunt our descendants for five generations."

"You had another child to carry the bloodline?"

A burst of birdsong silenced the whispers of the men. Above the sweet trills that greeted the dawn, came the hoarse croak of a jackdaw.

The door was thrust open so violently it bounced against the stone wall. "All right you miserable beasts. Up. Everybody up." Harelip stood outlined in the doorway, begging someone to challenge him so he could mete out punishment with is whip.

Why don't we just jump him? Jack thought. Thirty men could strangle him before he raised the bloody whip.

"Not ready," the jackdaw cawed. "Ye're not ready."

Jack slid his gaze toward the door. The stupid bird hadn't really talked to him, had it?

Still affecting a daze of incomprehension, Jack stood mutely beside his hammock while a second guard unlocked his chain from the post. Fraank stood beside him, patiently waiting to be partnered with him.

"You two been gettin' chummy, I hear. Can't have that." The guard with grime embedded around his neck like a necklace yanked on Jack's chain to lead him several paces down the line to a new partner.

They chained him to the scrawny newcomer with the patchy beard. Jack almost opened his mouth to protest. A warning glance from Fraank kept him quiet and docile. Harelip was watching for an opportunity to uncoil his whip.

Patchy-beard wrung his hands in anxiety, then scratched his face in a habitual manner. A few strands of mud-colored hair fell to the floor.

Out in the yard, the day crew marched through their regular routine. A trip to the privy—an open trench in one corner of the fenced compound. Then a bowl of thin gruel slurped from wooden bowls without benefit of a spoon. The food was enough to keep the men alive and working, but not energetic enough to plot or risk escape.

The jackdaw fluttered to the top of a fence post and watched the pot of gruel for an opportunity to steal some. The white tufts of feathers above its eyes twitched.

"Look. Look," the jackdaw mimicked words.

A guard laughed at the bird and held out his arm for it to perch on. The jackdaw ignored him and continued to instruct Jack to "Look, look."

Certainty that the bird was speaking to him alone, drew Jack's gaze to the high wooden fence. Eight feet high at least. Smooth planks that would defy a man to climb. What was he supposed to look at?

"Through my eyes. Through my eyes." The jackdaw cocked his head and looked directly at Jack.

A wave of revulsion almost brought the gruel back up from Jack's stomach. Invading another creature's mind had to be the worst form of violation.

The jackdaw shook himself. Dust flew from his wings.

"Filthy bird!" Someone picked up a loose stone and flung it at him.

"Craaawk!" it squawked and jumped into flight. Two flaps of his wings and he perched on top of Jack's head. "Look," it repeated.

Jack remained absolutely still, as if he didn't know a black bird was tugging at his hair with a sharp beak.

"Always knew that Muaynwor was a scarecrow," Harelip guffawed, flapping his arms like grotesque wings. Jack looked right through his antics as if they didn't exist. He hoped the men wouldn't start throwing stones at him as well as the bird.

Without knowing how or why, his thoughts blended with the bird. The color spectrum shifted and he saw colors he'd never seen before. Colors that revealed temperatures. Men became layers of overlapping reds and yellows. Buildings revealed neutral grays.

His perspective shifted upward and then flew with the bird over the fence. He knew a moment of dizziness and spinning colors. Then the terrain below came into focus.

Trackless mountains still covered in snow, that revealed iciness in shades of blue, spread out to the horizon in every direction. Snow blocked the valleys between peaks and ridges. A few scraggly everblue trees appeared pink and yellow as sap began to flow and bring them out of winter dormancy.

Together, he and the jackdaw skimmed over black rivers and pale blue lakes still choked with darker blue ice. Ice that cracked and thinned as the rising red and orange sun touched it.

"Not yet. Not yet," the jackdaw reminded him. They soared upward, along another pass where the melted snow had filled the nearby river to overflowing. At the western end of the pass, a trader caravan camped. Their train of surefooted mules was loaded with supplies for the prison mine.

Escape needed to wait until Jack could load one of those mules with enough supplies to last him several weeks. By the time the caravan arrived, the worst of the storms would have passed. He'd be able to walk away from the mine and survive.

Jack's consciousness plunged back into his own body with an abruptness that sent his senses reeling. He forced himself to remain upright, still, blank-faced. Escape would be doubly difficult if the guards suspected he was aware.

Chapter Eighteen

"Respond to me!" Neeles Brunix screamed at Katrina, withdrawing his hand from her naked breast. "I've had your maidenhead. You have nothing left to lose. Respond to me like the whore you are."

She turned her face away, biting her lip against her tears of humiliation. She wouldn't give him the satisfaction of evoking any emotion in her.

Owner Brunix heaved his long, naked body off the bed. Frustration radiated from him as he paced his private suite on the topmost floor of his factory. He seemed oblivious to his nakedness, concerned only with the emotions that roiled within him.

"You just lie there, pale and elegant, beautiful beyond imagination and numb. Making love to you is like fucking a corpse."

Katrina resisted the urge to recoil from his lecherous stare at the tuft of pale hair between her legs.

Brunix paused in his rapid prowl to stare at himself. Limp. As unresponsive as Katrina.

"All true-blooded women are whores at heart—titillated by sex because it is forbidden outside the bonds of marriage. But you refuse to show your true feelings out of some perverted need to punish me. You punish me because I have saved your life, fed you, clothed you, and allowed you to make lace for three years. Why should I keep a slave who can't satisfy me in bed?"

"Do what you will. I don't have to enjoy your rape of my body."

" 'Twasn't rape, Katrina. You came to me willingly, or out of duty, I don't care. But I didn't rape you, and you can't take this to my clan. Besides, you enjoyed it. Didn't you!"

She turned her face away from him. His touch reminded her too much of King Simeon's erotic caress and lewd suggestion that she might do this with P'pa.

"Tell me you enjoyed it!"

"How could I?"

"Like all true whores, you're holding out for marriage." He snapped his fingers as the idea occurred to him. "I could invoke the ancient laws of my mother's people, the natural laws that governed this land before the pale-eyed northerns conquered all. I told the palace guards that you are my wife, a clear declaration before witnesses. Your virgin's blood stains my sheets. The two make a legal marriage."

"I am required by law to make myself available to you. Marriage would not change my feelings," she whispered, afraid he would see her inner pain and become aroused by even that small display of emotion.

"I have no trouble with the whores I can buy on any street corner. I perform admirably with the other women in my factory. But with you, the only one I really want . . . nothing," he raised his hands over his head in exasperation and dropped them limply to his side. "I should have ignored my bargain with The Simeon and taken you the first day you came into this factory, taught you to enjoy my body while you were too young to know differently."

"A bar . . . gain?" Katrina tried very hard not to stammer. Hesitancy was an emotion Brunix could latch onto.

"The Simeon made me vow not to touch you so that you would

return to him as pure as when he sold you to work in my factory. I have saved you from his ritual at least. He needed you virginal to tap some unknown power he sensed in you. A power my Rover instincts cannot find." To emphasize his words, he leaned over her and pinched her nipples hard.

She refused to flinch or recoil.

"But The Simeon has broken his part of the bargain in pursuing you." Disgusted, Brunix returned to his pacing. "Therefore, I do not have to honor my part of the bargain. You are mine by right. *Mine!* I have wanted you for a very long time, and I have had you and you don't satisfy me."

"I see." She remained stone still. Inside, questions plagued her. What had triggered this new round of persecution from Simeon? The man at the parade, was he an agent of the king? Perhaps he owned a lace factory and wanted to deprive Brunix of his premier lacemaker. No, if he wanted that, he would have promised Katrina employment.

"Is there nothing that excites you? Nothing that raises your passion?" Brunix leaned over her, his eyes nearly glowing red with his frustration.

Katrina didn't respond. She had worked so hard at controlling her anger and hatred toward Simeon and the fate that sent her into slavery that she doubted she could show her true feelings ever again.

"If I can't have your body, Katrina Kaantille, I will have your mind and your talents." Brunix pounded his fist into the mattress beside her naked body.

A faint glimmer of hope sprang to life deep in her heart. She didn't dare let it flare too high.

"That lace shawl you wear, the one your mother made for the queen . . . the one the king identified you by."

Katrina nodded her acknowledgment. He'd studied the piece of lace thoroughly, even tried draping it erotically around her body to evoke something within her. He couldn't know that this unique piece of lace was all that she had left of her mother. Wearing it kept her keenly aware of all that she had lost.

"You will make a pattern from this lace. A pattern that is difficult to duplicate. I will not have my business rivals stealing the design."

She didn't tell him his business rivals already knew about the shawl and offered her freedom in exchange for it.

"Will . . . will you consider my obligation to service you in bed canceled?" She couldn't look him in the eye.

"The pattern will postpone your obligation to me. You have until you finish making a sample shawl to . . . develop some enthusiasm for me."

"The pillow I use in the factory is engaged with another pattern. The homespun cover is too rough for the fine silk M'ma used for the shawl."

"You will use the pillow in my office."

Excitement flared deep within Katrina. A real pillow, covered in soft velvet, stuffed with unspun wool. And slender bobbins that clicked and sang as she worked. Some of those bobbins had been made for her. Just to handle them again was a reward beyond her daily hopes for escape from this man and his grim factory.

"Light? The workroom is too dark to see a fine pattern. And pins? They must be delicate, sharp, and free of rust."

Brunix narrowed his eyes as he gazed at her with longing and speculation. He nodded briefly. "If I am pleased with the design, if it makes me as much profit as I think it will, you may consider the pillow and the bobbins yours. The light and the pins I will investigate. White paint on the walls perhaps."

"Oh!" Katrina gaped at him in surprise and delight.

"So you do have passion within you, my dear. Passion for lace, true lace instead of the rudimentary garbage the others turn out. We'll see if we can translate that enthusiasm into gratitude to me." He grabbed her roughly by an arm, pulling her to stand close to him. He pressed the full length of his naked body against her as he ground his mouth over her lips in a cruel and possessive kiss. "Remember, Katrina Kaantille, you and your work belong to me, body and soul. And I will never let you go."

Queen Miranda lies near death. Her court is in chaos. The princess hides in her suite. Dour councillors and advisers cower in the lesser audience chamber, wringing their hands in panic. In Coronnan, the nobles would seize control and continue to govern with little or no interruption. Lucky for King Simeon that in SeLenicca a royal wish is absolute law.

Miranda's council doesn't know how to act, only advise and hinder decisive action as being too rash. Miranda hasn't had time to revoke her Edict of Joint Monarchy. Simeon is now in position to seize the throne for himself, without Miranda's dithering. Once in control, he can allow Miranda to die and remain king without passing the crown to Princess Jaranda.

The coven, through Simeon, is now in total control of one of the Three Kingdoms. My agents move into place. Soon the entire continent will be mine—except for Hanassa. No one can rule that haven of outlaws, rogues, and thieves. And Rovers.

An alien presence brought Jaylor to full wakefulness. No light of moon or stars crept through the smoke hole, around the shutter or beneath the door. Yet he could clearly see every object in the crowded cottage. Moving only his eyes, all his magical senses alert, he surveyed his home seeking the *thing* that had startled him out of a sound sleep.

A ball of witchlight glowed at the foot of the bed he shared with Brevelan.

Instinctively he raised armor around his sons sleeping in the loft. The ball didn't move or flicker. Jaylor risked a little probe into the light. His mental arrow encountered no resistance, no menace, nothing. The light just hung there, waiting.

Waiting for what?

Carefully Jaylor swung his legs over the side of the bed. The ball of light shifted so that it continued to face him. As he stood, Jaylor grabbed the extra quilt to wrap around his shoulders against the night chill. The ball of light didn't object or move.

"What are you?" he whispered into the darkness, afraid to rouse Brevelan or the children in case the light turned hostile.

No answer from the light.

Jaylor took one step toward the central hearth. The light moved with him, remaining a few feet in front of his face.

"Who sent you?" Jaylor probed with his mind as well as his words.

The light bobbed a little, as if the question almost triggered a response but not quite.

"Are you a message?"

The light quivered and wobbled, almost joyfully.

A strange summons indeed. Magicians were trained to send a flame through a glass to a designated person. What if Robb or Marcus were in trouble and couldn't build a fire or reach a glass? The witchlight might serve the same purpose. He had to give the boys credit for ingenuity.

"Give me your message," he ordered.

I AM YAAKKE AND I AM ALIVE!

A long-handled shovel came readily to Jack's hand. Several men had hefted it and discarded it without knowing why. The balance was wrong, the grip too large, or they preferred a pickax to a shovel.

Jack allowed himself a small, secret smile. His staff, fixed as the handle of the shovel, didn't like to be touched by anyone but him. The more he used it, the stronger his bond with this basic tool of magic became. Each day, the staff fed him memories and knowledge. Each night he practiced a spell or two. But still there was something he had to do. Something that compelled him to escape, beyond the need for mere survival.

The iron chain around his ankle resisted magic. He was still bound to a partner or a pillar. Patchy-beard remained his chain-mate, someone who was too observing, always touching him, distracting him from his act of blankness.

The supply caravan should be close. Soon Jack would have to take his chances and escape. He'd be able to complete . . . something. If he couldn't break the chain, he'd have to drag his partner with him. The scraggly little man with bowed shoulders and patchy beard would slow him down, hamper his movements. If he waited a few more days until he was rotated back to being Fraank's partner, his chance of survival improved. Fraank was trustworthy and still reasonably strong—though his mine cough worsened each morning. Patchy-beard made the hair on the back of Jack's neck stand on end.

Jack wished the cranky jackdaw would come back and show him how far the caravan had come, how much time he had to plan and work on a spell to unlock the chains.

Aided by the strength of the staff, Jack stabbed his shovel at the nearest pile of rocky debris. As the blade clanged against solid rock, a new perception opened to him. A sound, so faint normal hearing could not detect it, whispered to him. Then the merest inkling of a vibration trickled through his toes to the soles of his feet.

Something bright and shining hovered on the sides of his vision. He extended his senses with magic and sent them in all directions.

"Rockfall!" he yelled with three years of stored energy. "Get out *now*." Without waiting for orders, he grabbed his chain-mate by the hand and lunged for the lift.

He broke the staff free of the shovel blade and tucked his tool through the cord that held his trews around his waist where it wouldn't get lost.

Fifteen pairs of men followed him without question, tripping over their ankle chains in their haste. Two-by-two they squeezed into the lift designed to haul half that many men out of the shafts. Jack took a moment to make sure that Fraank was with them. The guard pulled on the bell rope signaling ascent. The lift stayed in place.

An ominous roar rose from the deepest portion of the shaft. Dread hovered over each man's left shoulder, like death waiting to pounce.

"Simurgh take you lazy bastards," the guard yelled up the shaft. "Pull us up!"

The rumbling beneath the shaft grew louder. The lift seemed to sway side to side within the wobbling mine walls.

Jack and his chain-mate, with surprising strength for such an elderly and scrawny man, reached for the emergency rope. Fraank and his partner on the opposite side of the crowded platform grabbed the companion rope. Together they hauled on the pulley device and lifted the crew an arm-length.

Dust replaced breathable air. Pulsing roars filled Jack's ears. "One, two, three, heave," he ordered. Four pairs of hands hauled again on the ropes. "One, two, three, heave." He may have lost his name, his memory, and three years of his life, but at least he remembered how to count.

"Three, one, two, heave," the guard ordered in a squeaky whisper.

Up an arm-length, then two more. Jack and his comrades found the rhythm and pulled in unison without the off-count commands of the guard.

Dust and smoke built to a choking density. Men coughed and sweated; hearts beat double time. No one spoke.

Arm-length by arm-length the platform rose. Louder and louder the protests of the inner planet swelled to enclose them, cut them off from reality. New tremors sent them rocking against the smooth walls of the vertical shaft.

The lantern dropped and extinguished itself. Direction became meaningless. There was only the burn of the rope upon sweating palms and the choking nightmare of once solid rock rippling like laundry in the wind.

And still the roar grew. Words lost themselves. Thought ceased.

Jack and his comrades pulled. *One, two, three, heave. One, two, three, heave,* he commanded them with his mind when words ceased to have meaning.

"Light, I see a light up there," someone croaked.

"Pull us up," the guard yelled again to the men on top.

At last the grinding tension in Jack's shoulder's and arms eased as the crew on top took over with a winch. He felt slack in his rope. The platform jerked upward. He clung to his safety line, fearful lest the main pulley snap under the stress.

Faster and faster they rose to the surface. Thicker and thicker the dust filled their eyes and their lungs. Deeper and deeper grew the roar of collapsing rock and screams of dying men who hadn't had enough warning to escape. At last the lift broke the surface. Torches still burned in the upper chamber. All but the pulley crew had deserted to the safety of outside.

Jack pushed older, weaker men ahead of him. He and his chain-mate lifted the cumbersome length of iron links and hobbled in their wake. *Find the rhythm. Outside foot, inside foot,* he commanded his partner with his mind.

As if he heard the mental order, the other man complied. Less clumsy, they sped toward light and solid ground. Smoke and collapsing tunnels followed.

Chapter Nineteen

T he lacemaker hides with a Rover. That is what Simeon fears. If he crosses the factory owner, the man's entire tribe will curse the crown of SeLenicca.

I have little use for Rover tricks or Simeon's superstitions. Yet Simeon was raised in Hanassa, where Rovers are welcome. He knows more of their ways and their abilities than I do. I know only Zolltarn, the Rover king, and his treachery.

I must bring the lacemaker to heel so that I can end Simeon's obsession with her. The spells of the solstice will be useless if he cannot concentrate.

How to circumvent the mysterious connections of Rovers? I must force a confrontation with Zolltarn. He witnessed Krej's backlashed spell. He knows the construction of the magic. He also deserted the coven for the dubious honor of membership in the Commune.

Chaos reigned in the yard outside the mine adit. Jack assessed the situation with two quick glances. Most of the men, prisoners and guards alike, were running for their lives.

"Bring ropes and lanterns. We have to get the rest of the men out!" the commandant yelled from the center of the yard. "Come back here, you cowards."

No one heeded him. Jack dragged his sluggish chain-mate toward the storeroom for survival equipment. They hadn't much time.

Without thinking, propelled by his need to escape the mine, he whipped out his staff and tapped it against his leg irons. The manacles loosened. He bent and easily snapped them open with his hands. He repeated the procedure for all the other prisoners he encountered on his way to the storeroom.

"The gate is open. This way." Fraank dragged at his sleeve, holding him back. Fraank's chain-mate, in turn tugged Fraank toward the gate, toward freedom.

Patchy-beard pointed to his own leg iron in an appeal for freedom. "We've got to escape before the guards come to their senses."

Jack scowled at the man's pleas. "We'll never survive without food and warm clothing," Jack yelled at Fraank over the din of men screaming and the Kardia collapsing within the mine.

"Blankets and food. A pack steed if we can find one," Fraank agreed with Jack. "What about him?" He pointed to the still manacled Patchy-beard.

"He's a spy for the commandant. We'd better leave him."

Both Fraank and Patchy-beard gaped at him.

"You might as well remove the entire beard, spy. The glue won't hold it much longer." Jack continued his trek across the compound to the storehouse.

"How did you know?" The spy ripped the false beard off in one smooth motion, revealing clean, healthy, skin beneath.

"You listened too closely and kept trying to touch me in a camp where men avoid physical contact as much as possible in order to maintain some semblance of privacy. As we hauled the lift up the mine shaft, you pulled with too much strength." Jack selected blankets and new boots, coats, and a tarp for a tent while Fraank stuffed another pack with food.

"You won't get far in these mountains without help and a guide. Release my chains, magician, and I'll take you to safety," the spy said as he added water carriers to the supplies.

"What makes you think I'm a magician?" Jack tapped the end of his staff lightly against his thigh. Power shot from the end of the wood down his muscles to his feet. An aftershock tingled against his feet. Moments later the Kardia shook again.

"The staff." Patchy-beard clung to the door frame for balance until the tremor eased. "I felt a surge of power the day you found it and came to investigate. Smart move keeping it inside the mine where the commandant couldn't sniff its power." The narrow-shouldered man straightened to his true height. With shoulders back and chin lifted, he was suddenly as tall and strong as Jack. And not much older.

"You are more than a prisoner of war, or a criminal culled from The Simeon's prisons," Jack said. He looked behind the man's left ear, judging the colors of his aura. The colors swirled and changed layers rapidly, defying interpretation. "I suspect you are a military officer on assignment. Perhaps you are one of the sorcerer-king's converts, seeking sacrifices to Simurgh."

Jack looked around for anything more he might need rather than make himself dizzy with the constantly shifting colors of the man's aura. Nothing important appeared nearby.

"We have enough. Let's go, Fraank."

"You haven't released me yet," the spy reminded him.

"You don't deserve release. You and the mine owners and King Simeon should be thrown to the bottom of the mine for what you have done to free men. No one has the right to own slaves and work them to death in that hell-hole!"

"If you release me and take me with you, I can take you to the coven. They have need of men with your power. They will reward you well."

"If you work for the coven, you must be a magician, too. Release yourself." Anger filled him for his three lost years, for the pain and toil of hundreds of men who had suffered in the mines, anger at himself for becoming a victim of King Simeon. He resisted the urge to plow his fist into the spy's handsome face.

"Take me with you. I'm not a magician," the spy cried. Panic tinged his voice as Jack dove out of the storeroom, Fraank in his wake. "I'm only sensitive to power. And I sense power in these mountains. The Simeon has hidden a dragon in this region. If you are the magician sent by the Commune to find the dragon, I can take you to her!"

Rejiia held her father's gold-rimmed circle of glass up to a candle flame. Slowly she recited the words of a spell she'd devised herself, pronouncing each word distinctly. The language was modern and didn't have the power of the ancient tongue of Simurgh, so she reinforced each syllable with magical energy from her mind.

The babe within her belly quieted his morning ritual of kicking and squirming, as if he knew the importance of magic and didn't wish to disrupt it.

Behind the glass, the green flame grew in size, broadened and stilled. The hot core of light surrounding the wick took on new colors. Gold and brown, mixed with ruby, silver, and pearl. Gold by itself. The colors became shapes. Reality faded. She sent her essence into the flame, to become one with the vision she called forth.

Rossemikka writhing in pain and grief. Darville silently holding her hand. Blood. Death?

Abruptly the vision ended. The present or the future? No matter. Rejiia had seen enough. She smiled. Something in the bizarre double aura surrounding the queen had caused the latest hemorrhage and kept her from giving Coronnan the long-awaited heir. She hadn't miscarried yet. But she would, and with enough damage to her internal organs she might never conceive again.

Plans appeared, full and complete, in her head. "I shall demand that Lord Krej's line be proclaimed heirs to Darville when I return to Coronnan in high summer. Why waste time with Simeon's pitiful efforts to rule through the coven when I can have it all myself?" She knew her child was male. As soon as he was born, she would arrange his betrothal to Princess Jaranda. That would put both Coronnan and SeLenicca firmly into her control.

Within the week she expected to hear of Rossemeyer's king being assassinated by poison. Poison on a letter from the young king's own sister, the queen of Coronnan. War would follow immediately upon the heels of that news.

Simeon had already proclaimed his right to Rossemeyer as the son of Rossemikka's father by his first and rightful queen. When the other Rossemeyer brat died of his long and lingering illness, the ruling party could turn only to Simeon to take the crown.

Rejiia had to make Simeon acknowledge her son as his heir to Rossemeyer. Once she returned to Coronnan as Darville's heir, she could afford to eliminate her lover. Her son would have Coronnan and Rossemeyer. Simeon's daughter would have SeLenicca. All three kingdoms lay within her grasp. She didn't need Simeon much longer.

The king had become so obsessed with finding one sniveling little lacemaker, he neglected all of his other duties to coven and country.

Her father would know how to manipulate the increasingly unstable king of SeLenicca. The two men had been raised together as foster brothers.Pappi knew Simeon's motives better than the king knew himself. Theirs was an intimacy Rejiia could never know as merely Simeon's mistress.

Simeon's mother, exiled Princess Jaylene of Rossemeyer, had died shortly after giving birth to him. Before she died, she had entrusted the care and education of her child to her best friend and the only person in attendance at the birth, Janessa. A few years later

Janessa had married the brother of the king of Coronnan, taking Simeon and another foster child, Janataea, with her.

Some said Jaylene had died of a broken heart when she couldn't return to Rossemeyer. Others claimed she'd been poisoned by her midwife, Janessa.

Lord Krej knew Simeon as a brother. He would understand why the king was obsessed with one ugly little lacemaker when he had a city full of nubile virgins willing to dance upon his altar in return for prestige and safety for their families. Rejiia's father would know how the little lacemaker had escaped them at the birthday parade and where she hid. Or, he would know how to get that information.

Ask who protects her and why.

Rejiia looked closely at the tin weasel sitting on the table beside her candle and glass. Had her father managed to penetrate her mind with his thoughts?

Rejiia returned her InnerSight to the flame. This time she positioned the weasel statue on the other side of the candle. Krej's red-and-green aura writhed within a tight case of alien magic. She couldn't see any breaches in the spell that trapped her father. Where had the thought come from?

Once more she repeated the words of the spell, seeking the secret of the tin prison.

"Where are we, Spy?" Jack surveyed the break between two rounded peaks. A dry polar wind whipped down that trackless pass, chilling his bones and burning his eyes. Above it, Corby soared, feeding him images of more wind-swept waste ahead.

"I have a name," the spy reminded Jack, shivering beneath the blanket he clutched around his shoulders. His lips were chapped to bleeding and ice rimed his new growth of natural blond beard.

Something in the silent misery of the man touched a sad

memory in Jack. He, too, had wrestled with the ignominy of being a nameless drudge. He'd had to earn the respect of others before they consented to refer to him as anything other than "Boy."

The spy had earned Jack's respect in his stalwart plodding through the mountains, a heavy pack of supplies on his back, in all kinds of punishing weather. Their weeks of trekking toward the dragon lair had left all three of them, Jack, Fraank, and the spy, hungry, lean, cold, and dependent upon each other for survival. Only Corby seemed to thrive in this treeless landscape. He taunted them now with his freedom to fly.

"Where are we, Officer Lanciar?" Jack repeated the question.

"I don't know where we are. Somewhere in SeLenicca, but so much of this land has been logged off and then eroded, all the landmarks look the same."

"Do you sense the dragon anywhere near?" Jack knew the lair had to be in the hills, at the bottom of a cliff with a wide waterfall. That kind of landscape didn't occur in the rolling plains and river valleys of SeLenicca proper.

"Sensing people with talent is easier. South, I think," Lanciar grumbled. He sank deeper into the folds of his blanket. There was no cover anywhere to shelter them from the punishing wind.

Lanciar's mind remained mostly closed to Jack. The secrets behind his mental armor still troubled Jack. Respect was there, but trust was a long time in coming.

"We should have stayed at the mine." Fraank edged closer to Lanciar seeking warmth or a windbreak. He didn't look well. His years in the mine had taken their toll.

"You sense power in people of talent," Jack turned his attention back to Lanciar. "Dragons emit a kind of power. Look for power in the air, in the ground, in the living rocks of these mountains."

"Look yourself. You're the magician," Lanciar snarled.

"I cannot gather dragon magic," Jack admitted reluctantly.

"Then why bother seeking the dragon? You should have run back to Coronnan where you belong. Or let me take you to King Simeon. Maybe he'll take you to the precious dragon."

"Shayla is the only hope for saving Coronnan *from* Simeon. I must find a way to rebuild the Commune and erect the magic border again," Jack affirmed. For the memory of his friends, Jaylor and Brevelan, and his beloved mentor, Baamin. "That is my quest. I must complete it in order to complete myself."

Though once he'd done that, he'd be an exiled rogue magician or a nameless drudge again. Because he couldn't gather dragon magic.

"Come, we must find shelter before the sun sets. I believe I see a cave up there," Jack pointed to a dark spot in the hills that guarded the pass. "And enough scrub to build a fire."

" 'Tis early yet. We can traverse the pass before nightfall. There is bound to be shelter on the other side," Lanciar argued. "Villages used to guard the western end of passes. Not all of them were deserted when the timber industry died."

"I have much to teach you tonight, Officer Lanciar." Before they reached the bedraggled village Corby saw on the other side. "Tonight, by the light of a campfire, you will learn to center yourself and align your body to the pole. Thus anchored, your spirit will be free to search for magic in all its forms. Tonight you will find the dragon."

One thousand pins and counting. Katrina stared at her mother's lace shawl stretched out on an inclined work board. The cream-colored wood pulp paper beneath the lace was marked off in a precise grid to help her determine the proper angle of pin placement. The intricate lace did not conform to any predetermined angle.

Katrina's head swam with geometrical equations, trying to discover the design. T'chon lace was worked on precise forty-five degree angles. Net-ground laces flowed at a wider angle. This piece defied geometry. She knew that science as well as her mother, or any lacemaker before her. She hadn't been taught to read but she *knew* mathematics.

She stretched her back and rose from her straight chair in the corner of Neeles Brunix's office. The owner was off on some errand, so she had the ground floor room to herself. She shuddered in memory of the night he'd taken her maidenhood. Her skin crawled whenever she thought of his hands on her face, breast, between her legs . . .

She deliberately pushed aside her revulsion. Dwelling on Brunix wouldn't draw a pattern from the shawl. Without his watchful eye pinning her to her chair, Katrina took the opportunity to walk around her new workstation and stare at the obstinate piece of lace from a different angle.

Spring sunshine filtered in through the two high windows covered with a mosaic of mica flakes. Fresh white paint enhanced that light and relieved the strain on her eyes. A stray beam broke through the heavy windows setting the lustrous silk of the shawl aglow in three dimensions. An entire garden of abstract flowers jumped to life before Katrina's eyes.

She tried to remember the weeks M'ma had spent designing the shawl. Tattia had tried to keep her work a secret, but during those days, the entire family had huddled together in the upstairs work-room for warmth and light.

A picture of Tattia bent over her design board flashed before Katrina's eyes. "She didn't use a straight edge! She drew pictures. Pictures of flowers connected by a variety of entwined braids and nets."

Inspired by this insight, Katrina perched over the board again, removing all of the one thousand and more pins she had used as markers. Carefully she placed each of the precious pins into a magne-tized box. A new piece of paper beneath the lace and she started over.

Pins in the top corners and along the fanned edge across the lace. Then several more along the side edges to hold the thing in place.

With a new vision of how the design flowed she traced the outside of each flower with pins at logical points. The center of each motif received appropriate pins, too. Tediously she traced each flower, following the lines of thread rather than any predetermined geometric pattern. The outside edges came easily. The inside motifs didn't seem to conform.

Again Katrina jumped up and paced the office, studying the lace from several new angles. The floral centers appeared too angular, too regular to match the rest of the design. They were almost like the ancient runes carved into the walls of the temple. Runes that represented the language before the Stargods brought the modern alphabet. The ancient writing was the foundation of the pictorial ledger language all women were taught to keep their household accounts. A forgotten language deemed too unimportant for those few men who needed to read.

The rune in the lower right-hand corner suggested something illegal. The one in the upper right-hand corner showed ashes. She knew the symbol as part of the recipe for making soap—ashes and lye. But it was different somehow. A mood of menace lingered in the runes.

How strange of Tattia to put such symbols in a gift for the queen!

The sun shifted. A shadow fell across the lace obscuring her insight.

'S'*murgh it!*' she cursed. "I need better light."

"You may not take the board to the workroom upstairs. I will not have the other lacemakers peering over your shoulder at the lace and gossiping about my newest venture." Owner Brunix placed a long hand on her shoulder and squeezed gently, affectionately.

"Oh, you startled me." Katrina jumped away from him. The hair on her arms and the back of her neck stood up in instinctive fear of his touch. She had been so lost in her work she hadn't noticed the sounds of doors opening and closing or footsteps.

Brunix frowned at the distance she put between them. He didn't say anything further until he sat behind his desk, in a position of unopposable authority. "You may carry your work to my apartment." The top floor windows of thinnest mica and a skylight of real glass— coarse and mottled but genuine enough to bring the sunshine inside —offered the best visibility in the district. How many fortunes had he spent on that luxury?

Katrina hesitated, reluctant to agree with him. He was right about the lighting. But she hoped she had escaped the necessity of ever returning to the intimacy of his private rooms. She looked at her board and the waning shaft of sunlight that now spread across his desk.

"I'll not press you to share my bed until the piece is finished. You may work in silent peace." He scowled.

His eyes were on an accounting ledger rather than on her, so she couldn't tell whether she or the figures displeased him. She peeked at the ledger, upside down. Unlike her father and other merchants, Brunix used the feminine runic language to keep his books. Where had he learned it? Not from any normal teacher.

Without a word she gathered her supplies under her arm. "You could thank me," Brunix reminded her, still not looking up.

"For what?"

"For saving your eyes from strain. For delivering you from King Simeon, twice."

Katrina remained silent.

"His Majesty thought the humiliation of being owned by a half-breed outlander would be greater than suffering through his perverted rituals." Brunix peered at her speculatively. "The Simeon thought you would choose him over me. He made the mistake of underestimating you. I will not make the same mistake. I find great satisfaction in owning you. Me, a dark-eyed half-breed owning a true-blood woman. I own a Kaantille, one of the greatest lacemakers in the world, and all of your work belongs to me. All of it!"

"You own my work, Owner Brunix. You will never own my soul. I couldn't respond to you, because you demanded it as your right, something you bought and paid for. When you ask me out of love, I will reconsider." She put more distance between them.

"Will you, really?" He stepped between Katrina and the door so fast she barely saw him move. "Will you give me your soul if I ask out of love?"

"Maybe. Maybe not. I said I would reconsider if you could ever raise your self-esteem high enough to risk *asking*." She looked up at his tight face. He stood head and shoulders taller than she—another indication of his outland blood. She didn't let his height or his authority intimidate her.

"Get out of my sight. Get up into the loft and work on that blasted shawl until you go blind. Work until your fingers are bloody and your back permanently curved. For I'll not release you from bondage until no one has any further use for your mind, your hands, or your body. Even The Simeon won't be able to use you."

Chapter Twenty

"**B**reathe in three counts, hold three, out three, hold three. Again," Jack instructed Officer Lanciar as he himself engaged the first stages of a trance. He wasn't about to send this unknown sensitive in search of a dragon alone. Jack intended to be right on his heels—psychically speaking.

"Still your mind. Breathe in, hold, breathe out. Again. Let go of your thoughts. Drift free of your body," he continued the monotonous litany.

The moon rose high and bright above the canyon. Frigid winds continued to howl and moan. Inside the long, narrow cave the three men were snug, almost comfortably warm. Corby crouched on a protruding ledge, head under his wing; oblivious to the proceedings. Fraank snored quietly on the other side of their campfire. The older man had feigned boredom from the long and repetitious exercises to cover his exhaustion. The mines had taken their toll on his lungs as well as his strength. If Jack didn't find the dragon soon, Fraank might not live to return to his daughter.

Lanciar fidgeted, like any first-year apprentice learning the basics of magic. Mental and physical disciplines were things he'd learned during his years in the army. But this control over heartbeat and breath was taxing his patience.

A vibration of power rippled from Lanciar. He had achieved the first stage of trance. His latent magic was set free of mental inhibitions. Jack's body hummed, seeking a resonance with the other man. When they were tuned, Jack was ready to follow wherever Lanciar led.

"Anchor your body with the *Kardia*. Make it one with the land beneath you so that you may achieve the *Gaia*. The oneness with all that lives and breathes and exists." Jack did the same. Automatically his blood pulsed in accord with the living rhythms of the planet and homed in on the magnetic forces of the nearest pole.

Lanciar took a little longer, not yet confident enough to release his body to instinct.

"Let go, Lanciar. Let your body find the *Kardia*. From the *Kardia* you were conceived and born. To the *Kardia* you will return. It is your home, nurturer of all life. Release your body to the loving arms of the *Kardia*."

"It's too much like death," Lanciar protested. At least he didn't break his trance. Five times they'd gotten this far and four times he had fallen out of rapport at the moment of release.

"What is death but one more phase of life? Touch it now, and you will never fear it again. Touch the *Gaia*. Touch all life." Jack's blood sang with power and joy as he followed his own instructions. Never before had he achieved such a sense of unity with life. He released his grief over the deaths of all those who had touched him with love and friendship.

Without listening, he heard underground water gurgling, the stones breathed, the soil mourned for the loss of the tall trees that had once anchored it to the planet. Jack knew where every bird nested, every mouse hid her burrow. He smelled the beginning of new leaves on the bushes. He sensed the stars wheeling in the great dance of life. He heard the moon pass through the sky.

He was a part of it all.

Lanciar followed him into the unity of life, death, renewal. Together they soared through the universe with their homeland.

Power beckoned them from all directions. Every living mote contained power, eager to be tapped and joined with the thriving life of the magician. Great blue pools and rivers of power surged through the planet beneath them. The power altered its internal resonance to match Jack's unique life song. It flowed through him as if he were another conduit, just like the planet.

He reached out with his senses, seeking his destiny. The image of a woman with hair graced by moonlight flitted past his mind's eye. A woman bent over a worktable with a single four-strand plait of hair down her back. He recognized the girl he had seen once before in a vision and many times in his dreams. Now he saw her grown to womanhood. Sad beauty touched her features and his heart.

Their lives were somehow linked. How? Why?

The vision faded. The future was an element he could glimpse but not know.

A shimmering crystal of power winked at him. *Now you are ready!*

All of Jack's past, good memories as well as bad, returned to him. He winked back to the core of crystalline power tinged with blue around the edges and continued his journey.

Enhanced by the land, he pulled more power from the moon and the sun, growing beyond them to the stars and distant galaxies. He saw more planets circling their suns, felt more lives that would never touch his own in real time and space. He joined and became a part of all life and rejoiced in the fullness of being.

Gradually the crackle of a small campfire, the cool wind and his stiff back touched his awareness. He sank back into his body, refreshed and renewed.

Lanciar's return was less graceful. His body jerked and slumped. He twisted his neck stiffly and stared numbly at Jack, mouth agape, eyes wide. "No wonder you were able to sense the rockfall before anyone else. If that is a sample of who you are, no wonder The Simeon sent me looking for you."

"That's . . . I never . . ." How could Jack explain that this was the first time he had *expanded* himself so far and so fully? "I saw the dragons. I know how to find them," he said instead.

"I didn't notice a dragon. I saw only a shimmering haze around everything and lines of blue crisscrossing beneath us." Lanciar stared at the remnants of the fire, still stunned by his awesome experience.

"Beneath us?" Jack glared at Lanciar with magic-sharpened senses. "There is no power in SeLenicca. Every magician knows that." So he hadn't looked for it. Suspicion grew in Jack. The power dimmed within him in response to the negative emotion. He didn't care. There was enough left in his body's reserves.

"You saw it, too!" Lanciar protested. "Not all over like in the rest of the planet. Pockets of power, raw power that hasn't been honed and fine-tuned by contact with magicians."

"We can't be in SeLenicca if there are ley lines. Where have you led us? We've twisted and changed direction often enough we could be in Hanassa for all I know." Jack controlled the urge to throw a truth spell over his companion. He wanted to know the depth of Lanciar's betrayal first.

"I swear to you, by the vision we both shared, that we are in SeLenicca. All you have to do is march to the other side of this pass and question the inhabitants of the village. They speak SeLenese. The men cut their beards square. The women braid their hair in four-strand plaits. This is SeLenicca!" Lanciar's aura flared with blue truth. He believed what he said.

"Then something very strange is happening in your land." Jack swallowed deeply while he organized his thoughts. "Nimbulan burned out all of the power in SeLenicca when he established the border three centuries ago. For three hundred years, none of the ley lines had begun to recover. Why would they now?"

"I hate this," Darville whispered to himself.

"Think of it as cauterizing a wound," Mikka whispered back at him. "If we do not cleanse the problem now, the poison will spread until all of Coronnan is diseased and crippled!"

"So fierce, my queen?" Darville kissed her hand, then placed it atop his forearm in preparation for their formal entrance into the lesser audience chamber.

"I enjoy trials and executions no more than you, beloved. Remember we seek justice not vengeance."

He was grateful for the gentle pressure of her fingers against his own. She gave him the courage to mask his anger. Justice. He had to remember that.

Margit, Mikka's maid, had detected an herbal combination in this morning's porridge. A healthy woman who wasn't pregnant wouldn't notice anything more than a strange taste to the cereal. Mikka would have miscarried, possibly with dangerous hemorrhaging if she'd eaten it. No one else in the palace reported anything strange in their breakfast.

The Gnuls had to be neutralized now.

The major officials of the court bowed as the royal couple moved toward the thrones on the dais. Lord Andrall stood to the right of the thrones. Jonnias and the Marnaks to his right. Behind the senior lords, Fred and a cadre of Darville's elite troops blocked any retreat through the back door. Another cadre had orders to move into position by the main entrance as soon as the royal couple passed through it.

No one smiled. No hands reached out with petitions. The mood of the court reflected the grimness of Darville's purpose. The full court would not have been assembled so hastily except in a dire emergency.

"They all have to know what is happening to Coronnan. I can't keep this private within the Council of Provinces," he muttered to give himself the courage to face the assembly.

"The lords would hide the ugliness behind secrecy," Mikka reminded him. "None of them have any concept of the reality or the consequences of their petty schemes and manipulations. You must force them to face this issue."

"Bring in the evidence and the prisoner," Darville commanded when he reached the dais.

The guards shifted position enough to allow a stoop-shouldered man of middle years wearing hand and foot manacles passage to the center of the chamber. Two grim-faced guards in palace green escorted him on either side. A ragged hole in the prisoner's tunic, above his heart, revealed to all the place where his badge of office had once resided. Upon first examination of the man's crimes, in the chill hours before dawn today, Darville had ripped the insignia away in disgust and despair.

"Where is the evidence?" Darville reminded his men.

The sergeant opened his mouth as if to protest. Darville scowled at him, daring him to disobey. The sergeant signaled to the privates waiting in the corridor.

Expressions carefully schooled, the foot soldiers carried a shrouded litter between them into the audience chamber. All around them, gently born men and women gasped in horror and withdrew from the stench of a three-day-old corpse. Escape from the grim proceedings was firmly blocked by battle-hardened men.

"You will all hear this prisoner's tale." Darville lifted his voice to parade-ground levels. "You will all witness my judgment."

Grimly he whisked the sheet off the dead body for all to see the wreck of a once human face and form. Patches of skin had been burned away. Multiple stab wounds had ripped open his chest. Blood coated the open mouth where the tongue had been cut out and stuffed back in backward. One eye was missing.

The king covered the body once more before he lost control of the hot bile in his throat. From the sounds at the far end of the long room, others succumbed to their revulsion.

"State your name and your former office, prisoner." Fred stepped forward and faced the man in chains.

"Caardack. I was senior magistrate of the city of Baria in the Province of Sauria," he whispered, never lifting his eyes from his chains.

"Louder. Speak loud enough for all to hear." Fred prodded the prisoner with a short club.

Caardack almost doubled over at the touch of Fred's weapon. Evidence that he'd endured more than one beating since being taken prisoner. He repeated his statement a little louder.

"Tell your tale, simply and clearly. The entire court needs to know how far from law and order our people have fallen." Darville sank onto his throne. Mikka placed her hand on his and squeezed gently. He had to endure this. For the good of the country, Caardack had to name his confederate in public. The court needed to see the perfidy of one of their own.

"I have been magistrate of Baria for twenty years," Caardack said proudly. He stood a little taller and straighter as he leveled his eyes on the king. "Always I have striven to be fair and just and maintain the laws of my king and the Stargods."

"Why, then, did you proclaim this man's death an accident not worthy of further investigation?" Fred pointed to the corpse.

Caardack looked furtively around the chamber, keeping his mouth firmly shut.

"Tell us why, Caardack. I promised you leniency only if you named those who ordered you to ignore death by torture. Illegal torture. Death perpetrated by a small cult of fanatics against a man in my employ!" Darville barely kept his voice below the level of a scream. He couldn't let the court see him lose control. Not yet. Not until the true criminals were revealed once and for all.

" 'Tisn't a small cult anymore," someone muttered to Darville's right.

"Numbers of followers do not make the crime of murder acceptable, Lord Jonnias." Darville stared directly at the man who had plagued him for years.

"I was told that the spy was executed lawfully," Caardack defended himself. "I was also told to proclaim the death an accident so as not to panic the populace."

"If 'twas a lawful execution, why wasn't it carried out in public by the king's order?" Fred threatened Caardack with the club once more.

"I do not question orders from the nobility."

Gasps and murmurs rose through the court. Men and women eyed each other suspiciously. Mikka bowed her head in sadness.

"As magistrate you have the right to question anyone," Lord Andrall said softly.

Caardack looked in fear at the four lords standing to the king's right. "If I had questioned Lord Marnak, I would have died as hideously as did the king's spy."

"Don't be ridiculous," Lord Marnak the Elder protested. "Baria is in Sauria. I govern Hanic. What interest have I in your city?" He stepped backward, hand on his sword. Two guards grabbed his arms from behind. He struggled to free himself from their grasp. "Hands off me! I am an anointed lord. You may not touch me."

"My orders supersede yours, Marnak." Darville rose from his throne and stalked to stand in front of him. "Laws handed to us from the Stargods forbid taking a life without due course of trial. The dead man was under my protection." On the day he died so hideously, the spy should have been fleeing Coronnan with Darville's gold to save himself from the Gnostic Utilitarians he had infiltrated. "You had no right to bring him to trial without my consent, so you had him murdered."

"He was a spy," Marnak spat. "A filthy spy sent to betray the rightful worshipers of the Stargods. Keeping our temples pure of magic gives us the right to protect ourselves from such as he. And you!"

"Father, no," Young Marnak backed away from the accused lord. His burn-scarred face took on a more horrible expression than usual. With no eyebrows or lashes left, his wide open eyes gave him a fishy look. "Our loyalty to the crown must never be questioned. Rejiia . . . my wife . . . ah . . ."

Hot anger narrowed Darville's vision to the elder Marnak's haughty face. The room and the gathered court faded from his awareness. His fingers itched to draw his sword and plunge it into the man's wide body.

Control yourself. Mikka's voice invaded his thoughts. Calm. Think quiet peace.

Visions of softly flowing water through woodlands. Calubra ferns swaying in the breeze. Shy wildflowers peeking out from shady glades.

"Lord Marnak the Elder, Governor of Hanic, I order your immediate arrest for the crime of murder. I will investigate charges of treason at the same time."

"Not treason, Your Grace." Lord Jonnias positioned himself between Darville and Marnak.

"Treason," Darville repeated. "When Caardack's full story is told at trial, all of Coronnan will know that the Gnostic Utilitarian cult seeks to set aside the dragon-blessed monarchy and the Council of Provinces. They want to set one of their own on the throne as absolute ruler of Coronnan. Since my ancestor, Darville I, ended the Great Wars of Disruption, the only person who can dissolve the Council of Provinces is a monarch consecrated by the dragons." He turned and stared at the entire court. "All of you saw and acknowledged the dragon at my coronation."

Shuffling feet and rustling fabric were the only sounds in the room. The story of a blue-tip dragon blessing Darville's coronation had grown into a legend, sung in taverns and on street corners across the land. Most of the people in the chamber had witnessed the event.

"Does anyone question that an attempt to assassinate me or my family is treason?"

Eyes opened wide with alarm and chins dropped as reality struck the members of the court. This was no game of gossip and intrigue for power and influence. Darville raised the question of murder of one of their own! By one of their own.

"We believe otherwise," Marnak interjected. " 'Tis treason to allow you and your witch-queen to rule. We must reestablish rightful government from the temple. The dragons have deserted Coronnan. The old laws protecting magicians are no longer valid."

"What right have you to accuse my wife of witchcraft? What evidence do you produce to back your claim?" A pulse pounded in Darville's temple. Not once in nearly four years of marriage had Mikka thrown a spell. Yet the rumors persisted.

"Everyone knows she has bewitched you."

"Everyone does not know that, Marnak. What everyone knows and the truth are rarely the same thing. I have had enough of rumors and whispers. There will be no more of them!" he bellowed, almost beyond control. "The next person to accuse the queen without evidence will follow you to the dungeons."

He swallowed heavily and breathed deeply, praying for calm. When the red mist cleared from his eyes, he leveled his gaze upon Marnak once more. "Speak no more until the trial, Marnak, lest you condemn yourself without the benefit of trial."

"I do not care for your petty justice, *King* Darville," Marnak sneered. "I shall die a martyr."

"Only if I let you die."

Marnak paled. Jonnias swallowed repeatedly.

Darville heard the gasps of dismay from the crowd. He didn't care if they believed him capable of the kind of torture his spy had endured. He wanted them to think about that horrible death and know revulsion against those who caused it.

"I promised Caardack a short term of prison and penance, instead of death, if he named the leaders of the Gnostic Utilitarians. I can offer you the same clemency, Marnak. But only if you tell us all who gives *you* orders."

"I take my orders from the Stargods."

"Perhaps you will tell us who you planned to raise up as ruler of Coronnan after my assassination?"

Marnak looked hastily toward Jonnias, then back to his king. Jonnias edged away, his skinny legs trembling.

"I have vowed to die before I reveal the identity of our sacred leader." Marnak bowed his head in submission to his fate.

"What about you, Jonnias? Have you taken the same vow?" Darville drew his short sword as he whirled to face the other lord. He stopped the blade a hair's breath from Jonnias' convulsing throat. Two burly guards kept the man from retreating further.

"I know nothing of this," Jonnias protested. His voice cracked with fear.

"Then you did not commission a new crown of gold and rubies from goldsmiths in Jhabb? Their ambassador thought you had. He also showed me a contract, written and signed by you, for ten thousand mercenaries to invade the capital city upon my death. They are to take orders from no one but you."

Jonnias slumped.

"Are you the sacred leader of this cult, or do you take orders from someone else?"

Jonnias remained defiantly mute.

"Take them away," Darville said. Sadness and relief dragged at his shoulders. He looked back to Mikka, still sitting quietly on her throne. A brief, sad smile touched one corner of her mouth.

"A formal trial against Marnak the Elder of Hanic and Jonnias of Sauria will begin at dawn. If they are found guilty, I will sentence them according to the law." He knew he'd have to order their deaths.

Marnak was right; they would die martyrs. Without leaders within the Council of Provinces, the cult would fade for a while . . . until some other power-hungry fanatic rose among their ranks. Whoever truly directed the cult would not remain in secret isolation long.

"What about me, Your Grace? I had nothing to do with the conspiracy." Marnak the Younger tugged at Darville's sleeve.

The king stared at the offending hand clutching the black silk of his shirt until the young lord removed it. "We will discuss your situation after the trial. If you are not guilty of aiding an attempt to put me aside in favor of Jonnias or any other potential leader, then you have nothing to fear."

Marnak blanched and bowed as he stepped hastily away.

Chapter Twenty-One

J aylor sat before a fire at the far edge of Brevelan's clearing. Years before he had cast a summoning spell from this very spot. Then he had held a multicolored cat in his arms. Mica's rhythmic purr had aided his concentration in guiding the tiny flame through the glass toward his mentor, Baamin, in the University of Magicians. Tonight he held a feisty tabby with a torn ear who was just a cat. No princess with magic in her soul had borrowed this cat body.

The purring tom dug his claws into Jaylor's thigh, bringing him back to the important task of stroking fur in rhythm with his breathing.

Mica had often done the same when she had aided his spells. For all of her human intelligence, Mica had adapted to her cat body and instincts very well. Rosse, the cat who had inherited the princess' body, hadn't been quite so adaptable.

And now the two spirits were joined in Rossemikka's human body.

He sighed, still missing Darville. The necessary silence between them had gone on much longer than either had expected. Margit's reports of the king's and queen's daily activities didn't feel the same as speaking directly with his best friend.

Enough speculation on the politics. Jaylor had news for his two journeymen. Yaakke was alive! The ball of witchlight had left a magic trace in the same direction Marcus and Robb had taken. He must contact the boys tonight, before they slipped around the armies guarding the pass and entered SeLenicca.

Jaylor had a feeling that his former apprentice was in trouble. Otherwise he wouldn't have sent such an unorthodox message after three years of silence.

I am Yaakke and I am alive.

Alive but not well; not returning; not capable of sending a normal summons spell.

Jaylor added another branch to the fire, to keep it going for the duration of the spell. As the flames caught, he breathed deeply, once, twice, thrice. The void beckoned him. He ignored the enticement of sending himself instead of his thoughts into the spell.

His trance settled comfortably on his mind and body. Cat purred and kneaded dough on the fabric of his trews. The flames grew larger, more animate in his mind's eye. A hand that might have been his, but seemed unattached to an arm, brought a large glass into view. The gold rim of the precious tool sparkled in the firelight. The images seen through the magnification grew even larger.

Carefully, Jaylor plucked one particularly lively flame from its greedy feeding on the wood. A thought melded the flame into the spells surrounding the glass. Then a gentle nudge and the flame surged outward, seeking. Seeking another flame hovering within a glass.

Down the foothills, through the forest and across rich farmland the flame traveled. Southward toward mountains. Mountains that were once rich in ore and covered in trees but were now barren and mined out. The flame traveled along blue lines of magical power. The magic trapped within the planet gave speed and ease to the journey.

At the mundane border, the flame hesitated. All of the blue lines ended abruptly—burned out centuries ago. The spark hovered, looking south and north, looking west and east. It wanted to retreat, back along the magic lines. Jaylor pushed it forward. The flame sputtered and tried to die.

Sweat broke out on Jaylor's physical body while his mind guided and fed the flame. *Another bit of fire.* He urged the traveling spark of his spell to seek another flame, any flame to renew itself.

He cast his senses farther, in all directions. No presence touched him with magic. No living person lived within a league of the spot where the flame flickered and tried once more to die.

Impossible. Last night Marcus and Robb had been camped on this particular ley line. Surely they couldn't have traveled farther in one day. Even if they had ridden fleet steeds, they should be within sensing distance of this summons.

He tried another direction. Hundreds of campfires dotted the landscape, separated by an invisible line. The front. Two armies faced each other in silent impasse. The flame brightened as it neared others of its kind. None of them were magnified by a glass, or a bowl of water, or a ball of witchlight. The flame flickered and hesitated.

Jaylor's body sagged, drained of strength. Hastily he pulled the flame back into his glass. He couldn't allow the spell to leave a telltale that could be traced back to him, should a magician from either army discover any residual power. The secret location of Brevelan's clearing must remain secret.

Robb and Marcus knew how to find the clearing and the sprawling buildings of the University just beyond.

Jaylor sent the flame seeking for a presence again. Nothing. What if the young men had been kidnapped or conscripted into one of the armies? Rovers or solitary rogues could overpower the two young men, not yet fully grown into their powers. Armor was easy to erect around magical minds. An adept rogue would know the boys were in touch with their master and would shield against future communication.

Jaylor looked closer for an *absence*. Sometimes the easiest way to find a person was to find the *nothing* they hid within.

The flame found vast acres of hills and river valleys, some lush, some barren. It skimmed around scrubby bushes and dipped into burned-out and charred power lines. Across and back it flew, still seeking. Together in spirit, the flame and Jaylor crisscrossed every inch of land within a dozen leagues of Marcus and Robb's last known camping spot.

The landscape was as it should be. There were no holes and no lives. The military encampment sheltered, among the soldiers of Coronnan, several latent talents who didn't respond to the whisper of the flame. Nor did the powerful magicians on the western side of the pass understand the address of the summons. Marcus and Robb had vanished, as if they had never been.

They had to have been kidnapped. By whom and how? Not just anyone could make two magicians disappear beyond the reach of the Senior Magician of the Commune. That someone was an enemy to be reckoned with.

How much coercion could the two journeymen endure before they revealed every secret they knew? Including Queen Mikka's magical talent. Secrets that could be sold to a frightened Council of Provinces and the remnants of the Gnul conspiracy.

With sickening abruptness, Jaylor dropped back into his body from his trance. No time now to cater to a bouncing stomach and reeling vision.

"I've got to hide Brevelan and the boys. We aren't safe here anymore."

Marcus and Robb! Jaylor choked a moment in grief. He was Master now. The safety and well-being of those two boys fell on his shoulders. He'd sent them on their quest too soon. Just as he had with Yaakke. None of them were ready for the responsibilities and rigors of a quest.

He rose to his knees and doused the campfire with dirt. He didn't have time for regret and sorrow. More lives than two journeymen who knew the risks were at stake.

"What have I done to you? Lost. Yaakke, Marcus, Robb. All lost." He sent a silent prayer for their safety even as he ran the length of the clearing to begin the work of moving his family and his University where no one could find them.

As Jack led Lanciar and Fraank down the far side of the pass, the wind died and the sun broke free of the early morning cloud cover. Corby squawked and sprang from his perch on Jack's shoulder into the air, flapping his wings noisily. His tail rose convulsively and let drop a smelly white blob, inches from Jack's boot.

"Filthy bird!" He stumbled slightly as he hopped to avoid the splatter.

"Crawk!" The bird answered back crankily.

"You're so ornery maybe I should call you *Baamin,*" Jack mused.

"Newak," the bird gave a negative reply, almost indignantly. "Corby, Corby, Corby." He resumed his flight path and quickly gained enough altitude to catch a rising current of warm air. Gliding effortlessly, he soared in lazy circles above their heads.

For a moment, Jack envied the bird its freedom. If he could fly like that, he'd be over Shayla's lair in a matter of hours instead of the week he estimated the journey would take. Maybe longer if Fraank's breathing didn't improve.

Lanciar didn't look too healthy this morning either. His first foray into the realm of magic had left him limp and drained, too tired to eat. Without food he'd never replenish the energy that magic depleted. The dry journey rations in their packs were unappetizing on a healthy stomach. Maybe the mountain village just below the pass would feed them, give them warm shelter for a night or two.

Fresh meat. Milk full of rich cream. Bread hot from the oven. Jack's mouth watered and he lengthened his stride in anticipation.

Ten more steps, around a boulder and under an overhang, brought him to a point where he could see far out across the lower slopes of the mountain range. Hill after barren hill rolled out in a wide vista. Pockets of morning mist clung to the valleys. A few small and isolated trees struggled toward sunlight in inaccessible ravines.

And not a rooftop in sight.

Jack looked up at the circling jackdaw, trying to peer through the bird's eyes as he had once before.

"Croawk!" The cranky bird chose that moment to slip into a new updraft and out of sight behind the boulders.

Jack's probe went astray. "Dragon dung! How are you supposed to become my familiar if you won't stick around long enough to be familiar?" He shook his fist at the last place he saw the bird. Corby didn't return.

"Where's the village?" Lanciar asked. His eyes looked hollow and his cheeks gaunt. He nibbled on a piece of dry meat, but not fast enough to feed his fading reserves of strength. None of the pockets of ley lines seemed to have revived in this area to support the use of magic and restore a body's reserves.

And yet a vibration hung in the air, almost like a *Song*. He listened closer, and the sensation faded like a perfume dissipating in the wind.

"That's what I'd like to know." Jack stomped forward looking for the jagged line of two dozen homes that were here last night. Both he and Lanciar had *seen* the village during their mystic journey. The bird had revealed the location to him earlier in the day.

"Villages don't just up and move overnight," Lanciar protested.

"Ley lines don't either. They're gone, too." Jack scratched the dirt with the toe of his worn boot. "We haven't time to puzzle this out. We need food and shelter. This was once heavy timber country. Where there was one village there ought to be another not far away." He shifted the pack on his back to a more comfortable position.

"There's a river valley." Lanciar pointed west by northwest. "The harvesters used to float the trees down the rivers to Queen's City and other ports. Maybe we'll find something that way."

"I prefer that path." Jack pointed to a different valley farther south. Mistrust of everything Lanciar suggested rose in him like a creeping poison. There weren't supposed to be any ley lines in SeLenicca. None at all. But a slender one tingling with raw power suddenly sprang up beneath his feet, begging him to tap into it

He didn't trust the line either. It could be an illusion. It could be a dragon-dream. *He* could be wrong in all his perceptions.

"The dragon is that way." Jack stepped toward his chosen path.

"But we'll find food to the west. We need to replenish our supplies," Lanciar protested.

"Then we'll hunt." Jack began walking. Fraank followed silently in his wake, too tired and hungry to make a decision on his own.

"Hunting takes time and energy." Lanciar stood firmly in place.

"So does lying and betrayal. How many of King Simeon's agents are waiting in that valley, ready to pounce on us and drag us to Queen's City in chains, or back to the mine?" Jack didn't bother looking at either of his companions. He expected them to follow; Fraank because he couldn't do anything else, Lanciar because his mission was incomplete without a magician to turn over to Simeon and the coven.

"I have to go this way!" Lanciar took a step in the opposite direction.

"Then you go alone." Jack turned his back with a hastily erected wall of armor around himself and Fraank.

Katrina knelt before the little side altar in the grand temple. Her hands folded in front of her, and head bowed, she hoped the crowd of

petitioners in the main sanctuary believed her lost in prayer. Like so many in the capital.

Queen Miranda still lay deep in a coma. Her citizens trooped into the temples daily to plead with the Stargods for a return of their monarch's health.

Isolated in the factory, with little free time or opportunity to travel outside the industrial district, Katrina hadn't realized how neglected the temple had become in the last five years.

The belief that SeLenicca was the land of the Chosen, theirs to exploit, was falling apart as the mines gave out and the timber did not regrow. King Simeon preached that the duty of all true-blood SeLenese was to conquer other lands, grabbing resources as they went and leaving behind everlasting evidence of the supremacy of the winged god, Simurgh.

Since Simeon's marriage to Miranda, attendance at the temples and contributions had fallen to mere pittances. Mortar crumbled and mold grew on the walls. The few priests left were ancient. They trembled with cold and nursed painfully swollen joints. Like the bent old man who shuffled behind the altar where Katrina knelt. His hands were so misshapen from the joint disease, he could barely hold his taper steady enough to renew the candles.

Worship of the Stargods hadn't been forbidden, but it had definitely fallen into disfavor. Until their beloved queen lay near death and her husband had named himself monarch. Not regent for the young princess, but ruling king.

Katrina wasn't the only one who had seen the magical bolt of blue fire that caused Miranda's steed to rear and bolt. All who had seen knew who had launched it. No one dared accuse the king, or the king's black-haired, outland mistress. Such an accusation was an invitation to a torturously long death. Iza had returned to the lace factory from Simeon's dungeons, with numerous bruises but no broken bones. Her mind drifted aimlessly and she spoke no more. She still wound bobbins and straightened pins, the chores of a lifetime not easily forgotten.

Surprisingly, Brunix continued to allow her to live in the dormitory despite her growing clumsiness.

The populace returned to their neglected temples with apologies and prayers and offerings. The Stargods were benevolent. Simurgh would not restore their queen and depose the bloodthirsty king. The Stargods might.

New candles on the altar cast flickering shadows on the walls of this tiny and nearly forgotten chapel. The geometric shapes, carved into the stone, faded in and out of visibility with each shift of the light. Katrina peered at them until her eyes burned.

The motifs in the lace shawl's flower centers were the same runes that decorated this wall, variations of the limited ledger language. She'd studied the lace shawl often enough to know the symbols by heart. Three runes out of the hundred displayed resembled the words for illegal trade; none of the others were familiar.

What did they mean? No one understood this ancient language anymore. Tattia Kaantille must have known something of it, or she wouldn't have included the runes in the shawl. A message or merely an unusual twist in the design?

Surely not the latter. The runes were interesting and in a different motif could have been lovely. The flowers surrounding the runes were too soft and flowing to support the hard angles and straight lines of this forgotten alphabet.

An ancient priest wheezed as he slipped out from behind the little altar. He wobbled past Katrina to replace the sputtering candles on the stand at the opening to the chapel. His threadbare robes had once been fiery green, but the dyes had faded with time and too many washings to muddy brown.

"Excuse me, good sir," Katrina whispered to the priest. "Do you know anything of these runes?"

"Eh?" He bent toward her, cupping an ear with his hand.

"The runes." She pointed to the chiseled markings. "Do you know what they say?" She raised her voice a little. Hope of a discreet inquiry and quick answer faded.

The old priest turned to face the wall, peered at the ancient writing, and shook his head. Then he bent closer, holding his lighted taper right up against the markings.

Sigils flared bright red against black stone as if gathering life from the flame. Seemingly random runes in a distinctive geometric pattern leaped away from the wall burning their image into Katrina's mind. The same symbols, in the same order as the ones Tattia used.

Katrina's eyes widened in surprise and excitement. The old priest backed away from the wall shaking his head. "I'm sorry, daughter. I can't see well enough anymore to read this wall."

"But you know something of the ancient alphabet, perhaps something of the old prophecy? Did you read the wall for my mother three years ago?" She rose in her eagerness to get to the bottom of this puzzle.

"Knowledge of the runes has been forgotten by most. Best you spend your time and energy praying for the queen." The priest wandered off again.

"Maybe the knowledge has been forgotten, but you read the wall, old man. I'll find the truth yet." She turned to follow, eager to pursue her questions in a more private place.

"A word, Mistress Kaantille?" A stranger restrained her with a whisper.

She knew that voice! The man who had offered her freedom for the shawl. The shawl had a message. For this man or another?

"Stay away from me." She backed away from him until the low altar rail pressed against her thighs.

"I can offer you freedom and passage out of SeLenicca in return for the shawl. Your mother promised it to me three years ago. But she died before she could give it to me. I have searched long and hard for it. And for you, Katrina Kaantille."

"The stranger who offered to buy the shawl? M'ma refused your offer. Why should I accept it?"

"Your situation is more desperate now. Your M'ma refused my first offer. Later, she promised to bring it to me. I waited for her until dawn on the night she died. Would she have committed suicide on the night she expected to gain enough gold to feed you all for a year or more?"

Confusion clutched Katrina's heart and mind. She turned her back on the man and knelt at the altar again.

"Go away. I must think on this. I don't trust you." She bowed her head until she heard the man walking away.

A long-fingered hand grasped her upper arm in a vicious grip. She jerked away, ready to scream at the stranger to leave her alone.

"So this is where you hide." Owner Brunix knelt beside her, crossing himself in the accepted manner as he lowered his long body to kneel on the stone floor.

"Not even you can deny me the right to say a prayer for the queen." Katrina dipped her head and closed her eyes. Her heart throbbed in her ears. Her skin burned where he had touched her. Had he seen her with the stranger? Would his jealousy drive him to such anger that he forced her to his bed again?

"Pray? Is that what you do for so many hours each evening?" he whispered in her ear. His breath fanned a stray tendril of her hair, just in front of her ear.

She shuddered and leaned slightly away from him.

"You have no reason to love our queen, or her outland husband," Brunix said. "They deserve your curses, not your prayers." Katrina schooled her face to immobility, her thoughts whirling in confusion. Had her mother truly promised to sell the shawl? Who was the stranger and why was he so desperate to get the shawl?

Silence sat uneasily between them.

"You are an educated man, Owner Brunix. What do those runes on the wall tell you?" Did he know more of them than the limited feminine alphabet used in keeping mercantile records?

"Nothing. The Stargods wiped out all knowledge of that form of writing. They considered it a service to *Kardia Hodos,* along with eliminating a plague and erasing the cult of Simurgh. But the three who descended from the stars were ignorant and considered all of the ancient gods and their arcane knowledge as one with the bloodthirsty demon Simurgh. We lost many unique and special parts of our culture. A thousand years have passed and we are not likely to reclaim any of it."

"But surely there must be a legend of old text that preserves the meaning of those symbols, else they would have been plastered over or sanded into oblivion centuries ago," she protested.

"Legends about a prophecy of doom persist. Yaakke, son of Yaacob the Usurper, is supposed to bring about the disaster." Brunix shrugged. "Why are you so interested, my Katrina? I thought you were lost in prayer for our queen."

"Beauty and symmetry," she answered too hastily. "I would like to incorporate some of the runes into a design—bed hangings or perhaps a table runner." Deep inside her, Katrina knew the sigils conveyed a message. An important message. She had to be the first to interpret it so she knew who to tell and who to avoid.

"Not bed hangings, please. The prophecy of doom might carry over into . . ." Brunix rose hastily, turning his back on her. "City curfew is upon us. The factory curfew is long past. You will return with me now," he ordered. "I don't remember giving you permission to leave the factory."

"But you did! You told all of the lacemakers to say our prayers for the queen."

"I told my employees, not my slave. Such a flagrant disregard of the rules requires punishment. No breakfast for you tomorrow. If I dared, I'd deny you sun break as well." He grabbed her arm again, hoisting her to her feet. His fingers remained clamped just above her elbow as he propelled her out of the temple.

As Katrina stumbled in Brunix's wake his words echoed through her mind.

Yaakke, son of Yaacob the Usurper. A prophecy of doom?

What could be worse than what she endured now?

Chapter Twenty-Two

Rejiia contemplated a water droplet on top of her viewing glass. The circle of gold-rimmed glass lay flat upon a tripod above a short candle flame. The water tended to enhance her visions of distant places and events to come.

Lately all she saw was death and destruction converging on a single point. There clarity ended and symbolism took over. Three feathers for the Rovers. A black bird for the dragon nimbus. Unnatural red flames must be the coven. What could the frothy sea foam covering it all stand for? Surely Rossemanuel's death by poison wouldn't be represented by that symbol. The eels that provided the oil to bind the ingredients of the poison lived in river bottoms, not in the tops of waves near the shore.

A summons spell hummed within Simeon's huge mirror on the wall of her private apartment before she found an answer. As tall as Rejiia, and nearly an arm-length across, the glass was incredibly valuable. Something only a king could afford. The images it revealed were imperfect, warped and wobbling, but better than polished metal and larger than the exact reflection from Krej's master glass.

Simeon kept the mirror in her quarters to feed his vanity. He spent more time preening naked in front of the mirror than using it to bring his ambitions to fruition.

"Since this tool was entrusted to me, I will answer the summons and act upon it." She stood awkwardly from her chair and faced the demanding mirror. The growing baby in her womb kept her from moving quickly or gracefully.

At the center of the glass, colors spun outward in a growing spiral until they filled the surface of the mirror. Greens and browns dominated the pattern. Gradually the spiral steadied and cleared. Lanciar appeared, life-sized against a barren landscape of scrubby hillsides.

Gray-green and greenish-brown were the signature colors of his latent magic.

Rejiia placed her hand against the glass in greeting, wondering where he was and who threw the summons spell for him. He returned the greeting with a raised hand, imitating her gesture image to image. She wished she could touch him across the distance of time and magic. Lanciar had such gifted hands. He was her favorite partner during the coven's ritualistic couplings.

"Lady, I have found a new magician. If we hurry, we can bring him into the coven." His voice sounded strained.

"Who? Where are you?" she asked. Excitement blossomed within her. A new magician. A new lover during the rituals. More power to funnel into her spells.

The face of a young man with Rover-black hair and beard flashed from Lanciar's mind to her own. Features fell into place. Long, straight nose, middle height, broad shoulders and burning black eyes.

"Yaakke!" she cried. Come back from the dead to haunt her. Her dreams of power faded. That wretched, incompetent boy had more power than the full coven.

"He seeks the dragon," Lanciar informed her. "He must not be allowed to reach the lair before we convert him to our cause. He might be able to break the spell that keeps Shayla captive in SeLenicca before he understands why she must remain."

"Yaakke will never willingly join the coven. We must kill him before he reaches the lair. Without the dragon, Simeon is nearly powerless."

"And so will be the others in the coven, Lady Rejiia. I will undertake the mission to destroy the magician. My magic has awakened and it is fueled by the dragon." Lanciar smiled in a sensuous way that sent Rejiia's senses lurching. He promised more in that smile than just magic. "Upon my return to the capital, I will request full membership in the coven. I will serve at your right hand to make certain you remain as the center of the eight-pointed star."

As long as Simeon believes the child you carry is his, he will be content to allow you to be the focus of the coven's spells. The unspoken words seemed to come from the tin weasel. Rejiia grinned, knowing her father had somehow managed to break through some of the barriers in his magical prison.

"My gravid body anchors the eight-pointed star to the Kardia as no other can," she replied. "I won't give up that position once your grandson is born." With Lanciar at full power to support her, she intended to remain the focus. Krej had fought for the center and lost it to petty bickering within the coven. Janataea, too, had been kept from the coveted role. Rejiia wouldn't relinquish it—especially to Simeon whose spells were increasingly erratic.

"The boy must be stopped, Lanciar. I shall send those I trust. Magicians from the coven who owe me much. Men who will not hesitate to kill the boy if he refuses to be recruited."

Jack heard the waterfalls before he saw them. Swollen by spring runoff, little creeks joined, became rivers and thundered over cliff tops in untamable torrents. Delicate mists drifted from the primary falls almost a mile up the valley. His ears roared as he entered the fog bank caused by cold, airborne water meeting thermal currents rising from the sun-warmed valley floor.

"Almost there, Fraank," he shouted to his companion over the sound of the booming cascades.

Fraank didn't look up from his concentrated trudging. Nor did he respond. All of his energy went into placing one foot in front of the other.

"Come, Fraank, you can't let King Simeon win. You've got to fight to get well."

Fever and lung-rotting mine dust dulled Fraank's upturned eyes. Sadly he shook his head and plodded forward, each step an effort.

Jack stretched his senses forward and back; a difficult task now that they were deep into SeLenicca and the pockets of rejuvenated magic were scarcer than the widespread villages. He sensed three large life-forms behind him, at least two days away. He couldn't tell if they were men, steeds, or deer. He didn't have enough magic to hone in on details and find out if Lanciar had summoned reinforcements.

Up ahead a different sensation sent his body tingling and humming with joy. LIFE! Vibrant, buoyant, joyful life. Dozens of lives, dominated by one, much larger than the rest. The primary mind picked up his probe and sent it back to him with greeting.

Welcome, Magician. I have waited long for you. Come, eat, rest. There is much work to be done.

Jack reared, propelled backward by the strength and clarity of the mental command.

"Shayla?" Jack asked the air around him. Who but a dragon could penetrate his armored mind?

Who else would live behind a waterfall and play with a dozen silver dragonets? The dragon chuckled. Her voice filled him with rich images of immature dragons frolicking in the rippling pool beneath the waterfall.

Feeling fresher and stronger than he had in weeks, Jack supported Fraank around the waist and marched the older man deeper into the rift between enclosing hills.

A path cleared by clawed dragon feet opened before them. Not a single pebble marred the surface of the packed dirt to trip them or lead them astray. Boulders had been pushed aside to allow passage of wide dragon bodies with delicate wing membranes. Above them, the mountain walls rose steep and sheer. What need had dragons of climbing upward when they could fly?

"Just a few more steps, Fraank. A few more steps and you can sleep," Jack urged his friend.

Half a mile farther, Fraank was drooping visibly, as if the end of the quest marked the end of his life. Stubbornly, Jack shouldered the older man's nearly empty pack, along with his own and continued to hold him up, almost carrying him as they penetrated the mist.

The valley corridor widened into a deep bowl ringed with cascades in many sizes. Sunlight struck water and sent rainbows arcing in all directions. Directly ahead, a huge waterfall thundered. The outline of a crystal dragon head pushed through the curtain of the falls. Sunlight struck water and dragon together, granting a wild array of colors to the mist.

Jack blinked. More of the dragon appeared outlined by the water. Rainbows danced around the crystal horns marching from forehead to tail. Then Shayla broke free of the main cascade of water. Droplets shone on her crystal-fur. Each tiny hair reflected the bright sunlight back to Jack's eyes, defying him to look directly at her.

And yet Shayla was so incredibly beautiful with her all-color /no-color fur, he couldn't look anywhere else but directly at her.

The male dragon who had shown young Yaakke a dragon-dream of this valley had been touched by blue along his wing veins and tips. Jack suspected the unnamed dragon's fur had held just a hint of color on the end of each hair too. But not Shayla. Every color visible to the human eye bounced off her body giving her the luster of pure, rare glass, a substance that could only be forged by dragon fire.

Gracefully, Shayla waded from her concealment behind the curtain of falling water through the pool to where Jack and Fraank stood. Jack watched her progress as the water lapped halfway up her side, splashing occasionally onto her wings and neck.

The pool was immense. And deep. At the shoulder, the dragon

was twice as tall as Jack, and equally as wide. The pool was at least six dragon-lengths across. Shayla didn't seem to be swimming. Jack wasn't certain dragons could swim. So the water was at least as deep as he was tall, maybe more.

We swim when the water is deep enough. The dragon answered him before he could ask the question. *We swam in the Great Bay often when we flew the skies above Coronnan.*

Embarrassment tinged Jack's cheeks and the tips of his ears. He looked into Shayla's half-closed jewel of an eye. The whorls of spinning color didn't seem to mock him. Did dragons have a sense of humor? He clamped down on that question before Shayla could answer him.

She cocked her steedlike muzzle to one side as if puzzled by the closure of his thoughts.

Don't you trust me to be honest with you?

"Of course I trust you, Shayla. I'm just not used to having my thoughts read and my questions answered before I've thought them through." He looked away from the compelling jewel eyes.

The dragon loomed so high above him that the only place he could look without overbalancing was along her side to the folded wings. The transparent membranes fluttered slightly for balance as Shayla emerged from the pool.

A twisting black burn, as long as Jack's body and as wide as his two thighs pressed together, marred the beauty of the left wing. Charred by magic that snaked along veins and bones, the wing hung lower, heavier and more painful than its undamaged mate. Unable to heal herself and unable to fly to a healer, Shayla was trapped in the beautiful prison of this valley with the rainbow waterfall.

Jaylor studied the misty colors of the clearing's barrier with his magic-heightened senses. A tiny crack in the armor glared back at him. A crack that might admit an enemy. Since Brevelan refused to move her family or the Commune, Jaylor had to make sure the protections of the clearing were intact, impregnable.

"How are we going to explain this to your mother, Glendon?" he asked his son.

Sorry. The boy hung his head and stared at his feet. No words escaped him now. No words had come out of his mouth since he suffered from the putrid throat. The healers said he'd healed. But he'd not spoken since. What need had the boy of words when his mind relayed all the information he needed to impart?

"What were you and Lukan doing?" Jaylor shook his head in dismay. Brevelan was the chosen guardian of the clearing and the dragons. She had been the only person capable of opening and closing the barrier until Jaylor's spirit journey with the dragons. As Brevelan's husband, the dragons had granted him the privilege of sharing the guardianship. As far as he knew, the boys were not included in the privilege of opening and closing the clearing.

Stargods help them all if Glendon got loose to wreak his personal havoc and tricks on the world at large!

Wrestling, Glendon replied.

"Wrestling with what?" The image the boy relayed to his father didn't mesh with Jaylor's idea of normal little boy activity.

Dead silence surrounded Glendon. Nothing escaped his mind.

"Have you two been experimenting with magic again?" Jaylor tried to keep the panic out of his voice. He had been denied admission to the Old University over and over because of his wild and unpredictable talent from the age of ten. His sons were only three and two and they'd managed to crack armor that even their grandfather, Lord Krej, had been unable to weaken.

Krej had managed to come through the barrier by shape-changing himself and his followers into small animals, then transforming them back into normal form once they were through. Glendon and Lukan hadn't figured out how to shape-change, yet. Or had they?

"If you don't tell me, Glendon, your mother will extract the information from you. Do you want her mucking about with your feelings?"

Glendon had the grace to blush. Somehow he turned the expression into a scowl at the same time. Brevelan had a unique way of making the boys feel guilty and regretful for their infractions of rules. Her empathy projected her own hurt and disappointment into her children.

"Well, son, what were you wrestling with?"

Witchballs.

An image of giant globes, almost as large as Glendon, formed of moss and dirt and leaves, held together by a magic glue, formed in Jaylor's mind. He'd made witchballs for the boys—small ones—among their earliest toys. The balls had the advantage of being as light or heavy as a child could handle, easily replaced, never lost, and could be broken down with a thought before they crashed into some fragile object.

Who would have thought the clearing barrier was vulnerable to a witchball?

"How many rocks did you put into the center of the balls?" Jaylor had a brief nightmare of the boys forming their latest toy around a boulder and rolling it into the walls of the house.

No rocks, Glendon replied.

"Then what did you put into them?" Jaylor tried not to shout. Sometimes the boy's cryptic remarks made him wonder if Glendon might have been fathered by Old Baamin or maybe by a dragon.

Armor wrapped around Glendon and he seemed to fade into the natural colors of calubra ferns and everblue trees.

Jaylor concentrated hard on pushing his hand through his son's protection and grabbing the boy by the scruff of the neck. He wasn't Senior Magician for nothing. The boys had yet to figure how to keep him out. They tried, often, and he dreaded the day he couldn't break apart any spell they threw.

"What did you put into the witchballs, Glendon?"

Lightning probes.

Bolts of inquisitive magic whose sole purpose was to penetrate a given object or person for information.

"What did you learn from your probes?" Jaylor asked, trying very hard not to shake the boy and frighten him into silence.

Glendon panicked anyway. The armor around his small body thickened and thrust his father's grasp away with a jolt of energy. Before Jaylor could reassert his hold on his son, Glendon disappeared through the crack in the clearing.

Jack jerked his eyes and his mind away from the hideous wound on Shayla's wing, back to her face. She seemed to wince—as much as she could show expression—with each slight movement of her wing.

"Does it hurt?" he blurted, too astonished for tact.

Yes. She folded the wing abruptly.

Of its own volition, Jack's hand reached out to caress her long nose in sympathy. Inches from contact with her iridescent fur he pulled back, uncertain he had the right to make physical contact with her.

You may touch. The dragon dipped her head, butting into his still outstretched palm. He cupped his hand around her cheek and stroked the velvet softness. Instantly his shoulders relaxed and his mind stopped whirling.

The cranky jackdaw, absent for more than three days, chose that moment to circle and land on his head. A series of earsplitting croaks informed both man and dragon of his jealousy.

Jack reached up to pet the bird and received a painful peck on his hand in return.

"There's no pleasing you!" He brushed the bird away.

It hopped to Jack's foot, pecked at the loose sole of his journey-thin boots then leaped to Shayla's longest spinal ridge. That perch didn't seem to please the bird either. From Shayla's back, Corby flapped noisily into flight up the cliff walls to one of the irregular knobs standing sentinel over the valley.

Knobs of rock or crouching dragons?

Almost invisible against the darkening sky, the jackdaw hovered over a looming shape, voicing his displeasure with life in general and Jack in particular. Finally, Corby landed and quiet reigned in the valley once more. The jackdaw began to preen, seemingly quite satisfied that he had thoroughly upset everyone.

"King Darville has a burn on his left arm that won't heal. It looks just like that." Jack pointed to the ugly black wound. "At least I presume it still looks like that. I haven't had any contact with Coronnan for three years," he babbled, unable to avert his eyes.

My king still wears the Coraurlia. His body continues to bear the wounds of his battle with the evil ones. He will not heal until I heal. He has learned to live with his pain, as have I. We both grow weary of the burden.

"I'm not a healer, but I have observed Brevelan. I helped her once when she tried to draw magic out of King Darville's wound. Maybe I can do something with the wing—enough to let you fly home."

That is why I sent for you.

"I'm sorry I took so long getting here." Jack hung his head. If he hadn't unleashed that terrible firebomb in Marnak's camp . . . if he had sent a summons to Jaylor earlier . . . if he hadn't been so arrogant and gotten lost in the void . . .

A million "what if's" couldn't change the past or bring back the dead. He could only try to improve the present.

You were not strong enough, or wise enough to heal anyone when my mate set you on your path. The passage of seasons has been long, but not without rewards. When you and your magic were mature enough, the dragons revived your mind so that you would once more seek to finish your quest.

"My staff? The dragons put the staff into my hand?"

We kept the staff hidden. It would have sought you earlier, but you were not ready to awaken. When your mind had healed enough to

*understand your mistakes and accept your destiny, we allowed it to
find you.*

Jack smiled as he fondled the length of twisting oak. The staff
was a part of himself, linked to his magic. Of course it would have
rolled through the mine seeking him when they were first separated.

Only then did he notice the dozen silvery shapes hiding in the
shadows of smaller side falls that fed into the pool.

"You mated again! Or are these little ones three years old?" A
smile spread through Jack at the sight of the pretty dragonets, all
silvery and dainty, climbing onto rocks to sun themselves. He
counted ten little dragons—if one could consider a winged creature
the size of a pack steed to be small—with pale colors beginning to
emerge on spinal ridges and wing tips. Two each of blue, green, and
yellow, the usual colors of dragon males. Still clinging to the protection of tumbling mist sat a shy pair tinged a rare purple. The last two
dragon children who swam to Shayla's side showed no trace of color
of their own. The immature females reflected light; sun and water
shimmering into a myriad of rainbows.

*My other children seek lairs of their own and will mate at the end
of the next century.* A note of maternal pride colored Shayla's mental
voice. She seemed brighter and her eyes more colorful as images of
the eleven older dragonets grown strong, flashed into Jack's mind.

"Two purples in this litter?" Jack asked. "Isn't that supposed to be
impossible to have two purples alive at the same time?"

Shayla hunched her shoulders in a dragon shrug. (*Destinies I
cannot control determine the colors of my children.*) She glanced at
each of her offspring. Love seemed to radiate from her in almost
visible waves.

*I do not wish to birth a third litter in this land. When you have
rested and eaten, we will begin the healing.*

"We don't have long," Jack informed her. "Someone approaches
from the south."

The Simeon comes but once a year to renew the pain. Shayla's eyes
grew dull. *'Tis not time for him.*

"Unless his spy summoned him. He seeks new recruits for the coven. He wants me to fill an opening."

Do you wish such a fate? No emotion touched Shayla's voice. Yet Jack felt the great anger filling her to near bursting. He didn't want to be on the receiving end of her fury. Stargods help Simeon when she broke free of this beautiful prison.

"I have no love for King Simeon or his coven. They wreak havoc with each spell they throw." Jack affirmed.

Then come behind the waterfall. There is time for you to dine and sleep. We begin our work at dawn. When the agents of my enemy arrive, we will be long gone.

"If I can remember the spell," Jack muttered to himself as he gathered the two packs and assisted the drooping Fraank around the edges of the pool. On the far left side, a narrow path led to a deep undercut behind the waterfall. A perfect hiding place or a dead-end trap?

Chapter Twenty-Three

I have found the lacemaker. She hides within an enclave owned by a Rover. She possesses knowledge damning to Simeon. Which does the king fear more, the knowledge or the Rovers? Zolltarn's clan does not frighten me. I will have the knowledge and the lacemaker. Then I will have control over Simeon, king and sorcerer, as well.

Fraank looked better already. He sat, huddled over a fire—ignited by an attentive baby dragon showing off his newly learned trick of blowing fire. The older man absorbed warmth while a meal of venison and tubers roasted over the coals. A yellow-tipped dragonet crouched beside the weary man, much like an oversized puppy anxiously protecting its master.

This was no puppy. Chromin, as Shayla had named the dragonet, stood nearly as tall as Jack and probably weighed twice as much. His wings were wide enough and strong enough to support his body mass while flying. The hooked talons at wing elbow, wing tip, and on all four feet could flay man or crush the neck of a goat. He was not yet telepathic with humans.

Jack watched his traveling companion lean against Chromin's flank. Tension left Fraank's spine and neck as his body slumped further against the dragonet. In moments Fraank was asleep against his warm and furry pillow.

Relieved at the ease Fraank had finally found, Jack relaxed against a nest of dried leaves and blankets, easy in mind and body for the first time in years. For a while they were safe, warm, and dry. He could turn his mind toward matters beyond survival.

"Your mate, the blue-tipped dragon who showed me this place in a dragon-dream, promised me information when I found you."

You desire to know of your family.

"I have a right to know my own history!" The familiar anger of his youth began to curl within Jack's empty stomach. He clamped down on a temper he knew could soon boil out of control.

Are you certain you want to know these things?

"I must. How can I know who I am if I know nothing of my parentage and childhood? I need to know if the name I chose for myself is truly mine and I am worthy of it."

You make your own life, your own future.

"But my past shaped me."

At moonrise, you may climb to the second highest peak above the waterfall. The dragon who wears magician blue on his wings and spines will speak to you there.

"Is there a path, or must I levitate up there?" Levitation took more energy than Jack thought he could muster right now.

A staircase exists. You must use your special gifts of sight beyond sight to find it.

Sight beyond sight. That meant magic and only his bodily strength to draw upon. Time to refuel. "I think that venison is cooked enough."

Fraank woke up as Jack approached the fire pit. Chromin looked at them both with a sparkle of mischief in his eye. Maybe it was just a reflection of the firelight. The baby dragon eyed the venison and then cocked his long head at the two men. Jack caught a glimmer of a thought.

"Don't you dare add any more char to *my* roast!" Jack lunged to restrain Chromin from breathing more fire upon the deer carcass. He wrapped both hands around the silvery muzzle.

Chromin's surprise jolted Jack off his feet. Telepathic communication dribbled into Jack's mind as Chromin scooted backward on the cave floor, closer to his mother. A few incoherent thoughts and a gibberish of dragon language fed a confusion of images. Still Jack clung to the dragon's muzzle, afraid to let go, lest he be the next target of fiery experiments.

Shayla appeared at his side, looming tall and protective over her youngster. Jack cringed away from her powerful talons.

You seem to have awakened the boy's mind. Now we must teach him to speak in words instead of baby pictures, Shayla chuckled. With a nudge of her muzzle against Chromin and a wink of her enormous eye at Jack, she sent the child to his nest for the night.

"Sight beyond sight," Jack muttered to himself as he stretched his hands above him, seeking the next handhold on the cliff wall. The moon rose above his left shoulder, nearly full in a hazy sky. Diffuse light washed the cliff in a uniform pearly gloss. "I need eyes in my hands and feet for this climb." He clung to the next narrow indentation.

Tired and panting, he pulled himself up another step. If the "stairs" were a little wider, he'd probably crawl. As it was, the indentations weren't wide enough to support one knee let alone two. The ledge he'd stood upon during his dragon-dream of this valley had been this narrow.

The moon rose higher. An irregular knob appeared above Jack, outlined in an eerie shimmer of magic and moonlight. A halo of deep blue hovered around the form. The dragon who wore magician blue.

Jack took another step and another, and then he was within the blue aura.

"Sir?" Jack tentatively probed the slumbering dragon with mind and words.

You are late again, Boy. The huge male didn't stir from his crouched pose, muzzle buried in a pillow of forepaws and encircling tail.

"I ran into some problems along the way," Jack defended himself. He wasn't a naive adolescent any more to bow to just any authoritative voice and manner.

Did you learn anything from your brash mistakes? The dragon opened one eye briefly, as if to verify his presence. Faceted points caught the moonlight and sparked with emotions Jack couldn't read. Then the translucent membrane dropped and the dragon seemed to slumber once more.

"My experiences taught me many things about the man I can be. Only you have the key to the child I was."

You won't like the story I have to tell.

"I don't like not knowing more. I have a right to know who I am, where I come from, what my true name is."

Jack suits you fine; more honestly than Yaakke.

"But what name was I given at birth? No mother would leave a child unnamed. You promised to tell me when I found Shayla!"

The lack of this knowledge burns deep within you. That yearning must be satisfied or you will not have the concentration to work the healing spells. Come. The nameless dragon heaved himself up onto his hind legs in a curiously graceful undulation for so large a creature. He stretched his spine and reached his shorter forelegs toward the night sky as if embracing the moon. Once more his eyes were open, light lancing from the facets.

Observe, Jack. Watch your past and learn from the mistakes of others.

Cold swirls of blue, green, and golden light closed around Jack. He fell through the dancing star points of the jeweled dragon eyes into a void. Falling, falling, farther and farther away from himself through the lives of dozens of people and into the past.

Endless moments flowed through the wheel of the stars. And still he fell. His body learned the streams of movement through this strange void, stretched out and flew.

Now you have enough of the dragon within you to observe the past. Remember the dragon within you and within every magician when next you have a need to visit with those who have gone before. Watch!

"Observe what?" A strange/familiar landscape took shape around him. He'd been here before. But not at this moment in time. The trees were not quite the right shape and the sledge-ruts in the road were too deep. "Where are we?"

He looked around again, sensing and smelling familiarity rather than understanding it. There was a road running toward the southern border, just outside Brevelan's village, that looked something like this. He scanned the horizon. Yes. The creek plodded along its path beyond the dip in the meadow and on toward the Great Bay.

The water was clear and clean, not choked with mud and debris from the floods that had plagued Coronnan when last he saw this place. Birds sang in the fully leafed oak trees that should have their roots underwater but sat back from the bank by several steed lengths.

He measured the angle of the sun against the length of the shadows. Early morning, past the summer solstice. Jack and Fraank had left the mine just after the Vernal Equinox, only a few weeks ago.

"Maybe I should ask, 'When are we?'"

The dragon said nothing. Jack looked over his shoulder to where he sensed the beast hovered. All he saw was the dim outline of an old man in colorless flowing robes. Then he looked at himself. Almost transparent and wearing the black trews and vest of a Rover. His shirt appeared to be pale yellow, but so much of the green fields around him shone through the fabric and his skin, he couldn't be sure.

Watch and listen, the dragon ordered.

Just then a man and woman riding double on a fleet steed appeared on the road, coming from the north. The steed was black and sleek, bred for speed. Sweat shone on its glossy coat. They might be proceeding at a stately pace now, but just recently, the riders had pushed the steed in an all-out race.

The man in the front, clad in shiny black leather to match his mount, kept looking over his shoulder for signs of pursuit. The woman, perched behind the saddle, clung to his belt. She rode astride with her brightly colored skirts hiked up above her knees. Shapely legs and bare feet clutched the heaving sides of the steed.

"Rovers," Jack spat. Three years ago, Jack had a few encounters with Zolltarn, king of the Rovers and his tribe. Rovers had their own codes of ethics and honor that had little to do with the rest of civilization. Jack was convinced the entire race of wanderers would gladly slit a man's throat just to prove they could.

Dragons observe and learn. We do not judge.

"But ..."

Observe.

The mounted couple moved past Jack and his guide seeking all around them with their eyes. The young magician started to greet the passing pair and offer them directions. A heavy hand on his shoulder stopped his angry words. A human hand in shape and size. Prominent blue veins stood out on the backs of that nearly invisible hand, much like the colored veining on a dragon's wing.

We are ghosts in this time. Our souls dictate our forms. They cannot see you. We cannot interact. Only observe.

"Who are they?" The couple must be important, or the dragon wouldn't have brought him to this place and time.

The woman is your mother.

"Mamam?" Jack dredged up a baby memory of the name he

called her. He took a step as if to follow her. His body didn't seem to move. "My mother is a Rover? But Rovers keep their children, even half-breeds and orphans. I was abandoned at the poorhouse." Confusion dominated the churning emotions within him.

Observe her past. You are not yet born in this time frame.

"Does she have a name?" Anger and curiosity warred within Jack. Mamam looked so very beautiful. He'd been deprived of that beauty, and her love, all his life.

She had abandoned her infant son! He tried to keep his anger dominant and failed. She was so beautiful.

Her father is Zolltarn. He named her Kestra for the kahmsin eaglet he spotted at the moment of her birth.

"Kestra." Memories began to tickle Jack's mind. He knew that name. Somewhere he'd heard of a missing Kestra and her mythical child. Was he the lost child the Rovers searched for through all the lands?

The scene changed before Jack's eyes. The road twisted and dipped into the deep shadow of trees. His ghostly senses allowed him to see the shapes of hidden men within the darkness. Men who killed for pleasure and for the few small treasures carried by travelers.

Bandits were rare in Coronnan. Travelers, the natural prey of the lawless, were almost as rare. After the Great Wars of Disruption, villagers retained their suspicion of strangers and fears of marauding armies. Merchants passed from city to city, stronghold to village, in large caravans. Other citizens remained home, where they belonged.

Where had these desperate men come from?

Hanassa, the dragon answered him. These outlaws know the magic border is already crumbling in this remote sector. The Commune is not yet aware of how far or fast their magic decays.

Nestled in the mountains is the deep caldera of an extinct volcano. Lava tube tunnels and secret pathways lead into this hidden city. Exiled magicians, outlaws, and mercenaries live there and watch all three kingdoms for signs of weakness. Outsiders are not allowed in or out of the stronghold alive.

The name of the forbidden city struck dread in Jack's heart. Legends of the harsh life there and the cruelties of its inhabitants were the stuff of nightmares.

His nightmares.

Sometime in the past he'd been there.

The bandits raised a thin rope across the road. The Rover steed stumbled to his knees, twisting and bucking wildly to recover his balance. Kestra fell to the ground, rolling, instinctively protecting her belly.

Unable to aid the woman his heart reached out to, Jack watched helplessly as the bandits pulled Kestra's man from the steed and slit his throat. His pockets and saddlebags were emptied before he was fully dead. Three men wrestled the girl to the ground and mounted her again and again, barely waiting for a comrade to finish before the next took his turn.

Kestra lay there, barely moving, not fighting lest her struggles lead to her death. Tears streamed down her face.

Disgust boiled in Jack's stomach as pain choked his throat and brought unwanted tears to his eyes. Despair made the air, his life and his body too heavy to manage.

"Which of the bastards is my father?"

Even as he spoke the words, the bandits carried Kestra off into the woods and across the already crumbling border, leaving her Rover guardian and the magnificent steed gutted in the middle of the road.

None of them. She was pregnant before she left Coronnan City.

Jack looked back at the dragon/man. Hope lifted his chin and his spirits.

"Who? The dead Rover there?"

No. She was ordered to lay with a great magician. The child was to give the tribe the magical power to open the border for the Rovers. They still seek that child.

"Zolltarn is my grandfather. My grandfather still lives! What about my father. Who is my father?" Jack tried to grab the dragon/man's shoulders and shake the information out of him. His hands slipped through air rather than touching solid flesh.

An aura of sadness clung to the old man. His eyes closed heavily. His long white mustaches dropped into this limp beard. *You have much to learn before you can know your father. When the time is right, you will be able to look within your heart for the answers you seek.*

Chapter Twenty-Four

Jack awoke to the predawn twitter of birds. The air around him smelled damp and chill. But he was warm and dry, his head pillowed on the foreleg of a dragon. A wide blue-tipped wing covered him better than any woven blanket.

He opened one eye to find the probing depths of a dragon eye staring at him.

You slept well?

"Yes, yes, I did," Jack replied, surprised to find his body free of stiffness and chill and his mind refreshed by deep, dreamless sleep.

A thousand questions assaulted his mind as he huddled next to the dragon for warmth. "Why do Zolltarn and the Rovers still seek the missing child of Kestra?" he asked the dragon. The magic border had totally disintegrated the moment Krej ensorcelled Shayla into a glass sculpture. When Jaylor had released Shayla from her prison, she had left Coronnan because Krej was still a power to be reckoned with on the Council of Provinces. The Commune hadn't been able to restore the border since. Rovers could come and go without Kestra's child to break down the magical barrier.

Rovers keep their own close. No one within the tribe is abandoned, exiled, or orphaned. The dragon answered.

"So how did I end up in the poorhouse as a toddler—maybe as old as three or five? Why wasn't Kestra rescued?"

Zolltarn was told that his daughter died after the attack. He mourned her but didn't have the heart to seek further news. Yet rumors of the child persisted. Zolltarn seeks to keep Rover magic within his Rover tribe.

"Those years in Hanassa must have been hell for my mother."

Kestra escaped through trickery. She fled with you into the teeth of a wicked storm. Merchants found her frozen to death on the road. You were still alive, sheltered by her dead body. They took you to Coronnan City, to the poorhouse, where you were cared for until you were big enough to work in the University kitchens. The merchants guessed you to be about a year old, based upon your size and inability—or unwillingness—to communicate. In truth, you were nearly four.

Now Jack couldn't banish the memories of cold and fear, of loneliness and bewilderment that his mother wouldn't wake up and feed him. Grief clogged his eyes and his throat. "She did love me!" he asserted. "She must have loved me to give up her life protecting me." Anyone could love a baby. Who cared for Jack as a boy and a man? Now that Brevelan and Jaylor were gone, he had no one except for Fraank's reluctant companionship and a cranky jackdaw who acted as a familiar only when the bird chose.

Shadows flickered across the dragon's eyes. Jack closed his own sight away from the shifting points of light lest he be enticed into another dragon-dream. The vision of his mother had shaken him more than he thought possible. For a few brief seconds he'd experienced a moment of kinship with her, a rarity in his lonely life.

He'd been abandoned again when Baamin died. The old man had given up on life too easily. Had Kestra given up rather than face the memories of rape and despair?

"I guess I'd better find Zolltarn when I've finished the healing spell." He resigned himself to facing the wily Rover.

The Rovers will keep you with them, bind you to their cause, but you will never be fully a member of the tribe. The dragon appeared suddenly alert. His wings spread slightly, almost protectively over Jack. *You have not been raised to their ways. The geas they will impose on you to keep you close will resemble the magic poison in Shayla that keeps her prisoner in this valley. A beautiful prison with ample food and space to breed, but she is chained here by pain and coercion, like a slave.* The blue-tipped horns above the dragon's eye ridges seemed to glow in the darkness. Unnatural blue sparks flared from each of his spines and wing veins.

"I have known slavery," Jack mused. "I will never succumb to that evil again. Nor will I allow another to. At dawn I will do my best to heal Shayla no matter the cost."

You may need more strength and wisdom than you are able to give.

"I'd rather die trying to help Shayla than be a slave again," Jack resolved. "Shayla's health and well-being affect more people than I ever will. Who will miss me if I give my all to this spell?"

The time has come for you to descend to the lair. Eat and drink well, for you will need all of your strength, and mine as well to throw the necessary magic.

"I can't gather dragon magic," Jack replied sadly. That inability had caused him to be rejected and shunned at the University. Because he couldn't gather the ethereal component of magic, he had been considered retarded, denied any rights, even the right to a name. He saw that, too, as a form of slavery.

The nameless dragon lifted one eye ridge in silent query. For a moment he looked just like the cranky jackdaw when he lifted those odd white feathers above his eyes, or like Old Baamin cocking a bushy eyebrow at an errant apprentice. Jack dismissed the image as he took the first steps down the almost visible staircase.

Jack paused, one foot extended toward the first step down. "Why didn't Shayla or one of the other males give Simeon a dragon-dream to lead him astray?"

He is immune to the visions we weave, as are all descendants of Hanassa.

"Simeon was born in Hanassa, son of the exiled princess of Rossemeyer," Jack sighed. He'd been born in Hanassa, too. Why wasn't he immune? His Rover blood perhaps?

The dragon didn't offer any more explanation.

"Shayla must be able to fly away before the next solstice." Jack recognized the growing need within him to confront the power-hungry king who had brought so much pain and suffering to the Three Kingdoms. "I will deal with The Simeon when I have healed Shayla and seen her safely home," he promised himself.

Halfway down the stairs, a sense of vertigo overtook him. The smell of woodsmoke on the wind and the rising sun over hilltops dumped him back into the dragon-dream he had experienced three years ago, the first time he had met the unnamed blue-tip. He sniffed the air, agitated that the fire might sweep down Shayla's valley and destroy her refuge as well as the pristine beauty of the place.

"I have been here before. In my first dragon-dream."

'Tis friendly fire.

"Friendly?"

'Tisn't wild. The chuckle behind the mental voice stopped Jack more than the command.

"Explain, please." Jack continued to stare out across the hills, seeking the source of the fire and the presence of the strangers who approached.

Villagers slash and burn to clear fields for planting. Not the most efficient means, but all they know. They defy The Simeon's policy of exploiting the land for export. That way leads to starvation for all— human, animal, and plant life. These people begin to work the land, to nourish it with crops and with their toil. A friendly fire can be the beginning of life.

"Margit! Damn it, girl, where are you hiding?" Darville yelled as he carried Mikka to their bed. "Margit!"

Mikka moaned and clutched her belly.

"Easy, my love. I'm getting help."

"Why now?" Mikka sobbed. "Why must I lose the baby now. I carried her so long, nearly five moons." She clung to her husband, not letting him leave her on the bed.

"Margit!" Darville gently disengaged Mikka's hands where they clutched his tunic. He rubbed at the raw wound in his left arm, newly aggravated by carrying Mikka from her solar where she had collapsed in a pool of pain and blood.

A sneeze betrayed Margit's arrival before she spoke. The only time the girl didn't sneeze was when she was out of doors.

"Yes, Your Grace?" Margit dipped a curtsy as she skidded to a halt in the doorway. She breathed heavily as if she had run from the cellars.

"Summon Jaylor and Brevelan. We need them now. Hurry, girl." He shoved her toward the alcove where she slept.

"What? What am I supposed to do?" She turned big innocent eyes on him, gray-blue and wide as the Great Bay.

"I haven't time for your deceptions, Margit. I know you are Jaylor's apprentice and summon him on a regular basis. Now do it again. We need Brevelan here. The queen will lose the baby if she doesn't get here quickly."

"How'd you know, sir?" Margit asked as she fumbled with a fire-stick to light the candle. Frustrated by her hurry, she snapped her fingers and brought flame to the wick.

"I've been dodging Jaylor's tricks and magical pranks since I was fourteen. I knew he had a spy around somewhere. You're the most logical person."

"Yes, sir." She closed her eyes a moment. When she opened them again, they were slightly glazed, looking through her tiny shard of glass into far distances.

"Darville, she mustn't. It's not safe for Brevelan to come," Mikka protested weakly from the center of the bed. Her face had no more color in it than the white pillow slips.

"I don't care. Brevelan is the only healer I trust to help you. If anyone can save you and the baby, 'tis her." He didn't dare think about the possibility someone had slipped her another abortive, deliberately murdering their baby.

"Shayla, can your brats . . . um . . . children sing?" Jack gently pushed an inquisitive green-tipped youngster away from his pack. The dragon extended his lower jaw in a good imitation of a pout.

As fast as he separated one baby dragon from the packs, another breathed fire on the coals and burned the warming remains of last night's dinner. One of the purple-tipped dragonets scooped up a mouthful of water from the chuckling stream that ran through the cave, and sprayed it over the now blazing fire.

Jack nudged the helpful baby aside with his knee. A curious sensation of affection spread through him at the brief touch. He dismissed it. The dragonets were cute.

Then he fished the soggy, charred meat out of the coals, wondering just how hungry he really was.

Sing? Why do you wish the children to sing? Shayla spread her undamaged wing in a gesture to gather the dozen curious youngsters to her. The females and the shy purples came readily to her side. The more aggressive males lingered around the fire, packs, and pallets.

A sharp, high-pitched command, almost above human hearing, from the mother dragon sent the reluctant children scuttling to her.

Jack almost heard the order to behave in the back of his head. He pushed aside the compulsion to join the baby dragons under Shayla's wing. Another directive from Shayla nearly sent him outside with the dragonets for the morning's hunt.

Only one purple-tip remained, hidden behind his mother's flank.

Why do you wish my brats to sing? Shayla captured his gaze with her compelling jeweled eyes. No rancor dwelled within the sparkling facets, only a mother's good humor.

"The only healing spell I know is the one Brevelan used on Darville. *Song* is her medium. I was hoping the little ones could aid in the spell by carrying the harmony."

Alas, dragon songs are not for human ears. Your hearing would shatter should they lift their voices and they are not yet old enough to control communication between minds. However, you should be able to gather a little extra magic from this one. With her muzzle, she nudged the shy youngster crouched behind her. The purple-tip dug in his claws and refused to budge.

"Let him stay hidden, Shayla. I can't gather dragon magic."

Anyone can gather magic from a purple-tip, boy. Even you! the unnamed blue-tip bellowed into Jack's mental ears. *That's why they are so rare and only one lives to adulthood. The fate of our two has not yet been determined.*

Jack cocked his head skeptically, staring at the shy dragonet. "Can I really?"

The baby dragon inched forward with more prodding from his mother. Jack reached out to gently pet the sensitive knob of his unformed spiral horn in the middle of his forehead.

Amaranth, the baby dragon nearly purred with pleasure.

Faint traces of power tingled beneath Jack's fingertips. Just like tapping a ley line!

"How much magic can I take from Amaranth without damaging him?"

As much as you can. You will not damage him. However, he is only a baby and you have no other magician to combine with you. You must remain in physical contact with him at all times during the spell, Shayla informed him.

"I'll take whatever help I can get.

"I used to be considered a decent tenor." Fraank roused from his pallet. A coughing fit overtook him. He rolled to his knees, slumping forward weakly until the racking spasms passed.

"Think you can support a note for the duration of a spell?" Jack asked skeptically. He waited for a reply that didn't come.

Fraank hung weakly in his kneeling position, drenched in cold sweat, panting for breath.

"When this spasm passes," he gasped, still too weak to stand.

"What about your mates?" Jack asked Shayla, not willing to accept Fraank's offer.

They may listen and try to support your Song. Human music is not a dragon talent.

Jack hastily swallowed a few more bites of his breakfast for fuel. Surprisingly, the meal wasn't ruined. He ate some more and washed it down with fresh, cold spring water and added a handful of dried fruit from his pack.

"Let's get started," he announced loudly, hoping a few of the male dragons might be listening. If they could harmonize at all, they'd help.

He knelt beside Shayla, touching her damaged wing with his left hand while his right arm draped around Amaranth's neck. A first deep breath cleared Jack's mind. The second breath on three counts sharpened his vision and brought out the auras surrounding everything within the cave, animate, plant, and mineral. The third breath triggered his trance and gave him access to the void.

Awareness of sight and sound, place and time faded. Only Shayla existed with him. She entered his mind, he became the dragon, they melded into one being, one knowledge, one soul. The horrible burning wound engulfed them both.

After the first jolt of sharp pain, awareness of the wound receded to a constant throbbing burn.

Jack sounded a deep note to counteract the hot ache and residual dull misery left by Simeon's evil.

A major fifth above the first note centered the black pain to a single location in his left arm. No longer did it radiate and infect his entire body.

Behind, above, and within him a second voice found the tenor note above his bass. Yet another male voice brought in the harmonic third.

A distant memory of Brevelan's clear soprano soaring through a melody lighted within Jack. He echoed the *Song* in his own vocal range.

The tune slid around and under the black burn, encapsulating it in magic. The wound lifted clear of delicate wing membranes, a visible entity pulsing and angry, yet contained by the magic of the *Song*. The wound sought to break free of the spell, sending new roots toward the dragon wing. Jack pushed it farther away, commanding it to dissolve. It resisted and drained strength from the *Singers*.

Jack fought the urge to collapse and forget his spell. He drew strength from Amaranth. He pushed on the living entity that sought to return to Shayla's wing, the source of its nourishment. A new root snaked free of the magic. He needed to send the blackness back into the void from whence it came.

He pushed harder with Amaranth's help.

The tenor notes cracked in a sputtering cough.

The second bass soared upward, beyond human hearing trying to compensate with a winding harmony. The earsplitting shriek of a dragon voice *Singing* shattered Jack's concentration. Amaranth broke free of his touch.

Jack fell, fell, fell, away from the void, out of unity with Shayla, back into his shuddering body. Shaking hands covered his ears in a futile attempt to shut out the new pain in his physical ears. He rolled into a fetal ball.

Blackness descended upon him as the black wound crashed back into Shayla's wing.

He had failed.

Chapter Twenty-Five

Jaylor and Brevelan crept quietly along the dank tunnels beneath Palace Reveta Tristile. Jaylor brought a ball of witchlight to his right hand. His twisted staff, held in his dominant left hand, hummed quietly. Wariness crawled along his spine like a swarm of dormant bees—ready to turn violent at any wrong move.

Brevelan inched behind him, drawing her shawl closer around her shoulders against the chill, subterranean dampness. Both of them stretched their senses for the presence of Council guards or witch-sniffers who might reawaken the zeal of the Gnostic Utilitarians.

"Mikka needs us. We have to hurry." Brevelan strode forward, ahead of the witchlight and Jaylor's protection.

"Slow down, Brevelan. Are you sure the transport spell didn't hurt you or the baby?"

"I'm fine. Now hurry. I sense her pain." She grabbed the witchlight from him and stepped forward with a determination that shouldn't have surprised Jaylor.

He shook his head in bewilderment. Only a true emergency

would pry Brevelan away from the clearing and her two sons. She wouldn't move when he believed their secret location compromised. But Mikka's health demanded her immediate attention.

Three determined apprentices watched Glendon and Lukan back at the University. Hopefully the apprentices wouldn't have to call in reinforcements to keep the boys under control and within the confines of the apprentice dormitory.

Jaylor gestured silently at a branch in the tunnel; their pathway lay to the right.

None of the ever-present algae marred the stone steps leading up to the hidden doorway behind a wardrobe cabinet. Recently scrubbed or well used? Since his teenage escapades with Jaylor's band of renegade town boys, Darville had been one to seek regular and anonymous escape from his royal duties. The tunnels had provided him with easy exits from almost every part of the palace.

How did the king pass unnoticed among his people now, with his damaged left arm in a sling?

Three raps on the thick door with the butt of Jaylor's staff, followed by two more short knocks, signaled their arrival. Only a few moments had passed since Margit had summoned them. A few desperate words, then she'd broken the communication to help the queen.

The heavy wood portal slid aside slowly and silently. Jaylor hesitated before stepping through the portal. No friendly face greeted him.

"Go on, Jaylor." Brevelan pushed him through the small opening. "I can't sense Mikka's emotions, only Darville's."

Cautiously Jaylor poked his nose through the opening, ready to duck beneath his armor should any menace greet him.

"At last!" A very pale Margit grabbed his arm and pulled him through the tangle of gowns and scarves that cluttered the cabinet. Worry creased her brow.

Jaylor turned back to give Brevelan assistance through the

wardrobe. The presence of twins in her womb made her bulkier and more awkward than usual.

His eyes sought Mikka and Darville as soon as Brevelan planted both feet on the carpeted floor. Mikka lay on the bed, pale and unmoving. Darville knelt beside her, holding her hand as if he could will his strength into her.

The queen's rich gown of rusty-brown silk revealed only the barest traces of the baby she had carried almost five full moons. The neckline dipped considerably lower than most thought modest, almost to the nipples. She was so proud of her pregnancy, she had reverted to the fashion of her home country, Rossemeyer. Among the desert dwellers who knew death's constant presence, a woman's breasts were considered a symbol of life. Mothers were granted the privilege of exposing their bosoms.

"At last. Brevelan, you've got to do something. Save her. Please!" Darville released his wife's hand and began pacing around the bed with his characteristic restlessness. His golden aura spread outward, swirling with the red and indigo of suppressed energy and serious thought.

Jaylor retracted his armor a little at a time while he watched Darville. Brevelan opened her satchel before she reached Mikka's side.

"Hot water, Margit. Fresh linens, and bowls to mix some potions. This isn't going to be easy. Maybe you'd be more useful keeping inquisitive courtiers out," Brevelan said to the maid. She rolled up her sleeves as she took Mikka's wrist, examining her pulse.

Margit left quickly, with a sigh of relief.

"She's afraid of cats," Jaylor whispered to Darville.

Concern shadowed Brevelan's eyes. She looked up at Jaylor and gestured for him to take Darville away.

"We're in the way, Roy." He guided his reluctant friend into the anteroom. Only Fred waited there, standing guard by the door. "Leave us, Fred. And keep everyone away. The king and queen need privacy."

The sergeant nodded and retreated. Quickly he brushed tears from his eyes before closing the door behind him.

"About time you two showed up," the king muttered. "I think someone poisoned Mikka to make her miscarry." The linen sling, dyed to match his black clothing, hung limply about his neck. Over the last three years, the support for his injured arm had become an accepted part of his wardrobe, almost a badge of honor. The constant pain had taken its toll on Darville. Much of his joy in living had faded. He no longer resembled the bouncy young wolf Brevelan had rescued from a snowstorm. He had become an impatient, prematurely old king.

"Who would do such a heinous thing?" Jaylor asked. Immediately his armor snapped into place. He lowered it deliberately to allow his TrueSight to seek traces of an alien presence.

"I don't know! Margit found traces of an abortive in Mikka's porridge a few days ago. Everything she eats is tested before she puts it into her mouth." Darville ran his hand through his mane of golden hair, forcing himself to deliberate calm. "We had word of a Gnul plot. I thought we'd taken care of them."

"The coven also has access to obscure poisons." Jaylor decided the rest of that story could wait.

Silence hovered between the men, the easy silence of long friendship. Even after three years of separation, the old companionship bound them together.

Darville flexed and moved his injured arm stiffly up and down, trying to restore movement and circulation.

"Sit down, Roy. You're making me nervous. I'll get you some wine." Jaylor pushed his friend into the nearest chair.

"No. I need all my wits about me. This isn't the first miscarriage. But this one is more dangerous. She hasn't been well." He ran his hands through his hair again. They met resistance at his queue restraint. He ripped it off and flung it into a corner.

"I've had reports." Jaylor handed him a cup of wine. "Drink. You aren't helping Mikka when you're near to hysterics."

Darville sipped at the cup and put it aside. He returned to rubbing his arm.

"Does it itch?" Jaylor asked. "That's usually a sign of healing."

"I irritated it carrying Mikka in here from the solar. Fortunately she was alone. None of her women will summon a mundane healer or the Council until I order it."

"Let me look. Maybe I can ease the discomfort a little." Jaylor rolled up Darville's sleeve, being careful not to brush the black wound with the fabric. He focused his sight beyond sight onto the twisted black wound. A vibrant tingling and disorientation swamped his senses. In the distance, a soft echo of one of Brevelan's healing *Songs* teased his hearing.

The difference between this *Song* and the one brewing in the royal bedchamber bothered him. Deeper, less certain. What was happening?

"What are you doing?" Darville stared at the burn that snaked up his arm, almost from wrist to elbow. "I feel weird, something akin to when you used to transform me back and forth between man and wolf." The king rested his head on the back of the chair.

Jaylor's eyes lost focus. He closed them and shook his head clear of the dizziness. He looked again at Darville's wound. The blackness lifted several finger-lengths above the level of his arm. It shifted and writhed within some kind of barrier. Slender rootlets stretched out toward the living tissue it fed on. Some broke off and dissolved in the air. One, thicker and stronger than the others, almost touched the arm before quickly withdrawing into the black mass.

"What's happening?" Darville stared at the raw muscle on his arm where the wound had resided for three years.

"I don't know. Don't move." Jaylor pushed at the blackness with his finger. An envelope of magic pushed back.

A scream knifed through his mind and his ears. The blackness dropped back onto Darville's arm.

"Mikka!" The king was halfway to the door before he doubled over in pain.

"Not Mikka." Jaylor supported his friend back to the chair.

Brevelan appeared in the doorway. Her eyes asked her questions. Jaylor shrugged his answer.

"Mikka?" Darville looked up from his deep contemplation of the wound that had become a part of him.

Brevelan shook her head. "I can't save the baby. If we're lucky, she'll recover." Her jaw clenched and released.

Jaylor watched her effort to control her emotions. Death always robbed her of vitality. He worried that the death of Mikka's child might affect the unborn twins.

"You're healing, Darville! Thank the Stargods for some good news." Brevelan rushed to his side and grabbed his arm.

The king winced and jerked his arm back.

"Not completely," he said through gritted teeth.

"But it is better," Brevelan said. "The wound is smaller, the edges ragged as if scabs had begun to peel away. Is this tender?" Brevelan touched some pink and healthy skin right next to the blackness.

Hope blossomed in Jaylor's chest. If Darville's wound healed, what was happening to Shayla?

Darville fidgeted as if he needed to continue his wolflike prowl. He kept looking toward the inner room, toward Mikka.

"Stand still, Darville," Brevelan commanded in the same voice she used on her young sons—the same voice she had used to order Darville about when he was enchanted into the body of a golden wolf.

"That still hurts, Brevelan." The king grinned weakly in acknowledgment of her authority.

Jaylor peered over his wife's shoulder to examine the evidence of healing. His extended senses caught a scent of rotten magic beneath a clean aroma of growth. So different from the whiff of magic-gone-awry coming from the bedroom.

"The strangest sensation came over me." Darville flexed his arm once more and resumed his pacing.

Jaylor propped up the door with his back, his staff at hand, ready to focus any spell he might need to throw in a hurry if anyone else responded to the unnatural scream.

"Then my arm stopped aching," Darville continued. "That was really weird, suddenly losing the pain after all these years. I almost missed it. It's become so much a part of me. . . ." The king's gaze drifted toward his bedroom and his wife. Then he frowned in worry.

"Evidence suggests you got caught up in a magic spell directed at someone else. I wonder who? And where?" Jaylor moved to a small writing table and pulled out his glass. "Shayla is linked to that wound. I need to know if my journeymen found her."

Darville stared at the injured limb again. "Shouldn't you be with Mikka?" He looked from Brevelan to the inner room once more. Then he stepped decisively through the doorway.

"The wound is smaller, Darville. Not all of it returned to you. Whatever dissolved is gone for good," Brevelan said as she followed him back to the bed where Mikka lay pale and thin. "It's possible that the brief removal of the poison allowed more healing to take place underneath."

Mikka shifted uneasily. Brevelan shifted, too, as if experiencing the same discomfort as the queen. Then her head came up sharply and she turned her full attention, physical and empathic, onto Darville.

"Stop looking at me as if I am your patient, Brevelan. Mikka is the one who needs you." Darville knelt beside the bed. Mikka reached a hand out to him. He clasped it gently, kissing her fingertips.

"What happened out there, Darville?" Mikka asked weakly. "What sent Brevelan running to you?"

Mutely, Darville showed her his arm. "We think one of Jaylor's journeymen found Shayla and tried to heal her."

"I've had a sort of message from Yaakke. He'd have the strength and ingenuity to try a healing. I have no idea how to find him, I only know that he lives." Jaylor shook his head in dismay. "I knew I should have gone after Shayla myself."

Brevelan shot him a wrathful glance. He didn't pursue the subject.

"You have to locate the boy." Mikka turned her face away from her husband. A single tear trickled down her cheek. "We have to help him." She rolled to her side painfully, and curled into a ball. "So Darville can be well. So we can . . . I must . . ." She stopped abruptly. Tears choked her.

"Mikka!" Darville gathered her into his arms, heedless of his still painful wound. She buried her face in her husband's tunic. A brief shudder of her shoulders and a quiet sob betrayed her tears. When she finally turned her face back to Brevelan, she was calm and her tears dried. "I have to know, has the poison in Darville's blood affected our babies?"

"I don't think so." Brevelan's hand began a rhythmic rubbing of her belly, as if the babes she carried had become unusually active.

"Is it the black magic in my body that kills our children?" the king reiterated the question.

Jaylor stood back to study their auras while Brevelan asked more personal questions about the nature of the previous miscarriages. His vision clouded a moment as he thanked the Stargods for both his sons.

Sadness and love for Darville and Mikka threatened to dissolve his objectivity. Images of him and Darville working together, laughing together, playing together slid around his control.

He brought clarity back to his magic sight and found Darville's aura. The layers of colors were familiar, healthy but for the one black spot on the left side. The evidence of Janataea's malice was reduced in size and intensity.

Mikka's aura bothered him. Double layers represented herself and the cat spirit who had shared her body for over three years. The joining of the two souls was an unexpected side effect of a major spell thrown that fateful autumn of Darville's coronation. At the time, Mikka's two auras were distinct with separate layers and colors reflecting two individual personalities. Now the edges were blurred and blending together.

" 'Tis not the magic in Darville that hinders the growth of your babes in the womb," Brevelan said quietly.

"No, please, no!" Mikka cried.

Jaylor caught Darville's gaze as he stroked Mikka's unbound hair. The two men nodded to each other in acceptance of the inevitable.

"Do you wish the truth, Mikka?" Brevelan asked. "Or do you need to wait until you are stronger?"

Darville brought Mikka's right hand to his lips. "I love you, Mikka. No matter the cause, I would never do anything to hurt you. We have to know the truth if we are ever to overcome it."

She nodded, once more the proud, decisive queen. Only the paleness of her face against the pillows betrayed her physical weakness.

"The presence of the cat in your body, Mikka, interferes with your natural rhythms and humors. You cannot achieve the balance necessary to nurture a babe until you are separated from the cat," Brevelan said sadly.

"Then you must force the cat out of me. You had to leave the capital too quickly three years ago when it happened. You must do it now."

"The cat will not leave you willingly, even if I can find a host body for it. The two of you are bound together in an intricate interdependence," Jaylor protested.

"Do it, Jaylor!" Mikka demanded. "I don't want to share this body with anyone but my children."

"I will need time to research the spells and find a host body. I'll have to find Zolltarn, because he directed the original binding spell. You need to rest and recover your strength. Think about this decision for a time, Mikka. It may cost you your life."

"Then my husband will be free to find a new wife to bear him the heirs necessary to secure the peaceful succession of the dragon crown. We cannot allow Coronnan to be thrown into civil war again for lack of a clear succession."

"No, Mikka. I can't allow you to risk your life. There must be another way," Darville protested.

"Who will give you an heir?" Mikka asked. "Who in your family line but Lord Andrall's retarded son is left alive with royal de Draconis blood? Do you honestly want Rejiia, Krej's daughter, to rule after you?"

They both looked at Brevelan and Jaylor. Darville mouthed a name: "Glendon."

Numbness spread from Jaylor's gut to his head. How could Darville even think of Glendon as his heir? "No. Oh please don't ask this, Darville," he muttered over and over, shaking his head.

"My son is not your heir, Darville." Brevelan stiffened. "I will never give him to you."

"You have proof that Jaylor is the boy's father?" Darville challenged her with equal stiffness.

"You will never take my son from me, Darville. Not you. Not your Council. Not anyone." Brevelan marched toward the wardrobe. She paused and turned to face them, proud and defiant. "King Darville, I will take my son to Hanassa before I allow you to strip him of his magic and turn him into a coddled and captive prince."

"We must return to the clearing." Jaylor clasped her hand in his own. He couldn't believe his friend could ask such a thing. Even making allowances for Darville's grief, he didn't think him capable of such a request.

"Is Glendon my son, Brevelan?" Darville demanded.

She stepped into the wardrobe without answering.

"You have another child, Brevelan. You are destined to bear more. Please, can't you share one little boy with us who have none?" Mikka pleaded.

Some of his friends' empty pain invaded Jaylor. Darville and Jaylor had shared their youth and many dangers and wondrous adventures since. They'd shared Brevelan's bed on that long summer quest four years ago. They'd risked their lives for each other and for

Coronnan. Could either of them deny Coronnan an heir because Jaylor loved the child with hair and eyes as golden as the king's?

"If you can't separate my wife from the cat, Jaylor, Brevelan, then we need Glendon. The boy should be raised here, to learn all he'll need to know as the next king of Coronnan." Darville reached a plaintive hand toward Brevelan.

"No." Brevelan retreated to the tunnels and the route home.

Chapter Twenty-Six

"Forgive me, Shayla!" Jack lifted his heavy head to plead with the dragon.

Forgive me, Jack, the blue-tipped male dragon apologized.

"Sorry, Jack, I couldn't stop coughing," Fraank croaked hoarsely.

Amaranth whined in distress, seeking shelter behind his mother again.

Shayla said nothing. Her steedlike muzzle drooped almost to the floor of the cave. Wings sagging and eyes nearly closed, she swayed and stumbled to retain her balance.

The spell to heal the dragon had failed utterly.

Silence reigned in the lair while Jack continued to crouch, nurturing what little strength he had left.

"Brawck! Strangers come. Strangers come," Corby croaked. He swooped into the cave, circling and flapping in an agitated frenzy. Harsh caws echoed around the lair with penetrating shrillness.

"Where? When?" Jack asked the bird, head throbbing with each new sound. He stuck out his arm, hoping the jackdaw would land and cease his noisy complaints.

Corby dropped beside Jack, pecking anxiously at his clothes. "Brawck. Strangers come. Strangers come," the bird repeated over and over.

Get up, son! the blue-tip added his urging to the jackdaw. You have only a few hours to get out of the valley!

"Who comes?" Jack shook his head to clear it. "Why must I run?" How could he run, as exhausted as he was?

The agents of Simeon ride this way in haste. They will enslave you again if they find you.

Lanciar, the spy from the mine, had found reinforcements!

"I can't desert Shayla. They'll hurt her. I have to try to heal her again, so she can escape." Jack rose to his knees. A wave of nausea overtook him. He dropped his head into the cradle of his arms as black spots swam before his eyes. "There is no one else left to do it."

You cannot heal me while we are within the realm of The Simeon, Shayla said. Her mental voice was weak with weariness and pain. There is not enough magic to support your spell and you do not know how to gather the magic we provide.

"I can't leave you here," Jack protested. "If only you could fly to Coronnan. With one strong ley line beneath my feet I could draw enough magic to work the spell."

You have helped the pain a little. Not enough to allow me to fly.

"What you need is a patch," Fraank offered.

"A patch?" Hope brightened within Jack. His stomach settled and his vision cleared. "A patch. Something light, but dense so it will float on the air like a kite, but strong enough to support the wing. What can we use?" Mentally he sorted through the contents of the packs they had stolen from the mine storeroom. An extra shirt apiece for himself and Fraank. A rectangle of rough canvas for a tent in rainy weather. Some food and cooking oddments.

"We don't have anything like that with us, Jack," Fraank told him needlessly.

"In the villages we passed through, the women were weaving. If we coat the fabric with a spell to resemble candle wax?" Jack tried picturing the looms and cloth. "Too coarse and loosely woven," he dismissed that idea.

"What you need is a piece of lace," Fraank suggested. "Lace made from Tambrin!"

"Tambrin?" Jack's mind sped faster than he heard and comprehended.

"Thread spun from the inner bark of Tambootie saplings. It's very rare and expensive, but it makes the best lace in the world."

"Tambootie saplings," Jack groaned. Memories of his triumph at stopping a smuggler's ship full of immature trees weighed heavily on him. He remembered a long conversation with Fraank about the investment syndicate and the seedlings. If the ship had won through to SeLenicca three years ago, then the precious thread, with magic potential imbued in its fibers, would be plentiful now.

But if the ship had won through, Fraank probably wouldn't have gotten into trouble with King Simeon anyway and wound up in the mines beside Jack to give him that precious information now.

You must travel to Queen's City, Jack, Shayla ordered. There you will find what you need. You will find your destiny. Find it before The Simeon comes again at the Solstice.

She is correct, son. Today the servants of The Simeon come for you, not for Shayla. The dictatorial tones of the blue-tipped male brooked no argument.

"That's barely two moons from now!" Jack protested anyway. "Fraank and I will need nearly a full moon to get to the city."

"Then you must leave me behind." Fraank straightened his shoulders with pride. His throat convulsed with a suppressed cough. "You'll make the journey in a week or less without me holding you back."

"I can't leave you for Simeon's men to find and enslave again." Jack stumbled to his friend's side.

We will protect your friend as one of our own.

"I won't live to see my home again, Jack. We both know I'm

dying. You must seek out my daughter, Katrina, when you reach the city. She will help you find the right piece of lace."

"Will she be able to get this Tambrin thread?"

You must take gold to buy the thread, Shayla advised.

" 'Twould be easier to transport the trees to Queen's City for spinning than to find gold," Jack muttered.

Not a bad idea, son, the blue-tip added with a draconic chuckle. But dragons have gold. We treasure it nearly as much as humans do. I will fetch you some from our secret hoard.

"I have a name, Master Dragon!" Jack nearly stamped his foot in frustration.

You chose a name out of legend, the name of a man who saved Coronnan more than once. To use the name 'Yaakke, son of Yaacob the Usurper' you must earn it. Bring back a suitable piece of lace made of Tambrin before midsummer.

That was why he hadn't dredged his name out of his memory upon first awakening in the mine, nor used it since: he hadn't earned it yet.

Curses on Darville and his queen. They have named my sister's oldest son heir to Coronnan. A proclamation of legitimacy has been dispatched throughout the land. Curiously, the boy is to be left with his mother because of his young age. I wonder if Brevelan and Jaylor are unwilling to give up the child.

The rift in their friendship continues. They cannot join forces against me.

I am next in line to the throne. I must be heir, me or my child. I know the babe I carry is male. If I return to Coronnan and my hideous husband before the birth, Coronnan will be reminded of the true heirs. The people will support me and a child they will come to know over the distant bastard who is rumored to have great magic. Danger lies in the journey so close to my time. If only I had the transport spell!

Simeon has become useless to me. He is obsessed with the little lacemaker. Night and day he plots and schemes for her death, neglecting his royal duties and his place in the coven. If he is not careful, Queen Miranda will awaken from her coma and denounce him.

I have not the time to puzzle over this.

"You cannot forbid me my right to worship in the temple!" Katrina screamed at Owner Brunix. "Even slaves have the right to worship in the temple."

" 'Tis not I who forbids, but King Simeon," Brunix replied. "I have had this day a letter from him. If you leave the confines of this building for any reason, you will be arrested for treason."

"Treason? What am I supposed to have done? All day, every day, I am here, working." She paced a circle around her pillow stand in the center of the owner's private sitting room. Sunlight spilled through the real glass in the skylight. More precious light filtered into the room from the thin slices of mica that covered the windows. "From dawn to sunset, I sit here, making lace. I sit here until my back refuses to straighten and my eyes are full of sand. I work until my hands cramp from holding the bobbins hour after hour. I work here in silence without even a time-honored song to relieve the strain."

"I have not been privileged with the exact charges against you." Brunix's eyes strayed to the nearly finished shawl on Katrina's pillow. "Perhaps your treason has something to do with this?" He lifted the free end of gossamer lace made from silk spun almost as fine as the best linen.

"King Simeon rejected the original shawl as unworthy." Katrina wandered to one of the windows, unconsciously putting distance between herself and the owner. Her owner.

"Yet he offered to forgive your treason and eliminate the restrictions placed upon me in your articles of enslavement if I will give him the original shawl, the pattern, and any copies we have made. I have also had an anonymous offer to purchase the shawl for a vast amount of money."

"What?" Katrina's mind whirled.

The runes! Each symbol told an entire story. Tattia must have woven information into the design, information damaging to the king. She had to find out how to read the ancient language.

How? She couldn't even go to the temple anymore to seek out a priest who could read the strange symbols.

"What is in the shawl, Katrina? I can tell by your eyes that you know something." Brunix closed the distance between them. His tall frame loomed over her. An implied menace rested in his clenched fists.

"I do not know."

"Do not lie to me, Katrina Kaantille." He grabbed her arm and dragged her to the corner window. "Look down there, Katrina. Look at the palace guard who stands watch on my doorstep. His companion stands at the river entrance ready to arrest you on sight. What does Simeon fear from you and the shawl?"

"I . . . do not know." She shrank back from the window lest the guard see her.

"You need not fear him *yet*. I have summoned a band of my relatives and warded the building with Rover symbols. Enemies know better than to violate tribal sanctuary."

"The three yellow feathers tied with black string!" She had noticed the strange adornment hanging over every door on the ground floor yesterday on her way to the temple.

"Tell me what you do know before I summon those guards inside."

"You would lose your best lacemaker and all the designs that are still in my head." She couldn't trust Brunix. His ambitions and resentments ran too deep and complicated. Katrina had no idea if he would use the knowledge of a secret code woven into the original shawl—but not into her new pattern—to help or harm her.

"But if I arrange your death, or turn you over to the king, the ghost of your mother will cease to haunt my factory. The ghost of a suicide always follows blood kin to their death. Without Tattia Kaantille floating through my workroom, I could hire better lacemakers and designers. Her presence frightens off all but the most desperate. I have tolerated the ghost for three years in hopes of possessing you, body and soul." Still holding her arm he captured her mouth in a savage kiss. The heat of his body, the moisture of his mouth and the fierceness of his grasp brought shudders of revulsion to her knees and shoulders.

She wrenched free and turned her back to him. Hastily she wiped her mouth dry. The taste of him lingered.

"Why is it that everyone in your factory has seen the ghost of my mother but me? I have heard she might have been murdered by the palace guard and not committed suicide." Katrina refused to look at him. "Tattia is supposed to haunt me, not your workroom. And yet I am the only person who has not seen or felt her presence. Perhaps she haunts those who enslave me?"

"That, my dear Katrina, is a question only your mother can answer. And perhaps King Simeon. Would you like to ask him about it? Tell me the secret of the shawl!"

Jack stepped off a transport barge cloaked in a delusion of sandy blond hair and watery blue eyes. The few people he'd met on his journey south to Queen's City had taught him early that dark-eyed strangers were not trusted in SeLenicca.

Men who talked to birds weren't trusted either. Corby had instructions to keep his distance on this trek.

Jack had made good time, once he found the River Lenicc. People and goods moved down the river on a daily basis. Hardly anything or anyone moved upriver. Almost as if the waters drained the interior of life along with its soil as it roared to the sea.

No timber remained to hold the soil in place. Without the timber to cut and float down to the capital for sale, the people had no livelihood. They hadn't the knowledge to nurture the cleared land and turn it into crops or pasture land. Only a few had the courage to try.

So Jack joined the flood of people pouring into the capital looking for work, for food, for hope.

The streets and pathways nearest the docks were crowded with swarms of hungry people. Ragged children held up pitifully thin arms, entreating a bit of bread or a coin. Skinny young girls with eyes too large for their faces exposed their breasts in the age-old invitation to sell their bodies in hope of earning enough to keep them alive one more day.

None of them wore lace, wove it, or spun thread. He hadn't time to help all those who tugged at his heart with their pleas.

Swiftly he moved away from the river district and the grasping poor. Two streets inland brought an entirely different scene. Steed-drawn litters moved up and down broad thoroughfares. Elegantly dressed ladies with servants strolled along clean wooden sidewalks. Shops displayed the wealth of the world for sale to the few wealthy nobles.

Jack observed from the shadows. Lace abounded in this district. On clothing, decorating windows, as coin in the shops. All of it was attached to something or someone and none of the pieces was large enough to patch Shayla's wing.

When he looked closely, he realized that large numbers of the people were trading well-used pieces of lace for food. Few others bought or sold any of the bright trinkets or furnishings on display.

He headed uphill toward the palace. Fraank had said the best lace was made in the palace—supervised by the noble ladies of Queen Miranda's court.

Two men wearing the black uniforms of the city watch fell into step behind Jack. His spell of delusion covered only his hair and eyes. He didn't want to waste energy cloaking the rest of his body. What had seemed decent quality clothing in the country was too rough and simple for this wealthy neighborhood.

Too late to change the spell. The guards increased their pace to overtake him.

Jack stopped and turned to face the men. "Good sirs," he greeted them politely. "I've been sent with a message for one of the palace lacemakers. Perhaps you could direct me?" He refrained from tugging his forelock. That subservience seemed out of place.

The black-garbed men halted in confusion.

"Country folk aren't allowed in the palace," the taller of the two guards informed Jack.

"Give us the message and we'll pass it on to the palace guards. They'll see the lady receives your words," the other man added as he eased behind Jack, fingering iron manacles that hung from his belt.

Jack shuddered at the small clinking sounds the chain made with each movement the guard made. He'd had enough of manacles to last two lifetimes.

"I must speak to Mistress Kaantille myself, good sirs." Jack side-stepped to keep both guards and their hideous manacles in view.

"Kaantille!" the tall guard hissed in angry alarm.

"No daughter of a suicide would be allowed in the palace. Her father's a traitor, enslaved for his crimes." The manacles clanked as the shorter guard pulled them free of his belt.

"What kind of criminal are you that you need to speak to *her*?" The tall man tried to capture Jack's wrists.

Jack turned and ran, revulsion deep in his throat. He'd never submit to chains again.

"Stop him!" the short guard yelled brandishing the manacles. "Bring him to the gaol. King Simeon wants to know about anyone who has any connection at all to the Kaantilles."

Chapter Twenty-Seven

No magic sprang to Jack's hands for defense. Without ley lines to augment his natural reserves, his mild delusion took most of his talent. But he couldn't allow himself to be captured and dragged before King Simeon. His quest was too important.

He dropped the delusion that masked his staff. Instinct brought the tool up against the guard's chin with a resounding crack. The stout man staggered backward, fighting for balance and consciousness. Before the staff completed its upward arc, Jack swung it down and around into the tall man's chest.

The guard ducked back from the blow so the staff merely brushed the buttons of his uniform. In return he lashed out with a foot to Jack's groin. Jack deflected the kick into his thigh. Bone-numbing pain sent him staggering backward. His delusion slipped.

The black-clad man gasped and stared at Jack's dark hair and eyes.

"You want street fighting?" Jack ground out between clenched teeth. "I grew up fighting for scraps in alleys!" Almost recovered, Jack took advantage of the man's momentary distraction. He stood from his crouch, bringing the staff upright with him.

Right, left, right, and down he struck the guard. Step by step, Jack pushed the tallest man into a narrow passage between two houses. In the shadowed privacy of a hedge he let his fists fly to jaw and gut. He caught his opponent behind the knee with a foot in a blow meant to damage the hamstring.

In moments the fight was over and Jack was running back the way he had come. Running toward the river district, where he could blend into the crowd and disappear.

As he rounded a corner, he heard the shorter guard gasp, "A magician! He changed his hair and eye color. A dark-eyed magician. He's the one with the price on his head. After him!"

Jack increased his pace. He elbowed merchants and shoppers aside in his headlong run. His foot caught the support pole of a market booth. Wooden poles and canvas awnings collapsed in the road behind him.

Guards stumbled. Ladies screamed. Men cursed.

Shadows from tall buildings invited Jack. He wrapped the growing darkness around him while he caught his breath. A cough born of mine dust threatened to choke him. He held his breath and melted against a brick wall.

The guards called for other men in black to assist them. A troop of seven stomped down the alley where Jack hid. He willed himself into silent immobility, knowing that color and movement caught the eye. His pursuers passed him by without a glance.

When the city watch turned a corner, Jack drifted away in a new direction. He had three more broad streets to cross before he reached the crowded industrial area. He tried a new delusion. Silver hair, stooped shoulders, a fine green cloak. His staff became a cane to assist his shuffling steps.

None of the agitated citizens looked at him twice. He crossed the first street. Large shops gave way to smaller stores with dwellings atop.

He crossed the second street and caught a glimpse of the marching troop of the city watch, now grown to twelve. He paused to cement the delusion in place.

The dozen men in black turned back onto the same route Jack followed. One man in the lead sniffed right and left, his right arm straight out before him. His nose wrinkled and he tested the air again. "There!" the witch-sniffer cried and pointed. "That old man, he's a magician."

"King Simeon has offered a year's pay for his head. Two years' pay for each of us if we catch him alive!"

Jack dropped the energy-draining delusion and ran.

The crowds increased. Jack found himself pushing and shoving innocent bystanders into the filthy gutters. Footsteps pounded hard behind him. The city watch gained on him. He needed a hiding place.

Large stone factories and warehouses crowded the narrowing streets. Shadows reached out to encircle him. He smelled the damp of the river and the tar used to coat ship hulls. Memories of Coronnan City assaulted and confused him. He stumbled on unfamiliar cobblestones up a curb into a green-painted door.

The latch was open and he fell into a narrow corridor. An unseen hand closed the door firmly behind him.

"A rather unseemly entrance for my new night watchman." An extremely tall and gaunt man dressed in fine black tunic and trews glared at Jack.

"Sorry, sir, I tripped on the curbing. I . . . I thought I was late and ran too fast," Jack stammered. His years as a drudge had taught him to dissemble rather than catch hell for imagined crimes and misdemeanors.

"Well, you are late. And you are short. The Rover chieftain promised me a strong man who could frighten off intruders, thieves, and spies."

Spies and Rovers? Jack wondered what he had stumbled into.

Was escape from the city watch worth the risk of an even more dangerous situation?

"Oh, but I am strong, sir," Jack found himself saying. He flexed his arms to show off his muscles. Three years of wielding a sledge hammer had added considerable bulk to his shoulders and chest. "And I know how to fight." To emphasize that point he put on his most intimidating expression and stared into the eyes of his potential employer. Eyes that were as dark as his own and full of Rover deceit.

That boy is here!

I cannot blame the mundanes of the city watch for losing him. He outsmarted me before with his transport spell. Lanciar lost track of him a week ago. How does he find enough magic in this cursed land to support such a spell?

I shall find out. Simeon must be forced to turn his attention to finding the boy. I have not the strength. The babe draws all of my energy and concentration. Perhaps I shall have to force an early birth so that I can devote my time and strength to something else. My father's wife will welcome the opportunity to raise my child in secret exile.

"Do you have a name, young man?" The dark-eyed factory owner asked.

"Jack." He'd learned at least that this was a factory, and rival factory owners had been trying to steal designs from the tall man who bore the heritage of the Rovers in his eyes. Just as Jack did.

"Jack What?" One long sandy-blond eyebrow rose above the dark eyes so that it looked like a sideways question mark.

"Just Jack."

"A bastard, eh." The owner shrugged and led the way down the long corridor. "Here on the ground floor are my offices and the warehouse." He flung open a white-painted, wooden door on the right to reveal crates piled high. The storage area took up most of the building surrounding the stark and utilitarian office. A much wider double door opened from the back of the building directly onto the docks. Six men milled around an open crate while stevedores from a waiting ship lounged upon more crates.

"Why aren't you men at work?" The factory owner's voice dripped disdain for his employees.

"Sorry, Owner Brunix." One nondescript man of middle age separated himself from the others and approached Jack and the owner.

Now Jack had a name to attach to his new employer. "Sir, this crate is short three reels of lace. That new design you wanted me to check special. It was in with the rest of the shipment yesterday when I packed it. But now it's gone."

"Cursed thieves!" Rage darkened the owner's skin to a dark sunburn. *Too stupid to respect Rover wards!*

The thought leaked through without Jack opening his mind. No further explanation followed the one angry explosion.

Owner Brunix's mind closed up once more. Rover tribes tended to have natural armor around their thoughts. What was so important about the wards that his thoughts leaked out?

So this was a lace factory. Luck or the Stargods had led him to a place to start looking for Mistress Kaantille. Or lacking her, he would have access to the delicate fabric he needed for Shayla.

His eyes searched every corner of the warehouse for clues. When the sealed crates revealed nothing but shadows, he allowed his other senses to open. "Listening" was much harder here, but easier than true magic. He only allowed himself to eavesdrop when he had no other course of action.

The stevedores were laughing among themselves at the free

leisure while the warehouse crew puzzled over the theft. The men who worked for Owner Brunix quaked inwardly in fear that they would lose their jobs. Work was hard to come by in SeLenicca. The only alternative to homelessness and starvation was the army. That life might provide a man with food and a tent over his head, but it provided nothing for his family unless they became camp followers. None of these men wanted their wives and daughters in so vulnerable a position that they could fall into the role of prostitute for an entire troop of battle-hardened men.

"I sent word to our chieftain that I needed a night watchman. Someone special who can stop these thefts. That will be your job, Jack." Owner Brunix closed his mouth as tightly as his mind. His eyes, too, searched the cavernous room for unseen thieves. Then his expression softened a little. "I had to fire the last night watchman. He drank and fell asleep once too often. I believe my rivals provided the whiskey."

"Whiskey has never crossed my lips, sir, and probably never will," Jack affirmed. And it hadn't. In Coronnan, the thick, sweet—and potent—beta'arack, distilled from treacle betas in Rossemeyer, was the preferred hard liquor. Grain had more profitable and practical uses in Coronnan—uses like bread and winter feed for cattle; it wasn't wasted on whiskey. Since Queen Mikka from Rossemeyer had married King Darville and increased trade without tariff between the two countries, SeLenese whiskey was much more expensive than beta'arack.

SeLenicca never traded with the desert homeland of Queen Rossemikka, so they wouldn't have beta'arack. Indeed, Queen Mikka's marriage to King Darville had precipitated the war between SeLenicca and Coronnan.

"I have no uses for drunkards, Watchman Jack. Remember that and report to me if anyone offers you a bribe. You," Brunix pointed to the warehouse foreman, "complete the order for that crate with the reserve reels of lace in my office. The rest of you, get back to work!" Brunix turned on his heel and marched out of the warehouse.

Jack followed the owner's rapid steps up a rickety wooden staircase to the first floor. Again he was met with a long narrow corridor running the length of the building. Two doorways on each side broke the bare walls.

"Male employees sleep on the right. The far door is the bath." Brunix gestured to the appropriate door. "Move your things into any empty bunk as soon as we finish this tour of the factory. Be ready to report to work at sunset."

"What are the doorways on the left, sir?" Jack hurried to keep up as they headed for yet another wooden staircase at the opposite end of the building. These steps were in better repair, painted and secured with a smooth railing.

"The women's dormitories." Brunix paused halfway up the stairs. "Flogging and dismissal is the punishment for any man who enters those rooms. Even I must ask permission. Remember that if any of *my* women tempt you."

The possessiveness of the owner's attitude grated on Jack. He wondered if Brunix owned the women like he owned the factory. Suddenly he disliked Brunix. Any sense of kinship he might have felt with his Rover heritage evaporated.

"The workroom is above the dormitories on the second floor. You will patrol this area after the women retire for the night, as part of your rounds. Stay out at all other times. Touching the lace or the patterns is forbidden."

Jack stalled a moment to watch the two dozen women bent over their work stations. He'd seen loom weaving often enough, but this process of moving threads on slender spindles mystified him, defied all logic. Yet the delicate fabric spilling off the bolsters gleamed with life like gossamer strands of magic.

A last ray of setting sun broke through the oiled parchment window coverings. Light set the strands of lace glimmering like moonlight on a dragon wing.

Fraank was right. The patch must be of lace. This wonderful airy fabric seemed akin to Shayla's iridescent membranes.

"Is any of this lace made of Tambrin?" he asked casually. There was enough lace in this room to purchase a kingdom.

"No." Brunix squinted his eyes as if caught in a lie. "Only palace lacemakers are licensed to work with Tambrin. We make lace for export. It needs to be as inexpensive as possible, made with common threads. Palace lace is made for our own nobility and no one else."

If Tambrin added expense and value to lace, the women Jack had seen promenading through the shops each wore a king's ransom on their gowns.

Brunix walked to a woman who sat close to the long row of high windows. In spite of the extra light from the windows, her work space, like all the others, was illumined by a candle lantern at the head of her pillow stand. Brunix examined the length of finished lace as wide as a man's palm. He unrolled at least three arm-lengths from a second, small bolster dangling from the larger workspace.

Owner Brunix produced a pair of scissors from a concealed pocket and snipped the finished length from the roll. "Take this to the foreman and have it added to the shipment going out tonight," he instructed the woman as he pocketed the sharp scissors and returned to Jack.

Together they mounted the last flight of stairs.

"This is my private apartment." Brunix flung wide the door. Brilliant sunlight flooded the room from six standard windows of mica and a skylight of decent-quality glass.

Neither the University nor the palace in Coronnan City boasted a single window with as much glass as that pane. The only bigger piece Jack had seen was the black glass table where the Commune of Magicians used to confer.

"You will have no need to enter these room unless I summon you." Brunix reached to close the door again.

Movement in the corner of the sitting room caught Jack's attention. He willed the door to remain open a moment longer. Brunix seemed to have difficulty pulling the heavy, soundproof panels shut.

A young woman stood up from another workstation set between

the windows. Moon-blond hair shone in the setting sun. Delicate fingers caressed a loose bobbin.

Her! The girl of his vision when he was lost in the void. The girl all grown up into a beautiful woman. The woman who had haunted his dreams when nothing else was real during those endless years in the mines.

"Go back to work, Katrina," Brunix admonished. "We will not disturb you."

"Your wife?" Jack asked still staring at the woman.

"My slave. You are not allowed to speak to her. Ever. She is mine. Do you understand? MINE!" Brunix finally managed to close the door, separating Jack from the woman of his vision, returning him to reality.

Chapter Twenty-Eight

Katrina checked the corridor outside the dormitory for any signs of the new night watchman. She didn't trust this dark-eyed stranger any more than she trusted Owner Neeles Brunix.

Three nights running she had tried to slip up to the workroom when sleep refused to overtake her. Each of those three nights the stranger had appeared at the end of the corridor as if summoned by her presence.

The first night he merely nodded to her, acknowledging her right to be in the building. The second night he'd followed her to the workroom, then returned to wherever he spent the night hours. Last night he'd slipped silently in and out of the room, watching her work for a few moments every hour or so.

Lumbird bumps rose up on her arms as she thought of his ghostly movements through the warehouse. What would he do tonight? Ask for lessons? She shivered in the chill darkness. Why did he watch her so intently?

She refused to admit that each time he left the workroom, a

terrible loneliness overcame her. Loneliness worse than that she had endured these last three years.

The corridor and stairway were empty. Soundlessly, and without benefit of a candle, Katrina slipped upstairs. She knew every creak in every unstable board in the building. She'd learned them well in three years. The watchman had learned them in one night.

She needed to lose herself in her work and find a kind of peace. Firestone brought her smokeless work candle to life. The bobbins came readily to hand. She caressed them and hummed lightly to herself. The old work songs sprang to life in her mind. She'd never let them die. In all these years of working in grim silence for Brunix, she'd gone over the songs in her mind, letting the gentle rhythms guide her hands.

Only at night, when she was alone and surrounded by darkness, did she allow herself to voice the words and tunes, very, very quietly. Brunix didn't believe in songs in his factory. Lacemaking was work and song made it seem like play.

The factory owner must know she worked alone at night, for he allowed her to keep a second pillow here in the workroom as long as the work was obscured from view by a large cloth during the day. A good pillow, covered in soft velvet, with bobbins as slender and graceful as the pattern she worked. The lace spilling off the bolster was the first design she'd given him. Other skilled women in the factory also worked the pattern. But they used a fine linen thread suitable for export. Katrina used Tambrin, as the design demanded.

She didn't know how Brunix acquired the thread or who purchased her lace. Did his Rover clan smuggle them in and out of SeLenicca? She didn't want to know, for if the palace ever discovered a factory using Tambrin, the owner would forfeit his license to make any lace at all.

The faintest whisper of sound reached her ears. Her eyes widened in alarm as she searched the shadows for signs of her mother's ghost.

"Don't you ever sleep?" the watchman asked directly behind her.

"Oh!" she gasped a little too loudly. "You frightened me." His presence always startled and intrigued her.

"Sorry, Mistress Kaantille. You are Katrina Kaantille aren't you?"

"I am mistress of nothing. Didn't Brunix tell you I am a slave?"

"He told me. Your father told me you were to be accepted as an apprentice at the palace and allowed to retain the family home. He wouldn't have sold himself to King Simeon otherwise."

"P'pa? You've seen my P'pa?" Wild relief and bitter anger roared through her heart, vying for dominance. Carefully she closed down all those confusing emotions, just as she had numbed herself the night she was forced into the owner's bed.

"Fraank Kaantille sends you his love. He wasn't well enough to come with me, but I'll take you to him when I've finished my mission here in the city."

"Then P'pa survived his years in the slave ships. I wondered if he would return when his servitude ended. That isn't supposed to be for another two years."

"Slave ships? Fraank and I met in the mines. And his sentence was life. If we hadn't escaped, he'd be dead with the mine rot by now. As it is, he's probably dying."

"The mines!" She shuddered. A long and bitter death. In her mind, Fraanken Kaantille had been dead for three years already. The reality of his condition brought new tears and a lump to her throat.

"King Simeon can't be trusted, even with his own laws." Her eyes blurred. Anger, born of three years of bitterness, covered her vision with red mist. Simeon was an outlander, just like Brunix and this new watchman. She couldn't trust any of them.

Neither said anything for a moment. She shouldn't see or speak to this dark-eyed outlander. She ignored the impulse to open her thoughts and emotions to him well beyond the realm of safety.

Katrina bent her head to the pillow, pointedly ending the conversation.

"Is this thread Tambrin?" the watchman changed the subject

abruptly. His fingers came close to the finished length of lace, as if to examine it more closely. Then he jerked his hand away.

"What difference does it make?" she returned rather than answer with a lie.

"A great deal of difference if you work at night, in secret, with a thread that is forbidden."

"Hadn't you better go back to your job, guarding the warehouse?" She stared at him, willing him away.

"If you are worried about another theft, don't. No man will get past my . . . er . . . traps."

"You have been forbidden to speak to me. Go back to your work and let me continue with mine."

"Or what? What can you do to me?"

"Report you to Owner Brunix. You will be dismissed, if he doesn't kill you first."

"But I am not a slave he can murder without question. You shouldn't be either. How did this come about?"

"Go!" She couldn't relive that humiliating night when The Simeon gave her a choice between slavery and a torturous ritual. Nor could she allow this outlander to discover all that went on between her and Brunix.

Perhaps he already knew. They were both dark-eyed outlanders. Only Brunix would dare hire another outlander when there were so many true-bloods out of work and homeless.

"Ssshh!" the watchman hissed. He extinguished her candle with a pass of his hand. "Stay here," he said so quietly Katrina wasn't certain she actually heard him or merely understood from the press of his hand against her shoulder.

Jack listened with all of his senses for the faint sound of movement. Nothing. Puzzled, he crept back down the stairs to the warehouse level.

He'd left Corby perched on top of a stack of crates in the corner, a ball of witchlight in front of him to keep the complaining bird awake. If anyone but Jack entered the cavernous room, Corby would set up a fuss loud enough to wake the entire factory.

Corby was quiet. Too quiet. Almost as if he slept. But birds did not sleep in the presence of light and they did not sleep with their heads erect, standing on both feet.

Jack stopped in the doorway, willing himself into invisibility. As his eyes adjusted to the shadows of the warehouse, he opened his senses to alien sensations. His nose itched, as if to sneeze. The scent of magic hovered in the air around him. A very small amount of magic, and it carried the distinctive musky flavor of dragons.

The softest of footfalls behind him brought his hand up to still any further noise from Katrina. His enhanced awareness of the building and all who dwelled within it told him she had followed, even before she descended the first step. He found her mouth with his left hand and gently covered it in a signal of silence.

With another thought, his staff sprang into his hand. Silently he moved into the warehouse, nose alert for a concentration of magic.

Light flared from the end of his staff, illuminating the room in a shadowless light and wrapping armor around Jack. He broadcast a very mild delusion of an ordinary lantern in his hand and another beside Corby. Best not to betray his magic with the obvious witchlight.

Every crate in the warehouse, empty or filled with reels of lace, stood revealed to his sight. Bent over one of them was a man dressed in the dark gray of the palace guard. Gleaming white tendrils of lace spilled from his hands.

Someone too stupid to respect the Rover wards at the doors? Or was he too strong a magician to worry about them?

Startled by the light, the intruder looked up, unblinking in the new brightness. Corby awoke from his trance at the same moment and set up a strident fuss guaranteed to bring Brunix and his burly employees running.

"So, since the queen is ill, has the palace stooped to stealing lace rather than making it?" Jack asked. He couldn't alert this barely talented man to his own magic.

He had to act fast and turn the matter over to Brunix, before his armor faded. Unable to replenish his magic from ley lines or from dragons, he had to rely on his own bodily strength to support his spells. Years of heavy mine work had given him muscles and stamina. These were not infinite.

"I seek a piece of lace more important than any of this paltry export trash. A piece made of Tambrin and designed by that girl's mother!" The magician in gray challenged Jack and Katrina. "King Simeon would give a life's pension for that lace. The coven will give even more!"

"How valuable is a life's pension if my life only lasts a day beyond giving over such a piece of lace—if it exists?" Jack returned.

"The piece exists. We have, this night, captured a Coronnite spy who seeks the same lace. I believe he offered Owner Brunix a great deal of money for it. He won't live until dawn. Our leader has seen the lace in the glass. A magnificent and unique piece."

He'd said *Our Leader,* not *The Simeon.* Interesting.

Katrina said nothing in reply to the man's statement, which sounded almost like an accusation. But Jack could feel her trembling in fear behind him. She was either very brave to remain there in the face of so much fear, or too stupid to know she could run.

Run where? The thought occurred to Jack that Brunix might not offer her the haven she needed. Her fear of her owner could be as great as her fear of her despotic king.

"I dispute The Simeon's ability to see anything in a magician's viewing glass. Else he'd know his enemy's movements ahead of time and would have conquered them years ago," Jack taunted, hoping the magician would reveal more.

"Simeon does not rule the coven."

"His black-haired mistress!" Katrina spat, coming out of her fear-induced paralysis. "*She* is responsible for Queen Miranda's illness. *She* leads the coven and corrupts the queen's government."

A clatter of footsteps on the stairs signaled the arrival of rein-forcements. Good. Jack's reserves were growing thin. He'd held the armor too long after several hours of stretching his awareness far beyond his normal limits.

Corby ceased his noisy fuss and swooped from his high perch to Jack's head. "Nasty man," he quoted. "Dragon man. Nasty man. Not a dragon."

Jack reached up to soothe the bird's feathers. He wished fervently that Corby would learn to keep his thoughts to himself. "Some familiar. You cause more trouble than you help me get out of," he whispered under his breath.

"Trouble, trouble, trouble," Corby repeated.

"What is the meaning of this disturbance?" Brunix burst into the room. He glared fiercely at Katrina. A gesture of his head toward the stairs dismissed her.

His dramatic dressing gown of black and purple draped around his elongated figure, and the arrogant gesture toward Katrina reminded Jack of Zolltarn, the Rover king, dressed in black and purple. Whatever blood kinship Jack might share with the two unscrupulous men, his armor remained firmly in place without conscious reinforcement.

The intruder in the gray of the palace guard seemed to assess the true authority in the factory within a heartbeat. Immediately all of his concentration turned to Brunix.

"I search this factory with a warrant from the king," the magician announced. "Rumors of the forbidden use of Tambrin have reached the ears of the palace lacemakers."

"Then search openly and honestly," Brunix defied the man. "I dare you to find anything in this building that is not authorized and approved by the king personally."

Really? Jack wondered. What about the Tambrin on Katrina's pillow? What about the mysterious piece designed by her mother?

Now that Jack had felt Tambrin, he knew he'd never mistake any other fiber for the shimmering white thread that glowed with magic. Katrina's lace sent tingles of power up his arms. His fingers had never made contact with the lace. He didn't need to get any closer to it than a finger-length to recognize the energy stored within the depths of any Tambootie tree. A tree that was poison to mundanes and led magicians into irreversible insanity. Only dragons consumed it with impunity.

Jack faded into the background. Let Brunix and the agent of King Simeon settle the issue of the warrant between themselves.

He found himself standing beside Katrina in the dim hallway. A faint tingle of power pulsed from the ground beneath her feet. He squinted and detected traces of silvery blue. A ley line? Interesting.

He edged closer, seeking the source. The girl or the land?

"Do not touch me!" she hissed so that only he could hear. "You are a *magician*. A dark-eyed magician. I saw the witchlight and your delusion! There cannot be two such as you. 'Twas *you* who interfered with the shipment of Tambootie seedlings. 'Twas *you* who bankrupted my father, killed my sister, and drove my mother to suicide."

Chapter Twenty-Nine

"Did King Simeon plant you in this factory to spy on me, to find some new way to torment and destroy me?" Katrina backed away from the magician. The anger and hatred she'd carefully nursed for three years burned cold and clear in her mind.

"The sorcerer-king is more my enemy than yours." He followed her retreat, never allowing more than two steps between them.

"I doubt that. Who has lost more, suffered more at his hands than I?" One step up the stairs. He closed the distance. She could feel the heat of his body, see a pulse beating anxiously in his neck. His pet crow had flown off when Brunix arrived. Now it landed two steps above her. She couldn't retreat much farther without disturbing the noisy bird and drawing more attention to herself.

"The soldiers who die by the dozens, cold and hungry, bogged down in mud up to their knees, with disease plaguing their ranks more than the enemy ever could, have lost as much. That goes for both armies. All because ruining SeLenicca isn't enough. King Simeon has to conquer more."

"We need trade to stay alive. Coronnan is rich with farmland and resources but has repeatedly denied us access to them, even though we pay for them!" The argument was old, repeated often. "Coronnan has to be responsible for the food shortages, the unemployment, the . . ." Her words trailed off.

"SeLenicca could grow its own food, become self-sufficient if Simeon would let you."

"No. 'Twould blaspheme the Stargods. *We* are the Chosen. The resources were provided for us to exploit."

"In Coronnan, we believe ourselves to be the Chosen and our duty is to nurture the land and ourselves, in memory of the bounty bestowed by the Stargods. SeLenicca has been methodically stripped, rather than nourished, for a thousand years. But this political argument doesn't settle the conflict between us. Why do you accuse me of the king's crimes?"

"King Simeon did not stop the shipment that caused P'pa's bankruptcy. You did."

"I stopped a foreign spy from escaping *my* country. A spy who had organized an assassination of my king on the day of his coronation. Would you have done less?"

Katrina had to think about that. Hatred of the man who had caused her poverty, hunger, grief, and humiliation had focused her desire for revenge. In the first years of her slavery, little else had kept her from following her mother into the river. She needed to nurse that hatred back into life. She had nothing, was nothing without it.

"What makes you think Simeon would have allowed your father to profit from that shipment of Tambootie seedlings if it had won through?" He mounted the step to stand beside her. In the cramped space, only a hair's breadth separated them. His quiet words caressed her ear while the closeness of his body threatened her senses as Brunix's lovemaking never could.

"There is only one use for Tambootie. Simeon needed my father to market the fiber for lacemaking."

"Tambootie feeds dragons. Simeon has a small nimbus of dragons to supply magic to the men of his coven. The palace guard arguing with Brunix gathers dragon magic. He admitted to being part of the coven. None of that Tambootie would have been made into thread."

"Dragons? Where?" Fear, or was it the watchman's nearness, sent shivers through her body.

"Your father is protected by the dragons. My quest is to send them home so that Simeon no longer has a source of magic. Without the dragons he can't work his evil on SeLenicca anymore. Without his magic, Queen Miranda will recover."

Jaylor opened the fragile book with tender reverence. How many times had he passed it by in the library of the new University of Magicians? He wondered if he ignored the book just as someone searching for the clearing would walk right past the proper path.

But the crack in the clearing barrier widened daily. Brevelan still refused to move. Jaylor feared that soon an outsider would stumble into the clearing without knowing he shouldn't be able to. An agent of the Gnostic Utilitarian cult would be as happy to find the clearing as to find the hidden University with its priceless library of magic secrets. The Council of Provinces and the coven had been trying to penetrate the Commune's defense of secrecy for years.

Darville knew how to find the clearing. Mikka could open the crack and snatch Glendon away. . . . Jaylor couldn't dwell on that possibility. Fear of losing the boy paralyzed all thought.

The library had grown during these years in exile because a few educated men feared for the safety of their private book collections during the height of the Gnul's fanaticism. The Gnuls didn't believe in learning to read. Since the skill to interpret the marks in books into language had been the exclusive right of magicians for many generations, the cult had decided reading was another form of magic and therefore evil.

Rational men who could not embrace the cult but found it politically expedient not to oppose it had found ways to insure the safety of their collections of books. Secret messengers left bundles of them buried in protective wraps near abandoned Equinox Pylons—festival landmarks that had been revered in Coronnan for so long even the Gnuls would not desecrate them. Only the coven did that.

Jaylor enjoyed quiet time in the library, meditating and planning. Physical and psychic quiet was a rarity in the clearing. Glendon and Lukan didn't believe in quiet, unless they were asleep. Lukan screamed at everything, with delight, anger, or frustration. Glendon tended to blast minds with his telepathic shouts. Anything done quietly, to them, was work. The same task or game completed with as much noise as their two young bodies could muster, was play.

So Jaylor sat quietly in the library and stared at this slim volume that had lain hidden in piles of books, overlooked, pushed aside and forgotten time and again.

"A book that doesn't want to be found might contain a spell that obscures a place," he mused. "Like the clearing." Since he couldn't persevere against Brevelan and make her move, he had to find a way to heal the barrier. If this book contained the spell that had originally set the protections, he might be able to analyze it and reset it.

Page by page he skimmed the volume. The penmanship flowed with delicate swirls and loops indicative of a feminine hand. An apprentice of old, recording for her teacher and mentor? Or Myrilandel, the fabled wife of the magician who tamed the dragons and the first known inhabitant of the clearing, perhaps?

If he could create his own protective boundary elsewhere, perhaps Brevelan would move and he needn't worry about that damned crack.

"It's worth a try." He ran his finger down a page and stopped on a poem entitled "Invisible Gate."

Spirit of air lift me high
With the dragons let me fly.
Protect us with a steady wind

That blows nowhere but here within.
Spirit of fire glowing green
Descend from air and wind unseen.
Heat my heart like purest gold
Cast off dross of lies untold.
Spirit of water, blessedly cool
Drop by drop fill this pool
Refresh my mind from life's pain.
Wash me clean of greed and gain.
Kardia gather with the other three
Root me through a mighty tree.
Anchor me with your knowing love.
Free to choose in the world above.
Altogether, the Gaia you are
bound as one, near and far.

The poem danced through Jaylor's mind with a familiar lilt. More a song than a chant. The words were similar to the spells the Rovers had used to bind Jaylor and his fractured magic together long ago, before Darville's wedding and coronation. Combined with a ritual of candles and dance, the massive spell had drawn magic from the fabric of life rather than simply from the planet below or the dragons above.

"I'm starting to think in song!" he protested to himself. "Brevelan sings her magic. Krej chanted his spells. There is power in the music, power in the singer."

A tune he swore he'd never heard before, yet was hauntingly familiar, trilled through his mind as he repeated the words of the spell. His tongue began to tingle and his feet vibrated in time with the pulsing life of the land beneath his feet. Too soon. The song only bound the singer to the four elements. He needed the spell for the boundary around the clearing before he unleashed that power.

Carefully he clamped down on his mind and pushed the

humming magic back where it came from, but not so far away he couldn't tap it again.

He turned the next page of the book and read carefully. "Six eggs gathered this morning. One-and-a-half buckets milked from the goat. Strung a line between the lower limbs of the everblues to hang washing." Jaylor nearly slammed the book closed. A bloody list of daily chores!

"One more page." Then another, and another all the way to the end. More lists. The author of this book was methodical in keeping records. Every person who visited, every cure dispensed, stores of herbs and catalogs of clothing washed and mended.

Jaylor nearly threw the book down in disgust. "Why do you work so hard at being ignored?" he asked the handwritten pages. "Maybe the spell itself is hiding just like the book. Hiding in an obvious place that I'm sure to overlook."

Carefully he pulled some magic into his eyes and lit his senses. Looking obliquely for patterns rather than reading individual words, he thumbed through the book again.

On the next page, the laundry list dissolved into a similar pattern, revealing words written by magic beneath the mundane chores. The poem leaped out at him.

Circles within circles.
Elements combined
Protect from eyes
Of the prying kind.
Keep this place safe for me and mine.
The Gaia's secrets carefully hid
Recited in order from bottom to lid.

Something of the writer's humor slipped through to Jaylor. With a jaunty air, whistling the tune that bounced from the first poem to his mouth, he returned to the clearing.

Just before the boundary, where the path's perceived direction wound around and around the widening crack, he halted and opened the book to the poem. In his joyful baritone he sang the poem backward, one line at a time—from bottom to lid.

The power of life tingled through his feet to his body core to his limbs and mind, opening every sense and pore to the elements. The boundary appeared before him as a humming wall of swirling metallic colors—copper, silver, gold, lead. In answer to his request, the drifting patterns coalesced and parted into an open gate.

Jaylor stepped through and sang the spell lid to bottom. The gate dissolved behind him and the colors disappeared. He reached out and touched a solid wall, invisible once again to his eyes and his magic. Just to make certain the clearing was once more inviolate, he wiped the spell from his mind and ran his hand along the barrier.

His fist fell through a chink in the wall wider than the crack left by Glendon.

Chapter Thirty

J ack followed the girl up to the workroom as quickly and as quietly as the rickety planks would allow. The sounds of the argument in the warehouse seemed to be winding down, and he expected the palace magician to come looking at the lace pillows for anything incriminating.

"What is Simeon looking for?" he asked Katrina.

She stared back at him without answering, eyes bewildered and accusing.

He could pluck the answer from her mind. He wouldn't. Not anymore.

"You magicians are all alike. How do I know you aren't in league with Simeon and that man downstairs? How can I trust anything you say?"

"You can't. But by the Stargods I hope you will trust me. Now, is this the only Tambrin in this room?" He gestured to the pillow where she had been singing and working earlier. If only he knew how to give back that joyful song rather than the ingrained bitterness she projected.

The stairs creaked and groaned under the weight of men climbing.

"It's the only piece I know of. I've got to hide it!" She looked anxiously around for concealment. There was only one door in or out of the room and the palace magician would soon block it.

Jack closed his eyes and sent the entire workstation, pillow, frame, stool, and candle deep into the warehouse. The magician wasn't likely to search there again. Corby flew after it. Jack caught an image from the bird's mind of plucking hairs from the magician's head as he swooped past him on the landing.

A screech and a curse confirmed Corby's mischief.

Jack stepped into the place where the pillow had been to disguise the blank spot in the orderly rows of workstations. Tendrils of raw power licked his feet—extensions of the ley lines he'd glimpsed on the ground floor. Katrina's workstation sat directly above them. Again he wondered at the source of regenerating power.

"What did you do?" Katrina gasped.

"I hid the evidence." He smiled and then drew the power into himself and faded into the woodwork. No transport for himself. A little invisibility would allow him to eavesdrop on the magician. The little blue ley lines beneath Katrina's work place fed him all the power he needed.

As an afterthought he drew Katrina into the circle of his spell. *If you move or utter a sound, he'll find us both,* he said into her mind. Then he draped his arm around her shoulders to keep her close and protected—something he'd wanted to do since his vision of a girl with pale, blond hair crying over the loss of her first pillow and bobbins.

Later he'd ask why she'd changed from the distinctive two braids to one.

She squirmed a little under his touch. He increased the pressure of his hand on her shoulder. She stilled, but he sensed her unease.

Filling his physical senses with her scent, her warmth, and the wondrous feel of her body next to his, Jack drew more power into himself in preparation for eavesdropping on the intrusive magician from the palace.

"Search for the Tambrin, search every corner of this building and you will not find any." Brunix threw the door to the room open with an expansive gesture of his long arms.

"Of course I won't find it. Your whore has had plenty of time to hide it." The thin magician sniffed in disdain.

Katrina stiffened beside Jack. He felt her indignation nearly as strong as she. Then her posture wilted in resignation. He pulled her closer, attempting to impart reassurance, respect, whatever emotions she needed right now. She didn't respond.

"You don't search, because Tambrin alone is not what you truly seek." Brunix narrowed his eyes and hunched his shoulders as if he were a vulture examining a particularly tasty morsel.

Jack had seen Zolltarn, king of the Rovers, assume the same pose of intimidation. It usually worked.

"I was sent," the magician leaned closer to Brunix as if imparting a great confidence, "to find a particularly fine piece of lace woven by the late Tattia Kaantille."

Katrina jumped. Jack stilled her movement and wondered at the guilt that seemed to pour out of her.

This was the second time the slightly built man had asked for that piece of lace.

Where is it? Jack whispered into Katrina's mind.

An image of Brunix's private sitting room, a secret wall panel that only the owner could key. The power engulfing Jack was enough that her thoughts flowed easily back into his mind without a conscious probe on his part.

Jack had yet to meet a lock or secret panel that refused his mental touch. He'd find the lace. If it was big enough, it might suffice as a patch for Shayla. Then he could leave this insufferable city and the sly, unreadable factory owner without delay.

He'd also have to leave Katrina. He was fairly certain she would not follow him to Shayla's lair.

You may not have it! Katrina's mind screamed at him.

How could she know he planned to steal it? In opening himself to her thoughts, he must have allowed her free access to his own.

"I know nothing of Tattia Kaantille's work. All of her designs were left at the palace, along with her pillow and bobbins, when she was dismissed by King Simeon," Brunix replied to the magician. His aura shot high white bolts of lightning filled with lies.

The glare from those lies left spots before Jack's physical eyes. He closed off that portion of his magic sight.

"Perhaps you should ask the ghost of Tattia Kaantille. She was a suicide and haunts her daughter here in this workroom," the owner continued.

The magician blanched and searched the shadowy corners for signs of a hovering spirit. His gaze slid over Jack and Katrina as if they weren't there.

"Th . . . there is no ghost here." He shrugged his shoulders as if dismissing his instinctive fear along with the ghost. "When King Simeon gave the girl to you, your duty was to pry her secrets from her. Three years have passed, and the lace is still missing."

"Nothing was said of secrets at the time. I was told to humiliate and frighten her so that she would be ripe for the coven's rituals. You are a member of the king's coven. You must know why he has not had the girl murdered so that her secrets die with her."

"He thought the lace lost with the body of Tattia Kaantille. But the girl wore it not a moon ago, at Princess Jaranda's birthday celebration. He saw it then. I saw it and so did our leader. We won't take action against Katrina Kaantille until the lace is turned over to Simeon or he sees it destroyed."

"If I were married to the girl, she would have the protection of my tribe. The king would not risk the wrath of the Rovers, I think."

"A knife across the throat would kill you as surely as the girl. This factory would then be forfeit and His Majesty could search for the lace at his leisure."

"My premature death would bring Rovers into the city bent on revenge more surely than the death of the girl. No. The king will send his thieves in the dead of night searching for the lace."

"*Where* is the shawl?"

"Only the ghost of Tattia Kaantille knows for sure."

"I . . . I sense no ghost. She isn't here. But she must be here. A suicide always haunts blood kin for five generations." The magician crossed his wrists and flapped in the ancient gesture of warding. Then, against royal policy, he invoked the cross of the Stargods. "With my head and heart and the strength of my shoulders I renounce the evil carried by this ghost." He scuttled out of the room and down the stairs like a beetle frightened by a predatory jackdaw.

Katrina hung her head. One of her tears touched Jack's wrist.

He sent his magic sight all over the room, followed by every sense he could summon. *There are no ghosts here.*

Katrina reared her head so violently she almost shredded the spell of invisibility. M'ma must haunt me. She threw herself into the river. Her spirit cannot pass into a new plane of existence until . . .

I'd know if she were here. There is no trace of a ghost now or the recent past. Perhaps your mother did not suicide.

Katrina was silent a moment while Brunix followed the magician at a more dignified pace. Jack kept her within the private circle of his arms and his spell, marveling at the telepathic rapport he had found with the lacemaker. The intimacy of the moment was deeper and more profound than the lusty satisfaction Rejiia had once offered him.

Perhaps my mother was thrown from the bridge by an agent of her enemy, King Simeon. The spy who dies tonight from torture suspected murder. M'ma was wearing the shawl that night. It was retrieved from the river by the City Watch. I washed the shawl and hid it lest P'pa burn it. It was all I had left of her. M'ma's body was never recovered.

If the lace had been around the woman's neck and shoulders, then why did it float free while the body sank? Unless Tattia had put up a great deal of resistance before entering the river, loosening the lace. The fall into the icy water had probably sent her into shock so that she couldn't climb out again. Only Tattia herself and the agents of King Simeon knew for certain how and why the lacemistress had died.

Jack added that piece of information to his list of tasks to complete before he left the city.

Katrina fingered the nearly finished shawl of her own design. Her usual patterns of edgings and insertions did not yet match her mother's in uniqueness and elegance. This piece surpassed the original. Mostly because the floral centers flowed with the weaving lines of the petals. She doubted any of the lacemakers in the Brunix factory could figure out the convoluted thread paths of the runes in Tattia's shawl.

But then Tattia had incorporated the runes for a purpose, never meaning the design to be duplicated. If only Katrina knew the message in those runes. After last night's invasion of the factory by a spying magician, Katrina had no doubt that her only chances of survival were to keep the shawl and its secrets hidden, or to learn those secrets and spread the information to the right people.

Was Jack the right person? Part of her wanted to trust him and accept his friendship. Another part of her didn't dare.

King Simeon must know the meaning of the runes, or he wouldn't be pursuing the shawl so diligently now that he knew it had not been destroyed. If he didn't know, he wouldn't have prevented the queen from seeing it when M'ma first offered it.

The murmurs of talk from the workroom below her rose to a roar of speculation. Brunix had not seen fit to disclose to his workers why the factory had rocked with arguments and pounding feet last night. Katrina hadn't bothered to explain her late return to her bed—though most of the lacemakers presumed she had been servicing the owner. Jack had not yet been seen today.

Jack. Those few moments wrapped in his arms and his spell had shaken her carefully-layered suspicion and mistrust. He had allowed her to eavesdrop and learn the depth of Brunix's involvement with the king.

She wondered briefly if the glimpse Jack had allowed of his own mind was the result of the invisibility spell he had wrapped around them, or another trick to win her confidence. He wanted her help in completing his mission. She knew that much. What kind of help and how dangerous would it be? There had to be danger or he'd have given her more details.

A special piece of lace, made of Tambrin. Was he, too, after the shawl? That piece was made of silk. Wasn't it?

Katrina needed to examine the piece more closely, looking specifically for evidence of Tambrin spun with the silk. Owner Brunix wasn't about to remove the shawl from its locked hiding place so soon after the palace magician had searched for it. She didn't have the key.

Jack might be able to open it with magic.

Her circling thoughts came back to the dark-eyed stranger again and again. She had to trust him if she was to find the answers.

Yet she knew she shouldn't trust the outland magician who had stopped the ship containing the precious Tambootie seedlings.

He claimed to know her father, to have aided P'pa's escape from the mines.

Brunix treated him as if he were a cousin—another untrustworthy Rover.

Jack had vowed his mission would deprive Simeon of magic and therefore his power over SeLenicca.

The arguments wove back and forth and around like a giant spiderweb. Katrina was the fly trapped at the center, waiting to be consumed, knowing her death waited just beyond the next heartbeat. Just like the insect trapped in the amber bead on her divider pin.

"I am tired of being a victim!" she shouted to herself, and the Stargods and anyone else within hearing distance. "If I am ever to cleanse myself of this web of lies and deceit, I have to take a risk."

Jack offered a solution as well as an escape. Brunix promised safety within the confines of slavery. How much longer would he wait to exert his rights over her again? Simeon offered nothing.

"I need Jack," she told herself. "I can use him as I have been used. I don't have to trust him." *But I do like him. I felt so complete, so right when he wrapped me in his arms.*

Decision made, she touched the single plait of hair hanging halfway down her back. With deft fingers, she rapidly released the tight weaving. A few moments later she had restored the two plaits she had missed for three long years. Assertive action began with simple gestures.

Tonight, when the factory slept and Jack was on duty, she would seek him out and offer her help. Until then, she would do what she did best—finish the shawl.

Rejiia watched through tired eyes as the Rover wet nurse fed her newborn son.

"Your son is strong but very small, born two moons early," the young woman commented on the infant's vigorous suckling.

Rejiia smiled in satisfaction. Too many plans relied on her strength and agility. The last two moons of pregnancy would have hindered her actions.

Old Erda, the Rover matriarch and mistress of all herbal medicines and the best midwife in the three kingdoms, wasn't available to assist her. But one of her apprentices had come with the tribe of Rovers that lingered on the outskirts of Queen's City. The bitter herbs Rejiia had drunk last night had forced the child into early birth.

"Your tribe will protect my son until I claim him," Rejiia commanded the young wet nurse.

"We will guard him as one of our own," the Rover woman murmured. She did not lift her gaze to meet Rejiia's.

"Only until I can claim him!" Rejiia hadn't the strength to

compel the woman, so she pushed as much authority into her voice as possible.

"We will welcome you when you claim him." This time the woman met Rejiia's look in a token promise of compliance.

"Your name, girl. Tell me your name so that I may find you again."

"I am called Erda."

"Nonsense. There is only one Erda."

"Each of us who nurtures a child can claim the title Erda."

"Your true name, then. What name were you given at birth?"

"No outlander may know my true name."

"Enough of this evasion. Give me your name so that I may find you when the time is right to reclaim my son." Panic generated enough energy to draw a tiny spell into her words. Erda squirmed in resistance.

"Ask for Kestra. All of the tribes of Zolltarn know of Kestra."

"Good. The prematurity of the boy's birth is our secret. No one in Coronnan must suspect that my husband, Marnak, is incapable of fathering a child. By law we are still married and the child legitimate."

"That belief suits the needs of the Rovers."

"Then take the child. I will inform the king that his son is stillborn."

For now I must garner my strength so that I am ready for the Solstice Ritual.

I will use the power of the Solstice to kill Darville through the lingering wound in his arm. Coronnan expects him to die from that witch burn. I shall hasten the process and step in to claim the throne for me and my son.

I am too weak at the moment to investigate the disturbance in the magical energies I sense within the city. I need a familiar to aid my search. Jackdaws aplenty nest near the palace. More intelligent than mere crows, their ability to mimic will develop into limited speech through the bonding spells. I will subvert one to my will. Tomorrow. I must sleep now.

Chapter Thirty-One

"Ley lines don't exist singly. Nor do they appear spontaneously," Jack mused as he wandered Queen's City shortly after dawn.

Cloaked in the face and body of the slightly built palace magician, he peered easily at the land beneath his feet with every sense available to him. His magic had recharged during the time he had spent standing above the pocket of power in the workroom. a relief from the weeks of weakened abilities.

Burned out ley lines rotted at every street intersection. If the land did not heal soon, the old channels would collapse, taking building foundations and street paving with them. Jack foresaw a shift in the riverbed and upheaval in the hills behind the city. Death and chaos would follow.

Simeon deserved whatever destruction the Stargods visited upon him. The innocents of the city didn't.

Everywhere he saw the signs of decay, heightened by the short-sighted belief that the land's resources were unlimited and meant to be exploited. When the belief proved false, no one knew how to rectify matters. Peopl abandoned shops and houses. Dirt and crumbling mortar were strewn through the streets from the collapse of a warehouse, and no one with enough energy to clear it away. No refuse for dogs to scavenge. And everywhere, the haunted eyes of the hungry and the hopeless citizens. Only the nobles seemed unaware of the lifeblood of the country bleeding into the river along with the land that no longer had trees to hold it back.

Having lost all sense of the Kardia, SeLenicca, its people, and culture were dying. Only the export of lace kept the economy alive. Lace was not enough to employ an entire nation.

Nowhere in his day-long search of the city did Jack discover any active ley lines. The city was as dead magically as it was economically. Shayla was King Simeon's only source of power. Did he and the members of his coven know how to combine the magic and make the power grow well beyond anything a solitary magician could throw?

Jack already knew he was incapable of gathering the dragon magic. After last night's confrontation with the palace magician, he had little hope he could complete his mission and escape without detection. In a magic duel, Jack's only chance of survival was one grouping of hair-fine ley lines beneath the warehouse.

If only he knew why the ley lines had sprung up beneath Katrina's workstation and nowhere else. Once he mastered that puzzle, he might be able to force more lines to grow and feed his magic.

Katrina was the answer. Katrina and the lace she wove for the love of the shimmering threads and the patterns that bloomed beneath her hands while she sang little tunes in the dead of night; not the lace she made for the owner to exploit.

Her gentle little work tune danced through his mind and gave his feet a lighter step. He hummed it lightly as he prowled the city. His mind cleared of puzzles and worries.

A crowd gathering on the bridge ahead of him caught his curiosity. The black robes and tall hat, crowning a city official, flapped in the wind like the wings of a jackdaw. Wearily the clerk intoned a prayer and scattered something into the water. Jack merged with the solemn listeners.

Two middle-aged women wept. Their sharp chins and close-set eyes suggested a strong family resemblance. Between them stood a tight-lipped man, probably husband to one, grinding his teeth in his effort to restrain his own tears.

A funeral, Jack decided. An all-too-common occurrence in a city where food shortages were a constant worry and lack of firewood kept buildings chill and dark. The customary sun break at noon seemed to be the only source of joy left in Queen's City.

Jack pushed past the funeral goers. He might as well check out the slums on the far side of the river for some trace of magical activity. The homeless and unemployed might have a better relationship with the Kardia than the elite of a mercantile city.

A winter chill filled his body with atavistic dread. He came to an abrupt halt. The day had been warm with a gentle breeze two heartbeats ago.

He scanned the center of the bridge with his already extended magical senses. A woman in soaking garments stood directly in front of him, flailing her arms as if fighting to the surface from the depths of the river. Her double plaits streamed down her back, dripping water. No drops or puddles formed on the wooden planks. For a moment Jack thought he was staring at a vision of Katrina grown into the beauty of maturity.

Only then did he notice the knife protruding from the woman's breast and blood staining the front of her gown. None of the mourners seemed aware of the injured woman or her plight. Instinctively he reached to withdraw the knife.

His hand passed straight through the woman. The hairs on the back of his hand and arm stood straight up. Lumbird bumps danced down his spine.

"The ghost of Tattia Kaantille," he whispered.

The apparition nodded at the sound of her name.

"Murder, not suicide?" Jack asked in a silent whisper.

Again the ghost gestured the correctness of his assumption.

"Who? Why?"

A shudder of effort seemed to pass through the spirit of Katrina's mother. She opened her mouth to speak, but no sound emerged.

Jack concentrated on the shapes her lips formed around soundless words.

"Simeon. Runes," he repeated the two words back to her.

She smiled and faded to wisps of water vapor.

"You were talking to that new man, Katrina. You are not to speak to any of the men I employ. And now you revert to the two plaits I forbade you to wear. To impress the new watchman? I'll not have it, Katrina. Why do you disobey me?" Brunix stood behind her left shoulder so he wouldn't cast a shadow on the lace shawl that grew beneath her fingers.

Katrina knew from experience she was not to interrupt her work while answering him. Lace provided the income that kept the factory going. Lace was more important than any of the workers within the factory. If a lacemaker fell short of her daily quota, Brunix would dismiss her without a second thought. If Katrina displeased the owner or made him angry he would sell her—possibly back to King Simeon.

"I was working and heard a noise," she explained. "I knew about the thefts and investigated. The watchman was already there."

Brunix moved in front of her, blocking her light so she had to look up to him. "The watchman was supposed to be there. You were not." He slapped her across the cheek, hard.

Pain lanced through her eyes to her jaw. The blow set her ears ringing and brought involuntary tears to her eyes. His violence shocked her senses and numbed her thoughts as his lovemaking had not. Never before had he hit her. The world centered on her pain and his burning anger.

" 'Tis not your position to put yourself into danger. You are *mine*. *My* slave. *My* possession." He backhanded her again across the face.

She tasted blood. This new blow jerked her head back, twisting her neck awkwardly.

"You are not to speak to any other male. You are not to venture below to the warehouse without my express permission." His long fingers grabbed her shoulders and he shook her, hard, rattling her teeth. "Do. You. Understand. Me?"

Katrina couldn't force words past her clenched jaw and reeling senses.

"Do you understand!" Brunix demanded again.

"Y . . . y . . . yes," she ground out.

"Good. I will find another watchman. This one broke my rules when he spoke to you." Brunix released her, seemingly oblivious to the blood that dripped from the corner of her mouth and the bruises forming on her cheek.

Katrina touched the back of her hand to the blood on her face, careful not to stain her fingers which might transfer blood to the nearly completed shawl. She had to think, had to overcome the shock that closed down her senses.

Brunix couldn't dismiss Jack. She needed the outland magician to decipher the runes. He was the only person who could help her bring about King Simeon's downfall.

"Before the evening meal, you will move all of your things into my quarters. I am tired of waiting for you. Henceforth, you live with me, eat with me, and sleep with me. I can make you feel pain. You will respond to me, if only in pain. Only one-quarter of my blood is Rover. I have observed their prohibition against rape more than one quarter of my time with you. I would take you now, but I have business that will not wait. This apartment and the workroom are the only places you have permission to be." Brunix stalked to the door of his apartment. "Do you understand, Katrina?"

"Do I have the right to a sun break?" she asked calmly, though her heart beat so loud and fast she could barely hear her own words. She couldn't allow him to see the panic rising to choke her.

"You will take your sun break with me. I allow you outside the building only because the law requires I must and a complaint from one of your friends would bring me ruinous fines." He left her alone, slamming the door behind him. A heartbeat later, the lock clicked, sealing her inside.

"I can't read runes," Jack muttered to himself. "I wasn't at the University long enough to learn that skill. Where would I find runes, if I could read them?" He trekked back across the bridge into Queen's City. A glance over his shoulder confirmed that the ghost of Tattia Kaantille had vanished once her message had been passed along to him.

His growling stomach reminded him that he hadn't eaten since last night's supper, and the day was half gone. He must return to the factory in time to share supper with the other male employees—after the women had eaten and retired safely to their dormitory. He had almost no chance of seeing Katrina before midnight.

The official with the tall black hat, who had presided over the funeral brushed, past Jack. His black robes flapped in the wind, reminding Jack once more of a giant jackdaw. The flowing sleeves of the black robe caught briefly on Jack's belt buckle. As the man tugged the fabric free with a deep frown of disapproval for Jack, the black embroidery on the black robe caught the magician's eye. Straight lines and slashes jumped into his perspective.

A primitive form of writing.

Runes!

This was no government clerk or judge, but a priest. Old temples sometimes had runes decorating tombs and icons.

Jack fell into step behind the man, thanking the Stargods as he kept a discreet distance.

A temple constructed of huge stone blocks, each as tall as a man, loomed before Jack. Bigger than the Palace Reveta Tristille, he'd never seen anything like it before. In Coronnan, the temples were small, little larger than a house, and scattered throughout the city for the convenience of each neighborhood, mostly taken for granted because they were an everyday part of life. This place of worship demanded attention by its imposing height and impossibly huge building stones. Men could not have built this place. It seemed designed for the entire population of the city to gather at once. The priest strode up the two dozen steps with the ease of long familiarity.

Jack followed him, stretching his legs to mount each broad stair. A long line of people dressed in sober colors filed into and out of the sanctuary. Jack joined them.

Inside the impressive structure, darkness ruled. No windows allowed daylight to penetrate beyond the porch. Hundreds of lighted candles lined the walls in banks of nine rows and nine tiers. The building was so massive in size, the candles lit only small areas around icons dedicated to one of the three red-haired Stargod brothers, or the painted canvases of the queen before her ailment. Nine tall candles in each of nine candelabras drew Jack's eyes to the altar.

One solid piece of lace spilled over the focal point of worship. Soft light reflected from the shimmering threads of the design. From the distance of one hundred arm-lengths, Jack knew the lace was made from Tambrin. The magic inherent in the Tambootie tree vibrated inside his body like a finely tuned instrument ready to sound the most beautiful note ever heard.

But it was a power he dared not draw into his body. Dragons were the only beings who could safely digest any part of the Tambootie. Madness trod the path of the Tambootie. Simeon's obsessive search for Tattia's lace shawl exhibited some of the signs of that insanity.

The line of worshipers in front of Jack moved forward. To his right, a series of tiny chapels bulged outward from the main sanctuary. Some were no wider than a single person. Others could accommodate three or four kneeling side by side before altars dedicated to images Jack couldn't identify. Incense hung heavily in the air.

A sneeze tickled in the back of Jack's throat. He held his breath. The sneeze subsided along with the thick perfume of burning herbs. Priests used incense in their rituals in Coronnan. Jack had never heard of them saturating the air with it, nor of using such heavy and exotic scents. Like so many things in this decaying city, the incense sought to hide unpleasantness rather than cleanse it.

He looked up, way up, to see how high the cloud of incense hovered. Four or five stories above the center of the sanctuary, the bowl of a huge dome separated the worshipers from the weather. Painted night skies with stylized stars decorated the interior of the dome. Most of the constellation groupings were inaccurate, broken by seams. Ah, the priests did do something traditional in SeLenicca. The panels in the dome opened, by a series of just barely visible pulleys and ropes, for observation of the night skies.

The architecture seemed to be centered on that dome. Did the entire temple date from the time of the Stargods or was the open dome added later to accommodate stargazing?

He sidled out of line to examine the side aisles and their stone tombs. Jack guessed the stonework was much older than the religion of the Stargods and the efficient alphabet introduced by the three divine brothers. The ancient runes should still adorn places considered sacred through all the changes of dynasties and worship. Somewhere in this vast building there must be some runes and he intended to find them.

Then he'd worry about a translation.

Katrina paced the circumference of Brunix's sitting room. Two burly warehousemen carried her trunk of personal possessions between them into the bedroom beyond. A third employee hauled her extra working pillow up the stairs.

"Where you want it?" he asked, not daring to lift his eyes to meet hers.

"By the window." She pointed to a cleared space beside the pillow where she worked the new shawl. Since the factory owner's uncharacteristic violence this morning, she hadn't been able to work, to concentrate, to think of anything but the night to come. The nights to come. For as long as Brunix desired her, she would have no peace.

"Think *he'll* let us have a go at her when he gets tired?" The two men with the trunk giggled and nudged each other.

Katrina felt all heat and sensation drain from her head to form a knot in her stomach. Brunix had promised her pain in order to force a response from her. Would he add the degradation of being mauled by these thugs as well?

The third man lifted one shoulder in a shrug. "What can I do?" he mouthed. His eyes pleaded for forgiveness from Katrina.

She didn't know how to reply to the man. Any attempt to help her escape Brunix tonight, or any other night, would result in his own dismissal from a job he sorely needed.

"Get Jack," she whispered. A ray of hope opened before her as soon as she whispered his name. Jack who persisted in his quest despite the dangers. Jack who held her tenderly and granted her the unique privilege of reading his mind as readily as he read hers.

If he had any secrets left, after that special rapport they had shared while eavesdropping on Brunix and the palace guard, those secrets were no danger to her.

"Gone, all day." The man ventured one step closer to her, casting about to ensure the other two weren't watching.

"Send his pet bird!"

"I'll try."

The three men filed out without a backward glance to Katrina. A loud click proclaimed they had followed orders and locked her in once more.

"Come quickly, Jack. I need you."

Chapter Thirty-Two

"Damned birds!" Rejiia cursed the flock of black birds that circled away from her window.

The aerial display of the flock separated and settled into individual birds. For the fifth time this morning, Rejiia concentrated her mind probe on a bird. Slowly she merged her consciousness with the creature. Her vision tilted, shifted colors to reflect heat patterns, and distorted to the perspective of one high above the city.

A moment of euphoric flight filled her. Contact with her body diminished. "Almost. Almost total blending." A thin silver tendril of magic tethered her to the person in the window. She absorbed more of the bird.

Eebon, the bird announced his name.

Mistress, Rejiia said. *You will call me Mistress.*

He was ready. Another moment and the crow would be her winged familiar, bound to her for life.

She tugged on the tether. The bird banked and circled back. Another tug and he flew faster toward her.

Rejiia regained enough of her own body to stretch out her arm as a perch for her new pet. Eebon extended his talons to encircle her padded wrist.

"Newak!" a second bird screamed. The menacing jackdaw with white tufts over his eyes dove between Rejiia and Eebon.

The slender silver tether shredded from the force of the bird's descent. Eebon jerked away from the villa window squawking his confusion.

Together the two black birds turned and flapped until they caught an air current that took them away from Rejiia.

"Simurgh curse you, bird," she screamed in frustration. Every time she made contact with a bird, the interloper shattered the spell. Who controlled the jackdaw? Only another magician could direct a wild creature to do such a thing. Who?

That boy! Yaakke had to be the jackdaw's master. "He's the only magician strong enough to thwart me. I'll have that bird. I'll torture it to death and enjoy every moment."

Jack wound his way among the temple alcoves as if seeking an unoccupied corner for private prayer. As he paused by each small altar, he examined all of the decoration for signs of the distinctive lines and slashes chiseled into the stone.

The sight of a pair of large boots sticking out from beneath a familiar robe halted his progress. A tall man knelt in the next alcove. Owner Neeles Brunix had worn a similar sleeveless green robe over his black tunic and trews when he descended to the warehouse in dignified silence this morning. His orders had been brief, almost as if his words were gold and he a miser.

Jack had seen the owner's aura flare with the red of suppressed, violent emotion as he viewed the scene of last night's intrusion. His reaction to Jack's presence had generated near flames in his spiking aura, but his face and tone had not changed. When the owner retreated to his office, he'd closed the door with precise control. Jack suspected Brunix might rip the painted planks from their hinges if he vented his true emotions.

That was when Jack decided to absent himself from the factory for the day. His next encounter with Brunix might end with Jack unemployed and no more access to Tambrin lace and Katrina. Keeping Katrina close and safe suddenly seemed as important as finding a patch for Shayla's wing.

Jack turned to go back the way he had come. Brunix would recognize his current disguise and the crowd was too thick to alter the delusion spell without drawing attention. The crowd was also too thick to allow him a safe retreat. Forward, toward the main altar lay the only open path.

On tiptoe, as silently as possible, he edged past the factory owner. Brunix remained on his knees, eyes fixed ahead of him. But he wasn't praying. His hands copied the wall etchings onto a sheet of parchment. Wall etchings that duplicated the runic embroidery on the priest's robes.

Surprised, Jack nearly stumbled over Brunix's feet where they protruded into the main aisle. There was little chance of coincidence that Tattia Kaantille's ghost would tell Jack to seek out runes on the same day that Brunix—who owned Tattia's daughter—would copy runes in the temple.

Brunix stirred from his fascinated study of the carved message. Slowly he levered himself up to his full standing height, using the altar rail as a brace.

Jack sought a hiding place amid the crowd.

A priest renewed a sputtering candle two alcoves along the aisle and then disappeared behind a tapestry. Jack pursued the old man in black robes, rudely elbowing his way through the throng of people waiting for the kneeling space Brunix had just left.

Peering from behind the woven portal covering, Jack watched Brunix stuff the parchment into an interior pocket of his sleeveless overrobe. The owner peered about him with a smile of contempt for those who prayed for the queen's recovery. His eyes gleamed in the candlelight and his aura flared once more, this time in a bright orange.

The man knew something important.

Following in Brunix's wake was easier than forcing a new path through the crowd. Jack itched to remove the parchment from its hiding place. The factory owner kept a proprietary hand over the concealed pocket. He'd notice if the crackling bulk suddenly disappeared.

Very slowly, Jack allowed his delusion to shift. Bit by bit, he absorbed the face and demeanor of a nondescript man he passed in the wide temple porch, shedding his old disguise in the same order. When he plunged after Brunix into the bright spring sunshine, no trace of his previous delusion remained.

Brunix stood unmoving on the top step, blinking rapidly until his eyes adjusted to the sunlight. Jack used those two moments of distraction well. He gathered the tattered remnants of extra magic left in his body and concentrated on the copied runes.

The single sheet of parchment weighed a ton inside his mind. It refused to budge from the fold of fabric that protected it.

Jack pushed his magic deep, struggled, and sweated. The cords of his neck stood out with the strain of moving the burden.

Brunix blinked and twisted his neck in preparation for moving down the two dozen stone slabs that formed the steps.

Near panic that his quarry might escape, Jack "grabbed" the parchment with a spell and dumped it into his own pocket.

The factory owner stepped down into the milling throng.

Jack's knees turned weak in fatigue and reaction to the hasty spell. Barely able to keep a delusion of light-colored hair on his head, he sought a quiet corner at the edge of the open square before the temple.

Very soon, he must return to the factory and stand above Katrina's little web of ley lines. A good meal would work wonders at restoring his talent, too. But first a brief nap beneath that clump of bushes.

Eyes still on Brunix's progress across the broad square, Jack edged toward his chosen refuge. The tall man strode in the direction of the factory, never turning around or looking back to see if he was being followed.

Still five stairs from the paved square, Jack caught sight of a pair of men in palace-guard-gray scuttling behind Brunix. A knife flashed in the sunlight.

"No!" Jack screamed as he dashed across the square. King Simeon couldn't succeed with this murder. If Brunix died, then the sorcerer-king could confiscate the factory and all his property, including Katrina.

The men in gray disappeared, as if they had never been behind their victim.

Screams erupted from the throats of a hundred people. A wide circle formed around the crumpled body. Blood stained the fire-green robe and black tunic an ugly and lethal red.

Jack skidded to a halt beside the groaning figure. Cautiously he extended his hand to the carved bone of the knife hilt. The outline of a winged god glared at him, defying him to remove the knife from the wound.

He'd seen that outline before. Lord Krej had created a huge stained glass window of Simurgh in the great hall of his castle. Not true glass, but a magical simulation formed of blood and the volcanic sands of Hanassa.

Jack's hand shook as it hovered above the instrument of death. A ritual knife. Wielded by the coven.

Frantically, Jack sought a healing spell, anything to slow the bleeding, repair enough of the damage to keep Brunix alive.

"Get a healer!" he yelled to the watchers. They stared mutely at him, unmoving.

Why waste a healer on an outland half-breed? The stray thought penetrated Jack's mind.

Outraged at the arrogant prejudice of these people, he found a small spark of magic lingering within him. Instinctively he sought to draw more magic from the burned-out ley lines beneath his feet. Blue sparks shot from his hand into Brunix's gaping chest wound as the empty ley line shuddered from the strain of his tapping.

Brunix's eyes fluttered opened, unfocused, filled with pain. "Save the lace!" he whispered. "Save her. . . ."

Jack leaned closer to catch the man's dying words. A long-fingered hand grasped the neck of his tunic in a futile attempt to communicate.

"Katrina. Save her and the lace from Simeon." A death rattle choked Brunix and he collapsed, staring into the nothingness of the void between the planes of existence.

The stone paving of the square trembled as if a hundred war steeds galloped toward the murder scene.

Jack looked up for the source of the disturbance. The instability of the Kardia beneath his feet faded to nothing. A sense of the familiar rocked his senses.

Just before the cave-in at the mine, a similar vibration had told him of the impending disaster. Had his instinctive reaching for power caused the ley line to crumble?

Instead of the prison of tunnels dug deep within the planet to trap him at the time of disaster, he faced a ring of grim-faced palace guards.

"You are under arrest for murder." The magician who had invaded the factory last night stepped forward, a pair of iron manacles in his hand.

"He removed some outland garbage from our city!" protested an onlooker. A verbal protest only. No one stepped forward to defend Jack.

Praying that his protective delusion of blond hair wouldn't evaporate, Jack visualized his armor snapping in place. Then he activated the spell with memorized trigger words.

Cold iron enclosed his wrists.

There was no magic left in his body or in the land. His staff was hidden back at the factory. Once more he was a prisoner and unable to save himself.

Hands slapped his body, roughly, in search of hidden weapons. The parchment crackled.

"What have we here, evidence of conspiracy with magic?" The slight man chortled at his public display of accusing Jack of more than just murder. He held the unrolled parchment up to the light for all to see.

Black ink sprawled across the page in a jumble of rectangular shapes and straight slashes. Under observation and bright sunlight, the runes flashed into unnatural red sigils. The parchment thinned. A bright circle of sunlight at the center charred and burst into flame.

Gasps of superstitious awe and fear rose from the crowd. A dozen hands signed the cross of the Stargods. Two dozen more crossed wrists and flapped their hands in the more ancient ward against evil.

In seconds, the parchment disappeared into useless ash.

"A trick with a glass," Jack murmured so that only the magician heard.

"Perhaps," he shrugged and scattered the last of the ashes across Brunix's lifeless body. "Tricks keep the peasants afraid and cost no energy."

The magician gestured for two burly men, easily a head taller than Jack, to take him into custody.

"Lock him in the warded dungeon. The rest of you come with me. We still have to capture the girl."

Katrina wiggled the long divider pin that had been a gift from Brunix into the tiny crack between two wall panels. The hidden safe was deep in this wall. The door would open under pressure upon a secret trigger at the same time as a key released the lock. The long pin would have to be her key while her fingers sought a sensitive place at the top of the crack.

In another portion of the factory, the sound of a door being thrust open with violence startled her. The vibrations from the wooden panels shattering against the wall traveled all the way up to the top floor. Katrina's feet tingled as the entire building shook.

A few more moments of privacy and she would know if the precious shawl had been made with Tambrin, or if Jack and King Simeon sought a different piece.

Heavy boots pounded upon the first flight of steps to the dormitory level. She almost didn't hear the click of the hidden lock over the noise.

Brunix would be anxious to claim her when he returned, but surely his large boots wouldn't make that much noise in his own factory.

The panel swung open. Glimmering lace spilled out. Reel after reel of precious white lace, ivory lace, and ecru. Slender insertions, square mats, round doilies, fans and flounces as wide as her spread fingers.

A fortune spilled out of the cavity. All of it made of Tambrin. Enough to hang the owner who cached the forbidden treasure.

The footsteps slowed as the stairs steepened between the dormitory and the workroom. A few screams from startled lacemakers rose through the flooring.

Hastily, Katrina fumbled through the vast mound of lace seeking the familiar texture of her mother's shawl with her fingertips. At the back of the safe, beneath a stack of fans she found it. Sensitized by years of thread work, she knew without looking that the shawl had Tambrin spun with the silk. Both fibers were so fine they had blended together, neither distinguished from the other unless examined closely by an expert.

A particular creak indicated someone had left the workroom and now sought the top floor of the factory.

Katrina bundled the spilled lace and shoved it into the cavity.

There was so much of it, she couldn't hold it all in place while she closed the panel.

The lock on the outer door rattled. A fist hit the immovable panels.

Heedless of damaging dirt and tangles she crammed the reels together, held them in place with her foot while she closed the panel.

An alien foot slammed against the locked door.

The secret panel clicked closed.

She returned the long pin to its customary place within one of her plaits.

The door to the apartment crashed to the floor. Six palace guards crowded the landing.

Katrina backed up, hiding with her skirts the telltale tendril of shimmering white filigree peeping from the crack in the wall.

"Restrain her," the slender man who had searched the warehouse last night ordered.

Fear robbed Katrina of speech and will. Two men, much taller than the magician in charge, stepped toward her. The manacles looked puny dangling in the massive paw of the broadest of the guards.

At the last moment she stepped back, coming up against the wall abruptly.

"Owner Neeles Brunix holds me in slavery. You must have his authority to—"

"Owner Neeles Brunix is dead," the magician interrupted. "Murdered by one of his outland kin. At least we presume the night watchman in his employ is kin," he dismissed her protest. The magician's gleeful grin killed whatever hope Katrina might have had. "You belong to King Simeon now. Or the coven. Take your choice, Slave Kaantille."

"Brunix is dead?" Katrina didn't know what else to say, wishing only to stall. She had no doubt Jack had a good reason for committing murder. Like preserving his own life. But he was too smart, too powerful a magician to be caught so easily. Unless he didn't do it. Unless . . .

The cold iron of the manacle slapping her wrists drained the blood from her head and the strength from her knees. White spots appeared before her eyes, as cold sweat broke out on her back.

All these years of keeping Brunix at bay, of avoiding Simeon and his evil rituals were for naught. The Solstice was mere weeks away.

What will Simeon do to me when he finds out I'm no longer a virgin?

"Yes, Brunix is dead. I made certain of it when I twisted the knife before removing and cleaning it," the magician gloated as if he had committed the murder himself. "Now where is the shawl, Slave Kaantille?"

"What shawl?" she asked. Her eyes darted to the just completed piece on her pillow. Never would she betray to anyone but Jack the hoard of lace inside the wall.

"This shawl." The magician lifted the lace gingerly between two fingers, as if afraid of being contaminated by it. "You aren't a very good liar, Slave Kaantille. Don't bother trying to fool me. A truth spell will force proper answers from you. Painfully if necessary. Bring her," he ordered the guards as he sauntered out of the apartment, a sneer of contempt on his face, the lace held delicately away from his body.

Katrina screeched and struggled against her captors. They ended her thrashing by simply lifting her by the elbows and carrying her between them out the door. Never once did the palace guard look behind them at the scrap of lace betraying the secret wall safe.

Chapter Thirty-Three

Jack's ribs exploded in pain. He slumped against the manacles that chained him to the wall of the dungeon. His resistance to imprisonment evaporated with white hot agony.

Hope died.

A gap-toothed jailer smiled, fondling an iron bar as long as Jack's outstretched arm. "Want more?" the man in black leather grinned at Jack. "Just keep up yer hollerin' and ye can have all the tickles Old Mabel here can give."

Old Mabel? The cretin actually had a name for his crude weapon. The coven must love this man. The Commune believed that Lord Krej and his sister had learned to use pain—in others or themselves—to create magical energy.

Jack wasn't desperate enough, yet, to dive that deeply into black magic. Blood magic. Simurgh's magic.

Blackness encroached upon his vision. The tip of the iron bar caressed his side, cold against the spreading fire of crushed ribs and laboring lungs.

"Don't pass out on us now, boy," the jailer coaxed with an almost seductive voice. "King Simeon and his lady have questions to ask ye.

Ye be polite now and stay awake. Otherwise Old Mabel will need to wake ye up again." With a parting chuckle, the jailer exited.

Jack invited the darkness of his unlit cell to soothe the blinding ache behind his eyes.

Little creatures scurried in the straw at his feet. He jerked back awake. The blood on his face and side had attracted rats. If he fell asleep, the disease-ridden rodents might take it as an invitation to feast on his still living flesh.

"*Stargods!* What did I do to deserve this?" he moaned.

"You chose to interfere with my dragon," a quiet voice answered from the doorway.

For a moment Jack thought he was hallucinating. The newcomer appeared to be Lord Krej returned to life. His red hair was a little duller with the passage of three years. His square-cut beard hid the shape of his chin. But the bay-blue eyes that peered at Jack with lusting evil were the same. Even his red and green aura was the same.

The magic permeating his body smelled different. Still filled with Tambootie, but overlaid with something else. Something Jack couldn't identify.

"Who broke the backlash spell, Krej?" Jack asked, his curiosity overcoming his pain, for a moment.

"*KREJ!*" the man yelled. "How dare you call me Krej? That insignificant son of a weak and petty Coronnite. I am *King* Simeon of SeLenicca and Hanassa, true heir to Rossemeyer and soon to be conqueror of Coronnan. Do you understand me, boy?"

"If you aren't Krej, then you're his twin brother," Jack accused. So this was Simeon the Sorcerer, King of SeLenicca. *Simeon the Insane,* judging by his reaction.

"Nonsense, utter nonsense." A new voice, calm and feminine and familiar, moved into Jack's field of vision.

"Rejiia," Jack whispered. Pale skin, smooth as ivory, black hair pulled into a sleek knot at her nape. Long and graceful body clothed in elegant black. There was a new sensuousness to her walk, maturity in her ample bosom and a seductive pout to her full, red lips. If anything she was lovelier than ever.

And taller. Rejiia at fifteen had been nearly as tall as her father, Krej. At twenty she topped the red-haired man beside her by a finger-width or two.

She deposited a lump of metal by the doorway. Jack squinted his aching eyes to focus on the talisman she had levitated to this cell. A tin weasel sculpture with flaking gilt paint. Krej.

"*Lady Rejiia* to you, boy," she lifted her arrogant little chin in contempt. Her nose wrinkled at the same time as she caught a whiff of the odors of the dungeon. She caressed the head of the statue before moving into the cell.

"Adding incest to your sins, *Lady* Rejiia?" Jack quipped, tired of their need to add insult to injury with the appellation "boy." Suddenly he was beyond pain, and fear. All that was left of him was a glimmer of hysterical humor and that wouldn't last long.

"What do you mean by that, *boy?*" Rejiia approached Jack, looking as if she would spit on him. Anger blazed from her eyes and some of her control slipped, changing her beautiful face into a mask of ugly hatred.

"I mean, that if Simeon isn't your father, then he's your father's brother. He's obviously your lover, you stink of him. Or don't you care about such things?" With the clarity of pain and knowing he wouldn't survive much longer, Jack saw it all.

Queen Rossemikka, who had been a victim of Janataea's and Krej's manipulations, had warned the Commune of the coven's dynastic plans. Royal marriages and births throughout the world had been arranged and scheduled along with appropriate assassinations. Generation after generation of alliances came down to one or two people eligible to claim multiple thrones.

Simeon claimed descent from Rossemikka's much older, exiled, half sister. Thus he should rule Rossemeyer. His marriage to Queen Miranda of SeLenicca had produced a princess who could claim both thrones. If she married the heir to Coronnan, the entire continent would be united under one crown.

Rejiia shared a common great-grandfather with Darville of Coronnan. She, or her child, could claim the Coraurlia, the dragon crown, if Darville and Mikka had no children. Jack wished he'd taken the time to catch up on current events since leaving the mines. He had no idea who was alive and well and who wasn't.

What seemed most important, now, was that the coven would control Queen Miranda's daughter, Jaranda, and whoever inherited Coronnan. Stargods help them all if Rejiia passed off a child of an incestuous relationship as heir and mate to Jaranda, another incestuous relationship.

Greedy madness shone in Simeon's eyes. He, like Krej, was too ambitious to wait for the coven's plans to come to fruition. He wanted to rule and exploit for himself and not the coven.

I have to end this madness, Jack thought. No matter the cost, I have to stop the coven.

A jolt of memory rocked his mind away from Rejiia's spitting indignation. Years ago, Jack had claimed the name of "Yaakke." A name out of legend. A name of power and great reverence.

A thousand years ago, Yaakke, son of Yaacob the Usurper, had united three clans in northern Coronnan to form the first kingdom. Yaakke had met the Stargods in the sacred clearing and vowed eternal fealty and reverence if the three red-haired brothers would save his wife and child from the plague. The plague was banished and Yaakke charged with the duty of eliminating the power of the winged demon Simurgh. He had succeeded but only after bitter and bloody battles. Yaakke died two days after the last battle.

Now Simeon's coven was attempting to reestablish the bloody rituals of Simurgh as the one true religion. Once more, the duty of preventing the deaths of innocents fell to a man named Yaakke.

If he was ever to earn the right to a name, Jack had to complete this quest, even if it brought him an ugly and painful death.

Katrina tripped on the slimy steps into the dungeon. Her guards grabbed the chain binding her wrists and yanked her upright. The strain on her arms and shoulders made her cry out.

"Careful o' t'at one. His Majesty wants her undamaged," warned a jailer who was missing at least three teeth. He caressed a long iron bar in his arms, as if it were a beloved pet.

"I know. I know," groused the guard who still hauled upward on the chain. "Won't be no cuts or bruises. Just enough pain to keep her in line." He pulled hard on the chain and Katrina stumbled forward in his path.

She had been brought to the same manor house on the outskirts of the city as she had been that night three years ago when King Simeon gave her to Owner Neeles Brunix. Apparently, the king didn't want to soil the palace with dungeons and torture chambers and prisoners who would eventually be sacrificed to the coven.

The odors of sweat and fear, of the midden that had never been flushed clean, and blood—lots of blood—assaulted all of her senses. She swallowed heavily to force calm on her stomach.

She stumbled again. This time she dropped to her knees, unable to hold herself upright any longer. Her hands rested on the straw-covered stone floor. A vibration passed through her hands, much like the one that had shaken the factory just before she was taken by the guards.

Alarmed, she looked up at the grim-faced men, who seemed to be hovering outside one particular cell. None of them seemed to notice the shaking. The hideous statue of a weasel that had once been in Simeon's study rocked with the trembling Kardia.

Before she could analyze the nature of the vibration, her guard lifted her by the elbows and thrust her past the snarling statue, into the cell.

"Never utter your blasphemies again, boy," King Simeon

screamed at a man, hanging by his wrists from the wall. "My mother was Jaylene D'Rossemeyer, exiled daughter of the late king. *Jaylene,* not Janessa. Janessa's children are all bastards and not a drop of royal blood in them." Spittle dribbled from the king's mouth and his eyes showed more white than color.

"Tell that to your aura," Jack defied him.

Jack! Oh, poor Jack. Katrina looked closer at the magician who had vowed to help her. He had shielded her from Brunix and the palace magician last night, and opened his mind to her. Her heart shrank and burned for him. If only she could ease his pain.

Blood and bruises spread an ugly stain across his left side up into his naked chest, and probably his back, too. His bare feet looked swollen and raw. More bruises marred his jaw and wrists. Arms stretched wide by the rings holding his manacles, he seemed to cling to consciousness by the barest of threads.

Death was the only way to ease pain now. There was no escape from Simeon's dungeons. Just as there was no escape from his mines.

But Jack and P'pa escaped the mines, a tiny thought whispered into her mind.

"What do you mean about his aura?" The black-haired beauty who was always at Simeon's side these days thrust the king aside and stood squarely in front of Jack. None of them seemed to notice Katrina.

"I mean that Simeon's aura is almost identical to Krej's, and his magic smells just like Janataea's. He's brother to those two, which means you've been sleeping with your uncle, Rejiia."

Rejiia reared back in alarm.

"And borne him a child," Katrina added from across the cell, noting the woman's now flat belly. "An abomination by anyone's standards."

At last they all looked at her. She almost wished she'd kept her mouth shut. The malevolence dripping from Simeon's and Rejiia's demeanor echoed that of the weasel, and was almost enough to physically push her back into the arms of her guard. A disgusting thought, almost as unpleasant as the thought of Simeon sleeping with his niece.

"You can't prove that!" Simeon defended himself. "My servant destroyed the runes that Brunix copied. I have the shawl with the runes woven into the flowers. I have unraveled it and burned the threads. No one will ever prove that Janessa was my mother. Therefore, I decree that it is not so. It is treason to say otherwise."

"You're insane," Jack breathed. His chest heaved and he winced in pain. "As insane as Janataea was just before she died. The Tambootie has rotted your mind."

Katrina agreed with Jack. She didn't know the people Jack spoke of, but she saw Simeon's eyes and knew that madness lay behind them.

"We will discuss this later, Simeon," Rejiia ordered. She edged away from her lover as if she, too, believed he had lost control of his mind. "These two must be kept alive and reasonably healthy until the Solstice."

"I can't allow him to spread treason," Simeon protested. "Tattia put the runes into the shawl to warn the queen. But I had the lace-maker murdered and the shawl destroyed with her. But the shawl survived to haunt me. I have finally burned it and all who know of it must die. I want him dead now. Guard, slit his throat. Now. I demand his death. Now."

Chapter Thirty-Four

"**D**on't be a fool, Simeon." Rejiia brushed the mewling man aside as she faced Jack once more. "He has the transport spell. While he is in pain, and hungry—totally vulnerable—I will strip his mind and have the secret. I will also learn where the Commune hides. This *boy* will be the instrument of their destruction!"

Jack bit back a retort. Why waste energy asserting his right to a name? He'd need all of his strength to combat Rejiia's mind probes.

Then he made sense of her statement. Some of the Commune had escaped the fire at the monastery! Fervently he prayed that Jaylor and Brevelan and the baby had been among them. If they had, then the remnants of the Commune might have retreated to the clearing or Shayla's lair. He had a place to send Shayla for final healing.

If he managed to save himself long enough to patch her wing. If he managed to think of something else during Rejiia's spell. He didn't dare consider what would happen to Katrina. He had to somehow survive until he was sure Katrina was safe.

"I am the king," Simeon asserted. "My will rules. This kingdom exists to serve *ME*. Kill the blasphemous boy."

"In this house, by your own decree, the coven rules," Rejiia returned. "And I am the focus of the coven." She stared at the red-haired man with contempt.

Good. Division within the coven reduced their power and purpose. And Rejiia was female, she couldn't gather dragon magic. She, too, was limited by her body's reserves.

"You were the focus only while you were pregnant. I allowed you to take the focus because of your connection to the *Gaia*. You aren't pregnant anymore, and you lost the child, so I take back the focus." Simeon pouted like a little boy. The reek of Tambootie on his breath intensified.

Jack guessed the leaves of the dragon tree had finally inflated Simeon's sense of superiority beyond all limits of reality. The same thing had happened to Krej and Janataea. Neither believed them-selves mortal anymore and had left their bodies open to physical attack.

"Don't push me, Simeon. The coven looks to me for leadership," Rejiia warned. Then she turned her attention back to her prisoners, authoritative and purposeful. "Loosen the girl's chains so she may sit or lie against the opposite wall. Then clear this room. I need space and concentration."

The guards obeyed, fixing a long chain between Katrina's right manacle and a ring in the wall. Then they backed out of the cell. Simeon refused to follow, but he did station himself against the door, leaving Rejiia free to work inside the damp stone room. She planted herself between Jack and Katrina.

An advantage to Jack. If he couldn't see the girl cowering in the far corner, then he wouldn't be distracted by her. Wouldn't allow his thoughts to linger on her and draw Rejiia's attention to her under the influence of the probe.

Jack blanked his mind, trying desperately to think of nothing at all. If Rejiia's spells had nothing to latch onto, perhaps they'd fly in one ear and out the other.

"What about this?" A new man wearing the uniform of an army

officer entered the cell. Lanciar, the spy from the mine, who had helped Jack escape and then betrayed him. He carried a dead bird by the feet in his outstretched arm. His nose wrinkled in distaste.

"Ah, the familiar. Throw it into the midden," Rejiia dismissed the man and his burden.

"No!" Jack howled. "You murdered Corby. You've taken my only friend in the world." Once before he'd scattered a mind probe into erratic bird thoughts. Maybe he could do it again. If they believed his grief and panic.

"That's right, boy." Lanciar smiled. "You have nothing left to live for. You might as well give up your secrets so you may die in peace. But before you die, I want to thank you. That little session we had searching for the dragon opened me to my full powers where the coven's rituals couldn't. I am now a master magician, one of the coven and eager to watch this spell so that I may learn to use it interrogating prisoners of war at the newly activated front. We won a stunning victory last week and captured or killed at least half of Darville's troops."

"Not Corby!" Jack yelled again, ignoring this latest disaster. Think like a jackdaw, remember the bird's scattered thought patterns.

"We've done this before, boy. Three years ago, at the coronation. That time, the stupid bird intercepted the probe. Now he's dead. There is only you and me and my magic." A small dart of glowing dark green appeared in Rejiia's hand. As dark as her magic, almost black. The same color he'd found in another dungeon, back in Coronnan. Rejiia had broken Jaylor's wards and stolen Krej from his cell. Krej, who lingered in his tin statue form at Simeon's side, blinked at Jack with knowing eyes.

Can't think of Krej and that one hint of animation. Can't think about Jaylor or Coronnan. Think like the bird. Random. Meaningless.

Rejiia lay the probe on her outstretched hand, murmuring an incantation. Eyes half closed, her face became a mask of emotionless concentration.

The probe grew in length. Its sharp point broadened into an

arrowhead, big enough to hunt wild tusker. Wide. Sharp. Barbed. Impossible to remove once it caught on meat. The meat of Jack's mind.

The hot sweat of pain turned icy on his back. The burn of scraped skin beneath the manacles numbed. All discomfort gathered in his brain, a concentrated mass of terror.

"This will only hurt for a little while, boy," Rejiia cooed. The lines of her face softened into sensuous pleasure. Her breasts strained against the rich fabric of her gown. Her body radiated seduction. "Give me your thoughts. Join your mind with my mind, your body into my body. Share with me the ultimate intimacy."

Jack's breathing deepened against his will, until it matched Rejiia's heavy rhythm of passion. His heart pounded in his ears and his body strained to fulfill her promise of the sexual delights.

His thoughts returned to Katrina and the few moments of openness they'd shared within the shelter of his armor. Sweet, innocent, honest. Reluctant to give herself to any man without love, with less than total commitment from both of them. A sweetness he'd never know.

Rejiia had offered herself to him once before. Not from passion, but in payment. She was a whore. A filthy, amoral, spiteful, selfish whore.

Sickened by her, Jack's body and mind lost all interest in Rejiia. But he continued the litany of her vile attributes. "Incestuous bitch! Adulteress. Traitor. I will kill myself before I betray my Commune. The transport spell dies with me as it should have died with the passing of the Stargods."

"I love to rape innocent *boys*," Rejiia sighed with pleasure as she blew the pulsing probe from her hand as if sending a lover's kiss. "They learn to revel in the *pain!*"

Jack slammed his eyelids closed, praying that the probe wouldn't gain entrance to his mind through a vulnerable eye.

A slight whirring sound circled his head. Pressure built, squeezing his skull, demanding he open himself. More pressure until he thought his head would explode with it. His eyes seemed to bulge and his ears filled with a roar of unnatural sound. He fought the urge to cry out, to open any part of himself.

Think of quiet. Peace. Solitude. A gentle brook babbling down a mountain side. Hot springs filling a pool with enough warmth to bathe. Calubra ferns screening the path . . . the path back to the clearing.

"The clearing . . ." he heard himself say. "Brevelan's clearing."

Katrina watched in fascinated horror as Jack twisted and writhed as much as his bonds would allow. He fought the slimy black arrow of magic with eyes closed and muscled hunched.

She knew the moment Rejiia's spell penetrated Jack's defenses. His body relaxed, his face lost all expression, and he began to speak. Incoherent words, gibberish, or a foreign language.

Rejiia flushed with embarrassment at this failure in communication. Then she screwed up her face into ugly contortions, concentrating her will on her victim. His words finally made sense.

"To find the clearing, take the path behind the pub, up hill to a large boulder split in two. The path seems to go around the boulder. You must step through the broken halves . . ." Jack recited in a monotone.

"Yes, yes, but what pub? Where?" Rejiia stamped her foot in frustration.

"Fishing village of no name. Step through the two broken halves of the boulder, under the fallen tree and onto a game trail . . ."

"Where is the fishing village?" Rejiia screamed. Her hands reached for her perfect hair as if to tear it from her scalp. At the last second, she thought better of her actions. "Fetch me some Tambootie, Simeon. I must press him harder."

"No name village south of the capital. The game trail ends at a creek. Wait for the opening. Brevelan opens the path to those in need of her healing." Jack sagged against his chains as if unconscious. Sweat ran in rivulets down his cheeks and chest.

Katrina hoped he'd passed beyond the pain and guilt of succumbing to the spell. When he awoke, he'd be chilled and she wouldn't be able to comfort him.

In frustration she yanked at her chains. Simeon glared at her for quiet. His lips curled in a feral snarl, exactly like the expression on the face of the tin weasel. Katrina ceased her struggle.

"We will come back to Brevelan's clearing, boy. Give me the transport spell," Rejiia demanded. A fat oily leaf as broad as her palm appeared out of nowhere and drifted into her outstretched hand. She nibbled the tip of the leaf and licked droplets of oil from the vein.

A smile crossed her face and her hands began to flutter with new animation. Katrina hadn't been aware of the sagging in the woman's shoulders until this new resurgence of energy.

Jack looked puzzled and upset at the newest question. He did not respond.

"The *transport* spell. How is it done?" Rejiia urged, more patient now that she had consumed the dark green leaf with pink veins. She snapped her fingers at Simeon to indicate she needed another.

The king pouted and folded his arms across his chest in defiance of the order. Rejiia's eyes rolled up in exasperation. Without taking her eyes off Jack, she pointed to one of the men hovering outside the cell. The short magician who had visited the factory last night responded. In the matter of two heartbeats, three more leaves appeared in Rejiia's hand.

"Dangerous. Too dangerous. Lost in the void," Jack mumbled. His eyes snapped open and several emotions crossed his face in rapid succession. Fear of the spell fought Rejiia's compulsion to recite.

"I will risk the void. I will risk a confrontation with the dragons. Give. Me. The. Transport. Spell."

Words that meant nothing to Katrina, but delighted Rejiia and Simeon, poured from his mouth. Words of time lapses, visualization, deep breathing, and trances. And then a lilting series of words to trigger the spell. When the last syllables dribbled from him, like drool on a baby's chin, he collapsed against his chain, knees unable to support him any longer.

"Wake up, boy!" Rejiia slapped his face.

Katrina winced at the sharp sound. No response from Jack.

"Very well. I have what I came for. Guards, loosen his chains so he may lie down and die."

"Wouldn't want to take a steed up this path, Your Grace." Sergeant Fred de Baker checked the backtrail for signs of followers. Margit, dressed in comfortable leather trews and tunic and looking happier than Darville had ever seen her, signaled that no one followed.

"It's been a long time since I ran back and forth from village to clearing without a second thought. I'm not in condition for this." King Darville paused for breath in their upward trek. He held out his good right hand to assist his queen over a rough spot. Thanks to Brevelan's healing spells, Mikka had recovered rapidly from the last miscarriage.

She had said little since they left the capital. No stronger wall could stand between them than this endless silence.

"We were friends, Mikka, when we considered Brevelan's clearing our home," he said quietly.

She looked up then, her eyes steady and clear. Hope sparked between them.

" 'Tis Brevelan and Jaylor's friendship that worries me, love. How could we let this one issue destroy the bonds we forged? There must be another way," she said quietly.

"Our enemies have sought long and hard to shatter the friendship of a lifetime. We withstood those assaults only to fall victim to our own pride and ambition. Come, Mikka. We have to settle this, no matter how difficult for all of us."

"Promise me, Darville, that if we find no solution to the succession, you will put me aside and remarry."

"I won't even consider it. I'll match your strong will against my stubbornness. We will find a solution." He kissed her palm with loving tenderness. The wall of silence crumbled but other walls threatened to rise up.

"You sure this is the right path, Your Grace? Seems to fade into nothing more'n it goes forward," Fred asked.

Margit moved up beside him and giggled. "The clearing wouldn't be secure if just anyone could find it." She strode forward with a masculine swagger.

"This is the right path, Fred." In more ways than one. For the good of the kingdom, Darville realized, he needed to make peace with Brevelan and Jaylor over Glendon. More important, Mikka needed to settle the issue of the cat persona sharing her body.

Only Jaylor and Brevelan could help. So the royal couple had journeyed to the southern edge of Coronnan in search of the magicians.

They had left their military escort in the foul-smelling pub of a fishing village near the foothills of the Southern Mountains. Fred and Margit were the only ones allowed to accompany them on the long climb uphill.

Both Darville and Mikka knew the trail well. Four years ago, they'd traveled it often enough. He'd been a golden wolf then, and she a multicolored cat, familiars to a red-haired witchwoman.

Now he was a king, with a kingdom straining toward stability and she was his barren queen. An heir to the throne would give the people of Coronnan the confidence to continue their quest for peace among themselves and with their neighboring kingdoms.

Darville had acknowledged as heir his own bastard son, Glendon, over the claims of Rejiia de Draconis, daughter of his father's cousin. Rejiia's husband had petitioned the Council of Provinces time and again to proclaim his wife heir. But Rejiia had been absent from the capital for nearly a year. Rumor placed her variously in SeLenicca, in

Hanassa, and in her home—locked up and beaten regularly by her jealous husband.

Rejiia's claim was tainted by her father's involvement with a forbidden coven of Simurgh. Glendon might never be allowed to ascend the throne because his mother was an acknowledged witch and illegitimate as well. So far, Darville's acceptance of the boy as heir had met with only minor opposition from the Council of Provinces. They still hoped the king would put aside his barren wife and make a new alliance to produce a better successor to the Coraurlia. Few outland kingdoms had come forward with prospective brides, but the lords themselves had dozens of noble daughters.

The broken boulder that signaled the approach to the clearing appeared before him. Both Fred and Margit marched around the split rock in the direction the path seemed to follow. Darville stepped between the two pieces, on the left-hand side of the tree that had grown between the halves. Fred and Margit were immediately lost to sight.

Twenty paces beyond the boulder, the path crossed a creek and died.

"Look over there, Darville." Mikka pointed through the trees.

"I don't see anything." He squinted his eyes to peer closer in the direction she indicated.

"The barrier to the clearing. There's a big hole in it. We can walk right in without Brevelan opening it for us."

"Come on." He grabbed her hand and dragged her toward the barrier. "Something's terribly wrong. We've got to get in there!"

Rejiia left in a sweep of black skirts, the men following in her wake. The door slammed closed behind them. The click of the lock tolled Jack's doom like a bell in the remaining silence.

Darkness descended upon the cell until the torches further down the corridor filtered light through the bars that formed the wall. Once Jack's eyes adjusted, he picked out the details of Katrina's huddled form on the pallet opposite his. The single chain binding his left wrist to the ring in the wall was obscured by shadow.

The building grumbled beneath his weary body. Every joint and muscle screamed at the least movement.

"Oh, Jack, are you alive?" Katrina whispered. She crawled toward him, as far as her chain would reach. When she could get no closer, she stretched her free hand, as if to smooth his brow. Inches separated them. He couldn't move closer to accept her gentle touch.

"Not sure," he breathed the words, careful not to jostle any part of his body.

"I'm sorry you had to go through that. It was awful to watch. I can't imagine how horrible it must have been to endure."

Her sympathy reached across the space between them, even if she herself couldn't. A little of the pain lifted free of his mind.

"Don't try to imagine it. You'd hurt more than I want you to have to endure." The thought of the girl's plight suddenly pained his heart almost as much as the jailers' blows hurt his body.

"She didn't have to kill your bird. I know he meant a great deal to you. That just added insult to injury so you'd be more vulnerable."

As soon as Jack was certain the others were out of earshot he flexed his now unbound right wrist to check for damage and grinned to himself in the shadowy twilight that settled in the cell. "Don't be sorry for me. That wasn't Corby."

"How can you tell?" Astonishment and the smallest measure of hope shone through her words.

In Jack's imagination she'd never looked or sounded more beautiful. Even knowing her face was marred with bruises didn't diminish his gladness that his imprisonment was lightened by her presence.

"That was a crow, bigger and no white spots on his head. My bird is a jackdaw. His white spots look like an old man's bushy eyebrows. I sent Corby back to the dragons this morning. He shouldn't be anywhere near the city."

"He obeys you so well?"

"He is my familiar." Jack shrugged and regretted the movement. As a magician he needed no other explanation for the bond that now existed between himself and the bird. "How'd you get those bruises?"

"Brunix. He slapped me for speaking to you last night." She paused a moment, rubbing her jaw. "Is he really dead?"

"Yes."

"Did you kill him?"

"No. Did you care so much for him?"

"I hated him. But life with him was better than death during one of Simeon's rituals. I don't care that I have a power the king wanted to release. If having power means being like him or Brunix, I don't want it."

"I've been a slave, too, Katrina. I know the limited choices you've had. But if Brunix left you a virgin, then he was a better man than I hoped."

She bit her lip and turned her head away in embarrassment. "What will Simeon do to me when he finds out I'm not?"

A new pain awakened in Jack. Brunix had raped her. Like all Rovers, the factory owner had no respect for anyone not of his race and clan.

"Brunix only took me once. Mostly to prove he could after Simeon violated some private agreement between them. But Brunix grew tired of waiting for me to come to him willingly. He promised to rape me tonight, after he finished his business. I wasn't as important to him as his business and his money."

"The business had something to do with the runes in the temple. They cost him his life. The coven murdered him in the temple square. I wonder if they knew what he'd done to you, and death was his punishment?"

Further conversation ended with the rattle of the door again. The gap-toothed guard with the iron bar entered with a bowl of gruel and a cup of steaming liquid. Light from the corridor chased away some of the shadows.

"Dinner time, sweetheart." He bent and placed the meal at Katrina's feet. "Ain't ye gonna thank me?" He reached out and pinched Katrina's breast hard.

She winced and closed her eyes but said nothing. Then a mask of total blankness descended upon her. No emotion betrayed the pain and humiliation she must be feeling.

"Frigid bitch," the guard spat and left. He made a great show of locking the door behind him, making certain the prisoners knew he was free and they were not.

"You need this more than me." Katrina shoved the bowl and cup as far as she could reach. By pushing gently with her toes, the food inched to within reach of Jack's fingernails.

"Just a sip of the broth." He grimaced and held his stomach. "Take the rest, you've got to keep up your strength to survive whatever Simeon plans for you."

"If I don't escape, I'll make sure I don't live long enough to face his rituals!" Hesitantly she fished the long divider pin from her tousled plaits. The thick portion, gathered close to her scalp from temple to nape, had hidden the tool during the guard's earlier search for weapons. Even when they knew her to be free of anything dangerous, her captors had continued to paw her breasts and between her legs.

How would she do it? A slash across the wrist and slow bleeding to death? No, the guards would find her and stop her. A stab to the heart? Her hand shook as she held the sharp pin up for inspection.

"We'll get out of this, Katrina. I don't know how yet. Simeon's insanity and Rejiia's arrogance can be turned against them. If I push Simeon hard enough, maybe he'll admit that he's a bastard and not descended from Jaylene of Rossemeyer. That will end his influence in SeLenicca and in the coven. They need his claim to Rossemeyer.

But we have to stay alive to escape." He stared at her pin with eyes that speculated and evaluated even as he pleaded with her. "I don't think I told her everything."

"We'll share the food." Determination to survive replaced her earlier despair. "You've got to eat, Jack. I don't know how long this will take, and that bitch may return at any moment. They got the wrong shawl. If we can get out of here, I think I have proof that Simeon is a bastard, with no royal blood and has no right to rule. M'ma coded a message to the queen into the shawl three years ago. Queen Miranda and her councillors would have annulled the marriage, and set Jaranda aside as heir, if they thought Simeon a bastard. I know where the shawl is hidden and I intend to use it."

She'd picked one lock today with this pin. The manacles shouldn't be that much more difficult.

"Rejiia is probably hoping that watching you eat will make me hungrier and weaker, hasten my death." He sipped at the cup and coughed, nearly retching. The spasm went on and on, wrenching his body and draining him of even more energy. At last he lay back groaning. His face flushed with the onset of fever from his injuries.

Katrina bent to her task with the pin. They didn't have any time to lose.

Chapter Thirty-Five

Jaylor stood before Darville and Mikka in the middle of the broken barrier into the clearing. With his arms crossed sternly, and his face totally blank of expression he presented a formidable barrier himself. Years ago, the king would have been able to read his friend's emotions by his posture. Too much time had passed. The bond of trust had been weakened.

"I come with an apology and a need to consult the Senior Magician, my chief adviser," he stated simply. Beside him, Mikka nodded her agreement with the statement.

A little of Jaylor's rigidity melted.

"You haven't needed to consult your 'chief adviser' very often in the last three years," Jaylor returned. "Why now?"

"I miss your friendship. I miss your wisdom. Most of all, I miss you and Brevelan. The thought of losing you forever pains me deeply." Eye-to-eye, he and Jaylor stood, assessing each other's strength and sincerity. So they had challenged each other time and again since adolescence. Each time they had ended with laughter and stronger bonds. This time . . . ?

"Could you please address the problem of Mikka and her cat? If we find a solution, the question of my heir might no longer exist."

"You have the right of it, Darville. The cat is the problem, not custody of Glendon. I think you need to meet my sons to know why." Jaylor turned and gestured at the impenetrable wall of the forest. Abruptly, the path appeared before them, straight and smooth. The three of them stepped forward, not quite side-by-side, not quite separated.

The open meadow, the planted garden, the flusterhen coop, and the goat wandering beneath the line of laundry were as familiar as yesterday. But the one-room hut that had sheltered an ensorcelled wolf, a witchwoman, and a strange little cat had grown into a large cottage. Two rooms below, a large loft above, and a shed attached to the side.

"You've made improvements," Darville commented, more to break the silence than to express himself.

Mikka smiled for the first time in weeks. Hope returned to Darville. The clearing had always offered healing to those in need.

Jaylor nodded toward the biggest improvement of all. Behind the coop two little boys stalked a beleaguered flustercock. The younger of the two, boasting a full head of red hair, clutched a bright tail feather that could only belong to the cock.

"He . . . they are wonderful, Jaylor," Mikka gasped, an anxious hand to her throat.

It was the older of the two, with golden hair and eyes, longer of leg and narrower of hip than his brother, who caught their attention. As they watched, Glendon launched himself in a flying leap onto the cock's back. He came up giggling and dusty but triumphant, a long tail feather clutched in his grubby fist. The flustercock squawked, flapped, and announced to the world his long-suffering displeasure.

Both boys dusted themselves off and ran back to the laundry line. Brevelan appeared from behind damp shirts in three sizes. She knelt on the ground to gather them both in a big hug as they showed off their treasures.

Darville smiled. This was his son, happy, playful, and handsome. He was growing up secure in the knowledge that both his parents loved him. Darville had not had such security. His parents had been monarchs with mountains of duties. As a young prince, he had been entrusted to a series of tutors and guardians, each more interested in his position at court than Darville's happiness and welfare.

How could he and Mikka take the boy away from all of this love?

"I can't get it, Jack," Katrina whispered some hours later. She shook her manacles in frustration and put the long pin back into her hair.

Jack roused from a fitful doze. He was sure the perverted guard with his pet iron bar named Mabel had broken some of his ribs. The hot stabbing pain all across his chest and into his back never dulled. Cautiously he tested his breathing. Painful, but not wheezing. Perhaps he had escaped a punctured lung.

"If I had any magic left, I could open all the locks with a thought." Now would be the time to do it. After midnight. The jailers were drowsy, the torches in the corridor sputtered and burned low.

The only things keeping the manor awake tonight was the irregular trembling of the Kardia beneath them. Something strange was happening in Queen's City.

Jack's time sense remained true and his alignment with the pole and all directions seemed intact. He had access to magic, just no strength to throw it. Rejiia's probe had failed in one sense: she'd viewed information but she hadn't stripped his mind as she threatened. And she'd had to renew her spell twice with Tambootie.

If only he were back at the factory and that little puddle of reactivated ley lines. Lines that grew beneath Katrina's workstation—the place where she sang as she worked in the dark of night.

His memory called up scenes in villages between the mine and the capital. Women singing as they went about their daily chores. Songs of joy, of love, of nurturing.

In those villages the ley lines had glowed with life, like newly planted fields of wheat. There had been a few areas where the magic was stronger, where there were supposed to be villages—groups of homes and people visible to Corby, but not to Jack. Could the women have *Sung* a kind of armor around their homes?

Brevelan *Sang* all of the time and her clearing had the best protection of any place he'd encountered. Except the time he'd visited there on his way to and from meeting the blue-tipped dragon. The barriers had been down then. Because she was dead? He prayed that merely her prolonged absence had opened the clearing to him.

Men protected their families with brute strength. Women were more subtle, and perhaps stronger, in their forms of protection. Nurturing and strengthening from within.

"*Sing* something, Katrina."

"What?"

"At the factory, you created a pool of magic beneath your work-station. You *Sang* the magic into life. That's the power Simeon sensed within you. But you awakened it by yourself. Please *Sing*." He levered himself to a half-sitting position, balanced on his right elbow, the side that didn't hurt quite so badly.

"I have no magic," Katrina protested. But she leaned forward, almost eagerly, to listen closer to him.

"You are a woman. Therefore you have the strongest magic of all, even if you can't throw it in specific spells. *Sing* me a lullaby. A healing lullaby."

Just then the foundations rumbled for the tenth time since Jack had been captured. The sense of a series of small collapses in the land filled him with a new anxiety. They hadn't much time before the burned-out ley lines gave way to the pressures of the abandoned and exploited surface.

All is quiet, all is still,

Sleep, my child, and fear not ill,
Wintry winds blow chill and drear,
Lullaby, my baby dear.

Katrina's thin voice whispered into the darkness. She nearly choked on the last line. "The last time I sang this lullaby was to my sister Hilza."

"The one who died?"

She nodded. Then she lifted her tear streaked face and sang again, stronger, surer.

Let thy little eyelids close,
Like the petals of the rose;
When the morning sun shall glow,
They shall into blossom blow,
When the morning sun shall glow.
Then the little flowers I'll prize
Then I'll kiss those little eyes.
And thy mother will not care,
If 'tis spring or winter drear,
And thy mother will not care,
If 'tis spring or winter drear.

Jack concentrated on the air surrounding Katrina. He didn't need magic to read an aura.

Healing green shimmered around her in increasing layers. Palest green of new willow shoots accompanied the first lines of her *Song*. Then a darker green of grass marked with dew at sunrise grew between the willow and the white afterimage surrounding her like a halo.

When she began the second verse, the white burst into yellow and the next layer, the color of mature ivy, climbed from the stone floor into the glowing colors.

Katrina came to the end of her melody and the colors dimmed

but did not disperse.

"Again," Jack coaxed, awed at the controlled power contained within this woman who knew only the magic instinctive to her gender.

> *The dark-eyed Rover came over the hill*
> *down through the valley on May-day.*
> *He whistled and he sang 'til the city rang*
> *and he sought the heart of a lady.*

Katrina's aura renewed itself with the first five notes of this slow and mournful tune. The layers deepened and Jack's magic reached out to embrace her power. He sensed the twisting of the lock on his manacles more than heard or felt the release.

He lay back and listened, renewing his strength and his magic. Eyes half closed, he watched for any further change.

> *Her father forbade the Rover's suit*
> *Her mother wept a malady*
> *They cried and they blamed 'til the rafters rang*
> *Never could he love the lady.*
> *They ran away to the forest's lure*
> *They refused her parents pity.*
> *But they wept and they died, alone and poor,*
> *Ne'er to return to the city.*

The last note of the *Song* hung in the air, an almost visible souvenir. And then she *Sang* the words again. The meaning of the lyrics penetrated Jack's weary mind. A love song. A man and a woman of different class and culture separated by loyalties and responsibilities greater than themselves. Typical of SeLenicca, the ballad was sad, pronouncing dire fates to young people who valued love over money.

In Coronnan, the song was joyful, and full of promise for the lovers. 'Twas a song he'd like to sing for Katrina—in better times and in a better place.

He allowed himself only one moment of poignant regret. Katrina sang it correctly. She could never love him. His life as a magician was destined to be more solitary than that of a Rover. Superstition would push him to the fringes of civilization, make him an outcast. Katrina deserved better.

The song built an ache in his heart as the notes climbed and lingered near the top of Katrina's range. The dark blue-green of an everblue in moonlight pulsed at the depth of her aura.

More blue burst forth and filled the gaps. Like quicksilver, the blue energy molded and flowed up and down and around. It slid into the floor and quickly filled the gaps in the paving stones, spread and formed a network of fragile ley lines.

Baby lines that needed love and care and nurturing to grow and fully integrate with the four elements to become part of the *Gaia*.

Katrina brought her song to a close and slumped against the wall. The power of her spell vibrated in the air. Some of the glow in the new ley lines dimmed, but they continued to pulse and throb.

"Can you see what you've done, Katrina?" Jack gasped.

"I sense nothing different. Only another tremor. But this one is smaller."

A crash and rattle of broken shutters and cracked wooden panels above them belied her words.

"Not smaller. You have stabilized the ground directly beneath us, for the moment." He continued to stare at the ley lines. His need to be free called to them. One tiny flash of blue stretched toward him, like a feeder root seeking water.

Jack stretched out his foot to touch the line. His skin crawled as if a hundred ants swarmed up his leg.

"Ah," he sighed in relief. He allowed the power to nourish him.

"You can open your chains now," he said to Katrina, still drawing the magic into his starved and battered body.

The rocking tremor increased in intensity. The iron bars rattled.

Shouts of alarm echoed along the corridor. Torches fell from their brackets and smoldered in the damp, filthy straw.

"I think we'd better make a break for it, Jack. This room might be stable, but the rest of the city is likely to collapse on top of us." Katrina hastened to the door, rattling it to see if the lock had sprung.

Jack pulled one last bit of power into himself, as if drinking the last few swallows of ale after a meal. He gestured the door open and crawled to his feet.

No part of his body was free of pain. Each breath stabbed in his chest. His vision blurred and shifted focus, spinning his head in six directions at once. He used a little of his careful store of magic to reduce the pain to manageable levels.

"Don't pass out on me now, Jack. We've got to get out of here." Katrina hauled on his arm toward the exit.

He groaned from the pressure on his ribs.

The last of the blue lines withered as a nearby building collapsed in a tumbling crash.

Katrina draped Jack's right arm around her shoulders, careful not to touch his wounded left side. Witches were supposed to be left-handed—that was one way to tell a witch from a normal person. So the guards had concentrated on Jack's left side, to weaken him further. She knew he was right-handed. Another superstition broken by fact.

Half-dragging his weight, she stumbled into the deserted corridor. The only light came from a fallen torch and the smoking straw beneath it.

As she watched, the filthy mess ignited.

"You've got to help me, Jack. I can't carry you," she pleaded with him. The twelve steps up to the next level of cellars appeared a mile high with his weight holding her back. She remembered how slippery and narrow the stone slabs were and how easily she had tripped on the worn centers.

Dutifully, Jack tried steadier steps. His right, her left, they wobbled and nearly fell.

"Together, Jack." She paused to regain her balance. "Right, left." They took two steps together and remained in rhythm.

They traversed the short corridor with relative ease. The stairs seemed another matter. Jack's bare feet recoiled from the cold stone. Katrina's torn indoor slippers didn't insulate her feet much either.

"If I had my staff . . ." Jack looked around him.

"Here, use this burned-out torch as a cane." Katrina picked up the nearest fallen brand. About as long as her arm, the handle was sturdy and whole. The oil-soaked rags wrapped around one end had ceased smoldering in the damp straw, but made a decent base.

Katrina stepped onto the first stair. Jack followed. They paused. She climbed. He climbed. Haltingly they rose to the next level.

"I don't like the sound of your breathing, Jack. You sound kind of wheezy." She paused while he took short shallow breaths, wincing with every intake.

"Got to keep going. Worry later." Grimly he took another step, putting as much weight on her shoulders as he did the improvised walking stick. "I can't waste magic on myself. Got to conserve it for the tasks to come."

The cellars above the dungeons were deserted. Barrels of dried goods and casks of ale lay on their sides, some still rolling against a new tilt to the floor. Ropes of onions and garlic had been flung from their ceiling hooks. One barrel of flour had burst when it collided with a wall. The white powder was scuffed and filthy from running feet.

"Looks like a band of Rovers wreaked havoc in here," Jack surmised.

Katrina just grunted and hastened to the next flight of stairs. She didn't like the way the outside wall bulged and water seeped through the gaps in the stonework.

These steps were easier, because they were wide enough to hold an entire foot and had recently been scrubbed clean of cellar-damp slime. But there were fifteen of them and Jack was already tired.

As she placed her foot on the first wooden plank, another quake shook the floor. They didn't bother counting stairs or pausing until they were at the top.

Jack's weight dragged against her shoulders. She loosened her grasp and he slumped to his knees. A new round of coughing claimed his strength. When he was done, he collapsed into a fetal ball on the kitchen floor. Each intake of air sounded like a boat whistle.

"Please get up, Jack. Oh, please. We haven't much time," she pleaded.

His eyes opened. Fever bright and unfocused he mumbled something. "Water," he repeated the sound, a little closer to a recognizable word.

Mercifully a pitcher remained upright on the long work table in the center of the kitchen. A cup rolled on the floor, handle broken, rim chipped, but the bowl was intact.

A few sips, most of which dribbled from Jack's mouth along his cheek to the floor, seemed to revive him. He rolled to his knees but didn't have the stamina to rise further.

Katrina placed the fallen torch into his hand once more and crawled beneath his other arm. Straining her back and thighs, she heaved him upright. They proceeded to the back door.

More painful steps up into the garden. Then a level path to the street.

Noise assaulted Katrina's ears as soon as they rounded the end of the manor house. Everywhere, people ran screaming. Children cried. Steeds wailed and dogs howled. Fires burned out of control. Houses gaped and split, while near neighbors remained intact.

A stream of frightened citizens clogged the broad street. All headed out of town toward the hills and safety.

"The river's broken its dike."

"Rovers fighting the palace guard."

"Flooding in the factories."

"Fire in the slums."

"Rovers looting the shops."

Comments flowed around them. How much was fact and how much was rumor?

She turned into the crowd, hoping the press of bodies would carry them.

"Turn back," Jack ordered.

"Don't be a fool, Jack. We've got to get out of town."

"I have to go back to the factory. I have to get some Tambrin lace to patch the dragon's wing." He wrenched free of her grasp, staggered and nearly fell beneath the feet of a frightened steed.

The rider hauled back on the reins. The beast reared. Iron-shod hooves lashed out.

Katrina dove for Jack, rolling with him out of harm's way. "Idiot. You'll be killed. You can't make it alone."

"Got to." He heaved himself upright again and pushed his way to the edge of the mob.

Katrina clutched his hand rather than be separated from him. "A piece of lace isn't important enough to risk your life. We'll come back when this is over."

As if to emphasize her words, the Kardia shook again. The roof of the manor they had just left collapsed, taking the walls with it.

"My life isn't important anymore. The dragons are. I've got to send the wing patch to Shayla now. Before Simeon can get to her again."

Fear tugged Katrina back into the crowd and the path to safety. But something more bound her to Jack and his cause. He was right. Their lives meant nothing if they allowed Simeon to continue in his insane path. The sorcerer had to be stopped. The only way to do that was to remove his dragon from SeLenicca.

"This way. I know a shortcut back to the river. If the flood hasn't destroyed the building. If Simeon hasn't found the stash of lace already. If we aren't killed along the way . . ."

All is undone. The land rebels against Simeon. His insane obsession with the lace shawl prevents him from stopping the earthquakes. The shawl he stole did not contain the runic message he fears will prove him a bastard—not even a royal bastard. While he screams and strikes out at all near him, the walls crumble. He has drained SeLenicca and its people of life. They can no longer serve him.

I would abandon him, and this cursed land, but I still need him. He can gather dragon magic in great quantities. I cannot. His dragon magic must be turned back upon its source to destroy the dragons once and for all. Only then will I feel safe enough to return to Coronnan and demand my rights as blood heir to Darville.

Chapter Thirty-Six

Jack endured the trek back to the lace factory in a haze of pain, eased only slightly by Katrina's unfailing support. Broken cobblestones tore his feet. Panicked citizens jostled his smashed ribs. Each collapse of an old ley line stabbed through his magic into his heart. He lost all sense of direction and time. Purpose alone carried him to the edge of the river.

He wished he dared summon a purple dragon. But the collapsing city and frightened citizens would be a greater danger to Amaranth than they were to Jack.

"We'll have to use the warehouse door," Jack grumbled as he eyed the rubble, including half of a wall from a neighboring factory, piled against the once proudly clean front door of Brunix's factory.

Inside, all was confusion. Laborers looted the crates of lace intended for export. Barter goods against hard times to come. Two stories up in the workroom, lacemakers rushed about, packing their pillows, bobbins, and patterns—the most precious possessions they could claim. With lace equipment and patterns, they could earn a living in any city in the world.

"Brunix cheated me time and again, snipping off arm-lengths of lace and not counting it in my wages," one woman screamed. "I claim the velvet pillow and bobbins in his flat!" She dashed up the last flight of stairs.

"The outland bastard demanded I sleep with him time and again without extra pay. The law says he had to pay me extra. I claim the patterns he hides up there!" another woman said as she, too, headed up the stairs.

"No." Katrina protested. "They'll find the stash of Tambrin lace!" She abandoned Jack to race after her rivals.

Just then, another tremor rocked the city. The staircase shook and the railing split. The lacemaker highest on the flight clutched at the cracked wood for balance. Her weight broke the remnants of the railing. She flailed her arms and crashed to the landing by the workroom.

Katrina and the second lacemaker stopped dead in their tracks. With the railing gone, neither dared test the stairs for stability.

Jack limped over to the fallen women. He didn't need to test her pulse to see if she lived. The awkward angle of her neck and the blankly staring eyes pronounced her dead.

"Katrina, I need the lace shawl made of Tambrin. We've risked our lives to get here for it. Where is it hidden?" he asked in the mildest voice he could muster. She couldn't freeze in panic now. They had to finish this.

She looked at him with wide anxious eyes. "Up there." Her head gestured slightly toward the apartment that covered the entire top story of the building.

One more flight of stairs, broken in places but passable, if one avoided the splintered railing. Surely he could manage one more. To free Shayla he had to endure one more flight of stairs. "I'll get it. Meet me in the workroom."

Lift one foot, put it down. Lift the other a little higher, put it down. He kept one hand against the wall, the other outstretched for balance. The world narrowed to the staircase and the pain in his side.

Two steps. Then three more. He collapsed, nearly blind with

dizziness. A broken rib had moved and pierced his lung. He could hardly breathe.

"No, Jack. I'll get the shawl. Wait for me in the workroom." Katrina dashed up to the landing and disappeared into the flat. Her rival lacemaker took the steps more cautiously behind her.

Jack lay still a moment gathering breath and the will to move. The well of magic was behind him. Nurtured by *Song,* the blue lines were firmly anchored in the Kardia. He had to return to them.

Like a bay crawler he edged backward on all fours. When his feet touched the landing, he braced himself against the wall and heaved his body upright. The effort almost knocked him unconscious. "Ley lines. I need the ley lines." Just thinking about the restorative power of the latent magic spurred him into the chaos of the workroom.

Oblivious to his presence, the lacemakers fled in groups of two and three. By the time he reached the window, the room was empty. The magic filled him at first touch. He drank greedily from the well. Strength and stability first. Then he pushed his ribs back into place and repaired the tiny hole in his lung.

His body demanded more. He dared not take it. This little puddle of magic had to transport Katrina and the lace to safety. He dared not drain it to help himself.

"The factory doors are blocked." Rejiia stared at the pile of rubble as if it were responsible for all of her problems instead of just one of them.

"We must enter by magic." Simeon announced.

"The spell will cost me too dearly," Rejiia warned, as she glared at him. He had learned the secret of the transport spell at the same time as she. He also had the dragon to give him extra magic. "You must work the spell of flight. The power within me is not enough," she ordered.

Another earthquake set the rubble trembling. Simeon jumped back from the danger pouting. Panicked gibberish leaked from his mind.

"If you told me what the real shawl looked like, I could grab it with magic and use my remaining reserves of power to escape this cursed city," Rejiia shouted at him. He didn't appear to hear. His hands fluttered over his heart as he anxiously searched a multitude of shadows for his enemies.

"The Kardia itself rebels against me. Why has Simurgh deserted me?" he wailed.

Rejiia repeated her question rather than screech her frustration. Simurgh was only a means to an end, not the all-knowing deity the coven believed. She had realized that the moment her father and aunt had fallen to Darville, a believer in the Stargods.

"I can't tell you! Only I must know the shawl's secrets," Simeon said around tight lips. His eyes rolled away from her direct gaze.

He wouldn't release the information even under coercion. She had to try the spell. Carefully she replayed the magician boy's rambling instructions.

Three slow breaths brought her close to a trance. Three more and the void beckoned. Carefully she visualized the place she must take herself and Simeon. The office on the ground floor. She'd been there before with a bribe to Brunix for making the silver lace she preferred on her black gowns.

A quick grab at the power of the void and a quicker release. Visualization of their bodies three heartbeats before the beginning of the spell, but inside the building.

The air around them shifted and shimmered. Blackness, cold, no sense of body or self. Five heartbeats she endured the sensory deprivation. Then the image of the neat, white painted office wrapped around her and Simeon. She landed heavily, body and head spinning. Her passenger began searching the office before she had fully recovered.

Katrina didn't waste time sorting and choosing lace. Making a basket of her skirt she gathered the shawl and as much of the Tambrin lace as she could carry. Her pillow, the one P'pa had sold to Brunix, fit under her arm, the patterns tucked neatly inside the cylinder.

Her coworker, Taalia, staggered into the flat, more intent on loot than her own safety. Katrina barely spared her a glance. There was a second pillow and piles of lace for any who cared to grab them. She hated the thought of this greedy, spiteful woman claiming anything. With Brunix dead and the city collapsing around them, possession didn't seem to matter anymore.

In moments she was back in the workroom.

Jack stood beneath the window where he had sheltered her from Brunix and the palace magician. An expression of relief, bordering on bliss, filled his bruised and filthy face.

"I'll need you to *Sing* again, Katrina," he said. His eyes were closed and his chin lifted as if listening to something far away.

"What . . . what are you going to do?" She couldn't bring herself to stand next to him. His entire body seemed to glow with an eerie blue light.

Ghosts were supposed to look like that. Once more she looked for signs of her mother's spirit. Half relieved and half disappointed at not finding her, she turned her full attention on Jack.

Sounds of more buildings crashing together outside dominated her senses.

"We're cut off. I have to transport you and the lace to Shayla," Jack stated.

Fear pressed against Katrina's chest. Transport? Magic! Where did he get the strength and the will?

"Now listen closely. Shayla is large and formidable. But she won't hurt you. Don't be frightened. You must secure the lace to her wing with touches of glue." He held out a pot of spirit gum he'd liberated from Brunix's office on the way to the workroom. "Small touches of the glue, just enough to hold the lace in position."

"I can't do it alone, Jack."

"You must. I have to stay here to keep Simeon and Rejiia from following you. I sense them coming closer. *Sing* while you patch Shayla's wing. *Sing* like you did in the dungeon. The dragon will take you and your father to safety."

"You have to come with me, Jack. I can't let you die here." She rushed to his side, dropping her pillow at their touching feet so she could grab his arm.

"I'll follow when I can." He opened his eyes and looked at her with longing. "Remember me kindly, Katrina. Now *Sing* as if your life depended upon it."

The only tune that came to mind was the work tune she hummed to herself as she worked alone at night. A few hesitant notes rose within her. Then certain that her songs gave this magician power, she opened her mouth wide and let the notes soar with her heart. If he needed more power to come with her, then she'd give it to him.

Jack felt another major ley line collapse. His preparation for transport faltered. The void appeared and disappeared before him.

Someone had thrown a powerful spell very close.

Rejiia or Simeon? How close were they?

He sent his awareness in a quick dart around the building. Two lives filled with purpose approached.

"The shawl is near. I can feel it. The runes threaten me!" King Simeon's voice.

"Upstairs. The source of power is directly above us," Rejiia said.

The king's mistress was close. Too close.

Jack faltered in his deep breathing. The memory of the pain she had inflicted upon him sent his heart racing. His mind went blank. He had to get away from her!

"Jack, what's wrong?" Katrina tugged at his arm.

Reality and purpose broke through his instinctive panic. "Rejiia and Simeon. Let go of my arm so I can send you to Shayla."

"No. She'll kill you this time. You must come with me." She held tighter as she changed her *Song*.

Jack ignored her plea and accessed the void. From memory, he built a mental picture of the field outside the lair. He added the waterfall and the pool, tall cliffs and clumps of stunted Tambootie trees. The dragonets and Shayla climbed into the picture of their own volition. Lastly he added the big blue-tipped male, Fraank, and Corby.

Then, he drew on all the power of the ley lines as he moved Katrina and her bundle of lace into the field, an arm-length from the edge of the pool. He'd better send her pillow, too; she'd risked much to salvage it.

He barely noticed the feminine arm clutching his shoulders. He heard only the love ballad Katrina *Sang* with renewed vigor.

"There they are!" Simeon called out. "She's got the shawl. We have to stop them!"

Cold blackness engulfed Katrina suddenly, painfully. She cried out but no sound emerged. For several heartbeats she lost contact with her body and her senses. Jack seemed to dissolve beneath her grasp.

Before she could panic, awareness of her feet returned. Spongy grass beneath her ragged slippers. Birds chirping. A roar in the background.

Instinctively she ducked away from the sound, expecting the ceiling to crash around her. Then she realized 'twas only water rushing from the mountains toward the sea. Were they on the riverbank?

Bright sunshine pierced Katrina's closed eyelids. Shivering and scared, she continued clinging to Jack. His body felt solid once more beneath her grasping hand.

Cautiously she opened one eye a tiny slit. A lush meadow filled with wildflowers sparkled with dew in the first kiss of the morning sun.

Bees flitted from flower to flower. A pool fed by a mighty waterfall lapped at her feet. Bushes rustled, and she was certain someone or *something* watched her with predatory instincts.

Born and bred in the city, she'd never seen anything like this wild valley.

"Jack?" she whispered. "Jack, where are you?"

He, too, opened one eye. "*You* are where you are supposed to be, outside the dragon lair. I'm supposed to be back in the city, preventing Rejiia and Simeon from following you."

"I . . . I . . ." Katrina stammered and blushed. Only then did she become aware that her arm was still wrapped around his naked shoulders. His arm held her close against his side as if he never intended to let go. A hair's breadth separated her mouth from his. Their hearts beat in unison as they breathed in counterpoint.

A long moment of awareness awoke within her. She stared at the curve of his full lips surrounded by a sensuously thick beard and mustache. A part of her needed to know if the silky hair was as soft as Tambrin.

"Jack! You're back," a quavering male voice called. The man, thin and stoop-shouldered, appeared from behind the curtain of the waterfall.

Jack stepped away from her and turned his head toward the man. A chill of foreboding planted itself in Katrina's mind as Jack removed the warmth of his body from contact with her—though only half an arm-length separated them.

Something familiar in the approaching man's voice brought Katrina's gaze away from the wonder of Jack's mouth to watch the man pick his way around the pool.

"What happened to you, Jack? You're a mess. Worse than in the mines. And who is this with you?" The man shielded his eyes from the increasingly bright sun with his hand. He blinked several times and then stumbled over nothing. "*Stargods,* is that you, Katrina?"

"P'pa!" Had his hair and beard always been so thin and gray? "Oh, P'pa," she rushed to his side, still cradling the treasure of lace in her skirt.

Father and daughter stared at each other for long moments, drinking in the sight of a long-lost loved one.

The pain and the anger against P'pa she had nursed for three years faded at the sight of his frail body. What she had suffered at the hands of Brunix was nothing compared to what he must have endured in the mines.

Jack had lived through the same anguish as her father and emerged strong and resourceful.

Her father had wasted away. Dark purple shadows made hollows of his eyes. Knots of pain gnarled his finger joints. His shoulders bent under the weight of the world.

"Katey, how you've grown! A beautiful woman now, tall as your M'ma and more beautiful than ever." Hesitantly he gathered her into his arms. Tears flowed freely from both of them.

"I never thought to see you again, P'pa. I never hoped to find . . . to find . . ." Her thoughts clumped in her throat unable to get around three years of unshed tears.

He doesn't know that you were sold into slavery also. Spare him, please. Jack spoke directly into her mind. His pain at having to watch his only friend waste away in a long death became her pain.

"But for Jack I wouldn't have survived. I owe him my life. I owe him more for bringing you to me." P'pa coughed. A great shuddering exhalation.

Katrina, with her ear pressed to her father's chest, was reminded of the tremors beneath Queen's City.

"P'pa," she moaned, holding him close. Frantically, she prayed that he had escaped the mine in time, that fresh air, sunshine, and rest would heal him.

"Fraank, Katrina, I must tell you that Tattia did not commit suicide," Jack said sadly. He didn't want to talk about death now. His own hovered too close. But he had to give these two people, the only people in the world he dared call friends, the slight comfort of the news. "Simeon had her murdered."

Fraank swallowed deeply several times as if Tattia's death had just happened, not three years ago. "How do you know?" he finally said.

"Her ghost sought me out. She was stabbed with a ritual knife by one of Simeon's coven. The same knife that killed Brunix."

Katrina hung her head briefly, then looked up. Relief smoothed the lines of grief on her beautiful face. "Thank you, Jack. I suspected as much. There is a little comfort in knowing she did not take her own life."

"Do you remember, the night before she died, Katey. She was almost happy that night. She acted as if she had found something to hope for." Fraank dashed a tear from his eyes.

"Sorry to interrupt with bad news. You can reminisce later, Fraank. We've work to do and enemies on our tail," Jack reminded them. A shirt appeared in his hands. He winced as he slid his arms into the sleeves. "Where's Corby?"

P'pa shrugged his shoulders. "Haven't seen the bird."

"I hope he's all right. 'Tis a long flight from the city." Worry furrowed his brow and marked his posture as he scanned the picturesque vale for signs of one noisy, black bird.

Chapter Thirty-Seven

"Oh my!" Katrina whispered. Jack watched her eyes grow round and her mouth open in wonder as two dragonets, Chromin and Amaranth, glided into the valley and landed at his feet. As tall and as long as he, either of the two were enough to frighten away most predators. Only the silvery softness of their fur and the ill-defined edges of babyhood made their appearance less intimidating.

Chromin greeted him with a joyous nudge of his steedlike muzzle. A nudge that nearly toppled Jack into the pool. The knob of Chromin's unformed spiral horn pressed painfully into Jack's still damaged side.

Amaranth tried to ease Jack's grimace of pain by fanning him with his silvery wings. The resulting wind sent waves of water from the pool back into the waterfall.

"Hi, 'gnets. Where's your mama?" Jack hooked his arm around Amaranth's neck, effectively curtailing any further pranks. And while he touched the purple-tip, he gathered as much magic as he could to repair and replenish his body.

He also looked through Amaranth's memories for the remains of

last night's hunt, properly roasted by dragon fire. A thought brought a
hunk of meat, big enough for him and Katrina to share.

He smiled at Katrina's rapidly changing expressions. First she
tried to giggle at the eager antics of the baby dragons. Then the
rippling sound died aborning as Shayla emerged from the lair. The
vastness of her crystalline outline reminded them that Amaranth and
his companion were still babies after all. Momentary fear, then awe
widened Katrina's eyes until he could see cloud shadows in them.

Welcome. Shayla nodded her head in greeting. *The children
missed you, Jack.*

"I missed them too, Shayla," Jack said around a mouthful of meat.

Katrina dipped a hasty curtsy. Her eyes were still glued to the
dragon and her mouth slightly agape. But the beginnings of a smile
tugged at her lips.

"I . . . I brought you some lace, ma'am," she stammered. "How do
I address a dragon?" she whispered aside to Jack.

A little of the strain of the last few days showed in the tight cords
of her neck and glazed eyes.

We prefer the use of names, Katrina.

"Yes, ma'am . . . I mean, Shayla."

"Our enemies will follow shortly," Jack interrupted. "We have to
set the patch without delay." He scanned the skies uneasily for signs
of Corby. An entire day and night had passed since he'd sent the bird.
How far could one lonely jackdaw fly in that amount of time?

While Katrina spread her treasure of Tambrin lace out on the
grass, Shayla hunkered down close by, wings slightly spread. Katrina
kept looking up at the dragon as if she expected to be eaten at any
moment. Fraank knelt beside her. Jack paced wearily, stretching his
senses for any sign of Rejiia and Simeon.

"No need to fret, Katey," Fraank soothed his daughter. "Shayla
and her family hid me from Simeon's agents. They've fed me and
kept me company. They'll not hurt you." The older man fingered the
lace.

Jack scanned the skies once more. He allowed his gaze to linger on the irregular knob atop the cliff. The blue-tipped male still perched there, surveying the vale.

I will keep watch, Jack. You may work your spell and then we will all flee to safety, the blue-tip said.

What about the babies? Can they fly well enough to reach a safe haven? Jack kept half his attention on Katrina and Shayla as they examined the lace. He kept munching the meat, refueling his body, even after the venison had lost its first savory appeal.

We've been practicing flying in the void. Don't worry about dragons. Worry about yourself and your lady. A chuckle rippled from the male dragon's throat.

Jack was about to contradict the dragon about his status with Katrina and changed his mind. Arguing with dragons just wasted breath. They never changed their minds.

Where's Corby? he asked, focusing his mental words on a tight line to the dragon.

I cannot find him. The dragon sounded puzzled but not worried. *He is a wild bird and did not bond with you easily. He fought my compulsion to aid you with many temper tantrums. He may have returned to the wild now that your quest is nearly finished.*

"I hope so. I'd hate to think Rejiia managed to capture him after all. She is the more powerful of our two enemies. Simeon's obsession with the runes within one piece of lace has narrowed his power. He sees only one objective and ignores all other possibilities and dangers."

Dragon thought exploded in Jack's mind. *Runes! What runes?*

"Part of a design Katrina's mother wove into one of those pieces." Jack gestured toward the selection of lace spread out on the grass in a prearranged pattern for attaching to the wing. "Nothing important."

The blue-tip spread his wings and glided from his perch into the meadow. The wind from his passage scattered the array of lace like sea foam on the beach of the Great Bay.

Shayla stretched her undamaged wing protectively over Katrina

and the frothy lace. Her high-pitched hiss of reprimand pierced Jack's
ears. He slapped his hands over the offended organs.

Too late he realized the temporary deafness obscured another
sound born on the wind.

But the dragonets heard it and greeted the invasion of their
peaceful vale by a flock of noisy crows with mock anger. Ten baby
dragons took wing, eager for a new game of chase and harry.

The crows were being herded by a purpose more fearsome than a
dozen playful dragons. Scout birds broke away from their arrowhead
formation and flew in the opposite direction, screeching defiance.
The dragonets left the main flock to pursue the individuals. Deep
within the birds' ranks struggled a wounded member of the flock.
They all dived together for the pool at the base of the waterfall.

"Quickly, Katrina, get the patch set. Anchor it with a *Song* and
the glue. Shayla, as soon as you can get air under that wing, take
Katrina to safety. Brevelan's clearing will shelter you until it's healed.
One of your mates can carry Fraank. Take the babies with you. Especially Amaranth and his twin. We can't take a chance that Rejiia will
trap them and gather their magic!" Jack barked orders right and left as
he erected his personal armor and settled himself for the battle of his
life.

"What about you, Jack?" Katrina asked as she shook out the
largest piece of lace in the collection. The shawl wasn't large enough
to cover the hole in Shayla's wing. She would need many of the
smaller pieces to complete the patch.

"I have to delay Rejiia and Simeon here. They're right behind the
birds. They probably followed the trail of our earlier transport. They
can't be allowed to follow Shayla." He turned his back on the
patching procedure.

The squawking flock of black birds zoomed downward with
increasing speed. They were close enough now for Jack to pick out
the weakest member. A larger, stronger bird flew directly beneath it,
preventing it from falling when its wings failed. Other birds circled it
in tight formation, protecting it from the worst of the wind.

As the mass of birds, a hundred or more, swooped low, Jack fought the urge to duck. At the last moment he opened his armor and caught the wounded bird with a touch of levitation. It dropped into his hands, exhausted and shivering. Above its eyes were two bald spots where tufts of white feathers should be.

"Corby?" Jack caressed the sleek black head with a gentling finger.

The bird tried to tuck his head beneath his wing. The effort of movement seemed too much. "Caged! Caged, caged," he croaked. "Big light."

"Someone caught you and caged you. They left you in the sun? Without water?"

"Reji comes, Reji, Reji." The last words drained the jackdaw of energy. He collapsed in Jack's hand, a heavy, inert weight.

"Don't you dare die on me, Corby!" Lonely tears swelled his throat. Through all his pain and years of toil only Corby had remained from his days as Jaylor's apprentice—the only time in his life he'd been happy and cared for. Loved. Until now. He had Katrina now. Maybe.

Light shimmered and distorted not six yards in front of Jack. He needed to cuddle and protect his companion, but urgency prevented that. Hastily he spared the magic to send the unconscious bird into a pocket between two spines on the blue-tipped dragon's back.

"Please keep him safe, sir," he pleaded as he ducked the first bolt of magic thrown by the now solid forms of Rejiia and Simeon.

"Take all your dragons out of here, Shayla," he yelled. "Without dragons, Simeon has no magic!" A flash of blinding white light followed his words.

Katrina held the last round doily in place over the edge of the ugly black wound in Shayla's wing. Never had she seen anything to match

Simeon's cruelty in maiming this magnificent dragon. She counted carefully to ten for the glue to set while her heart hammered rapidly.

The skin on the back of her neck crawled with the sense of impending danger. She smelled the difference in the air when Simeon and his mistress materialized. A sharp scent of foliage beginning to rot.

Now! Shayla commanded. We must leave now.

"But it's not set. The patch will come off when you fly." Katrina held the doily in place, willing the liquid wax to congeal faster.

No more time. I must fly as it is. Come. The last word commanded the babies as well as Katrina.

The lacemaker wasted no more time. Shayla was too weak to take her. With a prayer and a leap she clambered onto the blue-tipped male dragon's back. Two spinal horns cradled her like a saddle. Corby lay between two smaller spikes in front of her, a black spot of reality in this fantastic adventure. She scooped the bird into her lap to keep him safe.

"P'pa, climb up behind me!" she called. Her father continued to stare at the three magicians.

"P'pa!"

My mates will see to him, Shayla explained. I must leave now.

Huge shoulder muscles stretched beneath Katrina as the male matched Shayla's movements. They spread their wings. Some of the dragon's joy in the movement filtered into Katrina's mind.

Too long since I have flown, Shayla groaned. Her wings faltered in their upward movement. Before they quite reached the peak of the arch, Shayla thrust them downward and gathered her legs beneath her. *Not enough strength. We'll have to run for it.*

Katrina's dragon moved into position behind Shayla, encouraging and protecting her at the same time.

Above them, the dragonets fluttered and chirped. Higher still, more dim outlines circled. The sense of urgency pressed on Katrina like a weight.

Rejiia raised her arms in preparation for an assault on Shayla. Simeon's spell was aimed at Jack.

Shayla and her mate sprang forward in unison.

"Look out, Jack!" Katrina screamed into the rushing wind.

A blast of magic fire burst from both dragon mouths, directly at the sorcerer-king. Rejiia's attack faltered as she diverted her spell to protect Simeon. Dragon fire ringed them both, beat at invisible armor and died out. Neither of them flinched.

Both dragons ran past Simeon, gathering speed with each long step. Two more steps, two more sweeps of the huge wings, and Katrina felt the rush of air flow beneath her. A sudden release of the weight that held her to the Kardia and she knew they were airborne. A sense of wonder filled her as the vale diminished in size beneath her.

She looked down one last time. P'pa appeared as a heap of rags collapsed by the pool side. A ball of dark-green flame crashed through Jack's armor toward his eyes.

The blackness of the void engulfed her senses and her heart.

Chapter Thirty-Eight

"We cannot deny you access to the child, Darville," Jaylor said quietly. "But taking him to the capital now would cause more problems than it would solve." The two men faced each other, arms crossed, similar grim expressions on their faces.

"Don't you think that once Glendon is away from all these magicians, these receptive minds, he would learn to speak?" Darville gestured to the pair of apprentices who occupied the children.

"Possibly. But not before the Gnostic Utilitarian cult had sniffed out the presence of his magic. The law forbidding magicians from being lords and lords from being magicians has never been revoked," Jaylor reminded him. "Legally, Glendon can't be your heir."

"Legally, Glendon is already my heir. No one on the Council has questioned that he is my illegitimate son."

Brevelan called the boys to their breakfast from the doorway of the cottage. She glared at the men, warning them not to bring arguments into her home.

Both men turned to drink in the wholesome beauty they had both loved for so long. Darville looked away first, seeking Mikka.

"If we do not find solutions to our problems, Mikka will not stay with me," Darville mused. "My love for Brevelan is strong and special. But it cannot compare to the soul-deep love I bear my wife. I am nothing if she leaves me."

"I have assigned a team of magicians to the problem and summoned Zolltarn, since it was his binding spell that caused the problem," Jaylor reminded his friend.

"Shayla!" Brevelan called, startling both men out of their preoccupation. "Shayla's come back."

Mikka appeared behind Brevelan within the hut, hair unbound, and a glow of relaxed joy on her face.

Jaylor looked in the direction Brevelan pointed. A hint of a shadow passed between the sun and the clearing.

"Are you sure it's Shayla?" Jaylor called as he bolted to his wife's side.

"If she isn't certain, then I am," Darville confirmed. He stared at his left arm, eyes wide and mouth agape.

"What?" Mikka rushed to his side. Without waiting for an answer, she freed his arm from its sling and rolled up his shirt sleeve.

"Darville, your arm!" Brevelan gasped. The twisting black mass of the old burn faded and shrank before their eyes.

"If my dragon flies, then she must be healed, and so must I." The king smiled as he searched the sky for signs of the dragon.

Suddenly the air was filled with dragons. Big and small, tipped with color and luminescent pearl. The central figure glided in lazy circles around and around the clearing. Each pass was narrower and closer to the ground.

"Someone's riding the blue-tip," Jaylor announced at the same moment the others pointed to the human outline atop the nearly invisible dragon. "Suppose it's Yaakke?"

"No, it's a woman. Shayla is tiring. She's going to crash!" Brevelan shouted. She dashed forward to rescue the two little boys standing in the center of the meadow, watching the spectacle.

Jaylor was faster. One son under each arm, he dashed for the safety of a bank of saber ferns. Sharp, jagged leaves stabbed at his ankles and dragged against his trews. But the boys were safe.

Two heartbeats later, Shayla stretched out her claws and grabbed tufts of grass. Her legs buckled and her nose nearly hit the ground. Her distress was evident in the drooping half-furled wings.

"Where are we, Shayla? Are we safe? Who are all these people?" Katrina scrambled off the male dragon's back to check Shayla's wing.

The male extended his wings in preparation for flight. Katrina grabbed Corby and cradled him in one arm before the dragon took off again.

Shayla didn't answer. Exhaustion dragged nearly transparent eyelids over the jewel of her eye.

"We are friends," the blond man spoke hesitantly in a strange accent. "I know a little of your language."

He was tall, with a commanding presence, Katrina shrank away from him. The solid wall of Shayla's side prevented her from retreating further.

Trust them.

Katrina gulped back some of her fear. Outlanders. Her ingrained distrust rose. Jack was an outlander and he had proved himself more a friend to SeLenicca than her own king.

The man was blond, like a true-blood. Only his golden-brown eyes betrayed his lack of citizenship. The woman who stroked Shayla's muzzle and crooned a healing *Song* had proper blue eyes, but her red hair and something about the shape of her chin made her look too much like Simeon. The other tall man, holding two small boys under his arms, looked the friendliest, but his hair and eyes were almost as dark as Jack's.

"Do you know a man named Jack? A dark magician." She formed her words carefully to make sure they understood her.

The dark man spoke a few words in a strange language full of lilting, singsong phrases.

"Speak freely." The blond man smiled reassuringly. "The blond child understands you and translates."

Katrina stared at the squirming children. She hadn't heard them speak. Jack didn't need to speak. Were these people magicians as well?

"Jack sent us here for healing."

"Jack?" All three adults shook their heads.

"Yaakke!" proclaimed the dark man after exchanging a long stare with the blond child.

"He said his name was Jack." Her Jack wasn't part of a legend, though he'd performed some pretty miraculous feats. He hadn't brought about the prophecy of doom. Simeon had.

Jack, Yaakke. Same man. Different attitude, Shayla interjected.

"Where is the man you call Jack?" the dark-haired man asked slowly but in perfectly accented SeLenese.

"I fear King Simeon and his witch killed him. They killed P'pa too. And they killed SeLenicca. Queen's City is in ruins," Katrina cried. Tears fell down her cheeks unchecked. "All is lost."

"The Simeon destroyed his own capital?" the blond man asked anxiously.

"Jack thinks . . . thought . . . said that the influx of magic put too much strain on the burned-out ley lines. They . . . the lines collapsed. Earthquakes. Fire. People trampled to death. Rovers looting everything." Suddenly the horrors she had witnessed during the last two days caught up with her. Her teeth chattered with unnatural cold. Her body trembled uncontrollably. She nearly dropped Corby. The second woman, the one with hair the colors of a calico cat, took the injured bird from the basket of Katrina's skirt. She caressed him gently, cooing and murmuring soothing phrases.

They come! Shayla proclaimed. The anger and fear in her mental voice proclaimed the approach of foes.

Jack felt more than heard an audible whoosh of wind and a crack of the sky opening to the void; the signal that Shayla had successfully departed the valley.

The resulting vacuum dragged the breath from Jack and destroyed his balance. Rejiia and Simeon seemed equally disoriented; balance off, eyes unfocused.

Jack used the distraction and the falling sensation to duck out of his armor and roll behind a scrubby willow shrub. He left the protective spell in place, around a fuzzy image of himself. Rejiia's next magic attack crashed through the armor but found no target.

The black-haired witch recovered with amazing speed. She held up two white feathers. A wicked smile played over her lovely face.

A magician was tied to his familiar beyond the simple bonds of a pet. More than that, the stupid bird was the only friend and companion Jack had ever truly known. *S'murgh it,* she was beautiful, even when she personified evil. Rejiia de Draconis enjoyed watching others suffer.

Rejiia wove a complicated gesture around the feathers, summoning the owner of those feathers to return to her.

But Corby was unconscious. He couldn't move. Would the spell levitate him back to Rejiia? Or worse yet, would it force Shayla and her mate, who carried him, to return to the vale?

Jack didn't wait to find out. An arrow-shaped probe formed in his hand. He threw it at the feathers and dove for a clump of tall grasses, armor returned, before Simeon found the spell to launch a new missile. The sorcerer-king looked dazed and distracted. His eyes kept wandering toward the sky.

The probe found the feathers, latched onto them, and yanked them from Rejiia's hand. In the blink of an eye, spell and feathers disappeared into the void. Hopefully they would find Corby and keep him in place.

Rejiia looked tired. She hadn't many spells left in her. But Simeon was still strong and filled with the need for vengeance. He'd conserved his spells for the lace shawl. His obsessive gaze landed on the heap of inert rags laying by the pool that could only be Fraank. Alive or dead?

Dragon magic was still in the air. Simeon gathered it and returned his attention to Jack. He stalked his prey, vision narrowed to one purpose, face set in grim determination.

If I can divert one more attack, Jack thought. Just one more assault, then Simeon will have used up the last of the dragon magic.

A blinding flash of sunlight on crystal flashed between Jack and Simeon. The big blue-tipped male dragon had come back. A huge supply of magic was at Simeon's fingertips while Jack's internal reserves were dwindling fast.

Then the bits and pieces of cloth and flesh moved, revealing Fraank's face. Neither the king nor Rejiia seemed to notice the man they had brought so low. The morning sunlight didn't reflect off the dull iron of the knife blade in Fraank's hand.

"You are bastard-born, an incestuous adulterer, and a traitor to your own kind, Simeon," Jack taunted, keeping the sorcerer's attention away from Fraank. "Even if you kill me, the coven will destroy you. You will have gained nothing."

Fraank staggered to his feet two paces behind the king. Jack had to distract the madman for two more paces.

"You betrayed the ship full of Tambootie," Simeon growled. "You were responsible for the economic disaster that followed. If the ship had won through, SeLenicca would have thriving exports once more. Food and jobs would be plentiful. The people would love me so much they'd welcome Queen Miranda's death so that I could rule!"

"Idiot!" Rejiia admonished. Her breathing was ragged and the strength had drained from her shoulders. "Stop talking and throw the *s'murghing* spell."

Simeon's armor flared a warning. If Fraank plunged his knife through the magic shielding, he'd die in an instant of blinding fire.

Jack flashed a warning to Katrina's father, his friend.

I'm a dead man already. The lung rot has worked into my bones and my heart. Let me kill this thing before I die.

Fraank raised the knife above his head.

Simeon whirled to face the new threat. With a flick of his wrist he dismissed the knife and its wielder. "No mundane can dare attack a magician, a king, a priest of Simurgh!"

Fraank staggered back a few steps as if struck, still clutching the knife. With the grim determination of a martyr he regained his footing and leaped forward. "You are a traitor to your country and my queen. Die like the miserable cur you are."

"Cease your attack or die!" Simeon screamed just before the iron knife plunged into his heart.

His armor had been set against magical attack, not a physical penetration. The armor ignited. Blood spurted. Smoke and flame and the stench of rotten Tambootie took them both into the void.

Not even a flake of ash remained of either man.

Jack flinched from the backlash of pain and death.

Rejiia absorbed it and swelled with a new source of magic. She seemed to grow and swell with dynamic power.

"Now it is your turn to die, boy."

His name is Yaakke! The blue-tipped dragon's bugling pronouncement echoed up and down the valley piercing mental and physical ears. Grab hold of my spines, Yaakke. Shayla and the little ones are safe now. I'll take you away from SeLenicca and the evil spawned by Simeon and this female.

"I can't leave. I have to finish this." Jack poured his remaining strength into his armor.

Another time. Your life is too important to waste on such as she. The dragon reached out his strong forepaws and clamped Jack around the waist without touching ground.

With a massive sweep of wing and a blast of dragon fire, they lifted free of Kardia's gravity and into the void.

My enemies have done me a favor. Simeon can never cast doubt on the rights of my son and Princess Jaranda to marry and together claim the Three Kingdoms. No one must know that Princess Jaylene's child, the true Simeon, died at birth, replaced by Janessa's bastard, also named Simeon. Jaylene's link to Rossemeyer is the key to dynastic unity. That wretched piece of lace with the runic message is attached to the dragon's wing. I must find Shayla and destroy the lace before the Commune has the opportunity to read the secret.

Shayla will most certainly fly to the Commune. Fortunately the boy told me how to find Brevelan's clearing. If I take my sister or her children hostage, the dragon will surely give up her wing patch.

Glendon would be the best hostage. He is tied to the dragons through his father's blood as well as his mother's. And if I eliminate the child, then I clear the way to name myself and my son heirs to the throne and the Coraurlia—the glass dragon crown.

All sensation fled Jack's body as darkness closed around him. Panic rode at the edge of his awareness.

We wait in the void, the dragon told him.

"Why?" The dragons knew the void better than any human. Maybe they wouldn't get lost this time. Maybe.

Colored umbilicals, symbols of life forces, drifted past him. Gold and crystal, copper and blue. His own silver entwined with white. White for lace and moon-blond hair. Jack and Katrina.

As he watched, the silver umbilical of his own life took on a glow of purple. "Just like Amaranth, my colors are silver and purple. I've seen my own aura color!"

A rare achievement among magicians. Only those tested and found worthy by the dragons were granted that privilege. He searched the glowing umbilicals for traces of his friends.

Come look. See the future and the past. The colored cords of life called to him.

He resisted the temptation. He'd been lost here once before. The last time he'd indulged in glimpses, he'd seen things he wasn't meant to know.

But you saw Katrina. You recognized her in your heart, the dragon reminded him.

"What good will that do me? We've shared an adventure and both escaped. Now we must go our separate ways. Magicians aren't meant to share their lives with a mate. Our path—my path—must be solitary." Some of his happiness at finding his magical signature faded.

Look again.

A tangle of colors wrapped around Jack and a new vista opened before his eyes. The clearing. But not the clearing he had known. The house was bigger. Two boys wrestled and played in the meadow. Brevelan *Sang* as she stirred a hearty stew of yampion and legumes. Jaylor came up behind her, wrapping his arms around her gravid body.

Love and caring filled the clearing.

"But they're dead!" Jack would have cried if he knew where his body existed.

Are they?

"The monastery was burned out. A soldier played with Jaylor's staff."

Many magicians passed into a new plane of existence from that monastery, over many centuries. Their staves were hung on the chapel wall in memory of their work. Magicians with the transport spell needn't be trapped by their enemies. The Commune escaped intact, Yaakke.

Hope blossomed inside Jack.

"Why didn't you tell me before?"

Would you have persevered to the end of your quest if you thought another magician could do it for you? Besides, you didn't ask. You assumed.

Jack had to think about that a minute. Would he have endured the hardships of the trek from the mine to lair, the betrayal of Lanciar, the disasters in Queen's City?

"I think I might have, dragon. I may not have been as willing to die for the quest if I knew I had friends waiting for me. But I would have continued to the end."

Then you have truly grown into the rank of Master Magician.

"Why are we lingering here? I need to warn my friends that Rejiia has the transport spell and directions to the clearing." Friends. What a wonderful word. His heart swelled within his chest. He needed to see his old friends, walk on familiar ground, speak his own language.

We wait so that the daughter of Krej cannot follow our trail through the void.

"How long?"

Time is not measured in the void by the passage of the sun. Time flows forward and back and sideways in the void.

Sideways?

Between dimensions.

"Great. So how long? I want my body back."

You don't want answers?

"I don't know what the questions are anymore." He'd escaped alive—so far. He hadn't planned to live beyond the magic duel with Rejiia and Simeon. Shayla had returned to Coronnan, Katrina was safe, and Simeon's tyranny had ended. Jack . . . Yaakke's quest was complete.

You have accomplished much. For your self-respect and peace of mind, you had to do it alone. Dragons are not allowed to interfere in these matters. But you are not complete yet, Yaakke. You have earned a name. Yet you still know only a portion of your heritage. I am allowed to tell you the rest now that you have succeeded in your quest.

"I'm half Rover. No matter who my father is, I can't overcome the prejudice against Zolltarn and his clan. They are thieves and malcontents, amoral nomads. Isn't that bad enough? Why should I want to know more?"

What if Baamin was your father?

"Baamin? My old master! Impossible."

Why is it impossible?

"Because it is. The old sot never . . . I mean he couldn't . . . he wouldn't. . ."

Perhaps he did. Kestra was ordered to seduce a powerful magician. Who more powerful than Baamin on the night before his installation as the Senior Magician of the Commune?

"But he would have told me!"

Not if he didn't know.

Sadness and joy threatened to split Jack in two. He and Baamin had been close. The old man had befriended and trusted Jack when no one else thought him smart enough to deserve a name. Of all the men he had known, Baamin was the one he would have chosen as a father.

But he had not known, had not done the things a father was meant to share with a son—the kinds of things Jaylor was doing now with his two little boys.

Will you deny your own children the right of a father?

"In case you hadn't noticed, I don't have any children. I haven't even . . . well, you know. Katrina's the only woman I know and we haven't gotten that far."

Yet.

"Not likely to either."

Time will tell.

"Not to change the subject or anything, but while we are sharing these intimate thoughts, how come you've never given me your name.

Dragons like names, use them all the time. But you don't seem to have one."

I have a name. The time was not right to tell you.

"When will be the right time?"

In another life I was called Baamin.

Chapter Thirty-Nine

Weakness assailed Rejiia's limbs and mind. "How can I follow that wretched boy and his dragons? I have no magic left for the transport spell."

There is Tambootie here in the vale, a voice whispered in the back of her mind.

"Pappi?" She looked at the tin statue resting on the grass beside her. Sometime during the battle it had tipped onto its side. Flakes of gilt paint littered the grass in a circle around the sculpture. Very little paint was left.

Set me upright. The imperious tone, without the whine Simeon had developed these last few months, told her the owner of the voice belonged only to her father.

"At last, you recognize that I have some purpose." She stared at Lord Krej without moving him. "You are now dependent upon me, Father."

And you must depend upon me to replenish your magic in time to follow the boy and the dragons.

"How?" She edged a little closer to him, not certain how she should feel toward him. "How are you speaking to me?" she amended her question.

The backlash wears thin.

"How?" she asked again. Her curiosity vied with her need to have her father acknowledge her as his equal in magic.

For many moons, I struggled against the spell. It fed upon the fight. I planned the spell to be self-renewing because I knew my intended victim would never give up. Once I realized this, the magic had no energy to feed it. Little by little it wears thin.

"How long before you are free?" Suddenly, Rejiia wasn't certain she wanted him animate, arrogant, ordering her and everyone else to heed to his slightest wish. Besides, if he was animate again, he might try to steal the Coraurlia from her.

I cannot tell. Once we have dealt with Yaakke and the dragons, you must take me to Hanassa. My mother's people might help us.

"Us? What if I decide to leave you here? I am a full magician, more powerful than any in the Commune. What if I don't need you?"

You need me, child. Because I am your father and you will never be happy until we face each other and prove ourselves equals in magic and cunning.

"You are right about that, Father. I'll eat of this stunted Tambootie and the food left behind by the dragons. Then we will confront our enemies."

She welcomed the chill and the darkness of the void after the heat of the magic battle with Yaakke. The sensory deprivation ended the residual fatigue and the little aches and pains of her corporeal body.

We cannot linger here, Father. We must finish what I have started.

She didn't regret Simeon's passing. In Hanassa, she could find sufficient believers to form a ritual star again. Lanciar could be persuaded to join her. He was such a magnificent sexual partner, she'd regret losing him to another.

The fishing village with no name must be near the foothills of the

Southern Mountains. She chose a spot near the decaying Equinox Pylon. Pappi had brought his entire family here the summer she turned ten. He didn't usually tour the forgotten reaches of his provinces. She'd forgotten what brought him here—something to do with witchwomen and dragons. The steep cliff down to the gravel beach and the Dragon's Teeth—a wicked rock formation in the cove—had stayed in her mind.

No one seemed to be active in the village yet. The fishing fleet would have left at dawn. Anyone else with sense was still abed.

The path behind the pub was easy to see. Many feet had pounded the dirt into reasonable smoothness. What was the boy's next landmark?

A boulder split in half by a tree.

The memory had been clear and precise in his head when she tried stripping his mind. Carefully she recreated the image of the broken boulder and launched herself and the tin weasel into the void.

This landing was more graceful. Practice, she told herself. Great magic took practice.

"Step through the split boulder, don't go around it as the path seems to indicate."

She lifted her skirts free of the dirt and moss that brushed against her and stepped through to a new path. Eight more steps and the path ended at a creek.

Bewildered, Rejiia searched the area with all of her senses. The boy had said to wait for Brevelan, but she didn't have time. She needed to find her way into the clearing on her own, without alarming the inhabitants.

Power tingled at the tips of her fingers, not quite entering her body. She reached out to find the source of energy. An invisible wall pushed her hand away. Finger-length by finger-length she followed the wall around, back to her starting place by the creek. Lives pulsed beyond the wall. The lives of her enemies.

She had found the Commune. And Darville. Her rival's presence taunted her, renewing her thirst for possession of the Coraurlia. "If he dies today with only a witch child as an heir, then I can put forth my claim to the throne without opposition." She giggled as she clenched her fist and pounded against the barrier, seeking access to the king who had stolen her crown.

Her hand and arm plunged through a hole in the barrier.

Ten dragonets landed in an awkward flurry of wings and dragging pot bellies. High-pitched squeals of distress pierced Jaylor's ears as the young dragons all tried to rush to their mother for protection and reassurance.

The clearing just wasn't big enough to contain them all without a talon or tail piercing the already damaged wall of the barrier.

A sparkle of black-and-purple lights announced the arrival of a magician by transport. "How dare you snatch me from my morning meal!" Zolltarn, king of the Rovers, bellowed before his body was fully formed. The tall man with silver streaks within his blacker-than-black hair raised a clenched fist and shook it at a vanishing shadow in the air.

"I summoned you the day before yesterday," Jaylor informed his colleague.

"And I was preparing to come. But a dragon snatched me from the privacy of my tent while I was still eating!"

You will be needed today, not next week when you would have arrived if left to your own schedule, a dragon voice announced.

There were so many dragon bodies in the clearing Jaylor couldn't tell which one had spoken. But the voice sounded familiar. Maybe Seannin, the green-tip he'd ridden once.

The reek of Tambootie smoke dragged Jaylor's attention away from Zolltarn, the frightened young woman, and the crush of dragon bodies. Green flames licked the edges of the small hole Glendon had made in the barrier. Jaylor's armor snapped into place without conscious thought. This was the stench of evil he had been reared to guard against. This was the signal that all of Coronnan faced danger from rogue magicians.

Zolltarn crouched defensively, his knife at the ready, as well as a spell in his open palm.

The hole burned bigger; oily smoke poured through it.

"Brevelan, summon the rest of the Commune. Darville, where is your sword?" As he asked, Jaylor remembered the sight of Darville's long battle sword in its plain leather scabbard propped upright beside the cottage door. He transported it to the king's hand. Fred and Margit had spent last night in the dormitory, an hour away. Not much help unless he wasted energy on a transport.

"Boys, into the cottage!" Brevelan commanded. No one, especially not small boys, disobeyed that tone of voice.

I must flee. I cannot stand against her. Shayla gathered her remaining energies.

"Her?" Darville and Jaylor asked at the same time.

Rejiia. Daughter of Krej, mistress of Simeon, witch of Hanassa.

"And mother of the next king of Coronnan!" The figure of a tall, slender woman, dressed in elegant black appeared in the flaming arch. Every sleek dark hair in place. She exuded calm confidence.

Overconfident, Jaylor reminded himself. Her father and her aunt had been defeated by their lack of wariness.

"Her!" Zolltarn spat. "She has been stripping SeLenicca of gold and power, and men of talent."

A shimmering sparkle of light rolled and gathered beside Rejiia. The tin weasel that was Lord Krej materialized at her feet. The statue's mouth opened a fraction and drooled venom.

"My father must watch the final destruction of his enemies," she announced. "But Zolltarn I will only maim until he reveals the reversal of the spell that holds Lord Krej captive." With her words she wove her hands in a complicated pattern. A dark green, almost black, lightning probe surrounded her.

"Stargods, she's going to burn the rest of the barrier." Jaylor ran to

stop her as the stench of burning Tambootie choked him. Three dragonets blocked his passage.

Rejiia laughed at his clumsy and useless progress. "You'll not stop
me, University man. Dragon magic is nothing compared to the
powers I control."

But she stood *between* two of the six ley lines that met at the
center of the clearing. Jaylor nudged a purple-tipped dragon out of
his way with a knee and planted his feet at the join. Zolltarn joined
him. Shoulder to shoulder they stood, united in purpose. The magic
welled up in Jaylor, eager to be woven into the fabric of the *Gaia*.

One small blond head appeared among the milling dragon backs,
between Jaylor and his target.

"Glendon, into the house!" he ordered. Curiosity touched
Jaylor's mind. The boy knew no fear.

"Glendon, come to me. I will show you what makes the barrier
and what destroys it," Rejiia coaxed.

Jaylor used the magic filling him to throw a wall between
Glendon and the witch. The spell hit a shiny metallic surface and
bounced back to him. He ducked the backlash and prepared a new
protection for Glendon.

Zolltarn threw the next spell. It, too, backlashed.

"Give it up, Rejiia," a new voice commanded. A strong and
assured baritone voice with hints of familiarity in it thundered
around the clearing.

Jack slid off Baamin's wing from the edge of the void into the
center of the clearing, right beside Jaylor, his old master, and Zolltarn,
his grandfather. Affection and a sense of homecoming almost pushed
the menace of Rejiia out of his thoughts.

"Jack, you're alive!" Katrina squealed in delight behind him. The
baby dragons stepped aside so that she could run to him. She plunged
the last few steps into his arms.

He held her tight for two heartbeats, allowing her joy to fill him
with purpose. He couldn't afford the distraction of her greeting.

Drawing renewal from the living ley lines he sent a spray of magic water to douse the flames still in Rejiia's hands.

Amaranth and his purple-tipped twin joined Katrina in a jubilant rush to get to Jack. Balance askew, Jack's spell dropped just short of his target.

His hands landed on the back of the purple-tipped baby dragon.

(*Iianthe.*) The dragonet's name appeared in Jack's mind without warning.

(*Amaranth,*) the other reminded him.

He stroked the silvery fur once in greeting and gave back his own name. Dragon magic jolted through his hands and up his arms. He gathered power from both dragons.

Energy from the ley lines rushed to greet and twine around the power granted him by dragon. The two magics combined and filled him to overflowing. Jaylor placed a hand on his left shoulder. Zolltarn touched his right. Dragon magic reached out to him and amplified both energy sources. A sense of overwhelming completeness and belonging flooded his being.

He was home, and this was his family. He didn't stop to analyze his emotions. He needed a massive counterattack.

Katrina's healing *Song* rose within him. A love song. Rejiia's evil was the only thing keeping Jack from Katrina's side. He *Sang*.

> *They ran away to the clearing fair*
> *They ran away to fight magic.*
> *They whistled and they sang 'til love overcame*
> *an enemy evil and tragic.*

A flash of magic counteracted the fire eating away at the barrier. The flame withered.

"NO! You can't do this to me. You're only an untried boy," Rejiia screamed. From the folds of her gown, she drew a wand, a miniature staff. She pointed the tool of focus directly into Jack's eyes.

Black arrows of magic sped from the tip of the wood.

They whistled and they sang 'til the clearing rang
Filled with love and magic.

Katrina raised her voice in *Song*. Beside her, Brevelan and Mikka joined her. Jaylor and Zolltarn raised their arms with a new spell fed by ley lines, dragons, and *Song*.

The offending black arrows dissolved into ashes.

Rejiia renewed the stream of magic.

Jack raised a wall of armor in front of them.

Rejiia's black arrows bounced off the armor and circled in confusion. Anxiously the witch stabbed at her spell with the wand. The arrows withered and fell back into the Kardia.

Jack raised a whirlwind of sparkling magic to circle around Rejiia and the statue of her father. Leaves and soil, moss and small rocks rolled into the tornado. The wind increased and lifted its burden free of the Kardia's gravity.

Everyone in the crowded clearing ducked and shielded vulnerable eyes from the blowing debris.

He whistled and she sang 'til the clearing rang
Filled with love and magic.

The magic storm winked out, taking Rejiia and Krej into the void. The burning arch collapsed and puckered, forming a ragged scar around the now-closed wound in the magic barrier.

Chapter Forty

Magicians and dragons filled Shayla's old lair with life and energy, laughter and love. Jack watched the flames from the campfire dance around the circle of rocks. He closed his eyes in contentment.

He stretched out his legs and shifted his back to a more comfortable position. Home at last, with a family of magicians gathered around. Katrina sat beside him on a nest of old blankets. Jaylor approached them, an odd bundle held close against his chest. Jack squeezed Katrina's fingers in reassurance, then stood to face the Senior Magician.

"Don't know why we kept any of Master Baamin's old robes." Jaylor kept one eye on the blue-tipped male dragon who embodied all of the knowledge, wisdom, humor, and spirit of the former Senior Magician. "But it seems fitting that his master's cloak be yours now, Yaakke."

Without much ceremony or ritual, the current Senior Magician handed Jack the cloak of fine blue wool with silver stars embroidered on the collar.

"My name is Jack." He looked around at the gathered assembly with pride and a swelling sense of family. His eyes lingered on Zoll-tarn and then Baamin. "Yaakke was a name chosen by a child to prove to the world that I was worth something. I don't need that name anymore. I'm Jack, just plain Jack."

A ripple of nervous laughter passed through the gathering.

"Knew you'd lose that childhood arrogance once we turned you loose." Old Lyman, the eldest member of the Commune, slapped him on the back.

Jack remembered hearing the old man saying that Yaakke should be locked up, for the safety of the kingdom, until he learned humility. He didn't correct him. He didn't need to.

"Yaakke is a name of power, for a man destined to lead great peoples. As my grandson, you will one day lead the Rovers!" Zolltarn pronounced in a voice that echoed throughout the lair.

"You have sons and other grandsons more deserving than I, Zoll-tarn. I have not been raised to Rover traditions and won't tolerate a lot of your ways." Jack didn't look away from his grandfather's piercing glare.

"What traditions won't you tolerate? We are an old and honor-able race!"

"I won't steal for a living. Nor will I rove the countryside. I want a home. A wife. Children." He glanced down at Katrina.

She blushed but didn't turn her head away.

"And now that you are a full Master Magician, Jack," Jaylor took command of the meeting again. "I have an assignment for you."

"If you want me to find Marcus and Robb, I'm sorry. I don't think they can be found until both armies are pulled back from the front and fully counted, magician and mundane. There have been some pretty strange things happening out there lately." Jack shook his head in dismay.

"I claim that quest, Jaylor. If anyone is sent to find Marcus, its me." The pasty seller from the coronation market jumped up from her place among the apprentices.

Jack recognized her, even dressed in boy's leather trews and vest.

If she had any magic talent to earn her place in this gathering, she hid it very well.

"You aren't going anywhere, young lady, until you've earned journeywoman's status." Jaylor frowned at the girl, then turned back to Jack. "I do want to find my journeymen as soon as possible, Jack. I have sent word to the battle mages at the front to look for them. If necessary, I'll send a journeyman in search of them. The task I have for you is closer to home and of some urgency."

"Tonight? Don't I get an opportunity to get drunk and sleep off the hangover with the rest of you?" Jack cocked an eyebrow at Baamin. "Seems that even my father had one night of rebellion before he accepted the saddle of responsibility."

More snickers. Jaylor gathered Brevelan and the boys close to his side, clear evidence that he, too, took some time away from his responsibilities.

"We must sing and dance to celebrate the return of my grandson!" Zolltarn looked ready to dance circles around the fire.

Enough, youngster, an affronted dragon commanded. If a dragon could blush, Baamin appeared to.

Jack drew Katrina up with him, wrapping his arm around her shoulders.

"Tomorrow or the next day will do, Jack," Jaylor chuckled. "Before His Grace is ready to return to the capital, we must deal with Queen Rossemikka's pesky cat." He winked at the queen, who looked very much at home in the rough camp. She'd made a comfortable nest for Corby out of her veil and left her hair loose around her shoulders as she dished stew from the communal cauldron.

"I knew she had a cat hidden somewhere," Margit muttered. "I hate cats."

"That's not going to be easy, sir. I'll need some time to study and experiment." Jack turned his gaze away from the grumbling girl apprentice and the smiling queen. Her double aura fascinated him.

"I can't be away from the capital much longer, Jaylor," Darville reminded them.

"The spells need to be thrown here, so we can guarantee privacy. Magic is not yet legal in Coronnan," Jaylor said. "For now, I'll send Jack with you, disguised as Sergeant Fred's assistant. You can all return here when you are ready, Jack. But you'll have to shave that beard. Square cuts aren't very popular in Coronnan City."

Jack fingered the growth of hair on his face. He liked the image of himself as a bearded, exotic foreigner. Katrina seemed to like touching it. Maybe he'd just trim it to a more rounded shape.

"You can also advise me about new ambassadors to SeLenicca, Jack." King Darville stretched and took a long sip of his ale.

"The best way to establish peaceful relations with our neighbors is to help them rebuild," Jack said more to Katrina than his king.

"We will no longer be enemies?" Katrina interjected. She fingered a bright agate in the palm of her hand. Jack had placed a translation spell into the stone to help her communicate.

"We'll be friends, allies. Family." Jack gazed deeply into her eyes. "We can begin breaking down the barriers right here and now. If you will be my wife, Katrina, you won't be alone anymore."

"Do the dragons come with you as part of the family?" A tiny smile touched the corner of her mouth, belying the glistening of tears that glazed her eyes and the trembling of her chin.

"Amaranth and Iianthe do." Jack reached to pet the purple-tipped dragon heads. Neither dragonet had been out of reach since the incredible swelling and combining of three forms of magic he had experienced in the clearing this morning.

Chromin grunted in jealous displeasure. The yelow-tipped dragonet butted his head between Margit and Fred into the sergeant's lap, begging for similar pets.

My boys are not yet ready to leave the nest, Shayla insisted. She stretched her wing and shoulder stiffly as if to gather her young to her side. A trail of loosened lace drifted to the ground from her hasty bandage.

Katrina hurried to rescue the doily. Jack followed her across the cave. He couldn't let her go without an answer.

Brevelan and Mikka stood beside him, looking over his shoulder at the damaged wing.

"I think we should remove the patches and work a proper healing for both Shayla and Darville," Brevelan mused. She began working the loose edges free.

Katrina reached to help. Her fingers seemed more concerned with preserving the lace than protecting the delicate membranes beneath.

"Don't bother," Darville laughed, waving his left arm freely. "I think the patch worked a miracle on both of us."

"We'll see about that, Darville." Mikka looked closely at his arm. "The blackness is completely gone!" she gasped in amazement, then turned her attention back to the lace-covered dragon wing.

Bit by bit the ladies handed Jack the lace. Square pieces. Round doilies. Yards of edging. Amazingly, it was all as white and pure as when it was first made. The Tambrin fibers vibrated mildly, reminding him of the power within.

"The wing is healed!" Brevelan and Mikka gasped together.

"Told you so," Darville smiled. The women grabbed his arm again and compared the newly pink skin against the dragon wing. All traces of black burns were gone.

"With our Tambootie and your lacemakers, we'll all be rich." Jack turned away from the healers and their patients. "Our farmers will replant the devastated trees if they can see a profit from selling the fiber to SeLenicca. The dragons will have Tambootie to eat. Coronnan will have a strong nimbus again and we'll all have peace!"

"And the Commune will have dragons to make magic legal and controlled again," Jaylor added.

"And Katrina will have the most beautiful wedding ever," Brevelan sighed as she lifted the last piece of lace from the wing. The shawl came free in a single piece, stretched beyond its original size into a frothy veil. Carefully she settled the lace onto Katrina's hair. "That is, if she ever gets the courage to accept Jack's proposal."

"We barely know each other, Jack." Katrina put her hand up to remove the veil.

Jack covered her hand with his own. "I feel like I've known you forever, Katrina. I hope you can come to care for me, a little. Please say you'll at least think about it."

"Having a lair full of dragons as part of my family will take some getting used to," she said with a shy smile and a wink of mischief. "When I was alone and friendless, you offered me help and love without conditions. I'll always love you for that. I think I'd like to share my life with the dragons, and you."

Jack gathered her into his arms.

"Well, prove your Rover blood, boy . . . I mean Jack. Kiss her!" Zolltarn shouted with joy.

A blush galloped from Jack's toes to his face. He wanted desperately to kiss his love. But they were all watching.

Shyly Katrina lifted her face. Again that glint of mischief in her eyes. "This is what having a family means. Sharing love and happiness as well as sadness. I never thought I'd have family again. Thank you for sharing yours with me," she whispered to him.

Accepting the inevitable, Jack lowered his mouth to her in a quick gesture of affection.

"Put more heart into it, boy!" Zolltarn laughed.

"Later," Jack whispered. "When we're alone."

The waning flames in the center of the lair highlighted denser sections of the lace shawl framing Katrina's face. Jaylor reached to examine the lace more closely. A puzzled frown crossed his face as he read the runes encoded in the lace. Then he threw back his head and laughed.

"What's so funny about a prophecy of doom?" Jack asked.

The runes name Simeon's true parentage, as the sorcerer-king feared. Baamin peered over Jaylor's shoulder, also reading the runes. *But they continued with the legend of Yaakke riding a dragon to the last battle that destroyed the coven of Simurgh. Tattia copied all of the runes into the shawl because she didn't know for sure which ones went beyond the intent of her original message. Seems we fulfilled the prophecy, Jack.*

"I brought the dragons home. Coronnan will learn that magic can be honorable and controlled. I fulfilled my quest. That is enough legend and adventure for one lifetime. Now I want only to be a Master Magician in service to my Commune and king. And a husband and father." He smiled at Katrina, still within the circle of his arms.

That's all we ever asked of you, Jack. Baamin winked at him again.

"Soon," Katrina replied.

Jack captured her fingers with his own, lacing them together. "Soon."

"Best if you take your vows before I send him to SeLenicca as ambassador to help rebuild your country." Darville remarked.

"Ambassador?" Jack choked.

"I'm willing to bet that the power in the shawl's runes severed the magical connection between Simeon and Shayla. He couldn't protect himself against that last attack because he couldn't gather any more dragon magic." Jaylor scanned the lace once more. "If we present it to Queen Miranda, as it should have been three years ago, this shawl could sever the magic that holds her in a coma."

"Who better to deliver the magic than Jack?" Darville pounded him on the back with his restored left arm.

"First he has to find a way to take care of my cat," Mikka reminded them.

"No problem," Jack shrugged, never taking his eyes off of Katrina.

"What makes you think the queen's cat will be no problem?" Jaylor asked.

Katrina smiled and kissed his cheek. The world brightened around him and his magic swelled in response.

"I'll have to study the problem a while." Jack continued to stare at Katrina, wondering if he dared kiss her right now, in front of the entire gathering. "I want to show Coronnan City to Katrina and rest my magic while I seek an answer. But if there is no spell in existence to solve the problem, then we'll have to improvise."

You do too much of that, boy. When will you learn proper procedures? Baamin glared at him as he had in the old days when he was Senior Magician, training a wayward apprentice.

"When you learn that I'm no longer a nameless boy, *Father?* But I won't have to work the spell alone. I have the whole Commune—my family—to help. I'll never have to work alone again."

Epilogue

The void does not frighten me. In the black nothingness, all pain, bindings, and disguises slip away. I see my father as he truly is, still alive, still thirsting for vengeance. His vitality fades along with the backlash. The nature of the spell surrounding his physical body becomes obvious. 'Twill eventually drain the life from him.

From the sanctuary of the void we flee to Hanassa. There we can research the backlash spell. Now that the void has revealed the secret, I can find a way to reverse the transformation. And I shall bring Lanciar to join me and my son.

Hanassa harbors others of our kind who long for an end to Coronnan and the dragons. We must entice Darville and the Commune into coming to the secret stronghold buried in the mountains to meet their destiny.

In the end all things come to Hanassa.

Acknowledgments

I wish to thank the members of The International Old
Lacers for helping me research this book over the
last thirteen years, even when I was having too much
fun to call it research.
Thanks also go to my editor, Sheila Gilbert, and her
staff of miracle workers for turning my rambling
prose into real books.
Most of all I need to thank my agent, Carol McCleary,
for believing in me before anyone else did.

Read a Sample from The Dragon's Touchstone

A lovely rising thermal current caught Shayla's wing as she glided one last time from the mountains to the Great Bay. A hundred dragon lengths below her, white-caps danced on the gentle spring breeze. Sunlight sparkled on the water, reflecting rainbows from her nearly transparent wing.

Mandelphs darted in and out of the water in a game of catch me if you can. One youngster leaped through a rainbow, laughing.

Join us, crystal-furred dragon. Play with us, the intelligent water-dwellers chirped. *Dragons cast interesting shadows and offer new hurdles to leap over and dive under. More interesting since you are nearly invisible.*

(*Thank you, friends. Not today,*) Shayla declined. Her lair was a long way away and the twenty babies growing inside her had become too large for her to be confident of her mobility. Tonight she would feast on a fat cow and build her nest. For the next few moons her five mates would feed and pamper her while she could not fly. At any other time, except during mating, she wouldn't tolerate the presence of her consorts within her hunting territory. The male dragons

wouldn't tolerate each other except during the cooperative effort to
support their gravid mate.

Five fathers for her first litter of twenty dragonets. Pride swelled
through her. The more fathers, the larger and stronger the litter.

She widened her circle of flight inland, enjoying the changing air
temperatures against her wings. The Great Bay dissolved into a chain
of islands then merged into a solid landmass split by a mighty river.

Curiosity sharpened her FarSight to spy on the humans who inhab-
ited this land. A bustle of activity in a wide-open space below drew her
attention. She dropped lower to spy on the strangely intelligent, yet
sadly immature race who had invaded this planet several millennia ago.

One of the humans below threw a ball of bright magic across a
field. The ball arced upward and burst into thousands of glittering
shards.

Sharp burning pain snaked from the tip of Shayla's tail up to her
haunches, numbing her muscles as it progressed. Without the maneu-
vering balance of her tail, she fell into a downward spin. Startled, she
didn't immediately compensate with stretched wings and extended
limbs.

Too late! Another pain spiraled around her left rear leg. Muscles
jerked out of control. She lost another dozen dragon lengths in
altitude.

Too low. Dangerously low. The humans came into sharper view
without the aid of FarSight. A cloud of magic residue hung above
them. As this fact registered in her mind, more magic flashed across
the field, adding to the residue. She barely escaped a responding flash
that hurled upward from the edge of the meadow before it fell toward
the opposite side of the open space.

A magic duel! How dare these puny humans battle with forces
they couldn't control!

Flame burst from her mouth with a roar of rage. She refocused
her FarSight, seeking a victim to atone for this outrage against her
body and the forces of nature.

Spells of varying complexity and strength continued blasting back and forth between the men. None looked up to see the source of her flame. They ignored her fair warning.

She dropped heavily through the air as a new pain reminded her sharply of the weight within her womb. No! Her babies weren't ready. No nest awaited them in her distant lair.

A new spell lanced upward. She veered sharply right, barely avoiding it. Fire burst forth as she bellowed her outrage. She folded her wings and plunged into a dive.

Her wing membranes snapped open at the last minute as she shifted and fought to regain height. Her flames drenched the field, turning the entire army, stubble, and nearby trees

to ash. No sense of triumph followed the obliteration of the threat. The pain in her womb enveloped all thought.

Shayla swung upward, slow and unwieldy with the extra weight in her womb. Greedy flames from the burning battlefield singed her belly. The babies twisted and fought for exit.

Not yet. Not until she found safe haven.

Where? Oh, where could she go? If she accessed the void long enough to find her lair, the babies would never survive the birthing. The void between the planes of existence would choke crucial air, light, and warmth from both her and her babies.

Who could shelter her? None of the males. Their lairs were small caves, barely large enough to secrete a single dragon; all of them too far away.

(*I come,*) an ancient dragon voice hailed her.

Iianthe. The oldest dragon of all and the only purple-tip known to have ever existed.

Shayla stretched her wings a little under the guidance of the telepathic voice, and she gained a little more control. But she kept dropping. She had to make headway. East. Where the mountains met the sea. Iianthe's lair, huge, designed to house many litters of baby dragons.

Barely skimming the tops of the trees, Shayla forced her wings to keep going. Her belly cramped in time with her downstrokes.

Iianthe appeared beneath her. His right wing supported the dragging leg that threatened her balance and her altitude. With the injured limb tucked back where it belonged, they gained elevation.

Everblue treetops receded from view. One dragon length, then two and three. They caught an updraft and glided east to safety.

The plateau in front of Iianthe's lair appeared before her, almost level with her sagging legs.

A heavy, awkward landing sent her nose into the spring beside the cave opening. Exhausted, she lay there, wishing she could cry as humans did.

Iianthe landed beside her, almost as tired as she. Near the end of his span, he'd lived longer than any living dragon could remember. Without moving, he crooned a *Song* of healing that only she could hear.

She could walk, a little, far enough to get inside the cave where a nest of leaves and soft sheep's wool awaited. Had Iianthe known she would need the nest?

No matter. She collapsed upon the bed as the first baby dragon squeezed from the protection of her womb into the waiting nest—an undersized mass of wiggling limbs the color of dark pewter. The tiniest hint of red touched its wingtips and the nubs of horns. A male. Alive and squalling for food already.

Shayla licked the last of the afterbirth from her son's fur. She paused a moment while she panted in rhythm with her labor. The miracle of new life filled her with awe. She stared at the tiny form in wonder.

Two more mewling dragonets made an abrupt entrance. Twin purple-tips. Purples! Rarest of all dragon colors, assigned only to personalities of great power or wisdom. What strange portent did their birth signify?

The cramping pains did not abate.

(*My replacement is born. I must die now. There can only be one purple-tip alive at any given time,)* Iianthe said from the cave entrance.

Shayla waited through the birth of two more dragonets before answering the hovering dragon.

(*Do not fly into the void just yet, wise one. We need your advice. The humans must be punished!*)

(*Your mates must not interfere. 'Tis not their destiny. This is a matter to be settled between your babies and the human magicians.*) Iianthe heaved a weary sigh. (*My next existence awaits, I must guard the beginning place of magic. The humans will find it within a century. Only those worthy of the power must find it.*)

(*The intruders have grown too strong, without the maturity of the centuries to guide them. They weave magic they cannot control,*) Shayla reminded him. (*The beginning place needs a powerful guardian until humans can use the magic properly.*)

(*'Twas foretold long ago by Purple Dragons wiser than I that your children must teach the humans what they need to know.*) Iianthe's voice faded as he backed out of the lair entrance.

(*But they are twins. Which one takes your place and which must be destroyed?*) Shayla panicked. Her babies were too small, not ready to grasp their destiny. Who would take on the task of dropping the extra purple-tip baby from the void into the Great Bay—to live or die as fate decided.

(*Seek answers in the void. Until you know the destinies of both purple-tips, do nothing to either. Perhaps they have been chosen by the fates to solve the problem with the humans.*) Iianthe gathered his wings for one last burst of energy and disappeared into the void. (*I can die now, Shayla. The lair is yours.*) Iianthe's voice faded.

Shayla caught a glimpse of winking amethyst crystal in the distant blackness that opened before her but did not touch her.

Shayla's wing folded protectively over all six pewter-colored dragonets that lived. Four males and the asexual twin purple-tips. No females. She pushed aside fourteen dead babies. No more infants awaited birth. A new kind of pain swelled within her. She lifted her muzzle in a mournful wail that pierced the silence and echoed through the mountains of Kardia Hodos. The sound lingered and replayed itself as sorrow overtook all of the dragons. The future seemed bleak indeed.

Too many dragons fell victim to the wild and aggressive humans who hated and feared all they did not understand.

Shayla nuzzled each of her babies, willing them all to live and grow. She had time to make a decision about the redundant purple-tip. Time to find a way to save both. Time to plot and persuade before dragonkind took drastic action.

Coming soon from Book View Café!

About the Author

Irene Radford is a founding member of Book View Café. You can find many of her books, both reprints and original titles, at the café, including her earliest books being released throughout 2023. She has been writing stories ever since she figured out what a pencil was for. Editing, as Phyllis Irene Radford, grew out of her love of the craft of writing. History has been a part of her life from earliest childhood and led to her BA from Lewis and Clark College.

Mostly she writes fantasy and historical fantasy including the best-selling Dragon Nimbus Series and the masterwork Merlin's Descendants series. Look for her writing new historical fantasy tales as Rachel Atwood, a different take on the Robin Hood mythology in *Walk the Wild with Me*, from DAW Books and the sequel *Outcasts of the Wildwood*. In other lifetimes she writes urban fantasy as P.R. Frost or Phyllis Ames, and space opera as C.F. Bentley. Lately she ventured into Steampunk as Julia Verne St. John.

If you wish information on the latest releases from Ms Radford, under any of her pen names, you can subscribe to her newsletter: www.ireneradford.net. Or you can follow her on Facebook as Phyllis Irene Radford.

About Book View Café

Book View Café is a professional authors' published cooperative offering DRM-free e-books in multiple formats to readers around the world. With authors in a variety of genres, including mystery, romance, fantasy, and science fiction. The Café has something for everyone.

Book View Café is good for readers because you can enjoy high-quality DRM-free ebooks from your favorite authors at a reasonable price. Book View Café is good for writers because 90% of the proceeds go directly to the book's author.

Book View Café authors include New York Times and USA Today bextsellers, Nebula, Hugo, Lambda, Chanticleer, National Reader's Choice, and Philip K. Dick Award Winners, World Fantasy, Kirkus, and Rita Award nominees, and winners and nominees of many other publishing awards.

BVC's Newsletter includes new releases, specials, author news, and event announcements. https://bookviewcafe.com/newsletter/

BOOK VIEW CAFE

www.ingramcontent.com/pod-product-compliance
Lightning Source LLC
Chambersburg PA
CBHW070348260626
47161CB00001B/60